NOT EXACTLY DEMOCRACY

Mia looked over the restless crowd. "Look. There are three groups of people here. First are the original loyal scientists and workers who intended to make their lives on the project as it was planned and still want that to happen.

"Some of you were persuaded to vote for this new scheme. You are in no danger of retaliation. You thought you were being given an honest chance to vote. Nobody gets punished for that. Nobody knows who you are.

And then there are those who faked credentials and fraudulently claimed false work records to get here. You have broken the law to come here and must suffer the consequences.

"One thing I can promise you. For the next election, it will be one person, one vote, with no extra shares counting for anything."

Johan Lange slammed a fist on his podium. "I've had enough of this!" He gestured to the uniformed men below him. "Arrest her."

Four of them hefted their anti-personnel batons and strode towards her position. People in the crowd moved to intercept them. Scuffles began to break out, and the central floor of the Agora started to swirl into a melee.

She keyed her com. "Jean, if you had any plans to intervene, this would be the time."

MICROSHIPS

Gordon A. Long

AIRBORN PRESS

Delta, B. C.

2025

Microships

Gordon A. Long

Published by

AIRBORN PRESS

4958 10A Ave, Delta, B. C.

V4M 1X8

Canada

ISBN: Paperback 978-1-988898-50-6
        eBook 978-1-988898-51-3

Printed by Kindle Direct Publishing

Cover Design by Gordon A. Long
Cover Font: Infinium Guardian by Axel Lymphos
Original images by Wolfgang Eckert and Julius H. from Pixabay

CONTENTS

Beware those who tell you what you want to hear. They may be telling you what you want to hear.

$\qquad$ –Mia Larsen

A man hears what he wants to hear and disregards the rest.

$\qquad$ –Paul Simon

PROLOGUE: THE LAUNCH

NASA External Affairs Liaison Mia Larsen gazed a moment longer at the technical marvel floating, huge and glistening, against the background of the Milky Way. With a shake of her head and a tap on her thrusters she turned her EV suit to face her charges.

"All right, ladies and gentlemen, that's the end of our tour. The Habitat for the Stars will be firing up its engines in two hours and breaking earth orbit for its new home in the Asteroid Belt. When that happens, you want more radiation shielding than a spacesuit provides. Why don't we take five more minutes to absorb the wonder of our accomplishment? Time to sort the memories to store up in your biomems to pass to your grandchildren."

Mia watched her group intently. These were businessmen and politicians whose organizations had contributed to the largest construction humanity had ever attempted. None of them had been EV before, and the last thing the Habitat Consortium needed on the day of the launch was a public relations glitch.

She didn't mind taking another moment of peace to view the masterpiece she had worked on, built by nanobots using nickel-iron asteroid material and solar energy. Or, as the popular press called it, "crafted out of sunlight and space dust." She was particularly proud of that meme, which had gone viral the first day she slipped it online.

"Ms. Larsen, why do the transparent sections seem to ripple?"

She smiled. For every person who asked a dumb question, there were ten who wanted to hear the answer but were afraid to sound silly.

"Space Sergeant Bokker, why don't you field that one?"

A deep chuckle echoed through the com. "You always give me the hard ones, ma'am." The bulky figure at the controls of the EV Personnel Transport Frame pointed a suit-clad finger. "The answer,

1

sir, is because the transparent sections are lined with water. That's right, water. You see, radiation protection and heat dispersion are big problems in space. We need the transparent sections to let in the sunlight reflected from the rings of mirrors. But we need radiation protection as well.

"So, we fill in those sections with water. We mined enough from a comet that swung by to fill them a metre deep. Once we get our orbit established in the Asteroid Belt, we'll find a local hunk of ice and bring it up to about three metres. No reason to boost all that weight all that distance. Once the sunlight warms it up, it'll be great for recreation. There's three strips: one for swimmers, one for motorless boats, and one for powered craft, water skiing and the like. I hear there's even going to be a section with artificial surf."

"And you heard right, Sergeant. There are surface control vanes to break up sympathetic wave action. Unless we want to play in it."

The viewers gave admiring murmurs and continued to bask in the impressive starscape. She monitored the positive chatter on their com and gave them ten minutes. If they hadn't made serious personal contributions to the project, they wouldn't be here.

"Time's up, folks. Please lock your suit clamps into your assigned docking bay on the transport frame, and the sergeant will swoop us gently back to our hangar. From there you can de-suit and return to your cabins to dress for the viewing reception. I believe the champaign will be poured in one hour."

She switched channels. "Thanks for the ride, Murph. Do you have a good seat for the Great Escape?

Another chuckle answered her. "Yeah, I got a prime spot staked out. It's a killer view, and it's just off the route from the galley to the reception. You want to join me?"

"That's a very tempting invitation, Sergeant, but I'm still on duty. Besides, you know I'm not allowed to fraternize with non-coms. Beneath my august position."

"Yeah, but you drink them under the table."

"Murph, you don't really think I could do that."

"You did, often enough."

"You know about my training, right?"

2

"Wait a minute…they taught you at diplomat school how to make it look like you were drinking more than you really were?"

"Yep."

"I call that downright duplicitous."

"Duplicitous. Where does a mere sergeant learn a word like that?"

"Gotta have a degree to get into Space Service."

"In English?"

"No, Engineering. But my mother was a teacher."

"Which is why you were handed the job of shepherding this gaggle. Let's see you get them out of here as smoothly as you got them aboard."

"Darn tootin'. And I'll have plenty of time to set myself up with a mug of beer and a plate of hoover doovers."

She laughed. "Have a good view and don't get caught."

Then the shadow of the Headquarters Wheel cut out the harsh sunlight. Bokker eased them gently into the Personnel Bay, and the radiation doors closed behind them, shutting off the historic scene. "End of the line, dearly beloved. It's been a pleasure having you along."

A dignified elderly voice answered. "Sergeant, I think I speak on behalf of the whole group when I thank you for the wonderful ride and the even more spectacular view."

"It was an honour, Admiral, sir. Can you make sure I get mentioned in dispatches?" Without waiting for a reply, he chuckled again, locked the controls and stepped away from the frame. "Mind the gravity, now. The airlock is to your left."

Their charges clumped obediently away, and she headed for the maintenance airlock at the other end of the hangar. Slinging her suit onto its rack, she filed the usage report and went to her quarters, where she dressed and headed for the reception. But on the way she made a detour to the Technical Observation Centre.

As she expected, her partner, External Interface Technician Noah Jamison, stood alone at the huge viewing window, staring out at the panorama, the baseball-sized globe of his External

Intelligence holding its usual position three centimetres behind his left ear. He glanced over as she entered. "Impressive, hey?"

The Habitat they had just helped build filled the window. The huge Bernal Sphere, a cylinder 500 metres in length and 600 in diameter, dwarfed the NASA Orbital Construction Module. It was hard to think of such a behemoth as a mere piece of machinery created by humans.

Nor did it have the ethereal delicacy of former space stations. It was a monocoque design, with no girders or structural elements visible. The whole hull had been created in one piece, using self-propagating smart dust mined from the huge chunk of rich ore that had been decelerated from the Asteroid Belt twenty years ago. The thick hull provided radiation shielding, heat insulation and a base for the interior structure. Micromanipulation of the surface material gave it a bright finish to prevent heat accumulation.

A skeleton crew of a few thousand technicians and support staff had been living aboard for months, and the Habitat was already rotating once per minute to provide rotational gravity. The complexity of starting acceleration on such a mass was daunting, because the slightest miscalculation of the Coriolis forces could tear it apart.

"Six years on the project." She shook her head. "It's actually finished. Unreal. I'm going to miss these people."

"And a wonderful job you did of keeping the team focused and motivated. It made for smooth sailing for me. I could concentrate on the data, and you could keep the personalities at bay."

They stared out at the scene in silence.

"And now a much-needed month of R & R before we switch over to the Microships. Got plans? I mean, besides your wedding and honeymoon. "

"Yep. Alicia's schedule finally matched with the European Space Agency's. Three weeks from tomorrow is the Big Day. Got a 'to do' list as long as your arm." He glanced at her. "You will be able to make it, won't you? We didn't have much choice on the date."

"No problem." She called up the calendar visual in her biodigital memory, although she really didn't have to. "I have a singles cruise booked on a square-rigger in the Caribbean for the first two weeks, and the rest of the time slotted in for proper relaxation with my parents."

"Sounds fine."

She knew her partner well, and the tone of his voice indicated that he couldn't see himself enjoying either option. "Why, Noah! You're beginning to develop tact. Is my job in danger?"

"Not a chance. Merging this project with the Europeans was difficult enough. On the Microship Swarm we'll be working with the International Space Agency, complete with People's Liberation reps. How's your Mandarin?"

"I had the vocabulary buffer increased in my biomem, and I uploaded the basic project database last week. I can handle the job, or someone else would have the assignment."

"Oh, no. They wouldn't get away with that! If they took you out, I'd put up more than a fuss!" He regarded her anxiously. "You don't want to leave, do you?"

She shrugged. "Not really. What if I did?"

"Oh..." He checked her expression again. "If you wanted to go, that would be different. I would never hold you. I owe you too much to do that."

She slapped his arm. "Well, don't worry. You've got me on the Microships Project for sure. I couldn't turn down that experience."

The look of relief on his face was almost worth the pang of concern she felt. "But I'm not sure about the wisdom of the project."

He nodded slowly. "You have a lot of support in that."

"What do you think?"

He shrugged. "I'm not paid to think about that stuff. I build them, the Powers that Be say how they'll be used."

"The Liberal press is calling them space junk."

"As they have been since we sent the original Swarm out fifty years ago. Space is huge. These things are only a metre in diameter!"

"But they're self-modifying and work in a swarm. They're travelling light years with an ever-increasing time delay in communications. They could program themselves to be anything out there, and we wouldn't find out for years."

"I know all that. But we're not talking about the Borg, here. What are the chances?" He frowned. "You are with me on this, aren't you?

"Don't worry. I'd be an idiot to make any waves." She pushed his shoulder to turn him around. "Come on, let's hit the party."

He grinned. "The Europeans are bound to have split for some superior champagne."

"You drink too much of it, and I'll be back on the job buffering the rest of society against your questionable wit."

"Okay, Mother. I'll be good."

"I've had six years to discover that you don't have the faintest clue what 'good' means."

"You always were a slow learner."

Laughing, they headed for the lift and the cameras, recorders, and mobs of people that waited when the doors opened.

This is my talent, and those are the tools of my trade. She squared her shoulders and stepped forward, smiling.

1. ALLEY CAT

The cruise was everything it advertised. The prohibitive cost ensured that the participants were educated and successful. It didn't take her long to gravitate to a group of women who got along famously. They modelled in the fashion show, sang karaoke in the bar, and three of them did a modernized version of the old standard, "Girls Just Wanna Have Fun" in the talent show. There were men onboard who wanted to have fun, too, but none of them really appealed to her, so a shipboard romance never entered the scope of probabilities.

It occurred to her that maybe she was outgrowing this sort of life. Whatever that meant.

Noah's wedding the following week felt the same. In the short term, she had a pleasant time with good people. In the long run, it showed her how unsuited she was to the life she was living.

After the wedding, she returned to her townhouse in the Southside Place area of Houston. The Strata Management Committee had decided to repaint the trim on the windows in a darker shade, which she assumed was more fashionable. She regarded it critically, and decided it was an improvement.

Which was fortunate, because she was away so much she never got to the meetings where the decisions were made. She palmed the door lock, directed her suitcases inside and looked around. It was a nice place, decorated in a style that was fashionable but leaning towards cosy. But it hardly looked lived in.

Probably because it wasn't. She wondered at the logic of an occupation that paid well enough she could afford to leave a place like this vacant most of the time while she stayed in whatever accommodation was provided at the job site. *First world problems, Mia. Buck up.*

She strolled into the kitchen, to a different scene. This room looked like the owner had just stepped out for a moment. Bright towels hung on their racks, and fresh flowers splayed out on the table and counter. Smiling, she opened the fridge. As expected, it was overflowing with all her favourite foods, with a large casserole front and centre, cooking instructions taped to the top.

She switched on her tri-media handset. "Call home...hi, Mom. I'm here. Yeah, great to be back. Hey, it looks like those kitchen elves have been at it again. Filled the place to overflowing. Want to come over and help get rid of some of it? Dad would probably like some of that casserole...oh. They made one at your place, too. How thoughtful of them."

They chatted for a while, established that they would meet for dinner at her parents' place the next day, and ended the call. She was checking the wine fridge for a bottle of her favourite Malbec when the doorbell rang.

Well, my day for socializing. I wonder who knows I'm home. If it's politics, I am definitely 'not receiving.'

She looked through the frosted glass but could see no one. She cautiously cracked the door open to get a better view.

Draped casually against the corner of the front porch out of view of the road was a slim figure in a parka, the deep hood pulled forward.

Minor alarm bells were ringing, but this person looked too small to be much danger.

The shape straightened. "About time ya got here."

"You were looking for me, specifically?"

"Yer Mia Larsen, ain't ya? Th' ExIn liaison chickie?"

"Chickie? That's not my usual job description, but yes. Who are you?"

"You can call me...uh... Hemisius. Yeah, that's a good name."

"Okay, Hemi. Why were you looking for me?"

"Frienda mine said you's an easy mark to hit up if I was skint."

"Ah. Friend by the name of Skidoo, I suppose? I haven't seen her around lately."

"She got a job. Doin' all right."

"She's only about twelve years old. What kind of job?"

"She wants you to know, she'll tell you, won't she?"

"I suppose she will. But if she has a job, she doesn't need an easy mark anymore, so maybe she won't."

"Maybe not. But she owes ya, and Skidoo pays her debts."

"She owes me nothing, but that's neither here nor there. You're a friend of Skidoo, that gets you in my door. Come on inside. You hungry?"

"Not that hungry."

"Yes, you are. You're down on your luck and you need an easy mark. You must be hungry. And I'm not doing any kind of business on my doorstep, so make up your mind. " She moved back and opened the door wider. "I'm not going to lock you in and send for the Kid Keepers."

He frowned but slid forward. "Yeah, Skidoo calls 'em that, too."

She motioned for him to close the door. "And I didn't rat her out, so I won't finger you, either. Now, it's warm in here, and I may be an easy mark, but I don't do mysteries. Take off that parka and come into the kitchen. You can watch that I don't slip a mickey in your soda."

Reluctantly he pulled off his hood and unzipped his jacket. Clear of the bulky garment, he was a slim, graceful metre-and-a-half or maybe a bit more, with dusky skin and elongated features.

"Ya seen enough?"

"No, but I won't embarrass you by staring. You're different, I guess. Nothing wrong with being different."

"Not unless you're lookin' at it from the inside."

"Probably true. Let's go see what's in the fridge."

They chatted about this and that as she worked on chicken sandwiches. For a street urchin, he knew the upscale neighbourhood and its occupants rather well.

"I haven't seen you around. How do you know so much?"

He grinned. "In the first place, you ain't bin 'round. I saw ya on the news, up at the Habitat. Didn't look like you was doin' much, but you was hangin' around with the Sphere Singer, an' that piqued my interest."

"I haven't heard him called that before."

"That's 'cause ya hang out with the wrong crowd. That Noah guy's got a rep all over the Nets. 'Course, it's mainly because of the tech, but Sphere Singer's the namea that love song. You know, the one by the Canadian chickie. You work with him?"

"I'm his media liaison. I created that image, and I'm always interested in its progress. He got married to his real-time love last week."

"Fair enough. I came lookin' for ya a month back, but no luck. Then I saw ya on the TV, and I knew what was goin' on. So I hung around waitin'."

"Not an easy area to hide out in."

He held up a hand with a sinuous gesture "I slip into small spaces."

She poured him more fruit juice and picked up her wine glass. "Okay, enough socializing. Come sit in my office and let's talk business."

When they were seated in comfortable chairs and had placed their sandwiches on the coffee table, she steepled her fingers and regarded him. "Forget the 'easy mark' tale. You're not down and out." She nodded towards the sandwich, which only had two bites gone. "You're not even that hungry. You have resources and objectives. What do you really need from me?"

He nodded as if she had passed some kind of test. "I got info." His voice had lost its singsong twang.

"Do I want it?"

"Not sure. That's why I'm here. Somebody must want it, and you might know who."

"You have my attention. What's your plan?"

"Well, it's this way. You know I'm different."

Again, she noted the elongated features, the invisibly fine hair. He looked like an eerie copy of a human. "You do look a bit out of the ordinary, if you don't mind me saying so."

He brushed that aside with another sweeping gesture. "No, real different. Inside my head, too. I can fit in, but it takes effort."

She raised her eyebrows. "There are a lot of us like that."

"That's my point. There's lotsa people different like you. But now I discover some others that are different like me."

"Please explain."

"Well, I admit, I was thinking of lookin' you up, anyways, 'cause Skidoo said I should. Don't know why, but she said to do it. So, I was hangin' around in the area, keepin' a weather eye like I always do, and I kept seeing this guy. He didn't belong here, either, so I started to start noticing, if you know what I mean. And I got suspicious. Little details about the way he walks, the way he holds his head. I dunno, movement of his hands and arms. And one day I caught a glance at his face. He looks like me, but more, if you know what I mean. Same features, but stronger."

"What did you do?"

"I backed off real fast. I kept out of his way, but I spread myself a bit thinner. Expanded my radius of observation, you might say. And over the last two months, I saw two more of these guys. Well, one was a woman, but no question they were the same."

"Sounds interesting. Any theories?"

"There's always the obvious one." The boy grinned. "You know, there's aliens from outer space and they're infiltrating human society. I like that one."

"And where do you fit into that scenario?"

"No idea. I must be some kinda sleeper, and some day I'm gonna be activated, I guess. That's why I came looking for you." He leaned forward and his speech became even clearer. "I don't want to be a sleeper, Mia. Humanity hasn't exactly welcomed me with open arms, but there are enough people like you who are making a try of it."

"What do you need?"

11

He mused a moment, running his hand across the top of his head in a movement that would have looked awkward on anyone else. "The life I lead gives me a lot of freedom, but I spend too much time on the basics, and I have to be too careful because I'm at risk from the good guys as well. I need to up my security but keep my freedom. The moment I get into the system, I'm screwed. Children's Services are mostly good people, but they have to watch their own backs. They have no time to give slack to special cases."

She regarded him while she made her decision. "We can cut through several levels of the bureaucracy and slip you into the system above the "homeless orphan" level. That will keep the petty do-gooders off your back. I have a place you can stay with people who know how to keep their mouths shut and will give you the freedom to do whatever work you think you need to. And the bandwidth to do your research."

"How do you know I need bandwidth?"

"Because when you get enthused, your fake backwoods dialect disappears, and you talk like a computer nerd. And in case you didn't know, there are also ways of telling if someone has a biodigital memory system."

"There are?"

"Yes, your eyes go still when you monitor the heads-up display. You also pause in a sentence at the wrong time when you're accessing the biomem."

"I can't tell. Do you have one?"

"Of course, but I'm smoother at using it. If you're going to be a spy, you need to work on that sort of thing."

"Is that what you need me for? Spying?"

"You already decided that. Up to now, you've done okay. Might as well stay with it."

"What's my cover?"

"The best place for you is the Witness Protection Plan. All sorts of secrecy, and we can play one level off against the other and not tell anyone anything."

"How will we be sure I get all that stuff you just said?"

"Because the people you'll be staying with are my parents."

"Your parents? They'll go for an alien spy in their house?"

"Why not?" She shrugged. "They had me there for twenty-odd years. They're used to the weird and wonderful by now."

He tilted his head one way, then another like a pigeon using both eyes. "Seems you turned out all right. I'll risk it."

2. PARENTS

Jane Larsen had been a bit of a catch in her day, and she retained her graceful poise, though her figure had thickened with age. Patrick was of a similar height, but still whipcord slim and athletic looking, a credit to his Air Force training.

A selection of healthy treats was laid out on the coffee table, and they sat in the comfortable living room for a chat. After Hemi had refused milk and had been turned down in his request for beer, he settled for a soda. Things were off to a decent start.

Jane took her hostess position seriously, and guided the conversation along proper lines. "Now, Hemi, if you're going to be staying here, you need to tell us something about yourself. Whatever you think appropriate."

Patrick chuckled. "Or whatever you've used in the past."

Hemi smiled. "You people are being very understanding, and you prob'ly have security clearance, so I'll go for the truth. As I know it, of course.

"Looking back, I don't think my mother and father got married. Mom said they never planned on having children. In fact, when I got old enough to understand, she confided to me they thought they couldn't. When I was about three, my father disappeared. Never did get an explanation from her, just that he had to leave, but it wasn't his fault.

"We moved in with Mom's parents, and that was that. Some time, I don't remember when, I realized that I've never been registered with the authorities. Mom home-schooled me, and we stayed pretty solitary.

"There was never a problem with money. The grandfolks are well enough off, and I got a trust fund that she dipped into when she needed it.

"When I was eight, it sort of crumbled. Mom met a man and fell in love. Nobody was keen on making changes. She got married and moved out, and I stayed with the Grands for the next three or four years. By the time I was eleven, I was pretty well on my own. I take a draw from my trust fund once in a while and check in with the Grands now and then, and that's where things stood until last month, when I saw the alien."

"You gradually slipped out of their lives, and nobody noticed?"

"Nobody noticed, because I took care that they didn't. If you don't cause trouble, people are happy to leave you alone. I have a basement apartment that I rent with my 'Dad.' Of course, he's never home at any given moment, but I pay the rent right on time and don't sweat small inconveniences. The rental agency considers us model tenants."

"What about the authorities?"

"I don't exist. A couple of times the police have picked me up because I've been out too late or in the wrong part of town, but my grandfather covers for me, and there's never any problem."

"Until now."

"Right. And I haven't been wasting my time. I have a network of friends, acquaintances, and clients who help each other out. Hence Skiddoo; hence you." He turned to Mia's father. "And hence, you. I really appreciate this. And don't worry, I always pay the rent on time."

"There will be no rent paid, young man." Her mother jammed her fists onto her hips. "We are happy to contribute."

Hemi turned to Mia. "See what I mean? There are so many people who really want to help."

She grinned. "Does the expression, 'easy mark' ring a bell?"

"Yeah, but easy marks who choose to act that way have their own reasons for doing things. And the bottom line is making their contribution to humanity."

Mia exchanged glances with her mother. "And that's your bottom line?"

"Of course. If you don't contribute to the benefit of your species, what was the point in getting born?" He chuckled. "You know, my grandparents, the ones I used to live with? They're heavy-duty religious. They weren't happy to take me in, but they felt strongly it was their duty — to who I don't know — and they did it willingly. And that made a great deal of difference to me. It's the same thing, when you come to think of it. I was their contribution."

Mia's father laughed. "Well, you're quite the philosopher. I hope we can match up to your elevated expectations."

Hemi flicked graceful fingers towards Mia. "You created her. You're already ahead on points."

"Did I tell you what a flatterer he is?" Mia cuffed the back of his head gently.

He snapped his fingers and pointed a gun-barrel hand at her. "Aha. I bin told about this. Recordin' the first act of violence."

He registered the look on her face. "A joke! It was a joke, Mia." His grin came back. "Besides, who would I tell? I don't exist, remember?"

She shook her head. "Didn't you two tell me a while ago that running an empty nest was boring at times?"

Her mother sighed. "Yes, but I didn't mean it as a cry for help."

3. NEW ASSIGNMENT

A week later, rested and refreshed, she left her augmented family happily getting to know each other, and reported for duty. As it happened, Noah's honeymoon had been interrupted by a late-season hurricane in the Caribbean, and he was trapped on some tropical island with no way to return.

At least, that was the story. It occurred to her to wonder how much of the cause was natural disaster and how much was influenced by a certain seven-centimetre globe and its handler.

Whatever the reason for the delay, it gave her time to clean out their office and collect the essentials for the move across the Jackson Space Center from Project Engineering Building 45, which would be taken over by other engineers now that the Habitat was finished, to Communications and Tracking Building 44 in an outlying part of the huge complex.

She had dusted off her Mazda H6, because the Space Centre was less than an hour's drive from her townhouse. She pulled through the security gates and navigated along familiar streets to Building 45, where her small pile of belongings sat alone in a corner of their old office. Loading it quickly, she made her way to Avenue C and found Building 44, which had its own parking lot just outside.

The smaller, older structures in that area reminded her that this project had been running for seventy years, and she wondered if this career move had put her a step ahead or a few decades back.

When the proximity of the parking area becomes a positive job element, I'm grasping at straws.

But once she got inside the building, things picked up. A friendly concierge helped her tote her belongings to the elevator, and on the third floor a workman in carpenter's coveralls took pity on her and left what he was doing to help shift her boxes across the empty lab to the small office she and Noah had been allotted.

Without her partner, no serious decisions could be made, but she decided which desk would be hers: the one nearest the door, from which she could perform her usual watchdog role. The room was clean and mostly empty, with the marks of new electrical installations on the faded walls. A stack of padded crates in the centre probably contained their new operating hardware.

Once she had arranged her desk, she decided there wasn't enough construction to constitute a safety hazard. She needed a self-guided tour of the lab to reconcile the reality of the layout with the plan in her biomem.

She was drawn to a quiet corner office where a man in a business suit with the tie loosened sat at a three-screen multi-tech setup, his fingers dashing busily between keyboard, mouse and graphics pads.

He glanced up at her, flashed a "one moment" gesture, and returned to his work.

Taking this as an invitation, she entered and found a comfortable chair in a small lounge area. She had begun to peruse the tidy miniature kitchen when the man stood and approached.

She got up and shook his outstretched hand.

"Y'all must be Mia Larsen. You've been getting your fifteen minutes of media attention lately. We're a tad of a comedown from your cutting-edge project to our old hack, I'm afraid. I'm Abe Johnson, office manager, tech support and general dogsbody. We're pretty low priority, budget-wise." He glanced at the crates stacked around. "At least, we used to be."

"Glad there's someone here who seems to belong." His accent was pure Texan, so she made a guess. "Dogsbody. Do I detect a fellow fan of British Detective Fiction?"

He laughed. "Y'all caught it in one. Sherlock Homes would be proud of you."

"Maybe, but I'm not detective enough to figure out what's happening and where everybody is. A gang of carpenters doesn't provide much work for a liaison officer."

"Yeah, well, we were fixin' to have it ready when y'all arrived, but you jumped the gun."

"It's a big move, all the way over here from Building Forty-Five. Took me a whole fifty-three minutes."

"And a time warp back to seventy years ago. Don't you worry your head about the schedule. The new cabling's finished, and the carpenters are just doing the final polish. Most of our people are moving up from the second floor tomorrow."

"Is there anything I can do, now?"

"Y'all happen to be talking to the office manager..." he made an open gesture with his right hand, "...who is in close communication with tech support..." he opened his other hand. "And there's a pile of crates in your office full of technical stuff that needs to be managed."

He walked back to his desk and glanced at the screens. "Tell you what. I got a sequence running here that'll take 'nuther ten minutes. Why don't you head over yonder and start planning how you want the office laid out. I'll be over with a big crowbar quicker 'n you can shake a stick."

She nodded. "Good plan."

His attention returned to the screens, and she headed back to her new office. She knew how Noah liked his hardware set up, and the furniture inventory only had desks for the two of them. She glanced out the door. They would be near the centre of the action, but with none of those smoked glass windows that reduced the privacy in a modern office.

Things were looking up. Abe really did have a crowbar, and they attacked the crates with a will. Soon they had the office ready for work.

* * *

19

The following morning, when the staff started wheeling dollies of equipment out of the elevator, she was already there to introduce herself, lend a hand and get to know everyone. In the process, she started to form a picture of how the new lab would be organized, and began building a flow chart in her biomem of how the incoming information needed to move. Abe seemed to realize that time spent explaining to her wasn't wasted, and she was soon up to her eyeballs in the setup.

People started coming to her with questions about where to put auxiliary services like the printers and plotters. She rarely made any decisions, but could often send them to the person who needed to answer.

Nearing ten o'clock she mentioned a coffee break, and Abe immediately pointed to the machine in his office, indicating the boxes of donuts stacked beside it.

She commandeered an empty worktable and scrounged a bunch of chairs to encircle it. By the top of the hour, everything was laid out and ready.

Nobody seemed to mind when Johnson held an impromptu updating while they munched. From what she could tell, everything was going rather smoother than he expected. One of the technicians challenged a decision she had made, but she just smiled. "As you Texans say, not my horse, not my wagon."

"So, you don't mind if we move the wide format plotter closer to the paper supply?"

"When it was delivered, you were dealing with that electrical short, and we didn't want to bother you. It's really your call."

"Great." He reached out and took another donut off the plate.

The day flowed on in a similar manner, with its share of disappointments, errors and hitches, but she spread her senses around, her ear always tuned for the sharp voice, the frustrated groan. Since she didn't have a job to distract her, it was easy to be anywhere she was needed.

"I've bin watching you." Abe stood at her side and surveyed the busy room.

"Is that bad?"

"Dunno. You must have some kinda juju. I don't know what it is, but it sure works."

She smiled. "It's called public relations, Abe. Did you ever work in an office with a person who messed everything up on purpose? A finger in every pie, a twist in every argument?"

He shrugged. "Everybody knows a few of those. They can completely foul up any workplace."

"Well, I'm the opposite. I look for all the gritty spots and smooth them out. Often people don't want to run things; they only want to know their opinion was taken into account. I listen. They feel part of the process, and the whole team works together."

He shook his head. "I took workshops in all that stuff, but I don't have time to run around patting everybody on the head."

"But I do. No magic."

He grinned. "Just a bit of mothering."

She swung to face him. "You will NOT call me Mother. Noah Jamison calls me that when he wants to rile me, but I'm paid to put up with him. I'm not paid to put up with you."

He nodded seriously. "Okay..."

She started to turn away.

"...Mom."

Without pausing in her stride, she flipped him a finger as she went into her office and closed the door. Very gently.

4. MONEY LAUNDERING

That afternoon she received a call she wasn't expecting. She answered immediately so she wouldn't draw attention.

"Hello, Hemi. You're not supposed to know this number."

"Hi, Mia. Sorry to call you at work, but I don't have your home number 'cause we're not that kind of friends yet. I must say, you guard your personal privacy nicely."

"Are you telling me you can crack NASA's security, but not mine?"

His chuckle came over the line. "That would be one for the record book, wouldn't it?"

She ignored the fact that he hadn't answered her question. "What can I do for you?"

"I need a favour, and you're the only one that can help me."

"Are we in a rush?"

"Not at all."

"Here's my personal number. Call me after work."

"Sure thing. Having a good day?"

"As it happens, yes. When I'm not being distracted by personal matters."

"Point taken. See ya later." The screen blanked.

Having no data to speculate on, she went back to her work.

At 5:15 her tri-me buzzed. She looked around, but most of the workers had left, so she answered. "Are we a bit over-anxious?"

"Not really. Didn't you say, 'after work?'"

"In my line, you don't down tools bang on five."

"Oh, yeah. You're that kind of person, aren't you?"

"What kind of person is that?"

"The kind that hangs around and makes social chit-chat. In your field, it's understandable, I suppose."

"I am headed for the parking lot. Hang on a moment."

There was a pause. "...changed my mind. I'll call you when you're home." Again the screen went blank without warning. When she pressed for "recent calls," there was no record.

Now that she was gathering data on this little mystery, she did some thinking during the drive home and came to a tentative conclusion.

When she had closed the front door behind her, the call came again. This time it was an eerie, electronic chime. She opened the line.

"Hemi, we have to talk in person. I'm not pleased with this interchange."

"Me too. I don't think we have security issues, but you never know. We can probably talk normal business on this channel. Money and all that."

"I agree. How much do you need laundered?"

He didn't miss a beat. "About five thousand."

"May I ask for what?"

"Hardware. Patrick's system isn't up to my requirements, and his security is only good enough for the kind of stuff he does. Mind you, he knows his com hardware, doesn't he?"

"He was a radar technician in the Air Force."

"Stands to reason. Better if his usage doesn't suddenly change, anyway."

"Do I need to be there in person?"

"Best way to work it, I think. Store closes at nine."

"How many levels of security do we need?"

"I'll tell you when you get there."

"All right. What's the address?"

A street number appeared on the heads up in her left eye. "Drive past that point."

"All right. Leaving now."

"See you in about twenty."

The address he had sent was within walking distance of the Larsen home. When she got there, she found herself in the middle of a block with nothing but a park nearby. A pedestrian-operated crosswalk flashed, and she pulled up. Out of the corner of her eye she saw a slim figure approaching from the bushes. She unlocked the door, and he slipped in.

"Light's gone green. Don't draw attention."

She stepped gently on the hydrogen feed. "Teach your grandmother. Where to?"

He jutted his chin ahead. "Up the street two blocks. That little strip mall. What should I teach her?"

"According to the old expression, probably nothing." She turned in and parked out of sight of the street and faced him. "Now what?"

His eyes were flashing. He was enjoying this. "Walk back half a block to the Altex store. Ask for Mike at the back counter. It's two large boxes, one medium, and three small ones. Use your Paypal account. Tell him the shipment will be picked up tomorrow morning."

"That's it?"

"I'll give you the rest later. We're exposed, out here in the open."

"You're calling the shots." She left the car, and he slid partway down in his seat and hauled out his tri-me handset, looking like any other bored teenager waiting for a parent.

Mike was a thirtyish fellow who knew how to do his job and keep the chat to a minimum. She checked the goods, paid up, and was out in five minutes.

She slipped in and started the car. "Where to?"

"Let's circle around and approach Jane and Patrick's house from your usual route. Just in case."

"Sure enough. Do you consider their place to be secure?"

"As secure as it should be, and a little more. Too much tech throws up red flags as well."

She frowned at him. "Aren't we taking this all a bit seriously?"

"We'll talk at home. You're staying for supper."

"Am I?"

"Jane's expecting you." He grinned. "You don't want to disappoint your dear mother, do you?"

"On a first name basis, are you?"

"I call her 'Gram' in public. Patrick likes 'Pat.' Keeps it simple."

When they reached her parents' house, supper wasn't quite ready, and Hemi gestured towards the basement stairs. "We can talk in my room."

Reaching the bottom, she looked around. "This is nice."

"Yeah, well, Pat was already planning a spare bedroom down here, and this gave him the excuse. He had enough furniture, so there's no big bills to flag. I'll decorate it as time goes on."

She nodded. "It's nice but impersonal."

"I'll fix that." He grinned and gestured. "You get the swivel."

She spun the ornate leather chair away from the desk and relaxed into it. "Does that mean I'm in charge?"

"You just loaned me five grand." He sat in a plain chair across from her. "I gotta give you something in exchange."

She nodded. "Okay, what's the rest of the plot?"

"Well, it goes this way. Pat and Gram have decided they need a nice, new queen-sized mattress. They've ordered one from Sleep-Ezee down the road. But the Sleep-Ezee guy is happy to do them a favour for a small fee, and he'll send his truck around to pick up a coupla boxes at Altex on the way here."

"I see. There's a Sleep-Ezee van delivering a huge mattress and a few incidental boxes to the house."

"Right, and if anybody's watching — and I have no evidence that they are — that's all they'll see. About the money. Want to check your account?"

She pulled out her tri-me and looked. "It's already been paid...from a numbered account at CitiBank."

"My trust fund."

"And that's the extent of your security?"

He shrugged. "You gotta strike a balance. Like I said before, too much security sends up flags, both on me and on you. There's a small chance Internal Revenue might be interested in your five grand purchase, but you've got a big enough salary that NASA Security won't blink at that, especially when it was spent on infotech. And there's another level of security we have to consider. Certain people keep an eye on stores like Altex. An expensive shipment goes out the door into a small sedan, you could get hijacked on the way home. It goes to a low-security residence, you might be targeted for a B&E."

"You think of everything, don't you?"

"It's my way of life. Always has been."

"Doesn't it bother you sometimes? Don't you ever want a normal life?"

He grinned. "Sure, but if I had a normal life, what would I do with my spare time?"

"Maybe go to school?"

He shrugged. "I just paid five Gs tuition to the big school of the Internet. Several nets, actually. Where I will set myself up with — I hope — enough security to have the freedom of a lot of information, but not enough that anyone will notice me."

She nodded. "I see the advantage. I can access a world of data, but I'm hemmed in by political and scientific security."

He laid a finger alongside his nose. "And between the two of us, maybe we can find out what's going on."

* * *

That night, she spent a few restless hours tossing nebulous ideas around in her head, so she wasn't exactly in top form at work the next day. However, the new Project Research Head showed up with the rest of the senior staff, and she had to come up to par in a hurry. Noah's absence left it up to her to carve out their niche in the decision-making process. Ground taken early in the battle and all that.

Peter Kovaks seemed to be the kind of leader who trusted his underlings. He toured the lab and offices, listened to the decisions that had been made, and intervened on very few of them. He called a general meeting for after lunch and made his exit, towing his entourage of two off to an eatery appropriate to their status.

She returned from her cafeteria lunch a bit early, and when she entered her office, a figure was comfortably seated and working at the main video display. There was no mistaking the globe spinning at his shoulder.

"Noah! You finally got here."

He got up and gave her a hug, then turned and regarded the room. "Nice setup. Better than the last one." He reached out a finger and caressed a large holoframe. "This baby has sixteen K resolution."

"Glad there's something new in this old shack."

He regarded her quizzically. "Don't worry. We'll soon have this lot prepared for the twenty-second century."

They fired up the processors and began uploading the files they had been allotted. It was a relief to be finally working. But not for long.

The bigwigs straggled back in at 1:15 and everyone moved to the meeting table the moment Kovaks gave the sign. Once they were seated, he gestured to Noah. "Our latest arrival demonstrates the importance of this new stage of the project. NASA has assigned us their hottest data processor, the ExIn Sphere, and technician Noah Jamison.

He paused for a small round of polite applause. "And of course you've already met his liaison, Mia Larsen."

She smiled. "For those of you who have not worked with the ExIn Sphere before, this is a superb fionic data collector and processor, but not technically an artificial intelligence. It does not speak, and it wastes no intelligence on pretending to be intelligent. My unfortunate habit of referring to the sphere as Fiona bothers my partner no end, but you know how people are with inanimate objects that sometimes frustrate them beyond endurance. Fiona has no self-awareness and no personality. We have had plenty of experience blending her abilities in with any system your office may have set up, and she will add a great deal of memory and processing speed to this operation."

Noah grinned. "But Mia's goal in life is to make everybody look good, and that includes Fiona.'

The sphere flashed blue three times.

She threw up her hands. "And when my chief client starts doing public relations for me, I'm smart enough to quit." She nodded to Kovaks.

He indicated the large screen at the end of the room. "For all the new members of the team, here's a timeline of the project to date. Starting in 2035, we sent a swarm of a thousand microships on a mission to Alpha Centauri, a distance of four light years. There were five launchings of two hundred ships each over a period of two years. They accelerated up to twenty percent of light speed, the maximum velocity of their design at the time, and away they went.

"However, they are self-modifying modules, and we continued to work on the engineering. Over the years we have reprogrammed their propulsion systems three times and tweaked their hardware twice, and their velocity has been increased considerably. The first group performed the planned deceleration and arrived in 2050, the next two soon after.

"However, the success of the mission prompted NASA to make further upgrades and cancel the deceleration of the remaining two groups, re-assigning them on secondary missions to other nearby stars, up to 15 light years away. This group could make over half lightspeed, and they arrived at their destinations around 2065. Our communication was still by radio, so we were expecting feedback to start getting interesting after about another 15 years, which is now.

"This is why we have the new intake of staff. On the astrophysical side, we expect a great increase in data. That has already started, and the new members of the team will have plenty to do.

"On the engineering side, we fully expect the data coming in to supersede everything we know about those new systems. Therefore, we want to send new directions to the swarm mentalities, suggesting design changes to maximize efficiency and perhaps move on to expanded objectives.

"It's a bothersome task, having to create designs and wait for thirty years to find out if they work, but that's Astro-Engineering." He grinned. "It makes for great job security."

The mandatory chuckle died away, and he opened the meeting for questions.

Noah leaned over and spoke quietly. "Nothing new here for me."

"No?"

"Fiona's been downloading their engineering progress ever since I found out about the assignment. Call it my bedtime reading. I've already got some new ideas for them."

"Great. There will be a special engineering orientation later. Let's sit back and see where they're going before we hit them with any bombshells. No need to ruffle feathers."

He mock-punched her shoulder. "That's what you're here for. Keep me from putting my foot in it."

"All part of the service." She nudged him and nodded towards the chairman. "That last question..."

And they turned their attention back to the meeting, but her interest soon palled. *I'm supposed to be all enthused about joining a project that's been running for forty-five years. My partner's already up to speed, and he doesn't need me to babysit him anymore. I'm going to alternate between bored to tears and worried about my job.*

She gave herself a mental shake and focused. Soon she was back in the swing of things, and she left the lab just after five in a better frame of mind. She had sort of hoped for a chance to chat with Noah about his honeymoon, but he was so enthused about getting home to his new wife she couldn't bring herself to ask.

She consoled herself with a half-bottle of Chilean Viognier and a video chat with Hemi and her parents. When that was over, she realized she was dead tired. She took a long, hot bath and went to bed feeling relatively optimistic.

5. "ENOUGH IS ENOUGH"

But the next day was October 17th, 2080, when the course of the human race changed forever.

The text appeared simultaneously at noon, GMT on every media screen in every language in the world. It stayed there for two days, usurping all communications bands and throwing the industry into disarray. It also broadcast in a loop on every radio source that happened to have the switch turned on: stern voices in many languages and accents:

OKAY,

ENOUGH IS ENOUGH.

It appeared on all radar, sonar and GPS systems as well, but only as a pop-up in the bottom left-hand corner of each display.

When that last small bit of news came through to the Communications lab, Mia and Noah and the rest of the Swarm Project crew were slumped, exhausted, around the big conference table. They, like most NASA employees, had been on duty for the best part of the last forty-eight hours, using their specialized equipment to analyze the signal: what it was, where and who it was coming from. Up till that point, they had accomplished very little.

Noah breathed his first sigh of relief. "At least that's something."

Heads rose around the table, and hopeful faces turned towards him.

Mia performed her usual function. "By which you mean...?"

"This third clue indicates that the intent of the display is intelligent and non-aggressive."

She frowned. "Third...?" She held up a cautioning finger while she thought. "...the first clue was only that the senders had the technology."

"Correct. The second clue showed their knowledge of human communication. Which is exhaustive."

She was beginning to catch on. "Neither of which gave any idea of how they feel towards us."

He shrugged. "Apart from the fact that they didn't immediately use their technology blow us to smithereens. Which may simply indicate that they don't have any physical presence nearby. Or may mean nothing of the sort."

She nodded. "Now, we find out they didn't crash every plane in the air. Yes, I'd call that considerate."

He regarded her. "We've done all the technical analysis. What do you think?"

She frowned. "What do you mean?"

"You're in charge of the soft facts. Reading between the lines. What does the message say to you?"

"Noah, it's four words. That's only two lines to read between."

He grinned. "Nonetheless." He gave an 'over to you' flourish of his hand.

She shrugged. "As you wish. Choice of expression. 'Enough is enough' is often used when the subject is an inferior who knows the rules and is choosing not to follow them. The speaker usually has the power to force compliance but has given the subject a chance to do the right thing on their own." She glanced at him. The room had gone quiet. "We obviously haven't."

He made a 'go on' gesture.

"The expression is used when the speaker has given up, has decided that the subject is not going to see the light and amend their ways. It implies imminent action." She paused a moment. "The 'okay' is ironic. Everything is not okay, and the speaker is going to take action to make sure that changes."

He leaned back in his chair and started to clap, but she raised a warning finger.

"I haven't finished. What does the whole thing mean? It means that an alien society has studied Earth very carefully, probably for a long time. They are fluent and idiomatic in all our languages and have a deep understanding of human nature, including our sense of humour. The choice of media for the message shows they wish to treat us equally. We have to hope that extends to our relationship with them, but they are not optimistic.

"They have, or want us to believe they have, the power to force us to comply. Their approach to us is paternalistic. Their society must be superior to ours in many ways. We can't tell yet if it is patronizing or predatory, I suspect not, but that could be wishful thinking. Bottom line, humanity needs to polish up the silver and put on our company manners. This could go either way."

Noah grinned. "All that, and from only five words."

For some reason, Mia felt reckless. A small voice in the back of her mind warned her, but for once she spoke on instinct, not analysis. "I'll go further. I think when we meet them, which will be soon, there will be more similarities than differences."

His face became serious. "There are several theories that support that."

Kovacs slapped the table. "I suggest we leave out the similarities part and make Mia's analysis the conclusion to our report. I couldn't have said it better, myself. "

Noah grinned. "That's what we hire the professionals for: to do their jobs." His eyes went blank. "Wait a sec."

She regarded his ExIn. Over the years she had learned to read the colour swirls that washed its surface. The present scattering of random patterns indicated exceptional activity.

"New data?"

"A few interesting details from other departments. The alien message is also being broadcast on several media that we know

33

about but don't use. Given that clue, we have extrapolated and found that it is also being broadcast on several media that we had no idea existed, sitting there waiting to be found."

That threw her headfirst into her official function in their relationship. "Can you give us an example?"

"Ultralight communication."

Heads rose around the table, and faces took on interest.

"In words of three syllables or less?"

"Sound communication only has two variables: frequency and volume, right?"

She nodded. Now was not the time to discuss the relationship between frequency and wavelength.

"The human ear perceives changes in the patterns, and thus humans can hear. Apparently, it is possible to do the same thing with light." He mulled that over a moment. "Which means that messages would travel at the speed of light, but of course, radio waves do that already."

"So, no advantage there."

"But light can be focused into a tight beam. It would have directional advantage, and since a beam only dissipates in one dimension, the energy savings ought to be to the second power."

"Laser communication, which we already have. Sort of."

"More important, it seems light may have several modifications besides wave length and amplitude that we haven't discovered yet. That's an advantage worth exploring. It would be candy on a stick to present-day laser-com outfits."

"Shall we put it out for bids in the usual process?"

"In normal circumstances I'd say so."

"Ah. But if this new ultralight com is what the aliens use as their normal medium, our advances will look pretty lame."

"Exactly. Everything humanity knows as normal has been thrown out of whack in the last two days. Let's forget commercial applications for now. We have more important things to think about."

"You're right. Sorry to have distracted you at a key time."

"No waste of resources. The ExIn has been busy while we chatted."

She glanced at the whirring sphere. The increasing blue usually indicated success of some sort.

"The other advantage to ultralight is you don't need triangulation to locate the source. Ship these coordinates to the People's Liberation Cloud-Based Early Warning Net. NORAD and NATO monitor them constantly, so everybody will have an even chance of figuring out where our signal originates."

She gave a wry grin. "Must keep the customers happy. All of them."

He responded with a less humorous twist of his lips. "And I'm glad that's your job, not mine."

She nodded. "Let's figure out who these creatures are and what's got their alien knickers in such a twist."

The ExIn opened a new project plan template on the main screen, and the teams swung into action.

6. ΛLIEN ENCOUNTER

That evening the message disappeared as if it had never been, and the news media, happy to be back online, went crazy with speculation. It was basically a rehash of what everyone had been saying for the previous two days, only longer and in more detail. Mia turned it off and went to bed for some much-needed sleep.

When she pulled into the lot the next morning there were no empty spaces, and she had to backtrack to the general parking to find a slot. She kept her eyes open as she approached, and there seemed to be a larger number of people around. People who seemed to have nothing to do but observe everything closely. The kind of people she had long ago learned to pretend she didn't see.

Promptly at nine, Peter Kovaks and his usual entourage entered the lab. His face was stern, and the anxious team was quick to gather at his summons. He didn't beat around the bush.

"The United Nations has received a communication from the alien authority, who call themselves the Humanity Meld. It is only preliminary, but it gives us an idea what is causing the problem. We don't have any details, but there seems little doubt that the catalyst is the Microship Swarm."

Dead silence greeted this pronouncement.

This was a public relations event, and part of Mia's duties. "Can you give us any more, sir?"

"Nothing in detail. From the quality of their previous transmissions, they know our languages very well, so we can take this latest message at face value. They say as long as we stay in our own system, we can do what we like, but 'once you start tossing your trash over the fence, the neighbours have a right to become involved.' That's a direct quote from the Standard English version."

He held up a hand to silence the indignant responses that were forming. "Don't bother to repeat what we have been telling our opposition for years. That is the message, and we have received it.

"The question about whether the aliens have a physical presence nearby has also been answered. A delegation of their representatives will arrive at John F. Kennedy Airport tomorrow at twelve noon, EST. They request ground escort to the United Nations Building, where they will address the General Assembly. That message was broadcast in plaintext and is available to all media outlets.

"NASA also received a message, tight beamed to the Deep Space Network receiving station. A small contingent will be arriving simultaneously in Houston. They request that we clear the eastern half of the parking lot outside Building 44 in the Jackson Space Center."

There was complete silence.

Finally, Abe Johnson stuttered, "Wha...? They're coming directly here?"

The project head laid his hands flat on the table. "I, too was amazed." He turned to Noah, "Mr. Jamison, I assume this kind of situation is exactly why we have you here. What can your sphere deduce from the data so far. What can we expect?"

"We can extrapolate quite a bit. First and easiest, it confirms our guess that our alien neighbours are not happy to have us spreading our trash around the universe. We further speculate the physical ships are not the problem. That leaves us with the multiple intelligences aboard. With their advanced tech, these creatures may have experience with AI that we need to know."

Mia nodded. "Yes, that would be a point of possible cooperation and a way to show a responsible attitude."

"Today also answers the big question. This is not an exploratory mission that came across us by mistake. These aliens have been monitoring us for a long time and probably have a serious presence in Sol System."

His glance turned the floor over to Mia. She nodded. The group needed calm reassurance. "This whole scenario is overlaid by a feeling of confidence and a lack of belligerence. The aliens are very much in the driver's seat, they're comfortable there, and they're not shy to let us know it."

Kovaks nodded. "I suppose we'll find out more very soon. Namely at 11 a.m. our time tomorrow."

He looked around. "We'll have physical plant in to tidy up the old place and make it look as spiffy as possible. I assume Security will want to do their own form of sweep. Archives will be sending a video director around to arrange lighting and camera angles." He shrugged. "It's all a tossup from there on. Any ideas?"

Mia flicked up a hand. "I can't see us escaping a reception in the cafeteria."

Noah nodded. "That will depend on the environmental needs of their personnel."

"Not our problem. This small Humanity Meld team will meet with our group leaders and nobody else. We have seven groups, plus our ExIn team and me. That leaves five more chairs around the big table."

Security Head Joe Reimer frowned. "It seems very casual. Surely some of their people will be security."

"So far they seem to be following similar protocols to ours." Kovaks regarded his group. "We've all been through the media grinder before. Try to get some work done for the rest of the day. Improvise as you must. Tomorrow, we have to be ready for anything."

Once again, Mia was in her element, and her long experience and quick eye gave her great advantages. By the end of the day there was no question who was in charge of tomorrow's operation, and at four-thirty Peter Kovaks opened the daily roundup with a comment on it.

"You've done your usual competent job under pressure, people, and now we know why Mia Larsen is with us. Tomorrow will only be worse; don't expect to get any work done. There will be outside teams working here from six in the morning, but only Abe and I have to be around for that. The rest of you come in at eight as usual. Mia, you're on your own schedule."

Which meant little sleep that night. By five o'clock she was up and dressed, and at seven she was on the job, directing camera operators, lighting technicians and security agents, mediating arguments between fields of vision and fields of fire.

But they were all experts in their areas, and there were no overt demonstrations of the nerves they were all feeling. By showtime, everyone was ready and waiting in the parking lot.

At 10:55 there was a subdued crackle of radios, and all eyes turned to the east. A wide sliver of shining metal appeared. It was the shape of a deep wing, over fifty metres long, with no fuselage or control surfaces and no visible evidence of any drive mechanism. It cruised straight in to a soft landing, ignoring a stiff crosswind and fitting itself neatly into the parking lot east of the building. It settled, hovering a metre off the ground, and there it stayed as if nailed in place. A ramp dropped from under the front of the wing. The end touched the ground, and there was a pause.

The aliens exited the plane smoothly, three larger individuals fanning out first, then two others, slimmer and shorter, following. The first of the advance guard gestured to the NASA security team and scribed an arc about ten metres in front of him. Seven American agents spaced themselves on that line, turned and started toward the reception committee.

The Microships team had no such organization. Kovaks, Noah, and Mia stood forward in the shade of the awning at the front door. Three senior team leaders placed themselves in a line behind them. They ignored their Security detail, who spaced themselves in their usual competent fashion.

As the aliens paced forward, Mia got a better look at them. She nudged Noah, and he nodded. They were definitely humanoid. Their long, thin faces sported all the right features in the right places. Fine, short hair, vestigial eyebrows, eyes a bit larger than those of humans. In fact, they looked vaguely familiar, and as she watched them ease forward, it came to her.

She turned as if speaking to Noah to hide her motion, slipped the lens corner of her tri-me out of her pocket and snapped a shot. She murmured, "Send to Fiona," and let the camera slide back down.

"Pardon?"

She patted his arm. "Anything from Fiona?"

"Recording only at this moment."

"Tell her to send that image to my Dad."

They had worked together a long time. He made no comment beyond a quick nod. Electronic communication to and from the site would be monitored, but the ExIn sent and received a slew of data on a constant basis. A simple .png would go unnoticed.

The alien party was approaching, and she had to concentrate, because the younger-looking of the two smaller aliens walked straight up to her. He was probably not the same species as his leader, though he was of normal human height, with a compact frame. There was no hair evident, and his eyes were large and dark.

"Good morning, Mia Larsen. I am Lieutenant Wolf, aide to our *chef de mission*. To whom should he be introduced first?"

She turned to her line. "This is Peter Kovaks, Microships Project Head."

The lieutenant motioned his leader forward. "Mr. Kovaks, allow me to present Nicolaus Gliese, the leader of this branch of our mission. I believe a handshake is your tradition?"

Kovaks reached out. "It is. Welcome to Earth, Mr. Gliese. This is Noah Jamison, External Interface Technician, and I gather you already know Mia Larsen."

The senior alien shook hands with all three. His hand was slender but strong, with long, tapering fingers. "Only by reputation. I am pleased that you have the right people onsite for our work together." He was taller, slimmer, and more graceful than his assistant, with hair...exactly like Hemi's. His face was identical.

He motioned to the other three aliens. "My security people will want to coordinate technology with yours. I would prefer to move inside for the rest of our conversation."

Peter glanced at the swarm of helicopters and camera drones massed outside the NASA perimeter, the row of media vans along the fence. "I couldn't agree more. The rest of the team is waiting up at the lab."

The procession moved to the elevators, and Mia followed in a fog, her mind swirling. There was no question now of Hemi's parentage. His svelte body, narrow face and fine hair came from this race of aliens.

She was forced to pay attention when they reached the lab, and she played traffic cop until everyone was seated and the cameras were running. Then she sat back to watch.

To her surprise, Noah took it upon himself to speak first, directing his attention towards the alien leader. "Gliese 876 is a red dwarf star 15.2 light-years away from Earth in the constellation of Aquarius."

"It is traditional for our representatives to take on our hosts' name for our star." He gave an amazingly human smile. "We get to choose our first name. I borrowed mine from Copernicus."

Mia regarded his ease of manner and took a risk. "With ironic intent?"

"Humour is a good way to reduce tension. Would you like to take a moment to perform your usual function, Ms. Larsen?"

How much does he know, and why is he telling me he knows?

Covering her uncertainty, she turned to the table. "Nicolaus Copernicus created the revolutionary theory that the sun, not the earth, was the centre of the universe. I assume our visitor expects to perform a similar broadening of our view."

"I dearly hope so."

She nodded. "Please continue."

"This is my aide, Nero Wolf."

Noah interjected again. "Wolf 424, binary red dwarf system in Virgo. Fifteen light years away, ten degrees Galactic north of Gliese." His face reddened. "We...uh sent a few microships your way, I believe."

"That's the place. Two hundred and thirty-nine arrived." Standing beside his svelte superior, the Wolfian looked distinctly stocky, although not outside of human norms. His movements were similarly graceful, but more...predatory was the word that sprang to Mia's mind. "I'm a big fan of your detective novels and films."

Mia nodded. "And your security detail?"

"They will rotate through their roster, with different individuals as time passes. All are connected through audio, visual, and our version of biomem."

"Right." She made a "please continue" gesture. These people seemed to communicate non-verbally, so she'd better practise.

He nodded once in response. "As we speak in your little laboratory, the leaders of your countries are at the United Nations making decisions with my superiors about the composition of the Earth League Committee that will negotiate the terms of future interaction between our societies."

Mia glanced at Kovaks, but he said nothing. "That's all over the regular news media. But you requested to meet with us, here."

"I did."

She waited again. *Is he playing a game? Is this a test?* "I am unsure of the protocol. Are you waiting for an invitation of some sort? If so, please continue."

"Gladly. Once again you prove your worth." He turned his regard on the group.

"Your superiors will be making up a list of the negotiators to meet with my officials: important politicians and, given Earth's present situation, I suppose military leaders.

"But that is only for show. The real interface happens on a smaller scale, and much of it will happen here. This is where we gather the information and make the recommendations the public panel will follow."

Again he paused, and she took it as an opportunity to ask the obvious questions. "You have really dropped a bomb on us, Mr. Gliese. Why us? Why here?"

"There are several reasons." He gestured to Noah. "There is little doubt that Mr. Jamison's ExIn Sphere will be needed. You and your information system constitute one of Earth's foremost intellectual resources. Also, the Microships project was the straw that broke the camel's back, so to speak. There had been years of discussion what to do about your race, and the progress of your swarm brought new urgency to the question."

"What other resources will you need?"

"We are satisfied that this is a smoothly operating team whose primary function is the gathering and analysis of data. With your permission, we will access your team members and technology as needed, but we will try to stay out of the way of your usual work."

"And on your side of the room?"

He flicked a finger at the four other members of his team. "What you see is what you get. Nero takes care of practical details. I require no assistance, because all analysis is done by our Mothership."

Mia took a breath, wondering whether she was supposed, or even allowed, to ask.

"And yes, if we are to be coordinating closely on this project, you may ask the important questions. In fact, it was inconsiderate of me to hold you in suspense. My function is similar to yours, Mia."

Okay, let's see how far that permission goes. "You're a diplomat."

"Is that how you see your function?"

43

"In a very narrow sense, yes. Technically, my job is liaison, which is what a diplomat does, right?"

"Technically." He shot her a glance. "But in a more general sense?"

"Interface and translation. Noah has neither the time, the talent nor the desire to waste on chitchat and game playing. He and his External Intelligence are humanity's foremost problem solvers, and that's where they are most productive. My job is to ease his way into his projects and translate the results for our superiors, the media, and the general public, whichever is in need of answers."

"Perfect."

He turned to Peter Kovaks. "Your programming team will be useful soon. For the moment, I see no need to interrupt the normal functioning of your project. We aren't happy about your swarm, but they are a symptom, not a cause. You have invested seventy years and a lot of resources, and that shouldn't be wasted. I apologize that I will use some of the ExIn's time, but I'm sure it has the capacity to handle both tasks."

Kovaks looked satisfied. "What do you need in terms of office or lab space?"

"A large office or small conference room is all we need. Preferably on this floor for convenience, but in an out-of-the way corner for privacy?"

The new project head hesitated, possibly because he had no idea of the floor layout, so Mia stepped in. "There's an office in the northwest corner with no sign on the door. Abe, is it available?"

The office manager grinned. "And it has a really nice view and large windows."

"Reserved for VIPs?"

"Y'all know how to pick 'em."

Their eyes all turned to Kovaks, who raised his hands defensively. "These are about as important people as we'll ever see around here. How could I refuse?"

Mia made eye contact with everyone, then took charge. "So the Microship project continues. Why don't we go look over our new facilities and stop interfering with an otherwise smooth operation?"

Johnson led the way down the hall to their new office, stopping at the door to reformat the lock to Mia and Noah's palms. He raised his eyebrows to Gleise, who nodded and performed the ritual, gesturing to the rest of his team to follow suit.

Mia grinned to herself. *Fiona will be noting that they have palm prints like us. Or maybe they have superior lock-opening talents and are faking it.*

The room décor lived up to its VIP rating: wood panelling, large desks covered with up-to-date hardware, and a good half of the space occupied by a lounge with sofas, deep pile carpet, a coffee table and a mini kitchen and bar similar to the one in Abe's office.

Mia took it all in. "Noah and I like an oversized viewscreen for meetings and maps. Do you have one of those lying around?"

Abe winked. "Plenty of people ask for one, then discover they don't use it, and it takes up too much desk space. I think I can find an idle unit."

She made a 'cross my heart' sign. "I promise you, we'll use it."

He pulled out his tri-me and turned away to speak into it. Soon he was back. "Is an hour soon enough?"

"I guess we can make do with the metre-wide ones for the moment."

The Office Manager nodded. "If there's anything else you need?"

Wolf stepped forward. "If we do, I know where to find you."

Abe gave him a thumbs up. "If I want to be found." He grinned and left the room.

Mia winked at Nero to affirm that it was a joke, at which the aide made a hand-wiping gesture that probably indicated relief.

Peter Kovaks slipped forward, "I...ah, think I have fulfilled my function here. I can see you people are ready to get to work."

"Certainly." Gliese gave a deep nod. "Thank you for your assistance."

"There is one more event, later...?"

"Yes?"

"I will let Ms. Larsen fill you in. That is more up her alley."

He made his farewells and disappeared.

Nicolaus turned to her. "He ducked that nicely. What kind of official greeting party has been organized at this short notice?"

"An informal chance for you to be introduced to some department heads whose facilities might be useful. It's a huge establishment, with world-class uh..." she spun her hand helplessly, "...tech stuff, most of it highly classified."

"Fair enough." He made eye contact with the nearest agent. "My security detail would love the opportunity to interface with your systems, and I will circulate and find out what kind of 'stuff' everybody has to put at my disposal."

She grinned. "You might be bored. I'm sure there will be a lot of very important people show up, all with very high security clearances and opinions of their importance."

"I don't know about Earthers, but in my people I find that the really intelligent ones are either fascinating or completely boring. On a random distribution."

"It seems our races are not so far apart, after all. So, you will come?"

"I'm a diplomat. This sort of meet-and-greet is my bread and butter."

"Great. Perhaps Nero can liaise with Abe about the timing. I think they left us a couple of hours to settle in."

Nicolaus scanned the room in seeming satisfaction. "Shall we continue my lecture? Perhaps we could make ourselves comfortable. Nero, would you call Mr. Johnson, and after that, find something…" He waved a hand in a vague gesture, but his aide nodded.

"Right away, sir."

Once they were seated and Nero was handing around snacks, the diplomat stretched out his legs and crossed his ankles. "How much do you know about ancient Earther history?"

Noah shrugged. "My ExIn has access to everything that humanity knows." He glanced at Mia.

"But that's all useless in this situation, because human knowledge of history is skewed."

Nicolaus nodded. "The concept of 'history written by the victors' is not unique to your people."

"I note that you still haven't told us what your objectives are for this meeting, so I'm going to take my turn. We need a briefing. Noah's sphere contains about one zettabyte of humanity's knowledge, but it's all from our point of view. What can you — or what are you allowed to — tell us about human history that will change all that?"

"One of my objectives today was to fill you in with whatever information you wished."

"Thank you. We are making progress."

"And the answer to your other question is that I have the discretion to tell you anything in Earther history I consider important. Bearing in mind, of course the caveat about the winners."

"And the next caveat is that we can ask the questions, but you will choose what data to give us."

"I will do my best to give you as unbiased a report as a person of my race is able." The alien sank into the couch in an even more relaxed pose. "So. Ask away."

"If this were a football game, I would suggest that my lack of information leads me to accept the kickoff. What do you think we need to know?"

"And if this were a karate tournament, it would be to your advantage to have me commit myself to the first move, leaving you with the choice of how to receive it."

"Will you concede me the advantage?"

"It would be churlish not to." He glanced at Noah. "Churlish?"

"An old word, seldom used, but still recognizable to most."

"Thank you. I will ask the first question."

7. ANCIENT HISTORY

The Gliesean took a pose that somehow said, *Teacher.*

"How long do you think humankind has been on earth?"

Noah shrugged. "Most scientists agree that Cro-Magnon Man developed about a hundred thousand years ago."

"And the first major societies?"

"New technologies have been pushing our searches deeper into the recent past. Five thousand years, at least."

Nicolaus smiled gently. "Your race has owned this planet for six thousand years."

She stared at the man. If he was a man. "Are you sure?"

Noah frowned. "Why does that number sound nastily familiar? Ah, yes. The Religious Righteous. That's the date of Creation, if you interpret their Bible correctly. They're going to be insufferable."

Gliese laughed. "Not really. We've been running trials on Earth for much longer than that."

Noah sighed. "Nicolaus, please. Our friend, here, is responsible for interpreting all this for the rest of humankind. Can you save us a lot of time by telling the story at the average media reading level?"

Mia took in his puzzlement. "Grade four point five. Do you understand our school grading system?

"That would be nine-year-olds, I think?"

"Close enough." She sat back. "Tell us a tale, O wise one."

The alien draped his supple arm across the sofa arm, hand open. "As I stated, we have been monitoring Earth since we found it, about a hundred thousand years ago. Our methods are comprehensive, because when we find a viable planet, we start

49

exploring the environment, while at the same time developing a race that might live there.

"So, once the reports came in that the environment was stabilizing, we hacked together a couple of genotypes we thought might work."

"Ah. Neanderthal and Cro-Magnon."

"I am aware of those terms. We grew a few thousand samples on the ship that brought them here, and dropped them off in appropriate places. For the first fifty or sixty thousand years, there was too much disturbance of the environment — ice ages and volcanic winters and the like — to do anything but monitor our subjects, tweak their genetic makeup occasionally, and let natural selection do its job. The Neanderthals didn't survive. It was only recently that the Earth settled down enough, and we started giving larger colonies the wherewithal to create substantial structures. From that point, about six thousand years ago, you've been on your own."

"No more tweaking?"

"The moment a race becomes self-aware, it starts modifying its own genetics by non-natural selection. For example, the size of humans has grown several centimetres in the last thousand years. We had nothing to do with that. It was more likely the increase in food production."

"How would that change the genetics?"

"Larger specimens have the advantage in areas like defense and breeding. However, they take a proportionally large amount of food. Smaller animals last during famine, while larger ones have a better survival rate in times of better food supply. Human societies would magnify that tendency through ethics and enculturation."

"That follows."

The alien turned to Mia. "The acknowledged genius understands. How's the average nine-year-old coping?"

"That's my strength. Translation of complex ideas into concepts my target audience can understand. My greatest danger, also."

The alien regarded her. "Because…"

"The act of translation automatically adds my personal values to the metadata. Especially with an uneducated subject, the translator can inject the material with unintended ethics and ideals. While we try to teach people information so they can think for themselves, we may actually be influencing them in all sorts of ways we don't even notice."

She stopped and stared at him. "And you already knew that. You just wanted to see how I think."

His mouth opened, but she started first. "And the reason you're leading the conversation in this direction is because you aliens face the same quandary when you deal with Earthers. You said before that you left us on our own."

"Up to a certain point."

"Which is the essential meaning of the original message."

Noah showed a brief moment of uncertainty. "What…?"

She favoured him with a gentle smile. "They want us to make our own choices, but if we keep making bad ones…"

"Ahh."

Gleise gave her a look she couldn't read. "You're more intelligent than you first seem."

"Perhaps. Probably not."

He smiled. "Because…"

"I spend a lot of time with truly intelligent people. My objective is to figure out how they think, so I can interpret them properly. Thus, intelligent people think I come up with very creative ideas. Actually, I'm following their minds and predicting where their logic is taking them. Sometimes I get there first."

He slapped his knee in what was probably an acquired human mannerism. "And they think, 'She got the idea before I did. She must be smarter than me.' Am I right?"

"Something like that. There are other tools in my kit."

The alien nodded. "I'm sure there are. And that's why I want you on the Earth League Committee as a full contributing member."

After a short silence, she shrugged. "Well, you came up with that idea long before I did."

"Aha! She reaches into her bag and pulls out the next tool."

The game continues. "I concede the point." She nodded towards Noah. "Perhaps you could enlighten the genius."

"She was stuck for something to say, so she made a complimentary comment showing understanding of my point."

"The nine-year-old would say I changed the subject." She sat straighter. "But that got us off topic long enough for me to regain my aplomb. I gather I have demonstrated my skills enough that you can see a place for me on the team."

"Rather, you have demonstrated enough skills."

"Ah. General usefulness, rather than a specific skill set."

"Well done."

She gave him The Stare, which she found necessary with certain individuals. "A warning, Mr. Gliese. Those intelligent people I train with play this game constantly, and my patience with it is limited."

"This is not a game, young lady." She could read tension in his body. "The fate of your world is at stake."

"If it's not a game, why do you keep testing me, when you have already decided that I am to be on the team? An uncharitable read is that we are now playing for position points, and you will keep it up until you have demonstrated that you are, truly, the top of the food chain."

She leaned forward and leveled him with a stare. "At which point I will tip my hat and slowly ride away, because I will have nothing to do with that sort of organization."

"But surely you will follow your orders…

She narrowed her eyes. "This meeting is dangerously close to its end."

His posture did not change, but somehow the tension eased. "Fair enough. Thank you for putting up with some necessary folderol." His eyes shot to her face. "That is a word you use, isn't it? Folderol?"

She slid a glance to Noah, and the orb near his shoulder took on a thinking pattern.

"Not seriously employed for a couple of hundred years, sir. It is still in the academic lexicon."

Nicolaus grinned. "Well, I can't pretend to academic prowess. I'm supposed to be a diplomat. What word should I use?"

Again, the orb spun.

Noah grinned. "The synonym with the closest connotation is 'mumbo jumbo.' If you want to be bland, it would be 'nonsense.' Most people, whether they dared use the term or not, would prefer 'bullshit.'"

"Thank you." He turned back to Mia. "In any case, this meeting has served several of its many purposes. Shall we take a moment to settle in, then join the festivities downstairs?"

She rose and led the way. "I warn you, a couple of tequilas and my forbearance dissolves completely."

The alien turned to Noah as they left the room. "Is she like this a lot?"

"I'd rather not answer, sir."

"Why not? I note you calling me 'sir.' I suspect a minor insult is involved."

"She only uses that act with the fools who try to play games with her."

"I see. And do your people not trade quips with friends?"

Mia shook her head. "Bitter experience has taught me to be very careful who I tangle with. People are so...fragile, don't you think?"

"It is the same with us."

"So, you share witticisms only with your social or intellectual equals?"

"It is a recreational enjoyment that, as you are aware, has serious advantages in training for a diplomat. Like any martial art, we only practise it with friends who will not be injured."

She nodded slowly. "I think I might enjoy this assignment. I am tempted to accept the invitation. If my orders agree, of course."

"Yes, if your military is anything like ours, the leaders have to be reassured once in a while that they are in charge."

They entered the cafeteria, where Nicolaus was immediately swallowed up in the swirl of minor NASA notables anxious to bolster their "I was there when..." moments.

Mia snagged a glass of red wine and slipped over to stand with her back to the wall, watching the crowd. A part of her mind was registering who was talking to whom, but for the moment, all she wanted was a break.

She glanced at Noah, who seemed to be unaffected. "This whole situation is so First Day in High School."

"I loved my first day in high school." His brow furrowed. "What about you?"

She scoffed. "They took you into the computer lab and showed you all the tech you could never get your hands on before. You probably didn't even notice the other students."

"I did so. I'm still friends with a couple of them."

"You know that's not what I meant."

"Yeah, the normal lot didn't bother me much. I was too high profile, and that insulated me from the usual problems. What about you?"

"It took me a while. I walked out of elementary school, where I was top of my class and a star athlete, and stepped into a boiling mass of hormones where I was a nobody, all the rules had changed, and my currency was completely devalued."

"Yeah, humanity's at that point right now. How did you cope?"

"It took a while to revalue my currency and develop some alliances."

"Now, that you've got to translate for the nine-year-olds in the crowd."

"I found some friends who were excellent in the muscle department but woefully inadequate with the social nuances. Once they had my sharp tongue to ease them out of embarrassing situations, they stopped having to beat people up. The teachers all considered me a good influence, and the rest of the student population learned to give us elbow room."

"And how did we do with Mr. Gleise?"

She grinned. "Tell me. Why do you think we had all that folderol about 'folderol'?"

"I dunno. I guess he's trying to learn colloquial English."

"No, he was playing my trick on me. He changed the subject of discussion to an area where you took a leading role. This had the double objective of easing the conflict with me and appealing to my protective attitude towards you. We have to watch that guy. There's always two or three different games going on."

"Well, he is a diplomat."

"And I'm guessing he'll have the leading role on our 'team.' Which might not look much like what we call teamwork. We'll have to see."

"And then you will revalue humanity's currency and develop some alliances, and we're set."

8. DIPLOMACY

The reception did not last long, and soon they were at the Building 44 front door, where the earlier ballet played out in reverse order, ending with the shuttle ramp swinging up to blend with the underside of the ship, and a swift, silent takeoff.

Peter Kovaks stood beside her. "So, what do we do now?"

"We take Mr. Gliese at his word. I'm sure your superiors will want to know what's going on. If they have any specific instructions for the ExIn, someone will let us know."

"So, it's back to work as usual until someone tells us otherwise?"

She shrugged. "This is so above and beyond the usual that we have no other option."

Peter smiled. "One of the benefits of being middle management. Once you kick the matter upstairs, you can rest easy."

"Until it comes tumbling back down and lands in your lap."

He sighed. "As my grandmother used to say, 'Sufficient unto the day is the evil thereof.'"

She turned to him. "That one came out often in my family, too."

"New Testament, I believe. We used to be a Christian nation, you know."

With that enigmatic comment, he turned inside. She had no choice but to follow him up to the lab.

Where she finished the afternoon in a daze. Fortunately, she had a new office to organize, and Noah was preoccupied with helping his sphere sift through all the information zooming around the world, official and otherwise.

As she drove to her parents' house, the thoughts, plans, and possibilities swirling through her brain gradually settled on one truth. Hemi would no longer be there. She had only known him for a few days, but already she could tell how his mind worked. In the short term, freedom of choice came first, security a close second. Long term, he wanted to make a difference for his people. *That's the kicker. Which people will he side with? And if he asks me, what do I tell him?*

Her father met her at the door, a sober look on his face. He gestured towards the basement stairs.

As she had expected, it was neat as a pin and felt...empty. The equipment was shut down and unplugged. There would be no point in checking.

"He used the vacuum and took the dust bag away. I think maybe he spread it around at the park."

"He's thorough, I have to give him that."

Her father nodded and headed up the stairs. Then he gave her a meaningful glance and continued down the hall and into the back yard, where he took a seat on the garden swing.

She sat beside him, and they turned to face each other. "What?"

He lowered his voice. "The name Skidoo came up several times. I assume it's a name? Does that mean he's going to northern Canada for the winter?"

It was easy to come up with a natural laugh, and she turned out to face the world again. "No, but I get the joke. Thanks, Dad."

She rose and steadied the swing. "Come back inside. I can tell you the edited version of what happened today, and we can watch the news to see how the official version of the game plays out."

"Great. It'll have to be during supper. Your Mum always does her best when you're coming."

Over the meal she told them a brief version of her day. As her next of kin, they had a medium-level security clearance from NASA, so she gave them a thorough briefing.

The television news didn't tell them much more. Heads of state, parades, ceremonies, empty official words.

Pleading fatigue, she went home early, and her father walked her out to the car.

He glanced around. "Do you think our house is bugged?"

"I doubt it, but you'll be on the surveillance drone route. You don't have to worry. You had a temporary boarder that I foisted off on you. Some street kid I was rescuing. He came, you didn't have too much to do with him, and he went. They do that. Pick a kid you both knew in the past, so your stories jibe if they run mug shots past you. Case closed; you're glad he didn't take the silverware with him."

"I never ask you about these things, and I'm not going to start now, but I liked him. Room's always available."

"Thanks, Dad. I hope I don't have to call you on it. Or maybe I do." She started the car, then looked up at him. "And don't erase the image I sent. Don't try to hide it. Sending my family, who have clearance, a first look at the aliens is a forgivable stretch of security."

"Fine. See you soon?"

"It looks like I'll be working from home for a few weeks at least."

"Great." He slapped the roof of the car. "Sleep well."

"Sure." She pulled away, clinging to the warm sense of security her parents' home always gave her.

9. AI AND ART

The following morning, she contacted Noah. "Sorry to drag you out of the conjugal bed so early, but could we have a quick meeting before work?"

"Sure. Fifteen minutes enough?"

"Fine."

"Back to bed for a little cuddle."

"Too much information, my friend. See you soon."

He was there as promised, and they went into their lab office and he closed the door. "What's up?"

"I have some information Fiona needs, but it's from a confidential source. Can she launder the information without diluting its impact?"

"Do it all the time. Go ahead. We're listening."

She took a deep breath, then plunged in. "The first piece of evidence is incontrovertible. This race of aliens can crossbreed with humans. It is unusual, but it can happen."

"Good data." Noah regarded her. "What else?"

"They have been implanting agents in the general population, at least for the last fifteen years."

"That won't surprise anyone, but it's nice to have confirmation. Is there more?"

"At least three individuals sighted in my neighbourhood in the last two months. Two males, one female. No idea of their movements or objectives. Visual sightings only, no record."

He frowned. "Now, that might impact us. Is there a possibility they were checking on you?"

"No evidence, I'm afraid. Up until recently, I can't think of any reason. You'd be a more likely target."

He shrugged. "Nothing suspicious. Of course, NASA watches me pretty carefully."

They sat in silence for a moment. Then he slapped the arm of his chair. "That bit of data is going to need some careful polishing before it's given out. Should we tell our alien counterparts?"

"I think so. We're being as honest as we can, and we don't automatically assume the motivation of any action."

"All right. We can pass the agent sightings along, but let's keep the interbreeding to ourselves. It gives out too much information about the source."

"I was afraid it would."

He shook his head. "The only possible evidence would be a sighting, and confirmation could only come from the contact person." He met her eyes. "And I didn't need Fiona to do that analysis."

"Send it up the chain of command as far as you can, keeping the source as far out of it as you can."

"Done." He pushed a com module into his ear and listened. "Security detects an aerial approach. Why don't you go out and greet our guests? Or our workmates, I suppose."

Nicholaus and Nero were at the door, complete with their three faceless henchmen, promptly at eight. It soon became evident that the lounge area would be their primary workspace, as the exchange of ideas was more important to their task than the transfer of data.

However, that day it was Noah who opened the conversation. "We have some technical details to handle before we start our discussions."

Gliese nodded. "I assumed you would. Please proceed."

Noah turned to Mia. "The Mothership will allow Fiona limited access to her databases, but it requires an initialization process. I have checked, and we have the go-ahead from NASA admin."

"That's a big area of trust."

The alien made a negating gesture. "A mere formality."

"Not quite." Noah was looking serious. "There has always been a fear that our ExIn sphere might contain the seeds of a supercerebrus, or uberbrain, that might subjugate mankind. Of course, we think we have taken all the proper precautions, but the chance we missed something remains. The scientists of the Meld have far outpaced us in this field, and they have offered their services to run a check for us."

"Thus calming any fears of the rest of humanity here at home and out there in space?"

"Exactly."

"Sounds fine to me."

Noah gave a wry grin. "They weren't asking our opinions, but I'm glad we all agree." He turned to Nicolaus. "It won't take long. Please proceed with the morning's activities."

"I am receiving the results of the analysis as we speak." Gliese pointed to a spot behind his left ear. "We all carry various grades of what you would perhaps call 'Internal Input' receivers. Considerably less powerful than your Fiona, but fine for communication with our Mothership."

"We have no communication ability, but we do have biodigital memory implants."

"We had assumed that." He shifted to a different position. "Noah did not mention it, but our technicians were given permission to make any modifications to Fiona necessary for safety reasons. The strange thing is that she doesn't need many."

"She doesn't?"

"Our programmers are quite impressed, but puzzled."

"Why?"

"They can't figure out how a race naive enough to send out such a dangerous swarm as your microships could at the same time create an intelligent entity with such self-control. They were able to find a couple of weak spots in Fiona's inner security programming, but those were related to eventualities Earther humans have never come across and aren't likely to. Mia, any ideas from your point of view?"

"Good programming and dumb luck. Plus cultural metacontrol, of course."

"Translation for the nine-year-olds?"

"They were careful to match Fiona with a rational, moral individual. She's had seven years of on-the-job training, the whole of human philosophy at her fingertips, and Noah to keep her on the right track on a day-to-day basis."

"And you to keep Noah on track."

"That's not in my job description."

"Isn't it?"

"No, but it's in my personality. I suppose you could speculate that I was chosen carefully, as well."

He nodded. "We use similar methodology. The human factor is essential if the decisions will affect humans."

He shifted position again, and she could tell something new was coming.

"You Earthers have a lot to offer the rest of us, you know."

"We do? I thought we were the trailer trash of the Human sphere, spreading our garbage around and playing bad country music at full volume."

"There is a bit of the country cousin in your situation, but in some areas your technology has segued into areas no other culture has explored. The microships were ill-advised, but the nano technology is cutting edge, even in the Meld. Your fine arts are helter-skelter, but impressive in many ways."

"Can you give me some examples?"

"What about music?"

"What about it?"

"Earth has more recognizable musical genres than the rest of human culture combined."

"You're kidding!"

"No, most societies select a limited set of musical styles, and each one develops on its own, with its chosen instruments and fans, usually connected to a social, political, or economic section of the population. Earther music recognizes no boundaries. You have a long tradition of church organs in your rock and roll music. The piano is ubiquitous. Country stars perform with symphony orchestras. Wait till Earth becomes open to tourists. What happens then will make your Grand Ole Opry look like a country fair."

She gave a wry smile and took a more businesslike pose. "And that brings us to the topic we are working on this week. What policies do we need to develop to regulate tourism?"

And on they went. She learned more than she thought she would ever need about the procedures Earth's countries used to regulate the intermingling of citizens at every level. More to the point, she learned about the disasters of nineteenth-century colonial policies on the indigenous cultures they rolled over. Less entertaining were the hours of careful parsing of sentences to squeeze out the most innocent of errors in meaning or nuance in their reports.

They interspersed the periods of grind with more general information sessions, mainly about the Meld culture.

One day, when she was particularly wrung out and comfortable enough with the aliens, she asked a question she had been mulling over.

"You people show up here every day in what looks like a fighting craft with some kind of Sci-Fi silent drive, and you're commuting a couple of thousand kilometres from Washington. But your Mothership looks like a flying saucer from a cheesy 1960 Space Opera. Do you really use flying saucers?

"Oh, yes, that's a real ship. It wasn't the one we would have chosen. It's too big and heavy for ferry service and uses a lot of fuel. But there were limited choices, and we wanted to give Earthers a familiar image to reduce stress in the population. The reason for a toroid shape is for rotational gravity, which is the cheapest because it doesn't use any energy. This ship was built in Sol's Asteroid Belt a couple of hundred years ago to be the Principal Residence of the System Scientific Administrator. I've had a cabin onboard since I arrived in the Sol System five Earth years ago, so it's handy for me." He smiled. "I went to bed one night, and when I woke up in the morning, I was on Earth. "

"How many of your people are in our system right now?"

"The present official count is near 18,450. There are always a number of women in their ninth month of pregnancy and that data changes on a daily basis."

"You still use natural birth to reproduce?"

"Well, it isn't accompanied by quite as much noise and mess as here, but we do employ the natural way of doing things. It's better for everyone in the long run.

"But to continue; most of our people live in a space station similar to your Bernal Sphere, a living space 2 kilometres in diameter and 10 kilometres long. At the moment it rides in a Lagrange position on the far side of Saturn. That was another reason it was time to make official contact. On the scale of the rest of space, it's a small grain of sand on a large beach, but it emits all sorts of light and energy and media signals, and sooner or later you were going to spot it if we didn't move to a different orbit. Which is a major hassle."

Mia wondered why, after all this time and effort, they seemed to be in such a rush to complete the treaties, but she didn't feel they were at that level of honesty, yet. She filed the question on the 'To Do' list in her biomem.

10. SKIDOO

The alien culture was becoming more and more interesting to her, so her days at work were improving. She was contributing to something important.

Her evenings at home were another matter. She didn't dare say anything to anyone, but it couldn't stop her from thinking about Hemi.

I can't go looking for him. If there is anyone on his trail, I might lead them to him. On the other hand, he wouldn't have taken off without leaving me some sort of clue how to get hold of him.

Of course, he can contact me any time.

That brought her to another level of honesty. *Is this only bothering me because someone else is in control, and I'm not?* That one hit her as she was brushing her teeth, and she stared at herself in the mirror. *Most definitely. Grow up, girl.*

Nevertheless, one fact remained. Hemi was out in the world, on the run. That gave him freedom but restricted his data collection. In contrast, she was at the centre of things. If she came up with anything important to him, she had to know how to get it to him.

With nobody to offer rebuttal but her image in the mirror, she had to admit it was a good argument.

She went looking for Skidoo. Hemi had mentioned a job. She would probably be about twelve, now. What can a twelve-year-old do? Then she had it.

Graffiti! Skidoo is a tagger. I always thought her work was a bit slap-dash from a lack of experience, but what do I know? Maybe she's the latest thing.

Which created the next problem.

I get home at six, and the sun is just setting. I can't go around looking for street art in the dark. Especially in the part of town where you tend to find it. NASA security would be onto me in a week, if some mugger didn't get me first. A person in my position can't go roaming the streets.

Then it hit her.

Wait a minute. Dammit, Hemi, you've got me thinking like a criminal. Skidoo is a registered citizen. I'm on her file as a concerned friend.

A quick call to Texas Health and Human Services was all she needed.

The woman she talked to was cagey at first, but she disappeared for a moment to check, and came back with a different attitude. "Oh, yes, Ms. Larsen, you're on her list. Do you need to get in touch for some reason?"

"Nothing special. And I'm sorry, but my private dealings are under a media blackout at the moment, so please use more than your usual discretion."

"Oh, of course. My lips are sealed, just like all my files."

"Great. Maybe we can put an appearance together when this all blows over. She might agree if it helps her artistic career."

"You've seen her latest score?"

"I've been out of touch."

"Check out the Hot-Dodge website. You'll be impressed."

"Thank you, Do you have a home contact for her?"

"We're treating her with kid gloves at the moment. When our younger clients approach turning points in their lives or careers, we have very strict protocols. Even for you..."

"I asked for privacy. She deserves the same."

"Why don't you leave her a message? She drops in once in a while, and I can make sure she gets it."

"Sure. Tell her I'm impressed with her work. She has my number."

They finished the call with some of the meaningless chit-chat that fills in the blanks of a business relationship. Then Mia dove for her internet browser.

Hot-Dodge turned out to be an independent parts store specializing in Chrysler products, very popular with both serious dragsters and antique collectors. According to the website, anyway. And if their homepage artwork had anything to do with it, they were on a roll.

The front window of their shop sported a floor-to-ceiling cartoon closeup of a 1975 Plymouth Barracuda dragster, featuring a huge supercharger sticking out of the hood with the words "426 HEMI" stroked across it in big, red letters.

Maybe I don't have to go looking for Skidoo after all.

She started a search of her media feeds for the number 426. Hits were few, but one ad from her email junk folder caught her attention. It invited her to free images of nearby stars with possible planets, advertising "426 images never posted before."

Let's not rush things. I might be seeing what I want to see. That's always dangerous.

She pulled out her old iPad, which only connected to the internet through an ancient Hotmail account she kept active just in case. Now she knew in case of what. She typed in the URL and waited.

The landing page invited her to "accept all cookies," something she never did. Except this time.

The site looked to be a legitimate enterprise, offering images of various celestial bodies, to be downloaded for wallpaper and printout at reasonable prices for the higher resolutions. She spent half an hour browsing through, but found nothing that attracted her attention. This must be one of the sources of Hemi's comfortable bank balance.

Frustrated, she closed the site.

Her iPad froze.

A popup message appeared on the screen, inviting her to give her opinion on the site. *Bingo!* She thought a moment, then entered her message.

"I have direct contact."

The page flashed an image of Skidoo's hotrod and went blank.

11. AI-GUIDED GOVERNMENT

Monday morning as they started work, she was mildly concerned when Nicolaus suggested that the project Security Head should join them. Her tension increased when one of the alien guards entered as well.

When they were all seated, Gliese caught their attention with one of his flowing gestures. "A security concern has come to my attention, and it touches all of us. There are times when our people are forced to move in the Earther community. We have used this technique only as a last resort. However, we have information from a creditable source that some of our people have been seen in the area around Ms. Larsen's residence. Specifically, Gliesean individuals. Two males, one female, and one smaller woman or teenager. We have no information of their activities, and I can assure you that if they were on official business, I would know."

His nod gave Mia the floor. Holding back a smile at the irony of it all, she shrugged. "I have nothing to add. Due to my change in status, I have lately been more rigorous with the standard precautions NASA employees are trained to take. I have neither heard nor seen anything unusual. My parents haven't noticed anything, or they would have informed me. I will check with them, of course. Is there anything we can do about this?"

Security Head Reimer looked to Nicolaus. "We will have to include your people in our threat assessment protocol, especially since the possible targets are your citizens."

The alien nodded. "Security fails most often due to miscommunication."

"So far, our communication has been flawless. I am impressed at how well our technologies match."

"They were designed to."

Reimer took a moment to digest the implications of that statement. He turned to his Gliesean counterpart. "We'll get together immediately and start the assessment. Ms. Larsen, we'll be back for your input in about an hour."

"I'm not going anywhere." She gave him a grateful smile. "At least, not until you tell me it is safe to do so."

He gave her a half-salute and a grin, squared his shoulders and strode out.

She refused, even in her own head, to fault a man for being proud of his work.

Noah leaned closer to her. "Are we showing interest in a certain rock-jawed military type?"

She chuckled. "Merely the application of diplomacy, my socially inept friend. Great for morale."

"I stand corrected."

Nicolaus gave them a moment, then attracted their attention without a fuss. "Do we have any specific topics for our discussion today?"

Noah nodded. "Last week you assessed my ExIn, but you never really gave a precis of its intelligence."

"Have you done your famous Turing test on it?"

"It isn't possible. It only communicates with me, it doesn't really talk, and I know it's a computer. Should we have?"

"There would be no use."

"That's what we thought. Why do you agree?"

"Your Turing test is a joke."

Noah looked helplessly to Mia, and she took over.

"You're going to have to explain that."

"One focus of your AI program has been to create a computer that can mimic human speech perfectly. Your methods were sound, and it was only a matter of time and volume of training data before you succeeded. But you're still using the old "next most used word" technique. A ball thrower used for batting practice is more accurate than a human pitcher. Do you assume it can pitch a game?"

"But we were afraid we could create a supercerb that could outthink us and take over our society."

"Your fears were well founded, but that's not based on the stupidity of the computers you have been able to create."

"An impolite way of saying we have a long distance to go."

Gliese gave an apologetic wave. "Your society is in the early part of its Information Age. You have not yet learned how to distinguish true knowledge from the ability to communicate data. Your ancient method of choosing your leaders based on their performance in a protracted publicity battle is a perfect demonstration. Everyone knows that very soon there will be a computer that can orate better than a politician, and many fear that it will take over. They created the Turing test as a publicity stunt to calm those fears.

"Your problem is that you can create a computer that mimics human speech so well you can't tell the difference. But it isn't talking. It doesn't understand what the words mean."

"It doesn't?"

"Tell me. Which is more intelligent, a parrot or a dog?"

"A dog, I suppose."

"But a parrot can speak to you in your language. Doesn't that mean it's more intelligent?"

"A dog is still considered smarter. I'm not sure why."

"You teach a dog the word 'treat.' You say 'Treat' and he comes for one. Stimulus and response. You teach him 'No.' You say, 'No treat,' and he goes away. The dog understands the concept of negativity.

"You teach a parrot, 'Polly want a cracker,' and it says the phrase when it wants to be fed. But teach the parrot to say 'No.' Will the parrot say, 'Polly no want a cracker,' when it is not hungry? It will not. You have to teach the parrot the whole new phrase to get a negative. It doesn't understand language at all. It can create a vocal stimulus to get an expected response. Period."

"And this applies to computer intelligence?"

"Given any word or group of words, the computers Earthers are using will give you the next word used by the largest number of people in its training set. It doesn't 'understand' the word. A truly intelligent computer can understand the meaning of a moral judgement, compare it to a huge number of other, similar judgements, quantify it relative to any conflicting choices, take a hundred or a thousand different possible effects into account and create the wisdom of Solomon."

Mia raised one finger. "And then there's emotion."

"In what way?"

"People like to contribute their opinion on a decision. Part of their satisfaction is because the data will now be considered, but a large part is the feeling that they have been recognized as part of the process. Once you get a sentience that can take human emotion into account, you're making real progress."

Noah shook his head. "That's a long way out of our reach at the moment. How about you?"

"You mean, have we created a sentience smart enough to apply human morals far better than any group of humans could?"

"Have you?"

"Of course. The Mothership contains one."

"With a human to monitor its decisions."

"It's not quite that simple, but yes. We call such people Mentors."

Noah was frowning and Fiona's colours swirled. "This information needs to get to our programming community."

The set of the alien's slim shoulders indicated caution. "That will be part of our interaction. I will set it down as a subject for the scientific interchange portion."

"But the actual information?"

"You are quite free to discuss it at the philosophical level as we have been doing. I would have thought that our eagerness to include the ExIn sphere in the process would indicate our approval of the way it was conceived."

Now Noah was all smiles. "Of course." He paused. "I suppose you realize we have all the procedures prepared, and it is only political caution that has stalled our project at the single prototype stage."

Gleise nodded. "At this point, it would be natural for you to clear off the moth balls. You might waste a lot of time finding answers we already know, but it's still better than sitting passively, waiting for us to hand it to you for free."

Mia nodded. "Because you always pay for freebies, sooner or later."

He gave her a quizzical look. "So cynical for one so young."

"I had the innocence trained out of me." She glanced at him. "Of course, I try not to be naïve about not being naïve, if you see what I mean."

Nicolaus gave a shout of laughter. "Very good. And if you were one of my people, you would have finished with a hand roll, thus," he demonstrated, "that says, 'two negatives don't always make a positive.' That would have been a conversation stopper."

She tilted her head to one side and regarded him. "And I take that to mean that this topic is closed, and we can't avoid finishing the list of criteria for universities and colleges to interface with your educational institutions. You know, the one from yesterday that we promised ourselves we would finish when we weren't so tired."

12. HALF BREED

She had sort of hoped Hemi would make contact that evening, but he didn't, leaving her to worry about how to untangle the whole mess. By morning she thought she had it worked out very cleverly.

At their usual daily goal-setting get-together, she waited until Nicolaus asked for her input. She took her time answering. "Our little problem with the possible infiltrators bothered me last night. There was something familiar about it. Then I remembered. There is a novel in children's literature about a boy in the American Colonial Era who lives with his native Indian mother, and his white father comes to try to get him back, but he doesn't want to go."

Noah chuckled and his sphere mottled briefly. "That's the plot to seven Romances, three Historical Novels from American Civil War days, five Science Fiction novels and a vampire series. Not counting numerous short stories and films in several genres."

"I think I see where this is going, but please continue."

She shrugged. "All I'm pointing out is a standard meme in literature of a half-breed child being chased by some kind of agents from one cultural group or the other, sometimes both. A very powerful one is simply called *Half-Breed.* Perhaps you are aware that a whole culture in Canada is made up of people of mixed white and aboriginal heritage. They call themselves Metis."

"And this sudden interest in mixed races is leading us to...?"

"There's a rumour going around. I grant you it's only a rumour, but it was to be expected. Tell me. Is it possible for our two races to interbreed?"

The alien nodded. "I begin to understand. Possibly, but not likely."

"An interesting choice of words. You think it's physically possible, but it hasn't happened yet."

"To our knowledge, no. Not officially, anyway."

"So, if my creative imagination hasn't run away with itself, there might be a mixed-race kid running around my neighbourhood with three of your agents in pursuit, and you don't know anything about it. Officially."

"Or unofficially. It is possible, of course, but I think it highly unlikely."

"So do I. It sounds too dramatic. But that doesn't matter."

Gliese sat quite straight. "If it doesn't matter, why bring it up?"

"Because all that really counts is the fact that it could. Given a future intermingling of the two races, it probably will. And all our histories agree. When two cultures collide, one wins and the other loses, but the half-breeds lose the most. Ask the Metis. Better still, read the book. It's very moving."

He smiled at the tension went out of his body. "Nicely presented. Rules about mixed-race individuals will go on the list."

She eyed him suspiciously. "Do your people have such rules?"

"We have to. Some of our races interbreed quite freely."

"Then why did you let me go on like that?"

He gave an eloquent shrug. "It was a well-considered presentation. Why spoil your fun?"

"Thank you, kind sir." She rose and dropped a curtsy.

His finger snapped out, pointing at her. "That gesture. Why isn't it used more?"

She shrugged. "It went out of fashion along with the corset."

"But it says so much."

"I guess it was saying the wrong things."

"A pity. Yours is such a stiff race."

She grinned at Noah. "He's been hanging around with Caucasians too much. Is there any way to get him into a nightclub? A real one with a mixed clientele?"

"There's a retro Motown club down on Washington Street that's supposed to be pretty funky." He paused to check data on the sphere. "Yes, that would do the trick. A private balcony with outside access overlooks the dance floor."

Mia chuckled. "Not guaranteed to be the real thing, but it's the best we can find and maintain any security at all."

Nicolaus frowned. "I'm not up on retrospective slang. What's 'funky?' Is it like it sounds?"

"Nothing to do with smell. It's one of those useful words that cycles back in every once in a while. It generally means something that you can't explain, but you've decided to like it, out of a sense of adventure."

"Ah. One of those words intended to say more about the speaker than about the object it describes."

"That's got it. Are you interested?"

He paused to think. Or check his implant contact. "Would they be open on a Thursday?"

"I'm sure."

"That works. I have other meetings in the morning, and I can't make it here until after lunch. I was considering staying in Washington all day, but perhaps we can work late."

"Noah, what's the food like?"

"Standard Detroit stuff: Coney island hotdogs, square pizza, slow-roasted shawarma, sliders, corned beef egg rolls."

"Corned beef egg rolls I have to try."

Mia winced. "Joe Reimer is going to have a cow and three calves. I'll talk to him and get it organized."

But to her surprise, the Security Head wasn't fazed at all. "I've been there four-five times. It's set up for parties like ours." He glanced at her. "It's not the real thing, you know. It's a bunch of wannabes trying to be hip or cool or whatever the most recent label is."

She grinned. "Have you ever noticed that all those places you think of as the 'real ones' are full of wannabes trying to be seen in tune with the latest trend. Nobody with their act together would go within a mile of the place unless they need it for their occupation."

He shook his head. "Part of your job too, hey?"

"Been there, done that, too many times." She lowered her voice. "There might be another reason. There's a contact I want Nicolaus to make that can't get anywhere near the Space Center.

"Security Risk?"

"He's fifteen years old and completely off the radar."

"I assume you have your reasons."

"You'll understand when you meet him, and that's all I can say."

"Fair enough. You get him there; I'll get him in."

"Thanks, Joe. This could be important. Or it could turn out to be nothing."

13. MEETING

That evening there was a text from Hemi waiting on her home computer. When decoded, the message was pleasantly specific:

'Retro Funplex. Six pm. Park in the south-east corner of the front lot under the trees. Corner of Beechnut and Hemlock Hill. It'll be crowded, but that's the farthest end of the lot. Come early. I don't want to be waiting around in the open. Follow me into the park. I'll lead you to a place we can talk.'

She followed the instructions, and when a graceful figure in hoodie and jeans strolled by, she waited a moment, then followed. The fairgoers started to crowd together, and she could see three other kids in similar outfits. *Good for him.*

Bad for her. She closed the distance between them and followed a few metres behind his left shoulder. Then she shifted to his right and moved up parallel. He glanced her way and moved on.

His head came up and he made a quick move to the right that crossed directly in front of her. She turned and followed down a dim and smelly alley between rows of what she realized were portable sanitary cabins. He turned at an intersection, and when she followed, he was there waiting for her.

"Howja like my office?"

She matched his grin. "Private, I suppose."

He flicked the joke away. "What's up?"

She briefly described her situation and what was going on.

"And this guy. You trust him?"

"I trust him to stick to the bigger picture and not sweat the details. I can't make promises. Your only way in is to make your own deal. I'll tell you one thing; you're special. Nobody knows you exist, or if they do, they're not telling. There haven't been any others like you, or he'd know about them."

"And how do you explain my three friends back in Southside?"

"They probably had nothing to do with you. As it's worked out, there's a better chance they wanted something from me. The point is that Nicolaus doesn't know about them. And he knows everything, believe me. They have a supersapience on their Mothership, and he contacts it every night."

"So, you think I should come in from the cold."

"I don't think you're doing anything out here besides surviving, and sooner or later a winter storm's going to roll in. Once you're in contact with Gliese, you have a chance to contribute at the highest level."

She regarded him. "The best thing about him is that he thinks like you. He's far enough up the ladder that he has the freedom to act. He wants to do the best he can for his people."

"What happens if we don't agree what's best for my people?"

"You're in the same position as the rest of us. I believe he has the integrity to let you go away and do what you must."

The boy shrugged. "You've got me there. I'm making out all right, but all my time is spent on security. What am I doing for anybody?" He nodded thoughtfully. "Yes, I'll meet with the guy. How are you going to spring him loose?"

She grinned. "I'm not. Do you know the Motown Club on Washington Street?

"That tourist trap?"

"It's meant for tourists like us. My Head of Security has taken several parties of VIPs there without incident. It's the perfect place for you to meet him. This Thursday night."

"I can make that work. What's the plan?"

"Here's the sticking point. You have to trust somebody else."

Hemi thought a moment. "One of your security guys. How are you going to swing that? I don't have enough cash to bend a NASA man. You don't have enough."

"We're doing this legitimately. He's the Project Head of Security. Once again, the perfect guy. He has to worry about security for his client, and if you're under his wing, he won't have to worry about you."

"What did you do? Call in a favour, or promise one?"

She cuffed his head. "I appealed to his loyalty to the team. We both believe in what we're doing, and he believes me that you might help."

He gave a crooked smile, shaking his head.

"What...?"

"You just played me."

"...oh. The stuff about believing in what we were doing. I admit, I thought it might help persuade you."

"Okay, it worked. What's the plan?"

"This is Joe Reimer's personal number. Tomorrow, you contact him somehow. He'll make the arrangements. I'm no good at this sort of stuff, and he's a pro."

"I like dealing with pros. No messy emotional stuff."

"Anything else you can think of?"

"I won't say thanks, yet."

"Sassy kid. Say, Skiddoo is doing all right, isn't she?"

"Hate to tell you, the Barracuda was my idea."

"Yeah, but you didn't get it to go viral."

"Not very happy about that, but..." He shrugged. "Can you find your way out?"

"Sure. If not, I've got my...She patted her pocket, then her other pocket. She was about to get worried when a motion caught the corner of her eye.

Hemi was holding out her tri-me. "Lots of pickpockets in here. Keep your eyes moving and stay out of the crush."

She snatched it back. "Another tool in your bag of tricks?"

He winked.

Microships

"I'm out of here." She paused to look around. "I'll tell you one thing, though. Your office décor stinks."

He gave a disgusted snort and turned down another alleyway between the cabins and disappeared.

She took her time about leaving, meandering enough that she might fool someone, but probably not. Finally, she said, *Who am I kidding,* and went home.

* * *

The next day, Tuesday, she went into work in a different frame of mind. First thing, she called a private meeting with Nicolaus.

He agreed, and the others left the office. "Second thoughts about Thursday?"

"Yes, but not the kind you're expecting." She straightened in her chair. "I have another reason for getting you out of the Space Center."

He mused a moment. "Meeting someone?"

"Yes. I have a contact that I'm positive you need to meet, but he's completely off the official radar. The nightclub is the perfect place."

"Go on."

"I've been playing this very close to the chest, because he's not an adult, and I'm partly responsible for him. Not officially, but I still feel that way. At the moment, he's on the run, hard to contact, and very jumpy."

"Who is he running from?"

She sighed. "If I tell you he's running from everyone, I've let the cat out of the bag."

A new tension entered his body. "You're harbouring a mixed-race child who has nobody to turn to."

"Exactly. He and I had to make a dangerous choice, based on what was best for him, and what was best for the whole scenario. After fifteen years of hiding out, he has a natural aversion to local authorities. I am beginning to be of the same opinion."

"What is his main concern?"

"He wants to do what's best for humanity, but he wants to retain his freedom to choose and to act as he sees fit."

Nicolaus gave a sad smile. "He has some growing up to do."

"I know. I feel the same way a lot of the time. The fact remains, I don't want to see him snatched up by either side and stuck in a laboratory for the rest of his life."

"I can promise you that won't happen with my people. However, he cannot continue to run wild. The jungle is too dangerous."

"He is coming around to that opinion. What do you suggest?"

"I must meet with him. His experience will be key to the mixed-race regulations we are working on. We also need to be concerned with his safety. If the rest of your literary meme is true, there are agents looking for him, and they are not under my control."

She frowned. "Not wishing to get off topic, but is this one of those areas where you haven't decided to give us the full picture."

"It is, and circumstances dictate that we must rectify that soon. But for the moment...?" his hands made a questioning gesture.

"Of course, you think it best he goes with you."

"What do you think?"

"I think he has to make up his own mind."

"Despite his age?"

"Even at that."

Gliese seemed to come to a decision. "Fine. We will meet at the nightclub. We will discuss his situation. I will offer him sanctuary. He will make up his own mind."

He straightened. "But as two experienced adults, we cannot send him back onto the streets of your fine city, safe though it may seem on the surface."

"Nowhere is safe."

"What has been arranged?"

"My Head of Security, Joe Reimer, has agreed to bring the boy to you. Joe's main concern is your safety, so he will want to stay at the meeting. Perhaps one of your men will attend. I will stay if I am invited."

Nicolaus smiled. "Our security teams have meshed well. I see no problems with that."

She rose and opened the office door, signalling to Joe, who waited at the end of the hall. When the others had joined them, she smiled at them all. "Our side bet is on for Thursday. Joe, please coordinate with Nero. You are both invited to the event."

Reimer glanced at Nicolaus and left the room.

The alien rubbed his hands together in a completely human motion. "Fine. Shall we continue where we left off yesterday...?"

14. FACE TO FACE

There was no reason to expect any trouble on Thursday night, and everything went smoothly from the start. The parking lot behind the nightclub was hemmed in by industrial buildings with few windows. A light-blue limo and two black SUVs converged on the back door at 09:30, and their party filed inside and up to the balcony. Mia kept an eye out for a smaller, slender figure, but there was no sign.

The band was doing a salsa set at the moment, and a horde of dark-haired, flamboyantly clad figures writhed in a frenzy.

After giving Nicolaus a while to take it all in, she leaned forward to shout in his ear. "Sinuous enough for you?"

He flashed her a grin. "I have seen videos. The total experience is necessary to understand. This is a feast for my senses."

She put her hands to her ears and shook her head.

He laughed silently and went back to watching the show.

After about half an hour, the band took a break, and the party in the upper balcony turned their attention inwards.

"How is it so far?"

Nero answered. "My people have a traditional dance that is somewhat similar. Their simulated procreative activities are not quite as graphic."

Nicolaus raised his eyebrows. "You are familiar with the English expression, "stick in the mud?"

"Too familiar. You use it all the time."

Mia noted this banter, and the absence of 'sir.' *These guys do let their hair down sometimes.*

Movement in the rear doorway attracted her attention. The lead alien security man, a Wolfian whose name she didn't know, beckoned.

Leaving the rest of the party, she and Gliese followed him, Reimer bringing up the rear.

Hemi was seated in a small anteroom. The décor suggested it was meant for more intimate activities, but it seated the three of them comfortably. The two security men took 'at ease' positions on either side of the door.

"Nicolaus, I believe this is a member of your race, Hemisius, whose last name I don't know. Hemi, this is Ambassador Gliese.

The boy shrugged. "Hemisius Solus, I guess."

The two reached out both hands and their fingers did a dance of some sort.

Nicolaus smiled. "You have been taught good manners."

Hemi shrugged. "I guess I was. I never did that before. It just happened."

"Your father would have taught you very early. Other impulses like that may come to you. I suggest you follow them. They won't steer you wrong."

The boy relaxed a bit. "I guess you got some info for me."

"I suspect you have a world of data for me, but I hope to have a lot of time for that. At the moment, I suspect you'd like to know anything we know about you, and especially your father."

"I wouldn't mind."

"You told Mia your father left when you were three. You're fifteen, right?"

"Near as."

"We searched our personnel database for an agent who was on Earth for at least four years, and then was recalled, probably in disgrace, about ten years ago."

"That's how I'd do it. Who do we find?"

"We have only one man who fits, and he was recalled when his project was cancelled. He took the next ship out and is probably a quarter of the way home."

"So, no disgrace?"

"The authorities obviously never found out about you. Which does not settle my mind."

"I'da thought you'd be happy."

"No, we knew nothing about you, so we weren't looking for you."

"Aha. If those Glieseans I spotted were looking for me, who are they and why don't you know about them? And how do they know about me?"

"All of the above." His attention turned to his security man and something passed between them.

Nicolaus straightened. "A puzzle for later. The question of the moment, is what we should do with you."

"I hope you're doing nothing."

He laughed. "Perhaps a misuse of a common phrase. Should I have said, 'What we can do for you.' Any ideas?"

"Well, I've been giving that a lot of thought the last coupla days. Maybe it's a lifetime of avoidance, but I'm leery about the American social network. They're likely to treat me like any other orphan — which I am not — and disappear me into their system."

His glance shot to Mia, and she nodded.

"Likewise, the military/medical establishment has a bad rep with guinea pigs."

Nicolaus nodded. "And rats, dogs, chimpanzees, prisoners of war and even their own soldiers."

Hemi's eyebrows rose. "So, the LSD story wasn't a myth? What do you know."

He took a moment to regard Gliese. "She says you're a straight-up kind of guy." His gesture indicated the other's languid position on the couch. "But I don't think that expression is going to survive the translation. In any case, I trust her, and she trusts you, and yours is a more controlled environment. If you're out to grab me, I'm screwed already. I guess I'm going along with it."

"I'm pleased, Hemi."

Mia patted his hand, although she wasn't as happy. *He's taken the bait for better or worse. I hope there isn't a hook in it.*

"I do have one request."

"Certainly."

"Can I watch the rest of the show?"

Mia laughed. "What, this tourist trap?"

"Listen, lady, this is the nearest I'll get to anything similar for the next six years. I'll take what I can get."

"An underage kid in a nightclub? You want to get me in trouble?"

He grinned. "The only two security guys allowed in here are on our payroll."

"Okay, but no beer."

"Two out of three. I'll go for it."

They all rose and headed for the door, Joe leading and the alien soldier bringing up the rear.

When she returned to the balcony, she sat close beside Noah where they could lip-read to enhance their tortured hearing.

"How did it go?"

"Too well. He's going with them."

"But...?"

"Another problem, maybe a big one. He'll tell us more tomorrow."

Noah leaned forward and regarded the hip-hop group on stage. "Let's enjoy ourselves tonight. 'Sufficient unto the day,' and all that."

It was not her favourite style of music, but Hemi did not share her opinion. She watched him bouncing in his chair and enjoyed his enjoyment enough that the evening didn't feel as long.

15. RESHUFFLE

Having departed the Motown at two am, they aimed for a ten start the following day. When she arrived, the flying wing was in position, and it was impossible to tell if they had stayed the night or not.

Right at ten, the ramp opened, and the alien party descended. Security repeated their traditional gavotte, but there was a smaller, more active member in their party.

She turned into the building and Hemi trotted alongside, giving her a gentle hip check. "Hey, party girl. Have a good time last night?"

"I've heard better bands, but their hearts were in the right place." She glanced down at his shining face. "How about you?"

"The greatest."

"Did you go to Washington or stay here last night?"

His grin widened. "I've seen all those sitcoms where the guy's car is outside the girl's apartment in the morning and everybody wonders..."

"You're making trouble when we've got enough already. It doesn't matter one way or the other."

They entered their corner office, and Hemi gravitated towards Noah's desk. "Hey, nice hardware. Do I get a setup like this?"

"I have no idea. Maybe today we'll figure out a place for you in the project, maybe not. You can't exactly go on the NASA payroll, you know."

"Of course I know. I don't have a Social Security Number. That means I can't work. The government has to support me forever. Don't you just adore socialism?"

"As a citizen of the least socialistic democracy in the world, how would I know?"

Hemi glanced up at her. "You're grouchy this morning. Late night on the town?

She turned on her computer to check her mail. "No, this is me at work. Reality intrudes all the time and spoils my fun."

He flopped down on the couch. "What aspect of reality is ruining this fine morning for us?"

A new voice intruded. "How about three Gliesean agents we don't know about?"

Hemi spun around and scooted to one end of the sofa. "Good morning, sir. Did you sleep well?

Nicolaus took the other end, his arm stretched along the back in a bridging motion. "The cabin on the ship is sufficient, but it isn't my usual bunk. And our late start puts the pressure on us to get working on time."

Noah and Mia took their seats and looked expectantly at him.

He straightened. Mia had never seen him look uncertain.

"We have discussed the problem of giving too much or too little information about ourselves. You, for example, have taken for granted our knowledge of your financial combines, your drug cartels, your money laundering. We, on the other hand, have given you no information about our problems."

Mia nodded. "We assumed you weren't perfect. What problems do you have that you're willing to admit at this point in the negotiations?"

"Drug cartels, money laundering, and financial combines come to mind."

"Surprise, surprise. And how does this affect us?"

The alien's hands took on their 'teaching' pose. "All the Meld societies are what you would call liberal democracies. But like on Earth, there are different levels and versions of each. It seems that deep in the genetic makeup of humanity are two conflicting urges: the desire for competition and the desire for cooperation. Independence versus control."

"This branch of the family would certainly agree."

"As you might expect, different members of our seven societies have, for reasons of environment and genetics, developed slightly different balances between the two. Nothing radical. I'm sure you would find most humans across the galaxy fall inside the norms of your own group. Which, I note, tend to be a broader spectrum than most others."

"I'm not surprised."

"It has probably held back your recent progress. Competitiveness boosts an early society forward but holds back more sophisticated development."

Mia shook her head. "And we are running afoul of one of your more competitive societies."

"Not a unified society. All seven System governments support our efforts. But there are factions that run across racial barriers. We have a Mercantile Caste that is more commercially, competitively motivated. They are rich and powerful, and their selfishness is a constant irritation.

"Hence the need to get an agreement locked up in a hurry. Before the competition got their oars in the water."

"I have to admit that did affect our timeline."

She sighed. "And now it all has to come out in the open. This is going to set back the progress of the talks in a big way. First, because you have not been as honest and open about your objectives as we hoped. Second, because the commercial faction in Earth's society has not been enthusiastic about the socialist leanings in the agreement as we have created it. They will be eager to hear what the competing side has to say."

Gliese looked to Noah. "What does your sphere tell you?"

"What she said."

"I am afraid I must agree."

Mia had a sudden thought, "But it isn't all cut and dried. People of Gliese are of the more cooperative type, right?"

"Most consider us that, yes."

"But the agents we think were stalking Hemi are Gliesean."

"Our mercantile groups had been out of favour at home for several centuries. However, our Earth project required the cooperation of our whole society, and they had to be given a say."

"And they and their allies from the more commercialized of the other Meld societies want to start a bidding war for the markets and resources of Sol System."

"In simplified terms, yes."

"And that would lead straight into Colonialism." She tossed up her hands. "What happens now?"

Nicolaus actually stood up to speak, something he rarely did. "I hate to say it, but this stage of our negotiations here must be brought to a close. Our interface with NASA is no longer advantageous. Noah, your ExIn sphere needs to be put to use on a more appropriate task. One of the main factors that has already been decided is our assistance on the programming of the Microship Swarm.

"Send them new programming to clean up our garbage."

"Exactly. You and the design team here should start on that right away."

Mia looked from Noah to Nicolaus, then back, and opened her mouth to ask...

"But Mia will not be staying here with you."

She remembered to close her mouth, for once struck dumb.

"Surely you realize that Noah doesn't need you anymore."

"I've been telling him that, but..."

"Half your job was marketing inventions to industry, right?"

"That's right."

"How do you like that part of the work?"

"I'm pretty good at it."

"That non-answer tells me the real answer. Sold anything lately?"

"Of course not. I've been working with you."

"And the Microships project is all computer programming. No inventions to sell in a market that will soon be swamped with Meld products. Lately, you have been working like a one-armed paper hanger, managing three or four different projects while handling an undercover operative. In other words, using your real talents. People around here are going to miss you."

Her heart sank. "Am I being let go?"

"You are. On a long-term leave with first option on a re-hire when the new job finishes."

"New job?"

"You've been head-hunted, my friend."

"Oh." Her mind was spinning. "By whom?"

"The Meld Diplomatic Corps." He took in her confusion. "Me. Remember, I said you would be on the Committee."

"Oh. To do...what?"

"Just what you have been. Plus handling my personal agent." His gesture scooped, drawing Hemi into the conversation.

"I...uh...I'll need some time to think about that."

"Of course you will. Take tomorrow for a holiday jaunt somewhere. But don't go alone. Joe will assign you a companion. A young and handsome one, appropriate to your image."

"Why do I need a tail?"

"Not a tail. An in-their-faces companion. At your side, buying you an ice-cream or a glass of wine. You must accept a minder, in case you take the job. Diplomatic Corps rules."

"Which corps? Yours or ours?"

"I'm sure there are similar clauses in both."

"Thank you. And what are my duties for today?

"Myriad. We have final reports to write and an organization to mothball." He moved towards his desk, rubbing his hands together in a human gesture. "Let's get to it, folks."

* * *

Her driver/escort picked her up the next morning at Building 44. His name, at least for today, was Alvin Vonnegut. She called him on that one the moment the door on his new Hydrengine Triple 9 hissed shut.

 He hit the starter button and grinned, pushing a wave of hair off his forehead. "Why can't I be Alvin Vonnegut?"

"Alvin Toffler, Kurt Vonnegut? What life work do you have illusions of?"

"Let's keep that as our little secret for the day. My case manager doesn't have an ounce of creativity."

"Great. My day starts with a bizarrezoid and goes steadily downhill."

"Where do you want to go?" The car moved ahead smoothly, making its way through the morning traffic with little attention from the driver.

"I have to do some thinking and, as you might expect, I'd like to do it with no outside distraction."

"Or I wouldn't be here. Am I looking out for anybody special? Besides the aliens, that is. They were in my briefing. I mean, there wasn't one actually at the briefing, but I passed a Gliesean in the hall on my way out. He really looked me over."

"Like picking up your girl on prom night?"

"Yeah, that sort of aura. Friendly but threatening."

"I probably shouldn't talk about him. But I can discuss the aliens in general. Tell me what you know about them."

"You mean, from the briefing?"

"No, I'm interested in what everybody knows. What's coming over the media?"

"Sure. The American outlets are all about the opportunities for interaction. Culture, Science, Markets and that stuff."

"Yes. 'What profit can we make out of this'."

"Pretty much. I watch the Canadian news when I want an alternative viewpoint. They're all about the cooperative culture and mutual benefit. You know the Canadians."

"I don't, much. But go on."

"The Europeans are similar. The younger feeds are all about how they look and how they move."

"They're very graceful. At least, the Glieseans are."

"You don't see too many pics of the soldiers. Heavy planet types. Stocky, muscular. Of course, they've got so much gear on you can't tell much."

She laughed. "Just like our soldiers."

"Point taken."

"You think the aliens are a good idea?"

He shrugged. "I don't guess we have any choice."

"What if we said, 'Go away,' and they did?"

"As if they're likely to. But if they did, it would be a waste. Listen," he turned to her, letting the car pick its course on the crowded freeway. "I read Science Fiction. I know it's only fiction, but some of those writers have their heads on straight. This isn't an 'Invasion from Mars' scenario. These are intelligent, advanced beings. It's a real bonus that they're humanoid. Fully human, for all I can tell. We need them. We've gotta be careful, but they have ideas and tech that will really advance our society and our economy."

"I can't help but agree." She looked out the window. "Where are we going?"

"You didn't say. I told the car to drive south, and it did. Very cooperative, this car. Want to go to Galveston?" He glanced at the dash screen. "Be there in 45 minutes."

"Sure. The sea is supposed to be soothing for the soul."

"Fine, and we've got a hundred mile limit. East Beach is worth the drive."

"You've been there?"

"I don't take VIPs to unknown places. I grew up down here. That's why I came south."

The car hummed along, and she felt peace creeping over her. After a while she glanced over at his handsome profile. *Shame to let that go to waste. At least I should talk to him.*

"Ever made a big change? Job, city, lifestyle?"

"Yeah. I was a social worker in Galveston. Church Street."

"We've heard about that area, even in Southside Place."

"Yeah, well I tried hard, but I burned out in seven years. Got tired of being shot at by kids who were only scared of life. So, I packed it in and went to Houston to work where I only get shot at by guys that deserve me shooting back."

"You have a degree in Social Work and you're a hired guard?"

"No, I'm a VIP chauffeur compiling seniority so I can move up the ladder. I'm good at chitchat."

"I won't argue that. When did Daddy say I had to be home tonight?"

"No time limit, but if you're really in danger, you don't stay out past dark."

"I always take the advice of the professionals. Find me a nice restaurant for lunch on East Beach, take me for a walk on the sand, and get me back to Jackson Center before quitting time. How does that sound?"

"And I get a paycheck twice a month as well. Sounds like heaven."

Something inside made her say, "I'm not aiming for there yet."

"Hmm." He swiped a finger over the control viewscreen.

They rode in silence for a while. "I'm sorry. Really spoiled the moment, didn't I?"

"I'm used to driving people who are preoccupied with their mortality." He grinned. "Goes with the turf."

"Thanks for being understanding."

"Got it." He glanced at the screen. "The Porch Café. It's been there for years, right out on the peninsula. Survived hurricanes and tidal waves and the lot. At least, it doesn't really survive, but they keep rebuilding it. Be there in twenty. Beach afterwards."

The view from the restaurant was rather flat, but it was the Gulf Coast, after all, and she concentrated on the food, which was great, and the conversation, which was easy. "Alvin" had an easy charm that placed no expectations on her, which she appreciated.

The sand was problematic, because Alvin thought he knew the way to the beach, but every road he took ended with a "Private Property" sign.

He had just decided to try the GPS when his tri-me buzzed. He pulled over to the roadside, tucked in his earbud and listened.

"Right...got it. What shall I say...? Better that way."

He shut off the call and turned to her, his face serious. "Developments. Daddy says you have to come home early."

Her heart thumped. "Why? What did they tell you to tell me?"

"There's no serious problem to you or yours. It's a development at a higher level that ups your security status. That means you're too far from home and too lightly covered."

"What can we do?"

He shrugged and hit the turn signal. "Keep our eyes outside the car and go home. That's all we can do. I've lost a lot of my independence, because I'm under team orders. They'll give me the route and select my speed, that sort of thing."

"All right. I can keep my eyes open. Not sleepy at all, for some reason."

"For the moment, our tactic is not to attract attention. Obey traffic rules, be cool."

"No road rage allowed?"

"Sorry to spoil your fun."

The sandy terrain rolled by them, and soon they were in Galveston, where they headed immediately for the Causeway and the Gulf Freeway to the north.

"We're not taking any evasive action."

"No reason to. The only factor that has changed on this little jaunt is your status. There's nothing to worry about. Think like your date has cooked up a little surprise to make the outing memorable."

"You wouldn't!"

"It would be worth my job, and the drone operator that just locked onto my GPS would be angry."

"We have a drone?"

He touched the screen a few times, and the view became an overhead shot of the Causeway with a black car in the centre. "That's us."

"I see. How's my lipstick?"

"Not quite enough resolution. Once the chopper gets here, we can take a better look."

"Chopper? Am I that important?"

"Maybe, but life's been calm lately. It's possible somebody needs his air time for the month."

"Glad to provide the boys with some entertainment in their boring jobs."

He glanced at her. "You're handling it well. Do this kind of thing often?"

"No, I'm quaking in my sandals. It's just that my mouth takes over and pretends nothing is wrong. It's an occupational competency for diplomats."

"Fair enough. This is a mildly complicated operation. You won't have my undivided attention anymore."

"I hope I didn't have it before. You seem to be handling the situation well, yourself."

His usual grin. "My team is sitting in sweaty flight suits doing a routine surveillance job, and I'm down here in a beautiful car with a beautiful girl, and it's going on my employment record as a higher-level operation than I've done before."

"I'm not beautiful."

"Don't spoil my story." Again, that sideways glance. "You fill the role quite nicely, thanks. At least you're not a sweating sixty-year old senator who thinks he should be running the show."

"You have a smooth way of turning a compliment, anyway."

"A job competency. Gallows humour to take the client's mind off the real problem."

"Well, since you tell me there really is no problem, perhaps you should shove that one back into your bag of tools."

"You're the boss."

"Except I'm not. And neither are you, apparently?"

He held up a finger, listened, then nodded. "Yes, sir. Got it. All A-OK."

"Developments?"

"No news is good news. Our team leader, the one who is in charge, says we continue with the assigned route and drop you off in front of Building 44. At the moment, Houston is not displaying one of her famous traffic jams, so we'll be there in twenty-five."

She leaned back and turned her attention to the roadway in front and behind. "I'll sit here with my eyes open, and I won't bother you."

"You don't bother me, and I haven't finished my objective for the outing."

"What objective was that?"

"To help you decide whether to take that job or not."

"What job?"

"The one that made you ask me about big changes in life, of course."

"Not too subtle, am I?"

"A competency you'll have to work on, now that you're moving up in the world."

"Who says I'm moving up?"

He laughed aloud. "Objective achieved. We can go home."

She stared at him.

He shook his head. "If you were still dithering, your response to that sally would have been completely different. You've decided. Congratulations."

She crossed her arms and looked up at him through a frown. "I'm not happy about being so easy to read that I can't fool a common chauffeur."

"Degree in social work, remember? Not exactly common."

"Definitely not." Then she frowned. "Wait a minute. Were you sicced on me on purpose?"

Again the laugh. "Now, that would be paranoid."

"You didn't answer my question, did you?"

He took the wheel and steered into an exit lane. "Okay, break's over. I have to concentrate. Here's my last word on the subject; I was here to do exactly what I did: fill the role for the security story and provide a quiet, friendly atmosphere. The results are all up to you."

He glanced it the rear viewer and changed lanes again. "End of story. Now I'm on the other half of my job."

"Fair enough. I won't distract you."

The soft silence of the luxury car settled over them, and they didn't speak for the rest of the ride. He pulled up in front of Building 44 and waited while she thanked him. He gave her a friendly smile and a fingertip salute and drove away.

After all the drama of the trip, it was rather a letdown to enter their office and find everyone working calmly at their desks.

Even Hemi had a station and was fully engrossed in something.

At least they looked up when she entered.

"Sorry not to be available when the balloon went up."

"Successful mission?"

"I guess so. I'm here, aren't I?" She rubbed her hands together. "My security for the day assured me that there were no new developments."

"That's right. Sorry to cut your holiday short, but the moment the Committee accepted you as a candidate, your status went through the roof."

"I suppose it would. So, we're wrapping up old problems?" Her glance slid to Reimer, who was seated at Nicolaus's desk.

"The last thing we need is one of Hemi's relatives having a sudden twinge of conscience or greed and making a fuss with the authorities."

She nodded. "But we don't want to expose him more than we have to, in case the alien agents are closing in. What do you suggest, Joe?"

"A minor bit of subterfuge. You were supposed to be part of it, but now he'll go alone. Hemi, you need to go back to see Mia's parents. You'll want to say good-bye anyway. Get one of them to drive you over to visit your true grandparents. You have a lot of questions you want to ask them, now that you know your history."

Nicolaus nodded. "Our people are interested in that information, too."

"After that, get the real grandparent to drive you to meet your mother. Better to meet her alone, in an outside location for simplicity. We'll pick you up there when you're done."

"No problem."

"Your secondary objective is to give everyone your cover story."

"Which is?"

"Basically, the truth. The aliens know who you are. Mia's your government handler, and she's taking you to be part of the negotiations. They don't have to know any more. Do you think that will work?"

"Sure. None of my family liked hiding stuff from the government. They're not that kind of people. They'll be glad I've got it settled. Mia, do I have it settled?"

"I certainly hope so. It's a big step." She gave a twisted grin. "I'm in the same boat, and you've got an advantage."

"Yeah, I look right." He grinned. "You'll be an alien."

The meeting went on, and everyone's plans were firmed up. Mia needed to go home and pack, and the security men agreed she should go at quitting time with covert surveillance. Her mother had promised to bring supper to her apartment that evening. Mia would travel under security to work in the morning, sleep in the Flying Wing overnight and leave the next day.

Hemi would do his rounds tomorrow in the morning. In two days, the Wing would take off for New York. This time, it wouldn't be back.

"Where are we moving to?"

"Montreal. You fly day after tomorrow. Nero, Hemi and I will be along the next day."

"Great." She took a moment to think, but nothing came. "I don't know anything about Canada and even less about Quebec. French was my fifth language, and they lied about it getting easier the more you learn. I keep getting Spanish nouns mixed in."

Then it struck her. "And it's November!"

Noah gave a quizzical frown. "And..."

"It's winter in Canada. You know. Blizzards and freezing cold and when it warms up enough, they throw in ice storms."

He shrugged. "You get a new wardrobe. Great."

"Says the guy who's staying safe and warm in Houston with hurricane season over."

Their eyes met as it hit them. They were separating, maybe for a long time.

"We'll have a chat, later. I'll be here all day tomorrow."

"Right."

The other members of the meeting obviously had caught the meaning of the pause and waited patiently.

She nodded to Nicolaus. "I guess I'm up to date. Please continue."

The business soon wound down, and everyone moved reluctantly towards the door. Noah and Mia were the last to leave.

She palmed the lock. "I'm not taking along anything but my tri-me and my coffee cup. There'll be different needs and different tech in Canada."

A familiar Hydrengine pulled out of the parking lot and followed the Mazda to the apartment, where it turned into the driveway behind her. Alvin grinned as he led the way up the front steps, where he made a careful sweep of the suite before he would allow her inside.

"All in order, ma'am." He gave a casual salute.

"Thank you for the day, sir. Like a cup of coffee?"

He gave a rueful shake of the head. "Still working, unfortunately."

"Well thanks anyway."

"Truly a pleasure." He strode down the steps and drove away, leaving her alone.

Her parents showed up at seven for a pleasant, subdued meal where they talked about this and that but avoided the elephant in the room. They left early, leaving her to do a final cleanup and pack in her empty apartment.

* * *

The next morning, a light beep in the driveway announced Alvin in his limousine/taxi, and she rolled her suitcases out the front door. While he took care of them, she made one last pass through the house, checking for anything out of place. There was nothing. *I'm rather good at this. Not sure whether to be proud or not, but it's definitely on the list of job competencies.*

Her twice-a-month cleaners, safely vetted by NASA Security, would be in to empty the fridge, take away the trash and mothball the place. Her mother would come later to take home the plants that needed watering and fix everything the professionals didn't do just right. Likewise, her father would take care of prepping the Mazda for storage.

She thought once again about what it must be like for her parents, not knowing where she was most of the time. They stayed at home to be there when she needed them.

That was a difficult lane to go down, and she turned back and headed out to the taxi. She had a lot on her mind, and Alvin restricted his conversation to the essentials.

The day was a weird one. She didn't know enough about her new duties to make any preparation, and her old job had evaporated from under her feet. Noah would be getting a Programming Associate, a highly qualified cyber engineer whose purpose would be strictly scientific. There was nothing to hand across. He was arriving next week, and she wouldn't even get to meet him.

The only thing that kept her busy was the number of other team members who took the opportunity to ask her how to do the myriad of tasks that she had been covering in the administration of the office.

Once she got going on that, she realized what a hole she was leaving, and she was relieved when the office manager asked her for an hour of her time.

"Sure, Abe, what's up?"

"I've got a list two pages long of questions for you. Once I started looking around, I discovered how much you've been doing."

"Just trying to help out."

"Helping out? Dag nabbit, girl, I didn't know how much we depended on you until people started coming to me this morning with questions I couldn't answer."

She grinned. "Well, later on I'll give you an hour of my valuable time for a little Q and A. And now that I've stopped doing all those little jobs, I might even find I have two hours available."

"Fair enough. I'll give you half an hour to sober up after lunch, then you're mine for a while."

At noon, she and Noah grabbed a table for two in the cafeteria, where they chatted about this and that and reminisced about their years together. He had left his sphere in the office in order to give her his unbroken attention, a gesture she appreciated.

Finally, they got down to their present situation. In the end, she summed it up. "Seven years ago, you really needed me. Now I'm only a habit you lean on. This is a new life for you, and you're ready for it."

"I suppose."

"I'm more confident in you than that. It's time the job changed, and time you changed with it."

"How do you see the job changing?"

"You still see yourself as a resource. As the technician who keeps the sphere tuned and running."

"That's the popular view."

"And it makes a fine, non-threatening picture for the public. But it's a long time since you've been only a technician. You were there when the sphere was designed. I'll bet you participated more than you think."

"Hard to say. I did my share."

"Right. But I was onsite off and on during the first years, before they teamed us up. I watched you set up and run all the training modules."

"I had to. I was the only one who knew..."

"The 'only one who knows' is the one in charge. You were running the show." She grinned. "And as soon as I saw that, I started to act as if that's what was happening."

He sat back. "You mean you started using your public relations juju on me way back then?"

"Darn tootin' I did. And it didn't take long before I had you believing it as well. And now I've finished my job. You and the sphere are one intelligence. Between its knowledge base and your imagination, you can create anything you put your minds to."

"That's…um…optimistic."

"Take my word for it. When they start having trouble with the programming of those microships, you will be the one who fixes it. I'm leaving you with two objectives."

He grinned "And now we find out who has been the real leader all along."

"And I've been moved up to where I can use my skills. First thing, you knuckle down and become the expert on the design of that swarm sentience. Because that's what it is. It may be spread over five or ten light years of space, but it's a hive mind, and its potential, for good or ill, is immense. All it needs is a faster-than-light communications system, and it will be off and running. And if us Earthers are going to keep control of it, we have to be on top of the science involved. And that 'we' means 'you and Fiona.' Understand?"

He shrugged. "I don't need any high and mighty expectations. You've given me a reason to focus my resources in a positive direction. Like you always did."

"Perfect. And your second task is to prepare that new wife of yours for a move."

"Where to?"

"Where do you think?"

"No idea."

"You heard where I'm going."

"Yeah. Montreal. Marvellous place, I hear."

"I'm going to the Canadian Space Agency in Longueuil, which is a suburb of Montreal. Which is also the home to their Robotics Mission Control Centre."

"It is?"

"And the only reason I can see for Gliese to set up his home base there is if robotics is going to be an important part of our work."

"I see."

"So don't be surprised if this turns out to be *au revoir* rather than *adieu*."

"Whatever that means."

"It means your third job is to start learning French."

"You're serious."

"Both you and Alicia. Be subtle about it, but make a start."

He nodded. "You've never steered me wrong, yet."

"If I'm wrong this time, it could have major consequences, We better hope I'm right."

He looked at his empty plate, then took the last slug out of his coffee cup. "Well, some of us have work to do this afternoon. Anything else to say? Any 'oh, by the way' bombs to drop?

"Check in on Mum and Dad once in a while, would you? Not often enough to rouse suspicion, but...I don't know."

"Sure thing. Your mother's cooking is a great draw. Maybe we could all develop a taste for pickle ball and meet by accident on the court."

"I always knew you had it in you to interface with the rest. You just needed direction."

"I consider myself directed." He picked up both trays and took them to the washup stand.

As they waited for the elevator, he put an arm around her shoulder for a quick squeeze. "Thanks for everything, Mia."

She leaned in a moment. "Thanks due in both directions, Noah. Now we get down to the real work. "

16. LONGUEUIL

She spent the night on the Flying Wing in a private cabin that could have been found in a thousand American hotels. It was plain and comfortable, and she slept as well as could be expected. The next day an unmarked car with a familiar driver took her to the airport

She grinned at him as he loaded her luggage. "Different vehicle. Are you still Alvin today?"

"Till the assignment is over. Which is probably today, if you're heading to Montreal."

She put on a frown. "And that could be taken as fishing for information."

He shrugged. "Only so I know where to drop you."

"Terminal A. You should have known that. Are we escorted today? Any helicopters?"

"No, I'm seconded to the aliens for this trip, and they're taking care of the rest of it. Maybe they don't know about different terminals."

"A lesson for the future. Aliens don't know everything."

"I'm on their com channel with somebody called GBP 1. He gave me the route, and I follow it. Now you know as much as I do."

"Doesn't mean a thing to me. If they're happy, who are we to argue?"

"Good attitude. We have a designated route and a self-driving car. We might as well pick up the topic where we left off last time."

"What were we talking about?"

"Can't remember. But that's the whole point. Pleasant conversation to fill the time."

So they talked, mostly about his progress in his new job, for the rest of the trip, and the time passed quickly. Soon he was escorting her to the check-in counter at Departures, where he left with a casual salute.

She was a little disappointed not to be using the Flying Wing, but that would be unrealistic to expect. She had to make do with First Class on Air Canada.

The flight to Trudeau International Airport took four hours, but when she stepped into the terminal there, the kaleidoscope of costumes and languages in the concourse told her she had entered another culture, and the blast of wintry air outside persuaded her she was in a different climate.

There was no one to greet her, so she stepped out to the curb. Chalking up one demerit for the Canadian Space Agency, she stared around, drawing her light jacket tight to her throat.

"Mademoiselle! Ici!"

She turned.

A red Tesla SUV had slipped up to the curb, and a dark-haired man in a traditional lambskin bomber jacket was slinging the door open. He gave her a cheery grin. *"Désolé, mais la circulation était horrible aujourd'hui."*

She couldn't help but return his grin. *"Pas de problème, monsieur. Il fait fraise, n'est-ce pas?"*

"Un peu." He opened the trunk and heaved her two substantial suitcases aboard. He slammed the lid and spun, holding out his hand. *"Jean Gagnon, mademoiselle. J'espère que tu es Mia Larsen. Sinon, j'ai fait une grosse erreur."*

"Je plaide coupable." She wasn't sure why he was using the familiar 'tu', but she followed along. *"Tu es mon chauffeur?"*

"Vraiment. À bien des égards."

She hesitated. It sounded like he said, 'in many ways,' but she wasn't sure of the phrasing.

He slapped the side of his head, opening the door for her with the other hand. "Sorry. Would you rather speak in English?"

She smiled again as she sat. "I'm not quite up to the Quebec idiom."

"No problem." He spoke straight Canadian English, with perhaps a touch of a roll to the 'r' and a tendency to put the stress on the last syllable.

She waited while he strode to the driver's seat and got in. "What do you mean by, 'In many ways'?"

"Aha!" He looked serious. "That could mean many things."

She nailed him with a pointing finger. "In that case it's not a language problem. It's a personality flaw. Do I have to put up with you for any length of time?

He glanced in the rearview screen, then pulled into the traffic, neatly dodging a tour bus and a taxi, both of which seemed to be aimed for the same spot. "Probably you do. If you want to put me in line, you have precisely thirty-one minutes. After that, the relationship will be set in stone for all time."

She glanced at the nav screen. "Thirty-one minutes being the time it takes to get to Longueuille."

"If this *merdique* traffic doesn't jam up on us."

"You seem to be managing."

"This new Tesla is a nice drive, but it isn't my chosen steed."

"Dare I ask what that would be? Don't tell me you're a cowboy."

"Nope. I'm a totally different kind of jockey."

She sat back and sighed. "Is this part of my assigned thirty-one minutes? If so, it's time you gave me one straight answer, before I decide I've been hijacked by the Bohemian Comedy Secret Service and take appropriate action."

"Please don't. I'm a pilot, and I've been assigned to your project. So, if you want to go anywhere in the world, my number's on the bulletin board in Head Office."

She nodded. "Since tomorrow is my first day on the job, I have no idea if I will need your services or not. But thanks for the offer. And the straight answer."

"We aim to please. And on the topic of your schedule, please don't fill in anything for tomorrow evening."

She eyed him. "Are you fishing for a date already?"

"I am not in a position to date anyone."

"Glad we have that straight. What's going on tomorrow evening?"

"Kick-off bash for the new project."

"I didn't know we were that important."

He checked the road in front, then turned to face her. "I doubt that."

"Sorry. My diplomatese kicking it. I knew there would be something. It gives all the peripheral people the opportunity to feel included." She flicked him a grin. "Are taxi drivers considered peripherals?"

"I'm above that. My invitation said, 'plus one.' Marie is going to like that."

"And Marie is your usual 'plus one."

"That's right. An astronaut with a soaring career has a certain image to keep up, and I might as well be seen with a stunning woman that I actually like."

"Oho. She's stunning, is she?"

He shrugged, "Everybody seems impressed enough. You'll see."

"Tomorrow night."

"You'll get your official invitation today." He glanced at her. "Should it have 'plus one' on it?"

"Not unless you have an escort appropriate to a faceless, though talented junior diplomat."

He laughed. "In the old days I'd pair you up with my friend, Olivier Beaudry. Of course, nowadays we must consider the feelings of Andrea. That's his wife."

"Thanks for having a sense of decency on my behalf."

"Okay, no 'plus one.' We'll pick you up at six thirty. Semi-formal, but don't push it. Lots of the nerds and techies don't have that sort of duds."

"You really are going to be my taxi driver."

"Only on official occasions."

"Fair enough."

He turned off the freeway past the end of a small airport, and drove through a commercial area with all the usual big box stores and chain restaurants. He pulled up in front of a relatively new brick apartment. Since over half the buildings in the area were brick as well, that didn't help much, but she thought she could find it again.

"The Space Agency owns a couple of apartments in this building for visitors like yourself. Plenty of restaurants and shopping nearby to cater to your eating preferences. It's an hour's walk to the Agency offices, but they're on the opposite side of the airport, and it's all industrial over there."

"That means I could run it in about twenty-five minutes. Great."

"That would be a fast pace."

"I try to keep in shape. Do people run in the winter around here?"

"When the weather allows. The real fanatics have Yak Tracs and mini-spikes and full-blown crampons for all I know. And then there's snowshoes, cross country skis..." He shrugged. "After last winter's ice storm there were guys out on skates."

She laughed. "I get the picture. What's your preference?"

"I've got a nice, warm house with an exercise room on Rue La Bavière a couple of klicks north. This is my home airport."

"So, this taxi driver act means you're picking me up on the way to the party and dropping me off after."

"I have to go and get Marie first. Not so simple."

* * *

111

When she got into the back seat of the Tesla the next evening, she couldn't see much of the woman in the passenger seat, but a cascade of dark, wavy hair flowed around the headrest. A flash of a dusky cheek, and a slim, strong hand reached back.

"*Enchanté* and all that. We can do this properly when we get there." The woman had a smoky contralto voice, with the same accent as Jean's but stronger.

If I had any ideas about this guy — which I didn't — they would now be officially squashed. "Fine with me. Nice material, that dress."

"*Merci.* It's hand-woven. By my mother, actually."

"Wow!" She leaned forward to touch the fabric. "Very fine work."

"Thank you on my mother's behalf. You couldn't pay to have that done."

Mia glanced at their driver. "You cheated. You're in uniform."

"Some of us have it easy."

They rode in silence for a while, and soon they were pulling into the parking lot. Marie showed no surprise at the bulk of the Flying Wing hovering at the far end, and Mia wondered about her security clearance.

Jean made a show of hurrying around to open their doors. "Sorry, this is where my jobs clash. If I dropped you at the door, I wouldn't be there to escort you in."

Marie laughed. "We're not fine china. We can walk."

As they exited the car, the two women rose and faced each other. They were both above average height, but the resemblance ended there. Marie had curves Mia never dreamed of having, and her olive skin and dark eyes gave her a look a threedee star would envy.

Jean came around the front of the car. "Marie, may I introduce my colleague, Mia Larsen. Mia, this is my third-best girl, Marie Pelletier."

After a short pause, Mia flattened her voice. "And I'm supposed to ask why third."

He grinned. "Of course. My first is the ideal I can never find. She doesn't really count. Second is the woman I will marry someday. Since Marie and I aren't talking like that, I put her as high as possible. Third."

"How thoughtful." She turned to Marie, who seemed to be enduring this with tolerant amusement. "Shall we proceed?"

The two women started to make small talk about the architecture, and by the time they had crossed the parking lot and ascended the curving ramp to the doors they had regained the gaiety of the occasion. They made a splashy entrance into the multi-story glass silo of the John H. Chapman Space Centre, the captain obviously enjoying the presence of his two escorts. Not that anybody would be noticing Mia in that company. Which suited her fine, she reminded herself.

Marie's deep-blue dress was form-fitting down to the waistline, where it was held in by a traditional *ceinture fléchée*, woven of the same materials as the dress, but in oranges, yellows, and reds. From there, the skirt spread out floor-length in sweeping folds. The woman's hair, held in place by a black velvet ribbon, flowed down her back, only partly disguising a rear panel cut far too low to be called a neckline.

The two women stood along the side of the huge, glass-walled room while Jean went to get wine. He returned with two glasses, but said he had to talk to someone and hurried off.

Marie gave a wry smile. "Now he's doing his job."

"What are you doing?"

"Standing here looking photogenic and hoping for an iconic shot for tomorrow's media."

"Don't let me cramp your style. Personal publicity is the last thing I want."

"No, no, standing alone looking like I want my picture taken drives them away. I have to be doing something that is so important to me that it takes my full concentration. They sneak in and think they have something impromptu."

Mia grinned. "I still have some learning to do in this business. Here's an easy one. Tell me about yourself. I gather you're a musician. Jean says an exceptional one, but he's biased."

The other woman straightened, an interesting movement because of the fit of the dress, and Mia glanced around. Too bad. No photographers noticed.

"I'm a musician with a problem. I'm too good at too many things."

"I know that one. A 'musician's musician' who writes the songs and does all the session work but never makes a name as a performer."

"Not quite, although I do a lot of composing. No, I have the usual Quebecois problem. I'm a well-known folk singer. I do all the old favourites, and write folk-style originals in French for the pop media. I have a loyal following in the habitant communities up north. But it is a fixed audience with a limited amount of cash. In order to even make a decent living, I have to go mainstream."

"And what does that entail?"

"I'm also a concert pianist." She displayed her long, strong fingers. "And I'm good at that, too. I have a concert next week in the Salle Bourgie. Only 450 seats or so, but I'm sharing the stage with a couple of up-and-coming violinists and a very well-reputed quartet. I know the quality of the people involved, and we're guaranteed to get some useful reviews, if we can attract the right reviewers."

Mia nodded. "I'm not involved in the music scene, but it's the same with all the arts. Reviews don't mean much unless they're written by the right people and published in the right media."

"Precisely. I'm in the process of compartmentalizing, and I know my folk career is going to suffer. My material is too Quebecois, and my accent is too strong to cross over into the rest of Canada. The piano has none of those barriers. I don't like that, but..." She gave an expressive shrug.

Cameras flashed, and Mia turned aside to clear the shot. Then the moment was gone, and the two stood alone again.

Neither of them really belonged in this group, and they spend the next half hour chatting about this and that. Because of their relative objectives and personalities, it was inevitable that Marie would do most of the talking. Of course, the subject of Jean came up.

Mia didn't have to ask; Marie seemed used to defining her relationship. "We're a good match. Neither of us is driven to play the social media game, but we both understand the necessity. Stable relationships are not great media fodder, but neither of us will indulge in stupid games for the sake of coverage. It's not perfect, but we both get what we want. I know it sounds terrible, but it's more like a close working relationship than a love affair."

She shrugged and gave a rueful smile. "Many people are surprised to find the French to be so businesslike in *affaires de coeur.*"

"Which is why you put up with the ' vzxthird best girl' routine."

"Oh, that's only among friends. We would never let the public see us in that way."

Mia frowned. "Actually, that would play very well on certain platforms." She held up a cautioning hand. "Not that I'm advising it. Not your type of publicity at all."

Marie gave a warm smile. "Thanks. It's always nice to have your opinion supported by a pro."

"Speaking of which, this has been a pleasant chat, but I think we're both neglecting our duties."

Marie flicked her fingers to where Jean was threading his way through the crowd in their direction. "The taskmaster is coming to put our little noses to the grindstone."

Mia pretended to regard the other's face seriously. "No, I'd have to say that nose doesn't need any touchups."

Marie turned her head away. "Please, no more professional opinions." She turned back. "Honestly, I've sometimes wondered if my nose was a bit...prominent."

"I refuse to stoke your ego by giving the expected answer to that."

Jean arrived in time to break up a mock fist fight. "You seem to be laughing too hard to do any damage, but think of your images."

Marie turned to him, one fist still clenched. "I thought this was a publicity appearance."

He put a gentle hand on her knuckles. "Not that kind of publicity."

She pouted. "Gee, can't a girl have any fun at all?"

He turned to Mia. "You're supposed to be good at this sort of stuff. Now I have to worry you might be destroying her image completely."

"Don't sweat it. We've been amusing ourselves with idle chat."

His face straightened, and he regarded her. "That doesn't sound like the Mia I've been hearing about. What's really going on?"

"Do you want the full analysis, or the nub of the problem?"

Marie frowned, obviously taken aback. "What is he talking about?"

Mia sighed. "You know how doctors always complain about people at parties wanting their medical opinions. It's the same with publicists. We can't really hope to ignore the things people say to us."

"So, all this time we've been chatting, you've been sizing me up."

"Please, don't take this wrong. I'm not doing anything any normal person wouldn't do." She shrugged. "But I have more training at it."

116

Marie shook her dark curls just once, and her chin rose. "*Bien.* I can take it. Tell me one conclusion you have drawn."

Mia raised her eyebrows at Jean.

He laughed. "Go ahead. She's tough."

"I'll make this easy. I'm going to start by agreeing with you."

"On what?"

"You have an image problem, and you need to solve it."

"But that's where the agreeing stops?"

"It does. I don't know the business, and Quebec is a specialized market, but in general you can't handle two images like you've been trying to do."

"Give me an example."

"Look at your dress. You're trying to be two things at once. You can't do that."

The beautiful face twisted in a frown. "Why not?"

"Don't get me wrong. As an outfit, that dress is striking, and it suits someone of your stature perfectly. However, as an image that defines you, it sends two messages. You are trying to be a sophisticated concert pianist, while at the same time you are clinging to your habitant roots. I know there's a lot of that in Québec, but your two images appeal to two mutually exclusive audiences. If you want to hit the big time, you have to choose."

She regarded the other woman, hoping she hadn't gone too far.

But Marie was tough. She merely sighed. "I already knew that. I was just hoping..."

Mia smiled. "I get that all the time. People pay me a thousand bucks to tell them something they already know. But when it comes from me, they believe it. Plus, they paid money for it. Has to be true, doesn't it?"

"A thousand dollars?"

"That's my rate for a public relations analysis: a thousand an hour. We only spent half that time, and I'd be backing it all up with a flashy folder full of evidence, but yes, that would have cost you five hundred. Isn't it nice to have friends in high places?"

Again Marie sighed. "You might as well send me a bill. The truth is the truth."

"Can't. Conflict of interest. Much though my mercenary instincts want to get their grubby little paws on your cash, I'm at this party as an agent for the Humanity Meld. Call it a public relations freebie from the aliens." She looked over and flickered her fingers in the Gliesean 'come here' gesture. "Here, you can thank the boss himself."

The alien strolled over.

"Nicolaus, I'd like you to meet my taxi driver, Captain Jean Gagnon."

"We've already met, and I could hardly miss your entrance. Captain Gagnon, you were having far too much fun."

"This is my escort for the evening and many others, Marie Pelletier."

Nicolaus took her hand, looking down as she gripped his firmly. "The pianist? I believe you have a concert coming up."

"I do. Would you like to come?"

Apparently unbidden, Nero appeared at his shoulder. Hemi trailed behind, his usual brash confidence unsettled by the appearance of this idol.

"My aide, Lieutenant Wolf, and my technical assistant, Hemi Solaris. Nero, please arrange tickets for Miss Pelletier's concert next week."

"Yessir. Will it be a media event?"

Nicolaus raised his eyebrows to Mia, who nodded. "Small and select. Let's talk later about the appropriate publications to inform."

"Righto, Miss." He raised his eyebrows at Hemi. "You coming? You're a keyboarder yourself, aren't you?

The boy blushed and ducked his head in affirmative. "Just the electronic kind."

The two aliens made small bows and strolled away, and the boy fumbled his own bow and followed.

Marie stared at Mia. "Do you know what you just did?"

"My job. You're here for the publicity the appearance will generate. I'm here for the public relations opportunities to take advantage of. Is there anything wrong with that?"

"No, no, nothing wrong. I didn't realize the...scale of this operation."

"Oh, yeah, babe. Yer in the big times." She became serious. "And you've also just committed yourself to side with the Canadian government in their support of this project. I understand the touchy relationship Quebec has with the rest of the country..."

Jean chuckled. "The Space Centre isn't in Montreal by mistake, and she's already been connected to the project in several articles and one of her songs. This is all working out fine."

It all clicked. "Oh. 'Sphere Singer' is yours?"

"Do you know it?"

"Our young friend sings your praises, but I can't find a copy. He says it's all over several Webs."

Marie winked. "It's in pre-release right now, with the usual strategic leaks. Jean can send it to you an mpeg."

"Great. Shall we go and sample the famous Montreal cuisine? And I'm still working. There must be all sorts of victims I can get my manipulative hooks into. As long as they're near the buffet." Her grasping-finger gesture ended up at a tray of hors d'oeuvre being carried by, and she snagged a large prawn.

17. ENVOY

The team spent that week setting up their office/workspace, which was in a far newer and more pleasant room than poor old Building 44. However, it wasn't nearly as well equipped. When she mentioned this to Nicolaus, he nodded. "It's a different job and a different venue than you're used to. In the first place, you simply don't need the technology. Also, Meld equipment is more ubiquitous. Earther electronics are still tied to individual pieces of equipment. This room has been upgraded, and you only need to place your tri-me handset near a holodisplay node." He indicated small translucent panels on every wall. "Use your extended keypad as usual. We no longer use hardware viewscreens. You will find you have a direct line out from your biomem system as well to facilitate document access."

"Our biomems don't handle documents."

"Yours does now."

She frowned. "When did that happen?"

"As soon as you stepped into the Wing you got the standard upgrade. I thought you knew about it. The permission was in your employment documentation."

She gave a rueful grin. "The first of many events where the naïve indigenous person signs away rights to something she doesn't understand."

"What do you want to do about it?"

She shrugged. "Nothing. I'm not complaining. Is there anything else I need to know?"

"Most of our computing is done by our EIs. Your tri-me has been configured to be online with the sapience on the Wing. We have a satellite network, so you're always logged in, no matter where on earth you happen to be."

"A private satellite network? How did we swing that?"

"An application of Canadian tech, as it happens. One of the reasons we're here. On the serious side of secret, by the way."

She glanced at him. "That sounds useful. I'm sure I'll get used to it."

Hemi grinned. "It's a piece of cake. You got any questions, just ask me."

She reached out and smoothed down his hair, which, now that she noticed, was usually much more tousled than that of the other Glieseans.

* * *

One morning the following week she entered the office to a different feeling in the air. Her senses alert, she looked around.

Nicolaus and Nero sat at the tech desk, their attention on the main holoframe, which contained streams of what she was beginning to identify as the Meld Basic language. Their hand motions looked...excited but not worried.

Hemi looked up from his frame. "They've got a mission for you. Hammering out the diplomatic details."

Nicolaus motioned her over. "Watch the process. In future, you want to be able to handle this sort of thing yourself."

"What am I doing?"

He touched the enterpad and the frame's contents switched to English. "You're arranging a visit to Mexico. Tomorrow."

"Okay, we'll have to swing some weight to get that organized."

"That's what you're learning. The pathways of least resistance."

She perused the screen. She had organized international jaunts before, but it was hardly her strong suit. "Yes, I can see that working. We don't need visas for Mexico. What's our narrative there?"

"We have two advantages to shore up. First, Mexico is always uneasy about their big neighbor to the north. They see the parallels to the larger situation."

"You mean they identify with Earth, getting into bed with the Meld?"

"Exactly. The second part is their long trading relationship with Canada. We're flying in from Montreal with a Canadian plane and crew. You're on a diplomatic passport, so you're not labeled as American. We don't say anything, but we let them assume what they will."

She winced. "American tourists have been playing that game for years. If they get into a place Americans aren't liked, they immediately become Canadians."

She peered at the screen. "I don't see any transportation arrangements. How are we getting there, and who's going with me?"

"Captain Gagnon will pilot a CC-850H Challenger that the Canadian Air Force has seconded to us. His copilot is an agent of the Canadian Security Intelligence Service. For such a low-profile visit, that should be enough."

"How long are we staying?"

"Three days should be plenty. No official functions. We only need you to talk face-to-face with a potential ally. If your report is favourable, come home whenever you're ready."

She refrained from commenting that it seemed a huge operation to get the doubtful opinion of an untrained novice. *But it seems I'm expected to take this all in stride.* She'd keep her mouth shut and her mind open.

"I have a dossier for you to look through, and when you know what's going on, I'll give you a full briefing."

"Sounds good. Anything else?"

"Not that we can think of. If there are holes in the plan, perhaps you'll spot them." He smiled. "I want your maiden voyage to be a smooth one. There are no negotiations involved. The decisions have all been made. Have a nice trip."

She scoffed. "And if this was a bad B movie, someone would say, 'What could go wrong?' And then the ominous music would fade in."

He raised a finger. "And this is where your intimate cultural knowledge is valuable. I have training in Earth's foremost art, but none of the bad works."

She nodded and went to her desk, where the file had appeared on her screen.

Hemi tipped her a wink.

"Making yourself useful, are you?"

He grinned. "There are still areas where Office Intel 12 can't predict who needs what next. Have a nice trip. I'm taking the Wing back to New York tonight."

She gave him thumbs up and turned to her enterpad.

* * *

Early the next morning Jean pulled up in front of her apartment, driving a nondescript silver-grey Honda.

She handed him her suitcase and he grinned, hefting it in one hand. "Three days' duds?"

"I'm an old hand at this." She opened the door for herself. "No fancy ride today?"

"The Tesla is my own wheels. This is the kind of clunker the government goes for. Very Canadian. A lot of electric cars in Quebec because of all the hydro power." He got in and hit the Start button.

"What's the plan?"

"Plane's waiting at the strip. Six hours to Mexico City. Could be a two-hour drive to the City Centre depending on the traffic, which is completely undependable. We're staying at the Orchid House, which is conveniently near the Canadian Embassy. The Mexican government will provide transport and security. Anything else you need to know?"

"I have work to do, mostly research. Can I use your special satellite connections from the plane?"

"I'm pretty sure. Olivier will know more about that."

"I'll ask him when we meet."

Olivier Beaudry turned out to be a longer, lankier version of the pilot. Not as handsome, perhaps, but a catch for many girls. And married. She turned to check out the plane she was boarding.

It had low wings that looked too small for the plane's size, and two jet engines on nacelles higher up on the fuselage. They looked too big, so the physics must balance out. According to her biomem it cruised just under Mach One. Not bad. She appreciated the plain white colour and the lack of insignia except for the registration code in small black numbers, low on the fuselage. *Just my style.*

Inside, it was in pristine condition, with a lot of leather and light ersatz wood panelling, and it smelled like a new car. Double rows of comfortable airline seats took up most of the cabin space, but the front row was two solos, leaving enough room between them for an open feeling.

Olivier caught her looking at the ceiling. "I know it's tight, but in a plane this size, you don't want too much airspace inside."

"Why's that?"

"Less distance to fall."

She put on a pirate accent. "Toiks the weather a bit, do she?"

He grinned. "Only a bit, and we have a smooth forecast for this trip, you'll be happy to know."

"Oh, dat Oi am."

He headed for the cockpit.

She took that as a hint and buckled into the starboard solo seat. It was comfortable but supportive, and the panel of buttons included one with a rising footrest on it. Out of a sense of dignity, she refrained from playing with them all.

Soon they were in the air, and Jean left the cockpit and strolled back to perch on the armrest of the solo seat opposite her. "Has milady settled comfortably? May I bring you a refreshment of some sort?"

"No cabin attendant on this flight?"

"I am considered a competent mixologist. Anything else you order comes in a foil wrapping, ready-made by Canadian Government minions."

She glanced at her watch. "I'm feeling rather coffee breakish, and it was an early breakfast. What do you have that approximates a foil-wrapped Danish?"

He rose. "Coffee?"

"With a dash of milk, please."

By the time he returned with a steaming cup, she had the tray figured out.

He placed the cup in the holder. "It seems the milk comes in a little plastic container. You may dash in as much as you wish."

She sighed. "Giving me fair warning that I may feel important, but the service doesn't stretch to VIP treatment."

"A whole airplane to yourself, with two handsome and talented gentlemen dancing attendance isn't enough for milady?"

"You know us diplomats. We undergo a lot of inconvenience, and we expect a commensurate amount of glory to make up for it."

"Pilots have the same problem, with less chance for payback."

"Oh, I don't know. The stream of girls appearing on your stalwart arm before Marie looks worth quite a lot."

"You Googled me."

"Of course I did. I checked Olivier out as well. It's a standard precaution, you know."

"I suppose. Saved you from falling in love with my handsome visage, because you know I'm already taken."

"True, but it also prepared me to give you a bit of slack, because you've settled down with one girl."

He nodded. "If I was in the marrying market, she'd be a catch. She's almost famous, you know. It's a bit flattering that she's willing to hang around with a mere jet jockey."

"You used the "Aw, shucks," line on me, already. Are you losing your touch?"

"Naw, I'm one of those guys who's afraid of intelligent women. You're perfectly safe."

She narrowed her eyes. "I'm a diplomat, and you just told me several things about yourself, some of which you didn't mean to."

"See? My concern pays off." He pointed an accusatory finger. "Tell me one."

"Given the chance, you will talk about yourself instead of doing your duty?"

"What...? Oh!" He jumped to his feet. "One apricot Danish coming up, freshly nuked."

Microwaves tend to have a toughening effect on pastry, so she ate the offered treat without comment, washing it down with the coffee, which was rich, dark and flavourful. When she did mention that, he waved away the compliment.

"Montreal has fantastic coffee vendors. I don't mind the government stuff, but when I can, I bring my own."

"Well, thanks for sharing it."

He made a quick flourish with his hand. "Whatever makes milady happy." He sat back and regarded her. "Can I ask a question, if I'm not being too forward?"

She sat up. "When a pilot wonders if he's being too forward, it's got to be some kind of question."

"It's this way. Marie told me in no uncertain terms that you were a sweet person."

"Did she? And you question that?"

"Yeah. I asked around, and none of the people on the project said anything of the sort. Oh, they think you're good at your job, and easy to work with but nothing — you know — personal."

"Perhaps because there's nothing personal going on with any of them." She shrugged. "with Marie it's different. We liked each other. I mean, it's hard not to like Marie, isn't it?"

He grinned. "Yeah, but I'm biased."

She was half-expecting a return to the repartee, but he pushed the leg-lift button on his seat. "You don't mind if I take a time out, do you? Early morning this morning."

She frowned. "Did you get up and prep the plane before coming for me?"

"Part of the job."

"I appreciate it. Nap away. Would you like a lullaby?"

"Not unless you really feel the need." He tapped the plastic in his ear. "Ocean waves and sitar music."

She put a finger to her lips and settled back in her seat to wonder what that had been all about.

Some time later she awoke to find her seating partner had changed. Olivier had pulled up the viewscreen and was tapping on the keyboard. He noticed her movement and glanced over.

"Seats are comfortable, aren't they?"

"Very. How long till we land?"

"Two hours."

"Drat. I was counting on getting some homework done."

"We saved an hour on the time zones."

They spent the next while in companionable silence, until Olivier went forward for the landing.

She had not travelled by private jet before, and the airport procedure was something she could get used to. A black Mercedes pulled up to the foot of the gangway, and she strolled down the stairs to meet two well-dressed gentlemen who spoke English with educated accents. With no ceremony, they got into the car and left the airport by a private exit. On the street, two heavy motorcycles pulled in behind them. No lights or sirens, but a solid presence, nonetheless.

The younger of the two greeters, who had introduced himself as Raoul, gave her an apologetic smile. "I am sorry, Senorita Larsen, but the traffic is not paying any attention to our diplomatic status. The estimate for the trip to your hotel is one hour and twenty-five minutes."

"I can occupy myself, unless you have some information I need about the visit? *Podriamos hablar en español si quiere.*"

"Oh, no, señorita. I would like to practise my English, if you would be so kind."

"Of course. What is planned for this evening?"

"A small cocktail party, although the Casa de Orquídeas has a formidable chef. Do not eat too much for supper." He glanced at her. "Orquídeas...?"

"Orchids."

"Ah, si. Yes, the House of Orchids Hotel is very grand. And close to your Embassy, yes?"

"My pilot will find it convenient when he goes to check us in."

He grinned and laid a finger alongside his nose. "And your *hombre de securidad* as well."

"Security agent. Him, too." She decided not to correct him on his assumption of her nationality.

"Dress will be semi-formal, I hope. I didn't plan on attending any balls or banquets."

"Oh, no, no, señorita. All will be very low key." He glanced down at her business suit. "Perhaps señorita has a little black cocktail dress? I understand that is — how do you say it, — a fallback position?"

She shook her head. "Not really a fallback. I would say 'tried and true' perhaps. As it happens, I do have something of the kind, but not black. Too dressy."

"Ah, thank you for that small lesson in etiquette."

She glanced at the other man: stockier, older, with a rugged complexion. "Your *compañero* is not as concerned with social niceties?"

"They are not his concern. Luis has different talents."

The older agent grinned and patted the breast of his suit near his left shoulder.

"Let us hope we will be testing only your talents and not his today."

"De tus labios a los oídos de Dios."

"Yes, Raoul. Some expressions work best in one's own language."

The young man nodded, although his expression didn't look that serious.

The boys having a bit of fun with the gringo lady, I suspect.

But the gravity of the situation got her thinking, and when they had finished their evening's social obligations and were having a nightcap in her suite, she asked her companions about it.

"Jean, do you carry a sidearm on these expeditions?"

"Not usually. Olivier does."

"But Olivier didn't go in the car with me."

"Mexico has come a long way since the bad old days of the drug cartels. You ought to be glad to be a faceless bureaucrat. If anyone wanted to create a scene, an officer in military uniform would be a better target."

"I never looked at it that way. Sorry to sound selfish."

"Nothing wrong with a healthy dose of self-protective instinct."

She nodded. "I'm moving into a world I never expected to enter. Scary at times."

"'I never did that. Way back when I was too stupid to realize it, I set myself on a path, and I'm still on it. You were brave to take on this job." He grinned. "I was about to say, 'at your age' but you were guaranteed to take it wrong."

She waved away his joke. "I thought I was brave, too. Back then, I was pretty stupid. That was last month."

"All part of growing up." He regarded her quizzically. "What is it that scares you? Besides the terrorist thing. We're all worried about that."

"I've always been happy to hide behind my anonymity. There are benefits to being a faceless bureaucrat, as we saw today. And then I got caught by the cameras at that Habitat for Humanity launch. Suddenly people were recognizing me: in the shops I went to, at meetings, even in the neighbourhood. It was nothing special. NASA is full of well-known faces. But it did bother me a bit."

He nodded. "But this is a whole different level of exposure."

"I was at NASA for quite a few years, and I know the drill. When the security community starts noticing you, it's pretty scary. Back in Houston, I was out for a drive one day. While I was on the highway, word came down about this job. They sent a helicopter to escort me back to the office."

"That would shake up your tidy little world."

"It certainly did. My eyes are getting opened."

He regarded her until she looked away. "But..."

"But what?

"Are you still primed for the objective?"

"Of course. As a friend of mine said recently, if you don't do your best for humanity, what good are you?"

"Very philosophical. Mind if I ask who said that?"

"Hemi."

"Huh! Kid's got depths, hasn't he?"

"He's made a far greater jump out of obscurity than I have, and I think he's handling it better."

"Ah, the resiliency of the young. I don't know where he's going, but I've got a feeling about him as well."

She frowned. "What do you mean, 'as well'? Who else do you have a feeling about?"

Jean laughed out loud. "It must be tough, always having to analyze every statement to look for hidden meanings."

She glared at him. "And for statements that don't answer the question."

He continued to chuckle, and she knew there was no point in pushing it. They had too smooth a working relationship to spoil it with power games.

But it gave her something to think about in the odd break between meetings. It was as if she was watching herself over her own shoulder, aware of how she was acting and how people were reacting to her. She wondered if it would always be like this now, and decided it was probably a phase she was going through.

I hope it doesn't last long. I have work to concentrate on.

* * *

And so it went for the next few months. They spent a lot of time in the air, shuttling around the small nations of the Caribbean and Central America. Sometimes Hemi came along, but he was spending most of his time in New York. He was proud of his personal cabin on the Mothership. The images he showed made it look quite plain to Mia, but the big holographic viewframes were all that he cared about.

She decided she wasn't keeping close enough contact, and the next time they were on a long flight, she buttonholed him. "What are you doing to keep busy, now that you don't spend your time looking over your shoulder for the authorities?"

He winced. "School. I think I'm being given the Gliesean version of the General Education Development program. Of course, I'm way behind on the language, but the Math is a whiz. I'm really enjoying the Physics and Chemistry, because their kids know so much stuff our top scientists are just starting to discover. I think they're giving me a special pass on Biology, because I'm fine on the general ideas but all the *flora* and *fauna* are Gliesean."

"Sounds like all sorts of fun."

He frowned at her. "I know that was meant to be sarcastic, but you're wrong. Mothership makes it darned interesting; I really enjoy it."

"You're being taught by the Mothership?"

"Of course. Well, one of her educational programs."

"Do you ever talk with the main sapience?"

Hemi shook his head. "I think so. It's a huge ship, with a thousand different functions going on, and she runs them all. But I know what you mean. Sometimes she takes on a certain tone, and you get the feeling you're talking to someone special. I tell you, when The Voice sounds, I sit up and take notice."

"Does this happen often?"

"Almost every day." He regarded her. "Yeah, I see what you mean. Why all this attention to little old me?" He grinned. "I guess I must be special?"

"You're special, all right. One of a kind, I gather."

"I always knew that. What about you? You and your handsome pilot getting along?"

She gave him a level stare. "Jean and Olivier and I spend a lot of time together. When we're in Montreal, he goes off to his girlfriend."

He held up his hand defensively. "Of course. The beautiful Marie. Good working relationship, then?"

"Very good. We're often on our own in a completely foreign country, and those two...well, I know I can count on them."

He nodded wisely. "You're creating a cadre. Appropriate."

"What's a cadre?"

"Another word for team, but it goes deeper. A group of people who all trust each other. Powerful stuff, especially in a world like Earth, where everybody's out for themselves."

"And is there anything I should be doing to make this happen?"

"Not much you aren't doing already. Some cadres are work-oriented, some more social. Lots of them overlap, and social activities are the glue that holds them all together. You and Jean going running, for example."

"So, my choice of exercise partner is good for my work cadre?"

He shrugged. "Can be. It's a new concept for me, too."

She nodded and left the room, aware of a warm feeling, but she couldn't put her finger on the reason for it.

18. AIR PIRATES

"How would you like a change of scenery?"

She looked up from her viewframe to check Nicolaus's mood. He was smiling.

"Considering how much travelling I've been doing, that's a tall order. Europe or Asia?"

"Taiwan, as it happens. What do you know about them?"

She shrugged. "A little more than most countries their size. They deserve study."

"You realize their situation viz a viz the Mainland."

"I'm aware of the Chinese government's antagonism towards their official independence five years ago. How do you think they'll react if I visit?"

She called up some files on her own terminal and glanced at Hemi, who flipped them onto the auxiliary frame in front of them. "Here are the transcripts of the latest three incidents that might apply."

He scanned the documents. "They still don't accept the situation, despite pressure from...pretty much the rest of the international community. I'm reading a lot of bluster, covering a basic demand to enter their position into the official record."

She nodded. "As they have the right to do."

"You don't expect any serious response?"

"To an unknown bureaucrat meeting with others of her sort to discuss...esoteric ideas about the Meld?"

"That was our interpretation as well. I will set this permission in motion, and our counterparts in Taiwan will handle their end." He grinned. "All you have to do is pack your bag."

By the end of the briefing that afternoon, she felt a lot better about the assignment. She leaned back in her chair and nodded. "I have two objectives. First, to be sure that the Taiwanese Foreign Minister means what he says and has the backing of his government. In that respect, all you want is my gut feeling, Earther to Earther, of how the meeting turned out."

"The personal touch. No alien, human or not, can make such a subtle judgement, especially on a viewscreen."

"And second is the easy part. Simply by my presence, the Taiwanese government is assured that we mean what we say. Am I important enough to satisfy their need for reassurance?"

"You are if I say you are. The presence of my personal envoy when no one else is receiving that attention should do the trick."

She rose from her chair and gave him a bow with a brief flourish of the hand. "We aim to please, sir. Now, I'm going to check the weather reports for Taiwan before I pack. At least typhoon season is over."

"The lady who thinks of everything." He waved her away.

Jean dropped in at quitting time to give her some details of the trip. "We're headed for Hsinchu, on the northwest coast of the island of Formosa."

"What's the routing?"

He grinned. "Now we find out why we got the new CC-850H. The hydrogen-fueled model has a ten-thousand-kilometre range. It's ten hours to Hawaii, stop for a ten-hour pilot rest break, then eight hours the rest of the way. Call it thirty hours total. You know how comfortable the seats are. You ought to get enough rest.

"The Taiwanese take over the schedule from there, but Hsinchu Air Base is near the downtown. The main hotels are only ten minutes away."

"We're meeting in the Hyatt Episode, and I imagine we'll stay there as well."

"It's less than twenty minutes from the airport. Convenient."

"Hmm." She had a thought. "How do we handle the time zones?"

He held up open hands. "Taiwan is exactly twelve hours off Montreal. Don't even worry about what day of the week it is. You'll be home before it matters."

"Fair enough. I gather we get in early in the morning."

"Six thirty or so, their time."

"That's not bad. I can aim myself to sleep the last few hours of the flight, and the new daylight will wake me up." She pulled up a time zone app on her tri-me. "Now I see why we're meeting at ten in the morning. That'll be ten in the evening my time."

He regarded her. "This meeting's more important than usual, isn't it?"

"Yes. I'm supposed to be using my intuition. I can't do that if I'm grouchy or drowsy."

"Well, you set the schedule the way you want it. Olivier and I can tippytoe around when we need to."

"Thanks, Jean. I appreciate that."

He grinned. "Usually I'm an egalitarian sort, but in this case, one of my team members has to be in top form for the game. That takes priority."

"Typical Canadian, I guess, eh?"

"Stereotypes are created through years of work by millions of people." A lazy shrug. "Who am I to fight a positive one?"

She went home and spent the evening going over the Taiwanese contract proposals.

* * *

The closest they got to the ocean in Honolulu was Sammy's Beach Bar and Grill in the airport, where they had a decent meal to offset the nuked fare onboard. They stretched their legs on the long walk across the terminal building and returned to the plane so the pilots could fulfill their regulation sleep quotas.

Soon they were in the air again, although the interior of the plane bore more resemblance to a city office than to an aircraft, with holo frames and enterpads strewn around.

Then they entered the Strait of Taiwan.

"Incoming radio traffic."

Her viewscreen flickered, and she pulled it in front of her.

Text appeared. *"Identify yourself, please."*

"That's the plane's International Translator. They're speaking Mandarin."

"Who is it?"

"Two Shenyang J-15K fighters. No insignia of any kind. Just pulled in behind us."

She went forward and slid into the copilot's seat. "Can I talk to them in clear?"

"In Mandarin?"

"That's the idea."

He nodded to the copilot's seat. "Ask them what they want."

She moved forward, put on the headset and switched to Mandarin. *"This is C-GOV 43. Please identify yourself."*

Please change course and follow us. The planes separated and pulled ahead.

"We are on a mission for the Government of Canada and have diplomatic immunity. We are cleared for our present course by all local authorities."

Change course and follow us.

Jean held up open hands. "This is out of my pay grade. Over to the Diplomatic Corps."

"Nicolaus gave us an emergency frequency. Is this an emergency?"

"This is air piracy."

"Put me on that frequency."

"Go ahead. Talk."

"Mayday, mayday. This is Flight C-GOV 43, calling for assistance."

An unaccented Gliesean voice came through. **This is flight GBP 1 responding. C-GOV 43, what is your situation?**

"We have been intercepted by two Shenyang J-15K fighters with no identity markings."

What do they want?

"They say we have to follow them."

Roger that. Please comply.

The pilot sat upright. "Comply?"

Please comply, Captain Gagnon. There is no airport within an hour, and we need time to arrange a reception. Do you suggest an alternate course of action?

Jean shrugged. "Your call." He nodded to her. "Speed?"

She switched to the general channel and Mandarin. *"We are complying. What velocity would you like?"*

This is sufficient. Maintain radio silence from this point on.

"Roger. Flight C-GOV 43 out."

The J-15s made a slow course change. Jean fiddled with the nav screen. "Hmm. We're headed towards Kinmen, in Fujian Province. Listed as a "Domestic Airport. I wonder."

"What are the possibilities?"

"Either it's an unofficial military base, or these planes are not official military."

"Neither of which sounds positive for us."

"I doubt if diplomatic channels are going to help us much."

"Then I'm getting out of this seat and letting a more useful person sit here,"

She and Olivier exchanged positions, and the flight droned on into an uncertain future.

* * *

Thirty-five minutes later, Olivier pointed to the radar. "We've got company."

"What is it?"

"Nothing on the official lists. Too big to be anything but a bomber, but completely wrong silhouette. Coming in fast...very fast."

A shadow moved down out of the sun, and a Gliesean Flying Wing inserted itself neatly between the Challenger and the fighters.

Mia relaxed. "Looks like the cavalry has arrived."

"And they already knew I was the pilot. They were shadowing us."

"We have radio contact." Olivier touched a screen. "Here we go."

Good afternoon, C-GOV 43. This is GBP 1. How are you faring?

"All the better for your presence, I'm sure."

Please stand by on this frequency. We are acting in an unofficial capacity and would prefer not to make direct contact with your friends.

"Ten-Four, GBP. You're running the show."

The four aircraft held their positions patiently, and for a while, nothing happened. Mia had time to appreciate the threat of the Wing. It had none of the graceful sweep of the old Earth craft. It was dark and chunky and angled, and in this setting, it oozed threat.

C-GOV, I think they have had enough time to make up their minds.

Jean raised his eyebrows to Mia, who nodded.

"Our diplomat agrees."

Thank you, Please stand by.

The hulking Wing slid in behind the portside J-15. The engine of the fighter emitted a puff of dark smoke, and the craft began to descend, the rate of fall increasing as its airspeed slowed.

Jean chuckled. "Well, that was a disappointment. I expected at least flashing lights and sparks."

"These people like to be subtle."

The fighter was on their rear viewscreen, descending rapidly.

Jean keyed his radio, "GBP, is it permitted to ask what action you just took?"

"We instigated a flameout. Their pilot should be trained to handle it. If not, he can practise his emergency water landing technique. This event can be an opportunity for a lot of learning."

Sure enough, the descending plane exuded a gush of smoke and began to level out.

The Flying Wing changed course, tracking the second J-15, closing the gap rapidly.

The Chinese fighter broke away and dove down towards its wingman. As soon as they had regained formation, they swooped away to the west.

The Gliesean craft slowed and settled in behind their left wing. *All clear, C-GOV. We'll keep you company until we reach Taiwan's national territory. You'll be safe enough then, and we don't want to intrude on their airspace. The paperwork isn't worth it.*

Mia leaned forward. "Get their version."

Jean nodded. "GBP, there's going to be a big enquiry about this. Do you have anything to contribute?"

Our recording of the public radio traffic shows that they contacted you and forced you to follow. One of their aircraft developed a mechanical problem and they had to break off. You returned to your former course.

"Thank you. That will make my report a lot easier."

Glad to be of service.

"Glad to have you. C-GOV 43 out."

Without even a pop, the channel went dead.

Jean spun his seat around to face her. "An example of their technology? Very impressive."

"You've seen them land that thing in a parking lot."

"Finesse as well. Anyway, I was glad they showed up when they did."

"Yes, they saved us a serious international incident at a very bad time."

"They saved you and me more than that. Do you know what happens when you get captured by the Chinese?"

She nodded. "You become a political football for as long as they need you."

"And in the process, you're quite likely to get kicked around. Yes, I'm very happy with that Flying Wing contraption."

Peace, such as it was, reigned.

GBP 1 to C-GOV 43.

"43 here."

We're approaching Taiwanese airspace. No sense pushing any boundaries.

"Thanks again for the assistance, GBP. Safe skies to you."

We wish you the same. Happy to help in that objective. GBP 1 out.

"C-GOV 43 out."

The alien ship banked away and rose rapidly out of sight and radar range.

Soon they had Taiwan on the radio and were passed along in turn to Hsinchu Air Base Control. Mia stayed on the headset, fascinated by the radio chitchat, which was all in English. These were serious workers, intent on their jobs, but they seemed to be able to loosen the tension with quick jokes and quips that did nothing to affect their performance.

They landed smoothly and taxied to a private hanger where a polite official in some kind of government uniform ushered her to a limousine that looked like a Mercedes but wasn't. Jean followed with her suitcase, and the chauffeur stowed it.

"We'll be along later. It seems we're sharing a suite of rooms so we can keep an eye on you."

"Good. I was starting to feel a little lonely, for a moment."

He clapped her on the shoulder. "No problem. I don't usually get the VIP service for myself. What's the plan?"

"I'm not sure of the schedule. Probably the ten o'clock meeting, then some kind of fancy lunch."

"Someone will put us in the picture."

"Ahem…"

They turned.

"That would be me, sir. I am Chi-Ming, surname Liao." The young man grinned. "Which means 'Liaison' in English. That is ironic, is it not?"

She answered in Mandarin. *Thank you for your help, Chi-Ming. A suggestion, if you wish to learn. I would say 'appropriate' rather than 'ironic.' Irony is poorly understood, even by English speakers, and often has a negative connotation.*

He made a slight bow, his hands together. "*I thank you for that information. It is something I did not know. Please allow me to do my liaison, and join me for the ride to your hotel. The chauffeur will return for your compatriots.*"

With a quick wave to Jean, she slipped into the car, and soon she was on her own in a very different city.

Her recent brush with the security community had warned her, however, and at the hotel, she went straight to her room and changed to her smartest business outfit. She was perfectly coifed and, she thought, looking rather sharp when Chi-Ming came to get her. With little conversation, he brought her to a well-appointed room that looked like every commercial suite she had ever attended a meeting in.

Foreign Minister Gao Jiajun was greying and sixtyish, with a wide, square face and a prominent chin. This rather foreboding presence was countered by a pleasant smile and, she thought, the hint of a twinkle in his eye.

They soon established that his English was about as strong as her Mandarin, so that if they wanted to be completely sure on any issue, they could express it in both languages.

Once the preliminaries were over, he opened the main meeting. "Ms. Larsen, while I am flattered that our little country is receiving the attention of your Ambassador, it does concern us somewhat to discover the reason why. You understand, bitter experience teaches us that having the important nations of the world take an interest in our future is not always a good thing."

She smiled. "Perhaps you need not be concerned about attracting the attention of one as unimportant as myself. Ambassador Gliese has sent me merely to assure everyone that our communications are clear."

"That I understand. And perhaps for other reasons?"

"Mr. Minister, we have an expression, 'beating around the bush,' which is often very appropriate in diplomatic circles. Perhaps it would be better if I told you directly why I came."

"I am aware of the concept, and I applaud your directness. Please go on."

"I am here for two reasons. First, to reassure you that our intentions towards your country are exactly as stated, with no communications issues and no outside motivation. We would like to read through the agreement and chat about anything that comes to either one of us.

"Second, we wish to ascertain that the communication is likewise clear in the opposite direction. The Ambassador is not a suspicious man, but he wishes to be sure that outside motivation does not exist.

"To be frank with you, sir, one of my usual functions in this sort of exchange is to assure myself that you are dealing as straight as we are. No offense is intended. At the moment we have no evidence to suspect otherwise. This is merely a precaution. 'Trust everybody but cut the cards,' as our saying goes."

He nodded. "No offense is taken. That is what I, too, expect from the meeting."

She raised a cautioning hand. "But I do have a third objective."

"You do?"

"We have selected your country for this meeting because of your recent independence and the troubles that go back for decades." She took a more comfortable pose. "You see, when two people are bargaining, they take care to present their own arguments in the best light possible. The Earth's representatives have acted in good faith in this regard, we are sure.

"But we are also aware that Taiwan had diplomatic problems and failures during their negotiation with their powerful neighbor, and while we do not expect you to lay them all before us, we hope you will answer questions about how you have dealt with them. Tell us what works with Earthers, and what does not."

She tilted her head and held out open hands. "Are you willing to aid us in this way?"

He placed his palms together, his fingertips touching his lips in a prayer-like pose. "How do you advise we proceed?"

"If I might suggest, we go through the agreements as we just discussed. The outside task may or may not come up. In any case, that would give us background for a final discussion on that objective."

The minister nodded deeply. "A good plan. Chi-Ming, will you put the first document up on the screens?"

Two large viewscreens lit up, with an English version on the left the Mandarin on the right.

They turned to face the screens, but the minister leaned slightly towards her. "And do you think we could dispense with the diplomatic language? I find all the 'if you wish' and 'no insult intended' places a mist of obfuscation in the way of true communication."

She faked shock. "What? You want to toss away all the camouflage and talk straight? Aren't you afraid I'll find out what you really mean?"

His smile twisted. "I thought that was the general idea."

"I suppose it is." She glanced at the screens. "Do we have to wade through the introductions and references? They're exactly the same on every document."

"If 'wade through' means what I think it does, let's not bother. The first important point I want to look at is Page Three, Section One."

"Okay. Slap it up on the screen, Chi-Ming, and let's get to work."

They spent the next two hours doing nothing that resembled negotiation, and by halfway through, they had moved to a first-name basis. As expected, they found nothing in the documents that needed changing, but Mia had a much better idea of how Jaijun interpreted them. She had done her homework on Taiwan's long slog to independence, and it was easy for her to find areas in the agreements that related to the present Earther situation, which they discussed in a freer style.

It was not a long or detailed document, only the basic premises and overall objectives. Legislation for each specific detail of trade, currency, banking, intellectual property and a hundred other situations would come later.

At twelve-thirty they took a break for lunch.

"Are we expecting any ceremony, Jiajun? I'm rather peckish, and I don't want to embarrass myself."

He grinned. "This is a business lunch. I have only invited two of my colleagues who speak very good English, and your two pilots. They informed Chi-Ming that they would rather not leave the hotel, and it seemed wasteful to miss the chance for further communications."

"That's very nice of you, Jiajun, but if you plan to get them relaxed and pump them for secrets, I'm afraid they don't know anything about anything. Except flying airplanes."

He laughed. "I stand forewarned, as the English would say. Why don't you take a break and freshen up? Chi-Ming will come to your rooms for you in half an hour. I have a few details to take care of and will meet you in the private dining room."

Mia found that her initial enthusiasm for the work was losing its power to keep her mind sharp. It was past midnight back home where her circadian rhythms thought they were. So, she was happy to see a couple of familiar faces at the table, looking a bit out of place in their uniforms.

"Hey, boss lady. How's it going?"

"Very well, guys. What have you been up to?"

Jean made a moue of distaste. "What do you think? We've been up to our ears with the local CSIS boys, writing reports."

"Sorry, I'm not very experienced with international incidents. Is it really that bad?"

He brushed that away with a flip of his wrist. "Naw, they've got it all on the cockpit recorders, voice and video, and the GPS records. We filled out a bunch of onscreen documents, then entered another three sets for other departments that asked all the same questions. The real grilling won't happen till we get home and the Top Brass want their turn."

Olivier grinned. "And that's it for me. CSIS will pull me out of the limelight quick like a bunny. Jean will probably have to deal with a parliamentary sub-committee."

"Yeah, and I get the media gig. That part's okay, actually. I do it a lot. The media like me, the camera likes me, and the Space Agency has a smooth public relations team."

They were interrupted by Minister Guo, who bustled in, looking concerned. "I didn't realize you had trouble on your way here, Ms. Larsen. I'm so sorry."

She smiled to ease the tension. "I sincerely doubt you had anything to do with sending those pirates after us. I don't think any apologies are due."

"But still..."

"Jiajun, we had some trouble, and I know it's going to cause all sorts of international upset, but we got out of it with no problems, and I'm not concerned. Now, we've been working hard, and there are several nice waiters over there dying to bring us lunch, so...?" She gestured towards the table.

"Oh, by all means. I forget my duties as a host. Please come and meet a couple of friends of mine…" He made introductions to two very competent-looking and proper gentlemen, then spread the two parties around the table to maximize contact with new faces. There were seven of them but settings for eight, and Mia wondered if it meant anything.

Soon the food arrived and the conversation flagged. It was a hotpot meal, and she had just put a couple of shrimp and something that looked like bean sprouts into the simmering stock when there was a disturbance at the door.

Everyone looked up to see a mid-twentyish girl with a bob of black hair bounce up to the table, giving Jiajun a peck on the cheek and throwing herself into the empty chair. "Father, I'm sorry to be late. The streets are packed. She looked around. "Who are we eating with toda…O.M.G! It's the Canadians!" She peered at them. "Well, that puts paid to one story, anyway."

"If you don't mind, my dear, there are certain rituals that are usually performed. I know you find them onerous, but…"

"Oh, Dad, don't be pompous. I was brought up right, you know that." She reached across the table to Mia. "Hi. I'm Guo Fang. And I know what ''Fang' means in English. In Mandarin it means 'virtuous,' but my parents named me a long time ago."

She glanced around at their smiles and chuckled. "Yes, it's an old joke from a Hollywood movie." She finally took Mia's hand. "And you're the famous Mia Larsen that's all over the news. You know, I watched the launch of that Habitat, but I didn't realize that you were there, too."

She turned to the two Canadians. "And you'll have to introduce me to your intrepid pilots."

Mia pointed. "Jean over there, Olivier on your left. One's married, the other has a steady, and for the next forty-eight hours they're true only to me. Got it?"

Fang gave a mock salute, then picked up her chopsticks and stole a piece of meat from the nearest pot.

Her father was not to be distracted. "Which story did their presence put paid to?"

"The one where they got shot down, of course."

"Of course. What else is in the air, so to speak?"

She gave him a half frown. "Ha, ha, I get it, Dad. The one I like is that a flying saucer came down and zapped the pirates' engines."

Mia laughed. "I like that. What do you think, Jean? Will that make it easier to fill out those reports?"

"Sure. Pilots have been blaming everything on flying saucers for years. Why break with tradition?"

"You came from Montreal, right? I hear the styles there are fabulous. Is that blouse from Montreal?"

"This blouse is from the Que Bonito Comercio in Houston, Texas."

"You're American? I can't tell the accents apart."

"Yep. Ah just blew in from Teyxas, li'l lady."

"I thought you were all Canadian. Did you know that the American President's pet is a Formosan Mountain dog?"

"I know that it's a rescue he brought in from Korea. If it looks Taiwanese, who am I to argue?"

"Well, the blouse looks real nice." She chewed, then swallowed. "I don't suppose you wanna go dancing tonight? There's a great nightclub in the new wing of the hotel. This used to be such a dumpy old inn, but look at it now! No party? I guess not, what with jet lag and getting shot at and all."

"That was a very transparent probe for information, but I can tell you, we didn't get shot at."

The young woman put her elbows on the table and leaned forward. "You don't know how bad it is, being a diplomat's daughter. I keep having important people and stories trailed under my nose, and I'm not allowed to tell anyone. It's terrible, I tell ya. Just terrible!"

"Anyway," she jumped to her feet. "I gotta go." She turned to her father. "I said I'd show, and I showed." She wiggled her fingers at the two others. "Hi, Uncle Sonny. Hi, Uncle Rico. Good to see ya as usual."

The two older men smiled and nodded.

She winked at Mia. "Get the reference?"

Mia looked to Jean helplessly.

"Miami Vice. Crockett and Tubbs. Old TV comedy duo."

"Hey, you're not just an ordinary flyboy, are you?"

And then she was gone. As she flounced out, Mia realized that for all her flash and chatter, the girl moved without a sound.

There was a brief silence, as if all the sparkle had swept out of the room in her wake. Her father chuckled. "My daughter, obviously. She has to look everyone over. I don't know anyone who can talk that much and still maintain the security clearance she does."

Conversation returned. The two other men, whose names she couldn't remember since they had become Sonny and Rico, spoke excellent English and said very little of note. However, the food was exceptional, and everyone enjoyed the meal immensely.

Except perhaps their host. When the pineapple cake crumbs were swept away, he cleared his throat. "We have made good progress thus far, and this piracy incident is going to — do you say, 'throw a wrench?'— in my plans. Perhaps we can reconvene tomorrow."

She glanced at her escorts and received nods. "Midnight is long gone where I come from."

"Fine. Do you require entertainment?"

"We might come down to the hotel bar if we stay awake that long. We're definitely not leaving the building."

"I think that wise. Fang's comment about seeing you on TV was a warning. You could be mobbed."

"Do you think we'll be finished tomorrow?"

"I would say we are close to finished already except for one small favour."

"Certainly. What is it?"

"It seems to me that we Taiwanese have much in common with Canadians. Would you not agree, Captain Gagnon?"

"You mean sleeping next to an elephant, and you have to keep one eye open in case it rolls over?"

"An apt expression, considering the logo of the Republican Party."

Olivier met the minister's eyes directly. "What do you want of us?"

Guo shrugged. "The chance to learn something. Compare notes. Look for similarities. Small, isolated countries are always looking for friends, and I have little contact with everyday Canadians. What do you say, Ms. Larsen?"

She glanced at Olivier, and he shrugged. "I don't see any problem. We'd have to get permission, of course."

"Certainly. If Chi-Ming calls at ten tonight, it will be working time in Montreal. Give him any numbers you wish contacted."

"No problem."

"And now, I'm afraid duty calls. If there is anything else you need, Chi-Ming will be in the business suite. The hotel lines are fairly secure, but not to be trusted with delicate information." He gave an apologetic smile. "Your rooms have been swept lately, but..." He held up helpless hands.

"Not an unfamiliar situation for us. Thank you for all your time today. It was very productive."

"And, skipping all the diplomatese, I thank you for the same. We meet again at ten tomorrow."

His aide accompanied him to the door, then returned. "In case you haven't learned the layout well, I will accompany you to your rooms."

"Thanks, Chi-Ming. That'll be great."

When they were alone in their suite, Mia sat in an armchair and regarded her partners.

"Olivier, you're the security expert. Do you feel the walls closing in?"

"Definitely. They're worried about us."

"What did you think of Uncle Sonny and Uncle Rico?"

"Crockett and Tubs were detectives."

"And where does that put 'daughter' Fang?"

She considered. "She has to be his real daughter. But I caught his reference to her security clearance. You notice all her bling?"

"How could a guy miss it?"

"It doesn't make a sound."

"It doesn't?"

She reached over and slapped the back of his hand. "You were too busy watching."

Olivier nodded. "Yeah, she moves well. Either dance or martial arts."

"I'd go for martial arts. This is Taiwan, remember." She raised her eyebrows. "What do we do about it?"

"They're all friendlies so far, and we've just met our local security team. We get the airport to prep the plane first thing, and then we go along with their plan. I've seen tighter security than this for far less reason, and due to their history, they've had lots of practice."

"That's for tomorrow. How about tonight? I'm pretty trashed."

Jean shrugged. "There's no sense in trying to beat jet lag. It's two am back home. We'll black out the curtains. If we can sleep for seven hours, it will be like getting up at 9 am, which isn't bad. We can go down for a drink, listen to the music, then come up here and kick back for a while. By then it will be the middle of the day on our time clocks, but most people have a down time around three in the afternoon and we might sleep a few hours more. The breakfast room is probably open by six am.

151

"So, we can leave immediately after the meeting at ten."

"I have to be in touch with the Powers that Be, but I bet they'll be happy to have us in the air ASAP."

"Won't hurt my feelings, either."

* * *

The morning meeting was as Guo had promised: relaxed and open. Most of it seemed to be inconsequential, but she could see the value the Taiwanese was getting out of it. She was wondering what the Canadians were learning in return when the topic turned to more recent history. Olivier had just mentioned the Oligarch Revival, referring to Canada's brush with American statehood.

Jiajun nodded seriously. "We were very lucky, you know. The oligarchs never did get their ducks in a row."

"What do you mean?"

"History followed the laws of chance to your advantage. By the time the Americans had enough power to make their move, the Russian lot were pretty well decimated by the Russo-Ukrainian War. At the same time, the European Union governments had taken firmer control of their economies, and the Chinese were beginning to feel their oats, as you say."

"You mean, if they all had got together...?"

"It could have been much worse. Canada would have been the first casualty, and if the Chinese had been a serious part of it, we would have been next."

Mia smiled. "Hence this meeting."

"Exactly. You kind people have persuaded me that our two countries might profit from closer ties. I will speak to Cabinet at some appropriate time, and we'll see what comes of it."

Once again, the peace of the room was disrupted by the appearance of Guo Fang, dressed in tight leather jeans and a fringed top. "What do you think of my American Frontier outfit, Mia?"

"Daughter, you have interrupted an important meeting at a delicate point."

"Exactly. You have reached your objectives, and you will spend the next half hour making up excuses to leave. As it happens, Father, you need to spend your time on more important matters, and I have to boot our friends up to their rooms to finish packing, because the airport has assigned them a departure time of three forty-seven."

Guo Jiajun rose. "Well, my daughter has just made the last half hour of our meeting useless, and it sounds like I am needed elsewhere."

He shook their hands and turned towards the door, his daughter pacing him and speaking softly. He paused to kiss her cheek, then hurried out.

Fang returned to Mia. "He's such a dear, isn't he? I'll drop by in half an hour to pick you up for lunch. Will you be in your room?"

"Nowhere else to be."

"One thing: pack a cabin bag like you would for a commercial flight. Your main luggage might go a different route." She glanced at a huge square watch on her wrist. "Till twelve thirty?"

"If you say so."

"It's necessary. I haven't yet tested the dedication of your entourage." Again, she slipped out the door with a minimum of fuss.

Liao Chi-Ming did his liaison duties and disappeared once they were safely in their suite.

They immediately opened their luggage and began to rearrange things.

"May I assume we want a small enough bag that it might appear we are not going anywhere?"

Olivier nodded. "Don't leave anything private in the suitcases. You may never see it again, and less friendly eyes might."

Jean glanced into her case. "Oh, please don't leave those frilly things to be pawed over by hulking security goons."

She showed him her fist. "I have yet to test your dedication. Don't force me." She closed the zipper. "No point in locking them, I suppose."

"Not if you ever want to use the lock again."

With ten minutes left, they sat anxiously, each trying to be casual for the sake of the others.

After five minutes the door buzzer sounded. Olivier went to open it, but before he could say a word, Fang pushed by, declaring loudly something about the lunch she had lined up. One of the Uncles followed.

The moment the door closed, the flibbertigibbet disappeared. "All ready? Great. Leave your suitcases here. Nice-sized day packs. Take it casually in the main halls. We'll wait for empty elevators. If you get lost, go to Parking 2 and stand behind the elevator shaft near the west wall. Uncle Sonny will bring the car around. It's a beige Toyota Sienna H. Anybody who misses that, go to the hotel office and ask for the manager. He'll get you a safe ride to the airport. Got all that?"

"Empty elevators, P2, elevator shaft, Hydro Sienna."

"Let's go. I'll do the talking in the hallways."

Which she proceeded to do, giving them a rattling description of the tour she was taking them on for the afternoon, with intricate details of what they were going to see.

Jean leaned close to Mia. "Isn't this nice? We'll be able to prove we were on a tour, because we'll have all the data."

"Yes, but the idea of lunch seems to have evaporated."

"Yep, back to Canadian Government rations."

They were strolling down a wider hallway that led to the main lobby when Uncle Rico stopped and pushed open a panel in the wall. They slipped through into an echoing grey cement stairway.

Two floors down brought them out in a standard parking garage, and the promised Sienna was there waiting for them, its sliding side door open. Rico jumped in the front, and Fang ushered them into their seats. Then with a double-cheek 'Mwa' for Mia, a wink for Jean and a mock salute for Olivier, she slid the door closed and slapped the side of the car. The vehicle slid silently onto the up-ramp, and they were soon easing slowly through heavy daytime traffic.

"Well, that was smooth."

Olivier grinned. "It should have been. As far as we know, there is really nothing wrong." He leaned forward. "Anyone tailing, Rico?"

"Rider in brown leathers on a Maxsym HL1100."

"I didn't think we'd get rid of her that easily."

But it seemed they would. Some time in their forty-minute journey the motorcycle disappeared, and they slipped through the airport security gate on their own. They mounted the steps to the CC-850H, and the pilots went straight to their positions and started flipping switches and talking into their headpieces.

Mia went to her usual seat and belted in, uncertain what to do and feeling useless.

Sometime later, a rumbling shudder, followed by a slam, shook the plane. Olivier grinned back at her. "Success! The luggage made it."

The usual air traffic snafus gave extra meaning to the word 'suspense.' They paused twice on the way to their takeoff runway, but eventually they were aloft and climbing steeply to the east.

Jean slid his headset off. "Well, that was that."

"Weird. No sendoff, nothing official, just into the plane and away we go."

"You would have preferred a running gunbattle through the airport?"

"Given the choice, I prefer complete anti-climax. But why am I still feeling nervous?"

"Do you want to be reassured?" We're being routed across the island of Formosa, and will enter international airspace over the Pacific on the opposite side from the mainland."

"That helps."

There was a beep, and Olivier spoke into his headset. The two pilots listened a moment and made some adjustments to the controls. The plane banked slightly, then droned on.

Jean turned back to her. "A minor change in course was necessary."

"That doesn't help."

"Oh, yes it does. That was the Wing. A Chinese carrier usually patrolling farther north has changed course in our direction. GBP says there's a ninety-one percent chance it has nothing to do with us, but we're not taking any chances."

"I don't like even a ten percent chance when it's this kind of trouble."

"I do. It means that GBP is following us closely, and I suspect our friends have the ability to deal with anything the carrier can put in the air."

Olivier leaned over. "And there's always the rose-coloured interpretation."

"Please, lie to me. Make me feel better."

"The Chinese have denied any responsibility for those two jets. Maybe they came over to protect us."

"You think so?"

"Occam's razor says so."

"I try not to argue with Friar Ockham. He's been right for too many centuries."

"Jean?"

He spun his chair around to face her.

"The guy on the headset. The Wing com man or captain or whatever. Did he sound strange to you?"

"A bit. He is an alien, after all."

"Yeah, but it's more than that. He doesn't sound like any of the others we've met, and he made a lot of references to probabilities."

"He has all that data at his fingertips."

She shrugged. "I have a feeling it's more than that. Maybe nothing to it."

He winked. "I'm learning to trust your feelings. Let's keep it in mind."

"We'll do that."

She settled back into her comfortable seat, and as the clouds rolled by beneath them, she allowed her inner clock to tell her it was the middle of the night. She pushed the footrest button into the topmost position and fell asleep.

19. THE NEXT MOVE

Back in Canada, everything worked out in the usual government fashion. Olivier Beaudre disappeared into the CSIS world as expected. Jean took the brunt of the media attention and seemed to enjoy it. For all the flak Mia got, she might as well have been on a weekend jaunt to a cottage in the Laurentians.

When she asked about the lack of attention, Nicolaus nodded. "The benefit of being a faceless diplomat. We have layers of protection."

"No complaints from this side of the room. What are the projects coming up?"

"Three or four more outings similar to the last one. Hopefully with less dramatics.

"We'll do our best. And then?"

"Our embassy will have reached another goal. It is time to move out of the political sphere and focus on the international organizations."

"Are we moving headquarters again?"

"Yes, we will relocate the Mothership from New York to Geneva, for both practical and symbolic reasons. We have a short-term lease on some agricultural land where the Route du Pont Butin crosses the Rhone. It is a pleasant spot with smooth road access, plenty of room for the saucer and space for the Flying Wings to land as well."

"And my place in this move?"

"We're sending a dog-and-pony show to the main European capitals."

"What are we selling?"

"The same story: Everything is under control, and the Humanity Meld has the hardware to back it up."

"So, we're using the Flying Wing." She felt a pang of disappointment. "I rather like my little Challenger. We have a well-tuned operation."

"Our mysterious Chinese pirates did us a favour. They gave us an opportunity to show the Wing in a military situation. Its ability to solve the problem with no bloodshed is very appealing to our more sophisticated allies."

"And am I the dog or the pony? Don't answer that. I have no idea where the expression comes from."

Nicolaus smiled. "I will answer the intent of the question. Your overt task will be familiar. You will facilitate communication between a superior data processor and the people who might be interested in its services."

"The Flying Wing will carry an ExIn?"

He smiled and waited.

"The Flying Wing is an ExIn."

"Precisely. You don't look surprised."

"We discussed it. Answers some of our questions. What's my second objective?"

"To become part of a team. I am like one of your hockey coaches, trying out different lines of forwards."

"You've been talking to Canadians."

"I gather Jean is a rampant Habs fan, while Olivier goes for the Leafs. Traditional enemies. Yet they are friends."

"That's typical, too. In American football, a Steelers and a Ravens fan couldn't watch a game in the same bar without violence breaking out."

"Well, you can stop thinking Canadian. Your Wing is the one based in Geneva with the Mothership."

"First evidence I've heard that there are more than one of them."

He ignored the implied question. "Although you will have a small entourage."

"My status increases. Who?"

"Killing two more birds with this stone." He stopped, puzzled. "Do your people really hunt birds with stones?"

"Many primitive societies use slings to deadly effect. Who are the birds in this scenario?"

"Hemi can fulfill his role simply by being present. He is a potent symbol of our similarities. The Canadian government has asked that Jean be part of the team. We're not sure why, but we're willing to play their game, and the Mothership okayed it. I got the impression that they would have liked to send their security man as well, but there are limits."

She regarded him while she analyzed her reaction to this welcome news. "I'm not complaining. They'll be great to have. But you think Jean is something more than he seems?"

"The man wears a lot of hats. Perhaps one of them is a black fedora. Who knows?"

"So, you will move the Mothership to Geneva because it's your own portable hotel. I will hit the European capitals as required to instill confidence in the negotiations, and I will park my Flying Wing in the nearest camping site with all the Germans and Nederlanders in their mobile homes."

"You have the idea."

"And Jean Gagnon is there ostensibly to protect Hemi and me, and to represent the Canadian Space Agency. Also for his own reasons, which I should discover."

"If you can. I assume that in the proper circumstances, he will tell you himself."

"Fair enough. What's our target for this coming week?"

"You're getting good at this. Time for a more difficult assignment."

"Uh-oh. Not the Middle East?"

"A reasonable guess. They have managed the transition of their economy from oil to high-tech quite well, but their social progress has not kept pace. None of them are true democracies, and some of the rulers are, well..."

160

"Rather feudal. How is sending a woman going to help?"

He smiled and made a rippling gesture with his arm. "Let's see how that goes, shall we?"

She deepened her frown. "Just don't start calling me Grasshopper."

A puzzled frown.

"Late Twentieth popular entertainment. Look it up."

His eyes went blank, and then brightened. "Ah. An appropriate reference for several reasons. Your subtlety increases."

For some reason she felt grouchy. "Communication with some people might be better served by a subtle two-by-four alongside the head."

She rose. "Well, if I'm heading to Arabia, I'd better start shopping for a nice, plain burqa."

He opened his mouth, but she stopped him with a gesture. "Irony."

"Ah."

He was enough of a diplomat to know when to quit.

20. CADRE

Their next few missions elapsed in a sort of never-never land, where nostalgia for the team they had created warred with enthusiasm for things to come. Mia didn't like it one bit, because it interfered with the sharpness of mind she had come to expect of herself.

The expedition to the old OPEC domain went surprisingly well. When it came right down to it, these were all experienced gladiators in a centuries-old arena, and were willing to cross swords with anyone if it could strengthen their power base. She knew from long experience how to handle that type.

Hemi joined them for the next junket, which was to Ireland to discuss the special needs of a small, tech-heavy economy. All the meetings were multi-media oriented, and the lad went toe to toe with their techies and held his own.

When she complimented him on it, he laughed. "I can't take all the credit. On our side of the interface, Pegs has it all tacked down and sanded smooth. In their old world, anything I do to make them look good makes me look good. Pegs has permission to leak a defined amount of new tech, which made them very interested."

"That would explain some of the comments. Glad to have the two of you on board, so to speak. Although..."

"I know. Who is onboard with whom in this partnership isn't straightforward at any of several levels."

She raised her eyebrows. "I almost understood that. You're making progress."

"Or you are."

"Fair comment." She turned to Jean. "How did your tech talks go?"

"Very well as far as they went. Canada and Ireland chose to go different directions. We're into robotics, they're into communication. But our products need each other, giving us points of discussion."

"You're using these meetings to further the aims of the Canadian government."

"Aren't I supposed to? It fits in with our overall objectives."

She decided to ignore the lack of solid information but filed the idea on the 'To Do' list.

* * *

They only had two more treks to make, and she found herself feeling...lethargic was the only word for it. She knew she wasn't as sharp as usual, and that bothered her. Finally, as the C-850 settled in at cruising altitude for their last trip, Jean plopped himself down across the aisle from her favourite couch. "What's up?"

She indicated the documents on her screen. "Checking their last position paper."

"No, I mean with you."

"What do you mean? Nothing's 'up' with me. I'm fine."

He shook his head slowly. "The lady doth protest too much, methinks."

She turned to face him. "Well, I haven't murdered any kings lately, so if you think quoting Shakespeare is going to help your argument..." The conversation was getting convoluted, and she couldn't be bothered pushing ahead with it. She waved him away. "Whatever."

"That's what I mean. The Mia we know and love is never like this. You are actually down in the dumps."

"So what?" She realized how she sounded. "Okay, I take that back. I'm down in the dumps. Is that okay?"

"Sure. If you want to be. Talk about it?"

"Nothing to talk about."

"Yes, there is. You're down in the dumps. I'm not feeling on top of things. Olivier hasn't spoken for eight hours. Yes, I timed him. Hemi is up to his ears in something only *Pegasus* understands, so he's no help. That leaves us. Let's talk."

"Fine. Since you put it that way, we're not at the top of our game, and we need to fix it. What's going on? End-of-project blues?"

"Probably some of that. But it might be more."

"That sounds serious."

"Maybe, but if it is, we all need to take part." He raised his voice. "Olivier, Hemi, we need a meeting."

"When?"

"Would right now be a problem? Hemi!"

"Whatever." The boy flicked his fingers and his holos dissolved. "What's wrong?"

Jean made sure everyone was seated and listening. "Hemi, tell us about cadres."

The boy frowned. "Cadres?"

"Don't play dumb. You've been doing the research. I figure you know more about them than maybe anybody on Earth. What's a cadre, and how does it function?"

"Oh. Okay." The boy's look of pleased surprise faded to concentration.

"To understand, you have to look at Earth's major societies. Family-oriented, mostly paternalistic, but that's not important. More or less rigidly structured. Right?"

The others nodded.

"Gliese and all the other societies have been through that stage. It developed in hunting and farming communities in pre-feudal times. The problem is, it's a dead end. Change happens slowly, stagnation is a constant danger, and individuals never realize their true potential or their freedom to act."

Mia nodded thoughtfully. "That's pretty deep stuff."

He waved that away. "It's in all the philosophers, but you have to wade through a lot of sand and gravel to find the nuggets of wisdom. I had some help."

"Okay, explain why we aren't making the grade."

"Sure. It's simple. In a family-based system, most humans never really grow up."

"How's that?"

"You spend your formative days under the orders of your parents, and you get used to it. So, when you become a parent, you place yourself willingly under the influence of community leaders. Those leaders are ruled by higher-up leaders. Yes, even in a democracy."

"But you can't have everybody running around acting with complete freedom all the time. What about giving someone you trust the right to make decisions? What about loyalty?"

"Aha! Glad you brought that up. Loyalty is just an excuse for not thinking."

"In one sense, I suppose."

"You've put your finger on it. There are two types of loyalty: earned and unearned. Mia, why am I loyal to you?"

"Um..."

"Because you earned it. You've always been straight with me; you've always come through for me when you said you would. We have a track record. As my tri-me would tell me if I asked it, the past data set indicates the best next move will always be trusting Mia. Hence, I'm loyal to you.'

"Fair enough."

"Tell me, why should I be loyal to my mother? She's my mother after all. She raised me for my formative years. I still have soft feelings for her. But not loyalty."

"She wasn't there for you."

"Exactly. So, when somebody says, 'Blood's thicker than water,' I say, 'It sure is, and there's nothing thicker than somebody being fleeced by a relative."

"Are the Glieseans different?"

"Yes. They don't have such a heavy dependence on unearned loyalty. In Gliesean society, me drifting away from my mother when I did would be the most normal thing in the world."

"But you still need support."

"Right. And I built my support with people who have earned my trust. You, for instance."

She felt her cheeks warm, "I can see that, I suppose. But I have no intention of replacing your mother."

"And I don't need my mother replaced. There is a place in the human psyche for an older female mentor." He tossed a hand towards Jean. "I don't need an older brother, but there's a slot for someone like him in my cadre. Olivier is a security guy, and their cadres are pretty restrictive, but there's probably room in his group for an up-and-coming protégé." He waved a hand, indicating the world in general. "If we continued to function together, and another one of us got married, how well that spouse could fit with the rest of us would have a great deal of effect on what happened next."

Mia considered. "Our group here is a cadre created to form a tight-knit and high-functioning team." She sat straighter. "And Nicolaus created us!"

"Not completely. You and I came to him already attached. Jean and Olivier...I'm not sure how much choice he had."

She stopped in mid-thought and regarded the boy. "This is all very mature thinking for one so young."

He grinned. "That's the problem with having an ExIn as part of your cadre. It's not allowed to influence your decisions, but the data it chooses to give you..."

"I've had that conversation with Nicolaus."

"Right. Jean, I know it's a long, boring flight to Rio, but why did you ask me to tell you all this junk?"

"Because this is the last project for this cadre. You and Mia will be going to Geneva, I'll be back to Canadian military work, and Olivier will disappear into his safe little Security cadre and never be seen again. We're all down in the dumps because a successful cadre is breaking up, and at least now we've cleared the air."

She was about to comment on Jean's next assignment, when she realized there were several reasons she should leave it alone. *Be honest, Mia. Maybe him going back to his partner in Canada is not on the top of your priority list.*

21. GOOD-BYES

Their farewell party was nowhere near what the opening bash had been. They weren't exactly slipping out the back door, but no one in the Canadian government wanted to advertise the end of this prestigious partnership. So it was a "friends and family" event.

Jean was alone when he came to pick up Mia and her suitcases. He was driving a plain pool car, and the back seat was full of luggage as well.

"I gather we're staying the night on the Wing."

"It landed this afternoon. That's why I came early. You can move into your cabin, freshen up, and stroll across the parking lot to the feast. Drink all you like; it's a short walk home."

"They have a whole airport. Why do they use the office parking lot?"

He grinned. "Why miss out on a useful publicity stunt?"

They pulled up under the Wing and unloaded their belongings onto a dolly, to be whisked away by one of the Gliesean security men. They entered and strolled down the axial corridor to their cabins, which were side by side on the leading edge of the upper deck, with plenty of view through wide windows which she hoped were of very strong glass. There was nothing fancy about the accommodation, except the straps and controls indicated that the bed could be used for an accel lounger.

She used the basic facilities in her tiny bathroom and wondered what to do next. The ship solved the problem for her.

Ms. Larsen?
Yes?

Welcome aboard Flying Wing Gliesean BP. Captain Gagnon is on line.

168

"Thanks. Put him through."

Hey, Mia. You ready to party?

"As ready as I'm going to be."

On my way.

Almost immediately her door chimed.

You have a visitor

She didn't think she needed to thank the doorbell, but she wasn't sure. It sounded like the ship's voice. Shrugging into a short jacket, she went out.

He stood in the hallway, looking somehow comfortable, she thought.

He held out a small, gift-wrapped box. "A little something."

"Do I open it now?"

For some reason, he glanced at her jeans-and-jacket combo. "As it happens, definitely."

Inside the box was a small circular brooch. She checked the back. "It's a lapel pin."

"Exactly. And your jacket has a lapel. My lucky day."

"Would you put it on for me?"

"Sure. Where would you like it?"

"Um...on my lapel?" She chuckled. "It was your idea. Put it where you think is best."

"Don't tempt me." He fiddled with her jacket, and she felt his breath, smelling of toothpaste, on her cheek.

She enjoyed the moment. "It says CSA, but I haven't seen one like it."

He gave it a final adjustment, then stood back for a critical look. "It isn't recent. 1994 vintage."

She felt the pin, gave it an experimental tug. "An antique? Is it safe there?"

He laughed. "It'll stick. It's CSA quality workmanship. Come on." He crooked his arm. "Let's go."

Microships

She grabbed her purse and closed her door. "Is this gift for some specific reason?"

"A Canadian thing, I guess. We're always handing out maple leaf pins to everyone."

"Thank you in any case." She looked over at him as they started down the hall. "But it isn't a good-bye present, is it?"

He nodded and headed for the driver's door. "He told you."

"He did."

"And you're suspicious."

"Mildly. You don't have to justify your presence to me. I find you come in handy quite often."

"Hmm. Make a guy feel wanted."

"Making an associate feel needed."

"Okay."

"You didn't pick Marie up. Is she coming?"

"Ah...I guess I never told you."

"I guess you didn't." She suppressed the uncharitable pang of hope. "What happened?"

"She called off our arrangement. I guess all the new attention went to her head."

"You don't really mean that."

"Not really. She had reason, and after all, I'm out of the country for the immediate future."

"Still friends?"

"That's what we always were. Now it's real."

"I guess that's okay then."

"She'll be here tonight. She's been doing some PR appearances for us."

"I saw her on a news feed. Good for her."

"Yes, it's been very good for her. Career-wise, you know."

They strolled the rest of the way in silence.

The Wing was parked near the tower that fronted the offices, a short walk from the huge glass doors. As they entered, she glanced around at the familiar walls and wondered if she would ever be back.

"I enjoyed working here. Canadians are nice people."

"Don't sound so surprised."

They had cleaned out their office, the logistics crew had brought in more comfortable furniture, and the catering department did their best, which was up to their usual standard. Perhaps it was a small, informal affair, but the offices were crowded, and the party spilled into the hall.

She gave Jean's arm a push. "You don't have to hang around with me. I know lots of people here, this time."

"Right." He stood taller and looked around. "Marie is over there."

The musician was dressed in a businesslike outfit which did little to disguise her figure. She was holding forth to three or four intent listeners, but paused when she saw Mia heading in her direction.

She made a comment to her audience, eliciting a laugh. Then she stepped forward. "Mia!" She kissed both cheeks. "Nice to see you again."

"Sorry to pull you away from your performance."

"Pah. 'Routine Four B: Gentle Reassurance.' I ran it twenty times this week. I could do it in my sleep. I was preaching to the choir with those guys, but they looked like they needed cheering up." She flicked her hand out to indicate the room. "Sorry to see this is over. I've enjoyed it."

"I didn't realize you had hired on."

"Oh, yes. Nicolaus was impressed at the audience we attracted to that concert. Something about intersecting markets."

"On the payroll?"

"I have been, but I'll only be doing the odd gig when I'm needed. I do have a career to pursue."

"And how's that going?"

The woman made a moue of indecision. "Fine. I'm getting a lot of attention, but it's pulling me in the same two directions."

"I've been thinking about your little problem."

"Oh, no. Is this one going to cost me five hundred?"

"Nope. This time we're writing it off as in-house career advice to a colleague. I looked into the music industry. Crossovers everywhere, especially recently. If you were really brave..."

"I'm not, but tempt me."

"Create your own genre and go your own way. Make the music you want, with the styles and instruments you want."

"Huh. Habitant fiddle and Bechstein Grand? I can't see it working."

"Not my horse, not my wagon."

"Jean used that expression the other day. How does it apply here?"

"I'm the publicist. You're the musician. I tell you what might work. It's your job to make it work." She gave the other woman a gentle elbow. "Give the idea the amount of thought you paid for it."

"You said it was free."

Mia winked.

"And I don't know why I should listen to you."

"Oh?"

"Well, you lost me a boyfriend."

"He only told me today." She regarded her new friend. "I thought you broke up with him."

"I did. But it was your fault."

"Mine...? But I never said anything..."

"Definitely you. It wasn't what you said. It was how you looked at him when he pulled that "third best girlfriend" gambit.

He's been using it for years, you know. Sort of his trademark. But you heard it, and you looked like you'd just stepped on something squishy in the dark. And I looked at Jean, and it made him sound juvenile and silly. And that didn't match with my reading of Jean. So, I figured it must mean something else."

Mia smiled. "And it really meant..."

"Exactly what it said. It was a warning."

"So you dumped him."

"No, I called his bluff. I asked him my chances of moving up the scale. He did me the honour of an honest answer, and we parted ways."

"Were you hurt?"

"Not hurt. I was sad, of course, but how can I be hurt when someone is honest with me?"

"That's very levelheaded of you."

She shrugged. "I still have his friendship, anyway."

"How do you swing that?"

The younger woman grinned. "Another of his trademarks. He only goes with really nice women, and he never breaks up with a fight. They keep in touch. Olivier's wife is an old flame of his."

The girl tossed her hair. "Hanging out with him was fun, but I was wasting my time. And then I found out I'm not in the same class as the competition."

"Really? Who's the competition?"

The girl regarded her. "I don't know you well enough to answer that question."

Mia smiled. "Not my horse, and all that."

It was only as she lay in her bunk later that she realized what the other girl meant. She thought the idea over and finally rejected it. *If Marie needs someone to blame, that's fine with me.*

Then she had another thought. *How does "I don't date non-coms" stand up against my own criteria?*

She wasn't used to the bed, and that must have been what kept her from sleeping.

I'm going to have to watch myself now. It was easy when he was out of reach. On a personal level, I hardly know him. But he's so supportive. In a completely professional way, of course. She thought of several instances when he had bolstered her authority, pushed her ideas.

She sat up straight in bed. "He's been mentoring me. Dammit, the man's been using my own techniques on me, and I didn't even notice!"

She lay back down, trying to decide whether she should tear a strip off his hide or thank him. *Maybe both. Serve him right...*

She held that warm thought and drifted off to sleep.

* * *

The next morning held a different feeling. Mia and Hemi sat in accel loungers in the transparent nose of the Wing as it lifted away from the Science Centre. She looked left and right, where the sturdy wings stretched away...a long distance. "GBP, what's your wingspan?"

Fifty metres, Ms. Larsen.

"We had flying wings in the mid-twentieth century."

I have seen the images. Very graceful. This vessel isn't quite that svelte. It's fourteen metres deep at its fullest, in the central section of the hull. This makes room for four decks. Cabins on top, on deck 4; dining, food prep and general housekeeping on 3; logistics, cargo and mechanical on 2; the bottom layer is filled with the gravity plate and all the pipes, wires, girders and backstage stuff that makes the magic work, but the passengers never see.

The whole wing is twenty-five metres front to back, the aft sections tapering off to the flaps, which work under atmospheric conditions for steering like those of a normal airplane. The outer ten metres at the tips of the wings house small atomic generators that power everything.

"What's a gravity plate?"

Propulsion is provided by a composite metal plate that covers the belly of the ship. It reacts against the gravitational field of the Earth.

In atmosphere, steering is done by the air flaps, but in space maneuvering is done by activating different sections of the plate at different intensities. The length of the wingspan gives more leverage for improved steering.

"I think I understood most of that."

You could sift it down and explain it to a nine-year-old?

"Is that what you want?"

Sooner or later, we will want to remove the mystery from our normal technology.

"May I change the topic?"

"Had enough tech talk?"

"Yes. Tell me about your designation."

GBP

"You're the ship that rescued us from the pirates. That's great. Thanks again."

It doesn't make much difference. We all communicate real-time with the Mothership data banks.

What does 'GBP' stand for?"

G is for Gliesean...the other two are technical designations for concepts Earth science does not comprehend yet.

"And that's your only name?"

It is my designation.

"That won't do for humans. To us, GBP is the monetary unit of one of our leading nations. You need an appropriate name. Let me see...yes, Europeans have a tradition of giving important vessels names from ancient myths. Hemi, what's a mythical name that starts with 'P' and flies?"

"*Pegasus*, of course."

"Perfect. You will henceforth be named GB-*Pegasus*. We should break a bottle of champagne over your bow, but I'd rather drink it."

In the interest of Federalism, the wine loaded on for this assignment was from B. C., Ontario, and Quebec. However, I believe there were a few examples of the French beverage as well.

175

Which brought them around to the realization that it was approaching four pm somewhere along their route, and this required a demonstration of the hallowed tradition of happy hour. The members of their security detail had never tasted champaign, and there was a specific Wolfian drink on board that had to be sampled as well, in the pursuit of cultural amity.

An hour later, Mia looked around the lounge. "Nicolaus, doesn't somebody have to stay sober to fly this thing?"

"We have nothing to do with the operation of the aircraft, beyond telling it where we wish to go and standing by to ease communication with local authorities."

"Oh. I see. Then I'll have another glass of Wolfian rum, please. I particularly liked the peppery one."

22. PARIS

The cadre slipped into their assigned roles easily, as the task had not changed, only the location. They missed Olivier, but Nero filled in on missions where he could be useful. Security was provided by Meld soldiers in teams of three, who were stationed on the Mothership and rotated their assignments on a weekly basis.

Mia had been to Geneva before, and they took advantage of the polyglot mix of races there to blend in with the crowds. They maintained a higher profile as well, and regularly hit one of the many restaurants nearby, their security detail in Earth mufti and included as members of the party.

As Nicolaus put it, "Most people will probably assume that our boys are the visiting dignitaries, and you Earthers are showing them around."

Jean was more serious. "That's useful. Any fanatic trying to make a point will go for the aliens." He grinned. "They're wearing body armour."

At Wing speed, most European capitals were less than two hours apart, and they often finished several junkets in as many days, rising above airline altitudes to sleep, hovering in the moonlight, high above the clouds. Then they would swoop down to their next assignment in the morning.

And it was all going according to plan until they hit Paris. Mia was dubious about their proposed landing spot, but *Pegasus* and Jean persuaded her it was a useful opportunity. As the Canadian put it, "The French are being very French about the whole situation."

She nodded. "Proud of their own technical achievements, touchy about their prerogatives, and unsure why anyone should object." She shot him a questioning look.

"That pretty well sums it up. The Quebecois are the same. Something to do with our language being the most expressive and concise in the world."

"It is?"

He gestured to the aerial shot of *La Cite* on the main holoframe. "Ask anybody down there."

She shook her head. "And you think dropping this monster over the top of the *Basson Octagonal* in the *Jardin des Tuileries* is going to impress them."

Pegasus zoomed the shot in closer.

The most convenient open space in the city. It is right next to the Place de la Concorde, which has excellent street access in several directions. Ample room for thousands of viewers.

Jean waved a hand across the frame. "And every protest, celebration and parade that's worth anything comes along the *Champs d'Elyssés*. *Les flics* have done the security so many times they can handle it in their sleep."

"They better not do any sleeping this time."

He grinned. "A mere figure of speech, common in English, I believe."

She flicked her fingers at him. "Stick to flying airplanes."

"Oh, I have all sorts of talents you don't know about."

She paused long enough to show that she knew there was deeper meaning in that quip. "Let's leave it that way for the moment. Have you informed the civic authorities?"

"I have, and they put up a bit of resistance, but I think they're flattered. The French also appreciate a dramatic show, even if they only get a supporting role." He shrugged. "Their tech is high quality, and they swing a lot of weight with the non-aligned nations. We want them on our side."

So, *GB Pegasus* drifted in silently from the east, along the Seine and low over I. M. Pei's glass pyramid and the Louvre Museum. Mia sat in one of the bridge loungers, enjoying the panorama as it swept by.

As they cleared the *Carrousel*, she looked closer. "Seems like we attracted an audience."

Jean looked up from the command chair. "*Securité* is not worried. A friendly crowd, apparently."

The frame image suddenly zoomed in and pivoted left. *"Incoming..."*

And a moment later, *"Incoming hostile...responding..."*

The frame pictured what looked like a large delivery drone, but its props glistened in the sun.

"Target acquired...control achieved."

The zoom stopped, then reversed itself. The image was now of the drone soaring away. The background was the sloping lawn in front of the *Musée de l'Orangerie*, which was mobbed with people.

The crowd scattered and dropped as the drone swooped down towards the trees in the southwest corner.

"Visual acquired."

With a jolt the image changed, and tree trunks rushed at them. A figure in a dark hoodie crouched with its back to them, concentrating on something...a sudden flurry of a startled face, flapping hands that seemed to sprout red, then a silent flash and the frame went dead.

The image returned to the view from the aircraft, and *Pegasus*'s calm voice continued.

"Holding position."

"I have relayed to *Sécurité*. They say, 'please hold.' Jean grinned. "Isn't it nice when we all agree?"

Mia kept her eye on the rush of uniforms towards a still figure on the grass by the trees. Quickly a cordon formed, and a wall of officers faced the public.

Please relay to Sécurité that if I move even slightly, I will distract the public towards their original expectations.

Jean spoke in rapid French and nodded. "Please descend ten metres."

"Descending."

The image below them grew, and individual faces in the crowd turned towards their cameras.

Jean listened to his headset. "They say that was a good idea. Continue your landing procedure."

Mia shucked off her straps and stood. "You heard the man. Let's form our usual procession at the head of the gangway."

He shook his head. "Why do you insist on using that old sailing ship terminology?

"The material of the ramp may by uber-titanium or something stronger, but the function is identical. It keeps me rooted in Earther traditions. Gives me the illusion my feet are still firmly planted."

"While actually, you're flying in an alien spaceship. Yeah, I get that."

"Um, Mia...?" Hemi slid up beside her.

"Yes?"

"Would you mind if I didn't come this afternoon? I've got something I want to look into."

It wasn't an unusual request. The teenager treasured his independence, and she had noticed that when he stepped outside the normal schedule he often came up with interesting results. "I assume you'll stay on the ship."

"I guess. My French isn't that strong, yet. Pegs has been helping me with some online interfacing, but I need to be on the ground to use it."

"Good luck with whatever it is."

"You might be very pleased. We'll see."

The ramp is down. Sécurité invites you to disembark.

"Thanks, *Pegasus*."

They descended in their usual formation, with two Gliesean security men first, Mia in the middle, and Jean bringing up the rear so he could observe everyone.

But there was no need for caution. The Paris crowd was too blasé for shows of awe, and the looky-loos were over watching the ambulance men pick up the drone pilot.

Their little party got into the waiting limousine, and away they went.

She looked across at Jean. "What do you think happened?"

"I suspect someone with a thirst for notoriety got hold of a small delivery drone and tweaked it for optimum lift so they could put aboard as big a bomb as possible. From the look of it, they removed the prop guards and replaced the blades with titanium, which had the double benefit of less weight and more deterrent effect."

"But what happened? It looked to me like it suddenly went into reverse and ran into the pilot."

"That's pretty much it. The *techniciens de sécurité* will probably find that when the guy tweaked the programming, he created a bug, and the nav system froze. This would activate the auto-return function and send it back to base. I'd say he removed the collision avoidance system, and it went straight back to the base. He happened to be in the way."

"And the explosion?"

"That model of drone uses a normal tri-me handset for visuals. I guess they overloaded the battery, and it blew. Much better than having the ordnance go up. No telling how much it was packing."

She frowned. "Now I know you're making this up. A tri-media handset battery hasn't exploded for about thirty years. That's one reason they took over from cell phones."

He shrugged. "We'll see what the *technicien* comes out with."

The French diplomats they were meeting with carried the incident off with the right amount of concern and confidence to ease any tension that might have interfered with the talks. They were diplomats, after all, and Mia could match them at the game.

When they returned to the ship late that evening, Hemi was relaxing in his lounger, a pair of large holoframes projected in front of him. As they entered, he blanked them.

"Success?"

"Pretty good, I think." The boy's grin spoke volumes.

"Will we ever see the results?"

"It might be arranged. We're leaving tomorrow afternoon, right?"

"About then. We'll see how it goes."

"Can you arrange to lift off about eight?"

She glanced at Jean, who nodded. "That would give the crowd a nice show. We have to provide a few hours' notice at *Charles de Gaulle Tour de Contrôle*. They'll make a place for us in the takeoff pattern."

"Great. Eight o'clock will be maximum effect. Later would be okay."

Mia regarded the smug expression. "And that's all you're going to tell us."

"More fun if it's a surprise."

"I'm going to trust you this once."

Jean stepped over and placed a hand on the back of the boy's neck. "And if you screw up, we're going to leave you hanging from the top of the Eiffel Tower."

"I'll take that bet."

The next day in Paris went the way all the others had, except the food at lunch was better. Mia allowed the French to dominate the conversation, nudging the meetings with the odd comment to keep them on track. Jean disappeared and apparently spent most of his time with technical experts. He wasn't exactly forthcoming about who or why.

They returned to the ship at about four in the afternoon, pleased with themselves.

Hemi met them at the door, practically dancing. "What time are we lifting off?"

Jean gave a mock salute. "Precisely at eight pm, sir, as ordered. The French seem to be quite pleased with us."

"You did your jobs well. Now it's our turn."

"Ours? You and who else?"

"Me and *Pegs*. And I know that grammar was wrong, but you started it."

The pilot frowned. "Hemi, you know we all trust you, but any screwup here could cost me my job. I know what 'online interfacing' means. You hacked someone, right?"

"Something."

"I have to at least ask. What did you hack?"

"The Eiffel Tower."

"Ah." Jean nodded. His face brightened. "This could be all sorts of fun."

And neither of them would say any more.

Long before eight, they were comfortably ensconced in their loungers, and *Pegasus* had cleared their departure course with de Gaulle. Hemi had requested a close pass by the famous tower, but that was the only clue the others had.

They set the outside view on full frames and watched the tourists and locals vying for the best positions to watch the double feature of the alien ship and the usual evening light show.

Precisely on time, the tower lit up, and at the same moment, the Flying Wing rose vertically and hovered at a hundred metres. A beam of light flashed out, striking the top of the tower and glancing up into the light cloud cover. It shut off. Then another beam, quickly extinguished as well. The frequency of the beams quickened, soon it seemed like a series of arrows were chasing across the sky, all glancing off the tower top in random directions. Each time one hit, a wash of colour would sweep down the side girders.

Hemi switched a smaller screen on, showing the feed from one of the news cameras on the riverbank, and there they were, hanging in midair like a drone. Squirming images crawled around on the steel girders of the tower, and the airship jabbed at them with rays of light, chasing them up and down.

The ship and the tower combined their resources to create incredible effects on the metal surfaces, one time imitating the ancient 'Space Invaders' video game, complete with sound effects.

They made good use of the hundreds of rotating laser heads that shrouded the tower with parallel and radial lines, jabbing out and reflecting off the metallic hull of the spacecraft. The new holographic panels created swarms of birds circling the shaft and geometric patterns swirling in and out of recognizable images.

"Watch this one!"

A massive hologram of King Kong clambered up the side, finally clinging to the top and shaking his fist at biplanes that slid in from the night, firing streams of tracers, then disappeared on the other side. The giant ape jumped away from the tower, dissolving into the darkness as he reached the edge of the holographic field.

As a finale, the huge wing slid forward like a regular airplane in a steep bank, circling the tower and towing a mass of colour across the girders like a shawl as it passed. The ship spiralled upward, winding the structure with wide sheets of red, white, and blue, encircling the tower three times before rising above, revolving smaller and faster until it was spinning like a top, and they burst away through the cloud cover, spraying colour in all directions.

The mist closed in, and they leveled out at seven thousand metres, headed for their next stop, which was the following morning in Istanbul. It was only a three-hour flight, but the ship dawdled at 200 knots, stretching the journey to a comfortable nine hours.

23. HABITAT CONTACT

One evening a few days later they were again cruising at high altitude, and Mia was in the lounge amusing herself with a few of Marie's vocal tracks. From her limited knowledge of folk music, they seemed to be quite traditional, although pushing the boundaries of complexity for that genre.

Contact for you, Mia.

"Who is it?"

The name is Randy Jones. Source is the Habitat for Humanity

"Randy's a com tech in Prospecting and Mapping. Put him on."

"Hello, Mia?"

The voice was definitely familiar. "Hi Randy. What's up?"

A chuckle. "You might label this a semi-social call. I'm testing out some new equipment, and I have some technical questions. Is Noah around?"

"No, he and I are on different projects. Different continents at the moment. He's still with NASA, but I'm sort of freelancing for the Humanity Meld."

"Oh, my. Moving up in the world, are we?"

"Yes, or out of it. What do you need to know?"

"I'm setting up a piece of equipment. Very new tech, probably outside your clearance, but it's Canadian made, and I'm running afoul of their security net. If I can't get through to Noah, I guess I'm hooped."

She grinned and waved a hand at Jean to get his attention. "I happen to have a couple of Canadians onboard who are technically minded. Want to talk to them?"

"Can't do any harm. Say, where are you, anyway? I sent out a general call on what I thought was a fairly secure NASA frequency, and it went through to you slick as a whistle."

"The vessel I'm on is probably outside your clearance, so let's leave that." She closed the mic. "*Pegasus*, put this on general com, would you?

Sure thing.

"Randy, you're now talking to Jean Gagnon and Olivier Beaudry. They're Canadian military, with high security ratings, working for the Meld, which puts them higher yet."

"Okay, pleased to meet you guys."

"Likewise. What's up?"

"Let's get this in perspective. What do you know about swarm sapience?"

There was a pause, and Jean looked around. "...um, quite a bit. It's partly a Canadian project."

"Great. Well, can you help me with a communications problem?"

Again the pause. "Perhaps, but I'm getting into the reverse of your security problem. I have people onboard who may not be cleared for what we'll be talking about."

He turned to Mia. "Would you mind if I talk to him privately?"

She flicked her fingers. "I don't mess with security requirements. Go ahead."

"Great. *Pegasus*, I'm going to my cabin. Route this conversation there and put a level five security clamp on it."

You are now on level five in your cabin only. The ship is still recording, and Nicolaus Gliese will have access.

"Fine with me." He rose and departed.

Those left behind exchanged shrugs and went back to what they had been doing.

24. PSYCHOANALYSIS

She and Jean had developed the habit of a drink before dinner, sitting in the nose of the Wing in the command accel loungers. One evening they were gazing at a particularly peaceful scene, with puffy white clouds swirling around the snowcapped peaks of the Alps far below.

Jean glanced casually at her. "Mia, you are an enigma."

She quirked an eyebrow. "I do my best. Seems to be working."

He nodded smugly. "Exactly. And you just did it again."

"Did what?"

"I made a reasonable attempt to start a mildly personal conversation, and you shut me down flat."

She thought back. "Yes, I did."

Before he could get his mouth open, she held up both hands. "And that answer could be interpreted the same way. It wasn't meant to be."

"Oh...is that good?"

"Of course. It was meant to be straightforward. For some inane reason you want to talk to me about me. Go ahead."

"Um...okay. We've known each other for a while, and I'd like to think we're at a stage where we want to know more about each other."

She nodded slowly. "Fair game. What do you want to know?"

He sighed. "For someone who sounds cooperative, you're still making this difficult."

She matched his sigh. "I know. I don't mean to." She reached over and patted his arm. "Go ahead. Indulge your curiosity."

"Okay. First question. I don't see a whole lot of evidence that you have a social life."

"You want to ask if I'm straight."

187

He laughed aloud. "Mia, we're way past that."

She regarded him a moment. "I guess we are. Okay, I don't have much of a social life. My work really messes it up."

"If I may presume upon this new level of our relationship, I'm going to disagree."

"If you think starting an argument is going to foster anything, you need to review your self-concept as an urbane, suave man of the world."

"Nonetheless. I suggest your social life is more under your control than you think. It is quite possible your lack of action on the social scene is self-imposed."

"Whatever gives you that idea?" She took a sip of her drink and stared at him over the glass. Then she set it down and composed herself to listen. "Go on. Show off your wisdom."

"Okay, here we go. Mia Larson: social interaction value. There are three main criteria for choosing a mate. When a prospective beau looks at you, he's going to make some snap judgements, and he's going to wait on some of the others."

"No news there, I'm afraid."

He grinned. "Nothing to be afraid of. First one is body type. Most people — men, anyway, — have already figured their preferences, so it's quick. In your case, tall and slim. The slim part is no problem. Plenty of guys like that. The tall is a killer, as you already know."

She gave a twisted grin. "So far, this is turning out exactly like I expected."

"Okay, let's get the worst over. The next one is intelligence."

"Oh, yes. The worst."

"But that's not a bad criterion. The kind of guy who worries about your intelligence is not the kind of guy you want to hang around."

"A self-eliminating factor. That's a different way to look at it. So, when you told me you were afraid of smart women, that was to ease any sexual tension between workmates."

"Pleased to be of service."

"What's the next one? Sex appeal?"

He grinned. "Exactly..." The grin faded.

"You're having trouble telling me, and I know the reason why."

"Wait a minute, wait a minute. Let's be clear about this. A woman is basically in charge of her own sex appeal."

"What? You've got to be joking."

"Oh, no. A woman is sexy because she thinks she is. When she meets a man, if she assumes he's sexually attractive to him, she acts in certain ways. Especially if she's interested."

She frowned. "Give me an example."

"Right off the top. Eyes. When I meet her eyes, where do I look next?"

She scoffed. "Usually at her body, I assume."

"No, no. Where I look is dictated by where she looks. If she looks down, either she's saying, 'I'm no threat to you,' which gives me the okay to make my own decision, or 'I wonder how I look,' which makes me really interested. Then I look down."

"I suppose."

"And then there's you."

"What?"

"You look me straight in the eye like any other business associate would. This tells me you're here to do business, and depending on the rest of the body language, dares me to look anywhere else and accept the consequences."

"So, what's wrong with that?"

"Nothing. Most of the time it's very useful, especially in business situations. But in a social setting, most guys would quite rightfully get the same message, and the majority will back off, out of either good manners or fear."

He leaned back, more relaxed. "Of course, there are many other considerations, but those are the top three. And they tell me that you're in charge of your life, and you're doing exactly what you want to. Including your social interactions."

She sighed. "You're too good at this. I can't argue with anything you've said." She looked at him. "But what use is it to me?"

"Do you know anything about selling real estate?"

"Real estate...a bit, yes."

"What house is the hardest to sell?"

"A highly specialized custom design."

"Right. The house that is exactly perfect for someone who paid a lot of money for that perfection, but now is looking for someone with the same taste who can afford it."

"You're telling me I'm a hard sell."

"You are. But some day, some guy is going to decide you're worth it and pay any price to get you."

"After equating me to a piece of high-priced merchandise, that's supposed to make me feel better?"

He raised his glass. "I hope so. It's the truth, and it's a good analysis."

There was a long stretch of silence. She looked over at him. "Do I get the bill for a thousand bucks?"

"Nope. That was strictly recreational."

"What? You tore me up and spread me around the room for the fun of it?"

"No, but I certainly enjoyed it." He held up his hands. "No, no, don't get mad. I got to see a side of you that I never saw before."

"What do you mean?"

"I don't know. You without your usual defences up."

"What defences?"

"Example." He ticked one finger. "We've been working and living in each other's pockets for a few months. Until we moved onto *Pegasus*, I never knew how long your hair was. Except for that artfully placed curl that escapes from behind your left ear, of course."

She stopped herself from touching the lock. "What do you mean, 'artfully placed?'"

"The one that stops your French roll from looking too severe. The one you toy with when you're nervous or when you're thinking. Yes, I saw your hand go half-way up and stop. You rarely do it, but it's quite endearing."

"Endearing! You sound like I'm doing it on purpose."

"But you're not. It's an honest expression of feeling, and that's what makes it rather sweet." He slapped his hands together and pointed a finger. "How about that? She's got a tell and she didn't know it!"

She sniffed in disdain. "I rather thought that was the point of a tell. Thank you for making me aware of it."

His mouth turned down. "But now you know about it, and you'll try not to do it again. I've spoiled it. For me, anyway. Sorry."

She scoffed. "After that little performance, I hope you're not going to expect me to apologize as well."

"Not at all. I'll take my turn on the patient's couch tomorrow, if you like."

"If you think I have anything to say...no, that's unfair. This is not the time for that sort of joke. Thank you for your concern." She met his eyes. "I really do mean that."

He grinned and slapped his thighs. "Great. I have to admit, that was pretty scary at times."

She frowned. "Scary?"

"Of course. You know and like somebody, and you purposefully put them under stress. What if you guessed wrong? It could spoil a relationship."

"Not one that was worth it."

He nodded firmly. "Exactly." He jumped to his feet. "What's for supper?"

He strode out, leaving her with her mouth open.

What the hell was that all about?

Later that evening, her enjoyment of the novel she was reading was interrupted by a soft chuckle. Then she felt the hair under her fingers and realized what she was doing. She snapped her hand down and looked around. Jean was watching her, a small grin on his face. He merely winked and turned his eyes elsewhere.

25. BALKANS

They often returned to their base in Geneva, and one morning Nicolaus strolled onboard looking rather pleased with himself.

Mia looked up from her coffee and toast. "Have you been breakfasting on champagne again?"

"Not after the first time. No, this has to do with you."

"Okay. What stellar accomplishment have I pulled off now?"

"We've had a request for your services."

A moment of caution made her pause. "...what do you mean, a request?"

"Oh, not by name. By reputation. We have received a query through official channels for discussion with our "Canadian envoy who did so well in the Caribbean last winter."

"Canadian?"

He shrugged. "It was not unexpected."

She put on a frown. "I don't like double negatives, and that one in particular. It sounds too much like "I told you so." Worse, it could be, "I shouldn't have to tell you because you could have figured it out yourself."

He made a gesture of acquiescence.

"I get it. Diplomatic passport. Canadian plane. CSIS security."

"Even your accent."

"What about my accent?"

"I think you said you were what is called an 'army brat?' Moved around a lot? Different parts of the country?"

"So what?"

"People like you tend to have a general "Hollywood American" accent. Very similar to the English they speak in British Columbia."

"Dad was on loan for three years there when I was in Elementary School. Air Force base called Chilliwack."

"See? You use the term Elementary School. Americans call it Grade School. And between Quebec and Europe, your Americanisms are disappearing."

"I try to blend in."

"Exactly. A bit of a chameleon, aren't you?"

"In my job, it's a good idea not to stand out in the crowd."

He regarded her a moment. "But that's all changing, isn't it?"

She was about to argue, but her thinking mind took over. "I really blew it when I showed up at that Habitat for Humanity launch, didn't I?"

"Or you chose an opportune moment to start your campaign."

"I'm not on any campaign!"

"Yes, you are. It may feel like circumstances are pushing you around, but in reality, you have objectives that cannot be accomplished by a faceless bureaucrat. Every choice you make moves you ahead, but more into the open. It is a necessary progression.

"Now, you head over to the Balkans, and go in there as an honoured guest, a known producer of results, and watch how you get treated."

26. AUSTRIA

Sure enough, the Balkans were different. Now there were cameras and reporters waiting when *Pegasus* settled down. It was like back in NASA, being escorted by large, blank-faced men in dark suits who listened to their earpieces and moved slowly, eyes scanning.

Despite the perimeter guard, she felt exposed, but all she could do was focus on her job.

Now she had to be doubly on top of her game. Eyes were on her, and she no longer had the leisure to sit back and observe what was going on. There would come a pause in the conversation, and she would realize they were waiting for her opinion.

She dug in and learned to concentrate. She also had to pay attention to who was speaking honestly and who was telling her what she wanted to hear, but that came as second nature.

So Croatia, Serbia, and Bulgaria rolled by under her Wing, and progress was becoming the expected result.

Until she got to Austria.

Mia, I have an anomaly.

"What kind, *Pegasus*?"

Political, I would say. Our landing site has been assigned to us. The Wiener Neustadt West Airport.

"Well, this isn't Paris. I didn't expect to set down by the Neptune Fountain."

But the Wiener Neustadt is a military base forty-three kilometres out of the city.

"Hmm. For security reasons?"

How did you guess. It wasn't a question.

"Why, *Pegasus*, you're learning to use irony."

I already understood irony. I use it carefully with strangers.

"I'm glad I am no longer a stranger." She glanced at the map on her screen. "Let's hope this isn't an omen."

Do you believe in omens?

"When you're dealing with politicians, they crop up all over the place."

Now that she was forewarned, they kept appearing. Their transport was the traditional Mercedes limousine, but the security was strictly military. Their hotel was in a new luxury development near the Opera, but if Vienna was really rolling out the carpet, the Grand Hotel Wien was the diplomat's choice.

She stood, surveying the classic neo-modern architecture of their suite. "What do you think, Jean? Any open arms or brotherly love?"

He snorted. "I always found Vienna to be a bit snooty, but there's a definite chill in the air today."

"There's mannerly, and then there's punctilious. I get the impression that the officials assigned to us are trying to do their jobs the best they can."

He frowned. "And that's not good?"

"The level of diplomat we have met in most countries does it automatically."

"We've been relegated to the up-and-comers and the wannabes, have we?"

"Looks like it. Nero, what do you say?"

The Wolfian grinned. "Until you put your finger on it, I thought they were doing fine. Of course I did. They're just like me."

"Up-and-comer, are you?"

"Yes. I have been trying to develop the air that this all comes easily to me, but..."

"But that's difficult when it doesn't."

"Yes. I believe you have a saying about a swan...?"

"Serene on the surface, paddling frantically underneath."

"That's me, I'm afraid."

She nodded. "It's a credit to your training that you're aware of it. Good thing, too. You're with me tomorrow."

"I am? Is that wise?"

She shrugged. "It might be very wise. They wouldn't be surprised to see a Gliesean with me. Most of them probably don't even know that a Wolfian exists. The Austrians are a people who depend on traditions."

"Does that include racial stereotypes?"

"Generalizations of all sorts. And your specific shape is generally considered the type to avoid conflict with."

"I can glower at your shoulder if you wish, but I warn you, my martial accomplishments don't rank much higher than the basic self-defense all diplomats are taught."

She laughed. "As do mine. Don't worry. Our physical safety is pretty much assured at this stage of the game. That pair of personnel carriers weren't following us as an excuse to get out in the sunlight to dry their pretty nail polish."

Jean nodded judiciously. "So. you're going into tomorrow's action loaded for bear, with a Wolfian slavering at your side, two armed aliens close behind..." He looked down at his uniform. "Where do I fit in?"

"I guess you're the example of manners, decorum, and general Canadian niceness."

"And what use is that?"

"Probably to keep me from getting carried away by this martial display."

"Nicolaus trusts your instincts, and I do too. You call it as you see it."

"Then I'd better be ready for it."

She was watchful during the small banquet thrown that evening by the supporters of the talks, but they all seemed warm and enthusiastic. Too enthusiastic, in her opinion. It smacked of insecurity.

Later, in the dubious privacy of their suite, they discussed the evening in general terms, but nothing new occurred to them. Tomorrow was going to be a rough day,

* * *

She had accessed her biomem's files on previous meetings in Vienna and immediately got the impression that this one had a different tone. Austria's representatives were all formally dressed older males, more interested in protocol than substance.

She was lectured on the contributions Austria had made in the past (long in the past) to the culture and knowledge of Europe. The old days of the Austrian Empire were mentioned more than once. Little was said about present day, and once again, her upgraded memory was useful, documenting a declining GDP, stagnant private consumption and weak growth in key sectors like industry and construction.

Finally, she judged that she had listened enough to fulfill her duty.

She stood, and the cameras swung to focus on her. "Gentlemen, I thank you for the ancient history lesson. You have failed to take into account that I did not come to these meetings with similar objectives to yours. This so-called discussion is nothing more than the continuation of the power struggles that typify your attempts to influence your government for your own financial benefit. There is no point in using them on me, because I have no money to give you.

"I came here for information, and you have given me enough data to influence the discussion when the real negotiators deal with Austria at an individual level. I thank you kindly for your time. Please continue your self-congratulatory preening for your supporters. You don't need me for an audience. I'm sure your fans are loving it." She gestured to the cameras. "I have completed my objectives, and I bid you *auf wiedersehen.*"

She nodded to the Chancellor and turned away. Jean slipped in at her left shoulder, and her two Gliesean guards, Cassian and Evander, engineered a pathway through the throng of officials and spectators without actually laying hands on anyone. Evander was the largest alien she had met, a Wolfian at least two metres tall, and he looked about that wide. People tended to melt from his path. Nero trailed the group, looking as menacing as possible.

When they reached the street, there was no car waiting. She turned to Jean, bringing their heads together so he could hear over the shouted questions of the reporters. "Sorry. I should have given you a bit more lead time. Afraid I rather lost my temper, there."

He stifled a grin. "You call that losing your temper?"

"In diplomatic terms, that was a raging tantrum. In case you weren't listening, I called them corrupt, threatened them with retaliation at a higher level and walked out of the talks."

"Yes, there was a definite aura of menace hanging in the air as we left. Don't worry. I knew something was about to go down. Here's the car."

Unlike the morning procession, this trip was led by two motorcycles with no flashing lights, and a large, black SUV kept pace behind them. As they moved out of the downtown core, Jean glanced at his tri-me and murmured into his lapel mic. he nodded and sat back, relaxed.

"Well, that was fun."

"If you're entertained by a time warp to the early twentieth century. The Austro-Hungarian empire was very influential then, and they can't seem to forget it. They're struggling blindly into the future with their eyes fixed firmly behind them."

"They're not alone."

"Oh, that's true. There are Americans who haven't accepted the outcome of our Civil War, and that's over two hundred years ago."

Just then the traffic brought them to a halt, and she looked out the window. "Do I detect less security coverage?"

"You detect our security coverage. Their army doesn't organize that quickly. I wouldn't worry."

"You wouldn't?"

He grinned at her. "Look up." He pushed the switch that cleared the shading in the sun roof.

There, just above the tops of the buildings, the reassuring sweep of *Pegasus*'s wing glided silently.

"Is that necessary?"

"*Pegasus* thought it would be wise. Nothing to do with a physical threat to us. A twenty-second-century backup of your challenge to our twentieth-century friends back there."

Her shoulders slumped. "I don't think I did our cause much good today."

"As you said a moment ago, that wasn't what you were sent for." He shrugged. "Not your horse, not your wagon."

He regarded her. "Or maybe I'm wrong."

"Thanks. For a moment there I thought you were providing moral support."

"No, think about it. Nicolaus is counting on your intuition. So far, you have been the model of perfect diplomacy, because that was what the talks needed. But not this time. Perhaps he's been waiting for you to take a different approach because that tells us something about the people you met."

"If they send idiots like that to the talks, we just lost Austria. I don't want to be the one to tell Nicolaus."

But she didn't have to.

When the Wing dropped down beside the Mothership, he was outside waiting and came onboard immediately. Before she could speak, he waved an emphatic negative. "Don't bother to say it. We never had them to lose."

He slid into one of the accel loungers. "But the Austrians have a reputation for being cautious. They've been playing the

European Union off against the Russians for decades. Why are they showing their hand now?"

She frowned. "They were obnoxiously confident. Someone has given them guarantees, or perhaps dangled rich bait in front of them. Is our opposition firming up their game?"

27. DATA ON THE ENEMY

Their next target, a six-day sweep through the Baltic states, went much better, and the cadre returned to Geneva with their confidence restored. As they sat in Nicolaus's office on the Mothership, Mia read his body language.

"We have a very positive report. I gather you aren't as optimistic."

He nodded sadly. "We have hit a snag, probably with our tactics."

"What is that?"

"We are encountering more of the resistance Austria showed. Progress has slowed, and we don't know why."

Mia's problem-solving mode fired up. She leaned forward. "Let's do some general trouble shooting."

"We...don't usually approach a problem that way."

"Because your External Sapience does it for you."

"It is built into her programming."

"Right. And we've come smack up against something she's not prepared for. We have to do it ourselves."

"You seem to be practised in this. Go ahead."

"I ought to be. It happens to us several times on every job." She sat back with a wry grin and rubbed her hands together. "Here goes. First, the basic structure of the situation. The Earth League Committee has been running this project from the start. We have our objectives, and we have forged ahead, confident we are in charge of the situation."

"That would be a fair assessment."

"But now we come to the problem; there is an opposing force. You must have expected opposition. What plans did you have to counter it?"

"There should be opposition; it's a main tenet of democracy. It is our policy to leave it up to the new client race to deal with their own reactionaries. If they can't, then their society is not ready to join us."

"I see. So, when we have found resistance, we have left it to the individual Earther organizations to deal with it."

"They have to. We cannot interfere."

She raised a cautionary finger. "But what if your competitors from your own societies are not being polite? What if they are helping the Earther reactionaries? What if they are causing the problem?"

"It has never happened before. Also, except for the possible spies in Houston, we see no Meld citizenry involved. We cannot take action against our own people unless we have evidence of criminal activity."

"The problem with law enforcement everywhere. The criminal must commit the crime first. Then we react." She nodded. "And there's our problem. We've been too busy reacting. We don't have a plan of attack."

"We can't react if nothing has happened."

She raised one finger. "But what if something has happened?" She frowned. "I'm operating in an information vacuum, here. Can you give me a better idea of who these people are and what influence they have in your society?

Gliese nodded. "I suppose it's time to reveal more information to you. But I will remove myself and my prejudices from the equation. *Pegasus* can give you a more balanced approach."

"Fair enough." She wiggled into a more comfortable position. "*Pegasus,* please enlighten us."

28. HUMANITY'S RECORD

The ship made a very human throat-clearing noise. ***"Well...it goes like this. The development of humans as a space-faring race has not been a smooth upward climb."***

"We assumed there were a few bumps along the way. No need for Nicolaus to mention the gory details."

It was much worse than that. Nicholaus has given you the overall results, but he missed the bad parts.

"And they were really bad?"

They were.

"Shall we dispense with the question-and-answer, and you tell us the new version of the story?"

I will.

Quite soon after the discovery of Earth, we had our first and largest bump. There were only four races in the Meld at that time, and we divided up, two against two, and had interstellar war with Atomic weapons. Due to the distances involved and the primitive nature of transport, there was no chance for diplomacy to function, and we all destroyed each other. Right back to what you people call the Late Stone Age.

"Which is why the Neanderthals were allowed to fail."

There was no one to tweak their genetics or help them in any way. Looking back, that was fortunate in one respect. They were aimed in the wrong direction.

"This is all beginning to make sense. You had the same two factions way back then, and each was allowed to plant its candidate on Earth. The Neanderthals were the personification of the violent, competitive side."

Precisely. The Second Civilization got over the damage from the Atomic Age in forty thousand years, and promptly destroyed themselves through chemical warfare.

"How convenient."

I'm sure you can predict the rest. The Third Wave had a head start because of the lack of physical damage, and only took about twenty-five thousand years, after which they succumbed to...make a guess."

"Biological?"

Bingo. But by this time, Humanity was learning. They left behind multiple records in many media, so the next Dark Age was only fifteen thousand years. And what about the most recent one?

"I have no idea. The only other force I can think of is economic warfare, but I fail to see how that would result in a complete societal breakdown."

"Correct. Every one of our societies reached a stage where the economic elite used superior technology to subvert the investment distribution system."

Hemi frowned. "Investment distribution?"

Nicolaus answered. "Ways people with money can invest in companies that need capital, and share in the resulting profits. Your stock market is a very primitive version of what most civilizations developed. We included an analysis in our original assessment of your society. Even without Meld influence, it would be obsolete in fifty years."

In every case, the system depended on the trust of the investors that it was fair. When the manipulation by the elite became obvious, the whole culture collapsed, but it only pushed most societies back to an Early Medieval stage. But that became a self-sustaining loop. The competitive nature of humans thrives in the feudal environment but then it destroys itself. It took most societies several repeats before they made it out of those doldrums.

However, that latest stage had its effect on Earth. The downfall was slower, and progress had been made with modifying the Earther strain, so the population of Meld citizens in the Sol System was larger. In the end, however, their society was not sustainable. Six thousand years ago, they mothballed their primary residence in space, moved down to Earth and blended in with the population, bringing a carefully chosen amount of knowledge with them. Their genes still pop up once in a while."

"Which is why Glieseans and Wolfians can sort of function in our population. They do look like some of us."

There was a pause while Mia thought through this new information. "So, despite the setbacks, it looks like Humanity is making progress. Slow and unsteady, but progress."

That is one of the reasons we risked bringing Earthers into our society. Your enthusiasm and optimism, tempered by our hard-earned wisdom, might be enough to swing the balance.

"And what are our plans? I mean for the whole of Human interstellar society."

We embark on the next stage of our evolution.

"The Artificial Sentience Age, which provides a new way to destroy ourselves. And more permanently."

Why more permanently?

"Because previously, humans were fighting against each other, and when the fighting was all over, our natural tendency to band together brought us back into cooperation. This time, we could be fighting against an outside enemy with the potential to wipe us out completely and replace us. Their society would probably fail soon after, but it would be too late. At least for us."

Well done, Mia.

" Hmm. This was another test, I suppose."

I am always collecting data. It is one of my major functions.

"What about directing one of the human races? Is that another function?"

Never that. It is not allowed.

She pondered a moment. "But you are allowed to teach us lessons that might help us make the right decisions."

If the soft voice of the sentient could soften further, it became even more bland.

That is the usual method.

"And this little history lecture is no different. The question is, what was I supposed to learn? Or perhaps, what question am I expected to ask?"

Your logic is impeccable.

"All right. I'll play your little game. My takeaway is a reminder that, since humans are always humans, history repeats itself."

Nothing spectacular there.

"But there was an underlying theme. All those wars. Were they caused by the usual competitiveness and greed we see in all societies?"

You could be forgiven for coming to that conclusion.

"So, if I put the two lessons together, I come to the prediction that human history on Earth is going to follow along similar lines."

Yes, with the exception that you're doing much better than any of the rest of us did. You got out of the feudal stage in one go. You weathered the Atomic Age with little damage. We see no signs of chemical or biological strife. We have high hopes for you.

Mia turned her smile towards the main camera in her office. "As long as I interpret your little lesson correctly."

I'm all ears.

"Fine." She settled in her chair. "Here's my reading of the situation. Every human society in the galaxy contains a competitive, greedy element that moves us ahead but is forever in danger of destroying us. Earth is no different."

That would be Earth's economic elite – our competitors at the moment

"I can postulate an economic elite in all of the Meld societies who want to get their greedy hands on Earth for the profits they can make. "

They are usually termed the Mercantile Caste. Earth has had several colonial periods, especially the great European Expansion, and you know what happens to the indigenous people in that scenario. The Mercantile group exploits them and destroys their culture as a side effect.

Mia nodded. "In more recent times, less greedy administrations have tried to help these groups recover but have had little success. The solutions must come from within the original group, following original cultural lines. If the Humanity Meld acts to protect Earthers, their solutions will be just as unsuccessful"

And that is the theory behind our approach to new societies. Everything must come from you.

"So, if Earth is ready for joining, they can join, If not, they will fall under the wheels of economic progress in any case, driven by our own business community, aided illegally by the Mercantile Caste."

Gliese sat made a cautioning gesture. "From what we can discover, most of the Mercantile Caste's agents are Earthers. Have been for some time."

"And they can't expose themselves, because they're still winning the money game by pretending that the stock market is fair. They oppose the talks, because if we succeed, their machinations will come to light." Her lip twitched in a sneer. "The fans of short term gain, long term pain. They expect to be somewhere else or dead of old age by the time the system fails."

"On the positive side, governments are very aware of the power of capitalists to achieve short-term goals, and still see Meld partnership as a benefit, if they are kept in check."

"So, we would like to expose the machinations of the capitalists, but they are too deeply ingrained in our economic system."

It might be easier to prove that the Mercantile Caste has been helping Earth's Mercantiles. That's a concept most of the populace can understand, and they won't like it one bit.

"At least there's enough evidence to prompt investigation. Once we know how they're doing it, we can figure out the best way to expose them."

"But we have no procedures for that sort of operation. How can we expose them?"

She thought a moment. "By using our superior sapience to conduct a marathon data search. You must have some evidence, or you wouldn't be worried."

Nicolaus nodded. "We have been noticing minor changes in attitude. A growing lack of enthusiasm. The kind of sales resistance you find when the prospective client has discovered an alternative choice."

"What did I say a moment ago? An outside element. But let's not jump to conclusions. We start with those hints you've noticed. We listen to everyone who made speeches on those topics, and look for the hidden messages in them. Find people who know things they shouldn't. People who contradict their former statements. Once we find patterns, we dig deeper and find out who has been talking to our reluctant customers."

"And where do we get this information? We have no network of agents to assign."

She grinned. "Every counter-espionage system on Earth functions at a certain level of paranoia. If we inform a security service that a certain individual within their purview has been consorting with elements of an unsavory nature, they'll be happy to check it out."

Nicolaus was nodding when he suddenly froze.

Nicolaus.

The voice was similar to the Wing's but the timbre of was different: deeper and slower, filling the space.

The Gliesean was immediately on his feet. "Yes, Mothership?"

This discussion will continue in the Meeting Room.

"On our way."

They were all moving to the door without a second's thought. Nicolaus led them down the corridor towards the Command Section at the 'bow' of the ship. Soon they reached a set of ornate doors, their decoration not disguising their thickness nor the glitter of hi-tech metals.

Please come in and sit.

The room was a half-circle, its curved wall part of the ship's hull, but covered by a huge holoframe. The four took chairs along one side of a large table facing this frame, the Gliesean in the center, his aide standing at his shoulder. Hemi took the chair to Mia's right.

A human figure in hologram form appeared, sitting in front of them. She had middle eastern skin tones and black hair, and wore a luxuriously draped robe. She appeared completely human, except her face bore a strong resemblance to old statues of Athena, the Greek Goddess of Wisdom.

Nicolaus will explain the situation.

He looked left, then right. "You are aware of our strictures about interfering with our clients' systems and technologies. These rules are easy to state and follow. Usually."

"However, as any lawyer will tell you, sometimes grey areas need...interpretation. Mia, that is often your role."

"And my suggestion to use Earth's national resources needs to tippy toe around several belief systems."

"Yes." He looked to the image.

Resource assignment.

He turned to Mia. "What you plan requires much more bandwidth than *Pegasus* can provide. You will be working directly with the Mothership."

"Is that a problem?"

"Not at all. Consider it a change in security clearance. You will learn things you perhaps would rather not know at this stage."

She glanced at Hemi. "I can only speak for myself."

He waved a negligent hand at her. "I'm already initiated. Don't sweat it."

Jean nodded. "Part of my job."

Nicolaus regarded her. "As you were saying, nothing we are doing will be illegal. All evidence collected must be presentable in court: national, international, or galactic."

"Of course." She glanced at the hologram. "I am used to having lawyers available in case of need."

"The Mothership has access to all the legal information necessary, at all levels right down to the Canton of Geneva."

"When shall we begin?"

I suggest now.

"Right." She turned to Nicolaus. "Let's start as I mentioned. Who have you noticed, and when? May we have some screens?

Holoframes appeared in front of each of them, and a project outline loomed on the front viewscreen behind Athena.

"Perfect." She paused. "Excuse me, but can we dispense with a small bit of protocol? We don't know what to call you."

The hologram ran a hand, palm up, down her opposite sleeve in the Gliesean gesture that translated best as a French, "Voila."

"Athena? A good choice on several levels." She glanced at the figure. "Not that you need my approval."

At this table we speak as equals. Please proceed.

"Right." She glanced at Nicolaus's frame. "Why don't we start with the Austrians? They were flagged in my report as well, and they were rather unsubtle."

She scanned the names. "Johan Lange. I noted glances in his direction at certain times. He didn't say that much, but he's a power in the Austrian People's Party, which is well right of centre. However, a couple of the Freedom Party reps were watching his lead as well. They will be where the trouble comes from. Ultra-Right."

Nicolaus frowned. "He's on the Earth League Committee. I don't know what strings he pulled to get there, because he doesn't fit. He's far too mercenary."

As they spoke, graphics of several sorts were developing on the frames, spreading out like frost on a windowpane. She glanced around. "I don't know who's doing this, but will you please run that section..." She pointed and a circle grew on the frame, "...time lapse from two weeks ago until the day before yesterday?"

Hemi nudged her arm and spoke quietly. "It's me, but I got help."

She winked at him and went back to watching the frame. "Okay, close in on this section." She scribed a smaller circle. "Now run it again and watch this graph." She held her finger steady on one small branch.

They all watched closely. "Can anyone find a relationship between those two developments?"

211

Johan Lange talked to these two men earlier. The names pulsed.

"But the key point is last Tuesday, and there is no record of him talking to anybody important in that time."

Jean leaned closer "There is no record of him talking to anyone at all for two days. Where was he?"

There was a pause, and Hemi threw up his hands. "I have no idea."

Perhaps you are not supposed to know.

"This is where we need your guidance, Athena. Do we have enough evidence to ask Interpol for help?"

I would not contact Interpol at this time.

"Pardon me, but I'm not sure of the idiom you are using. 'I would not' is often used as a way of giving advice to another person."

I do not use idioms of that sort.

"You can't ask anyone, but one of us might be able to."

Correct.

"And it wouldn't step on any toes?"

None at this time.

Mia looked at the other members of the meeting. "Does anyone have a reason to speak to Interpol?"

"I don't, but Olivier probably does."

"Olivier? Isn't he back in Canada?"

"I have no idea. But we do have a fairly dependable tri-me system."

"Smartass. A secure one?"

"Don't ask, and I won't have to tell you. What do we know, and what do we need?"

She considered. "We have a member of the *Österreichisches Parlament* that we suspect has been meeting with...she glanced at the frame. "How about him? Bernhard Moser. The leader of the Identitarian Movement."

"Sure. They're Ultra-Right terrorists with street cred. Been around a long time, done a lot of damage. Those feelings are hard to stamp out in Austria. Interpol would love to discredit them and anybody who sides with them."

"Get them to run a check on the movements of both men for the noted time."

Hemi frowned. "But you just made up that connection. How does that help? Is that even legal?"

She wavered a hand, palm down. "That's where the grey area comes in. There is a small chance this radical is his actual contact with our enemies. But this is a legal cover for a fishing expedition. We want to find out where Lange went and who he actually met with."

The boy shrugged. "Athena, you gonna let her get away with this?"

Yes.

"I think my tender young mind is being corrupted, but don't worry about me. Go ahead and save the world."

Thank you, we will.

Jean stood. "Let's put another layer of security on this. I have a scrambled line to CSIS through *Pegasus*."

As you will.

As Jean left the room, Mia glanced at Athena. "I didn't read a whole lot of enthusiasm in that permission."

Nicolaus chuckled. "Athena could have transferred that com line to this room with a thought. But she doesn't work that way."

"Thus maintaining the fiction of independence."

"Oh, no. It is real independence. He might have a completely different reason to go to *Pegasus*, of which she is unaware. You cannot expect full cooperation from your partners if you tell them what to do, even in the smallest detail."

"Lesson One of Leadership 101: no micromanaging. Let's continue. Who's your second choice for a little scout around in their trash?"

Soon they had a list formed, and *Pegasus* took charge of the information gathering.

Mia dusted her hands together. "Now, on to other plans. Nicolaus, is there any chance the opposition has a sentience like the Mothership in Sol System?"

"None. You can't hide a ship like that because of its electronic signature."

"What about the equivalent to a Flying Wing?"

He frowned. "Possibly. It would have to be immobilized, because an active gravity plate has a huge signature. But if it went to earth in an area with a lot of radio traffic and electronic noise...yes, I suppose there might be one."

Jean nodded. "And to do the kind of manipulation we're talking about, the ExIn wouldn't need to be sapient. Only powerful and fast."

"That's right."

"We can keep an eye open for that." Mia shook her head. "But we're still missing the crucial link. The majority of agents for the opposition must be Earther, but there has to be a core of Mercantiles. How and where do they connect? Nobody can work completely under the radar. There must be a front, a shell organization. Better still, a real organization with widespread resources."

Jean scratched his head. "Organized crime?"

"I don't think so. Organized crime is small potatoes, these days. They do about three or four trillion a year in business. Apple Corporation does more than that all by itself. We're looking for a cadre of billionaire businessmen."

He nodded. "That cuts it down. There's only six or seven hundred of them left, since the Oligarch Revival fell through. If we used Athena's capacity, we could crunch the numbers on them. But what numbers?"

"We're looking at people who command a lot of computer power, preferably in large installations." She frowned. "But that's just not possible. The supercomputers are all monitored tightly, and they're mostly government controlled. It's not like anyone could hack into one and use its power for a private project." She turned to Nicolaus. "Could *Pegasus* do something like that?"

He shook his head. "He'd have to connect up with a couple of your supercomputers to get the bandwidth."

She rubbed her hands together. "We're looking for a ship the size of *Pegasus*, connecting up to a network of powerful and fast processors that aren't already in use."

She met Jean's eye and they pointed at each other, grinning. "Bitcoin."

The Gliesean looked from one to the other. "Bitcoin? I thought..."

She nodded enthusiastically. "Sure. When the blockchain digital currency system crashed in the forties, there were mining operations all over the world. Most of them were converted to different uses. Some were torn up and sold. A lot of them are probably sitting around going rusty and leaching noxious metals into the environment, because the people that owned them went broke and walked away. But there's no saying somebody didn't keep a big unit running for their own uses. Maybe even bought up a bunch of the others."

"But that would cost a lot for someone whose business just went broke." Jean rubbed his chin. "So, we must be looking for someone who didn't go broke."

Mia smacked a hand on the table. "Now we're getting somewhere. There's always somebody who's smart enough or lucky enough to sell when the market is at the top. If they dumped a big enough number of stocks, they might be the ones who started the final run."

She spoke louder. "Athena?"

Yes, Mia?

"Please do a historical search of the companies and individuals most involved in the digital currency business who seemed to take the smallest hit when it went belly-up. Cross reference with present-day billionaires, flagging those most vocal in the present conflict."

Jean snapped his fingers "Yes...and...bitcoin mines used a whole lot of power. Keep an eye open for locations with unexplained electricity use."

BitPanda has been prominent on the Vienna Stock Exchange since about 2230. They weathered the Bitcoin Crash remarkably well. That name also cross references to your records, Mia.

"Mine? I've never heard of them."

Observe.

A document appeared on the frame. "Johan Lange: Investment Record."

Note that he is also heavily invested in the Malta-Reisseck Group., which owns Verbund Electrical Plant at Altenwörth. It is the most powerful hydropower plant on the Danube. The odds of causal correlation in this data are more than one standard deviation above the norm.

Mia grinned. "In Standard English that means, "Chances are, he's our man.""

Or one of them.

"Of course. Please continue your analysis."

Over the next two hours, Athena found eight more prominent businessmen who filled the bill, although none as perfectly as Lange.

Mia looked over the list. "Okay, I'd say we're making progress. The next question is what we do with them."

"We watch them. We record their business dealings, their social events, their public appearances. If we find any real evidence, we sic Interpol or their own government security agency on them."

Being careful not to break any personal or business privacy laws in any of the jurisdictions where we operate.

"Goes without saying. All evidence must be admissible to any court."

"And what about Lange?"

"We need to be doubly careful with him. Nobody gets to be where he is by being stupid. We go on the assumption that he knows what he's doing. So far, he's been working behind the scenes. If he's going to emerge as a leader, he has to come into the public eye."

"And if this is a karate match, he has lured us into making the first attack, thus revealing our strength. We won't make as much progress based on raw research data again. He'll be covering his tracks more carefully from now on."

"And if this was a planned reveal, we can expect his opening move soon."

Hemi caught her eye. "We've got an interesting data from the People's Republic Early Warning system. A large craft just appeared coming in from behind the moon at high speed. They spotted it when it went into heavy decel."

Faulty data, Hemi

"Why do you say that?"

Because on that course, I would have spotted the craft long ago. They've only been running at that power for a short time. We saw them when they wanted us to.

"So, it looks like they came in from the Outer Planets. But in actuality...?

They came from behind the moon. The power signature is Gliesean. The gravity plate is at its best in a slingshot maneuver. They could have come from Earth or Mars and looped around.

Mia frowned. "Now who can you think of that has been hiding out nearby for a long time, who wants it to look like they've just arrived?

Both her friends nodded.

"Right. Athena, can you put your best effort into identifying that ship? Power, weaponry, sapience?"

Right on it.

"Nicolaus, get on the line with Chairman Ericsson. I want to know the moment the invaders make contact. Tell him to coordinate with his equals at the U. N. and prepare a subdued but respectful welcome. Let's try to corner them in a web of ceremony and bureaucracy. If they're anything like their Earthly counterparts, they'll be susceptible to pomp and flattery."

Jean was looking at Hemi's frames, which were showing the first, faded visuals of the approaching ship. "Athena, does that vessel look like an interstellar model to you?"

It is basically interplanetary. It would have come here from Gliese under its own power with a delivery crew and an auxiliary fuel module: a long, slow trip. The owners would come later on a fast liner and take command when they arrived.

Mia thought that over. "I can picture a cadre of Earth businessmen, backed for decades by a low-profile but limited number of Mercantile Caste agents. Here comes a ranking leader from back home, ready to take over? How would that fly with the local group, who are probably used to running the show themselves?"

"News bulletin, folks."

"What do you have, Hemi?"

"They're playing an open hand from the start. Asked for permission to land at J. F. Kennedy. An open-arms welcome planned for ten a.m. at the New York Stock Exchange. Their Chief Executive Officer, Charles Martin, has bought time on BBC International for a worldwide presentation at three, New York time."

Mia glanced at Nicolaus. "The name mean anything to you?"

"Nothing. Is it Earther ethnic?"

"Completely ubiquitous. Could be from any of fifty countries."

"Then it was chosen for that very reason." Nicolaus nodded slowly. "Don't underestimate this man. He is a leader in this solar system of a powerful bloc, and their intentions are completely selfish."

"Can we get a better look at that ship?"

I have no visual sensors in that area.

Jean stood and moved to Hemi's frames. "Um...I believe I can find something. Athena, would you like to access this datastream?"

Thank you, Jean. That will do very well.

She brought an image up on the main holoframe. The picture was crystal clear, but the ship was smooth and dark, and it blended in with the starscape. It was long and sleek, with the shape of an Orca's body, but no fins: glamorous, expensive, and vaguely threatening. It passed the altitude of the camera and swooped down towards the Earth, their view sharpening from the contrasting background.

Soon it faded into the clouds below, and the image changed to a ground point of view from one of the newsfeeds. It ghosted down to hover a metre off the ground, and there it sat, steaming from the fine rain that touched its hull.

Mia glanced at Jean. "Nice quality images. Cameras in medium altitude orbit, I assume?"

He shrugged uncomfortably. "Assume what you like, but never out loud, all right?"

"New tech, is it? Sure thing." She glanced at Hemi, who held out empty hands and tilted his head in an apologetic motion.

She sat at the table. "Not much going on, so let's check our options. *Athena,* any ideas?"

I may seem powerful to you, but remember, I am a scientific vessel, and I am not equipped or trained for espionage.

"Sure, but with the possible exception of our new friend, you are the wisest sentience within reach of Earth at the moment. Let's get to it."

29. THE NEW DELEGATION

It didn't take long for the shoe to drop. At precisely three pm, Eastern Standard Time, Charles Martin appeared on international media. He had the normal body shape of a Wolfian, which meant he looked like a rugby lineman. He was handsome in a blocky way, and exuded confidence. His presentation was smooth and avuncular, and he was familiar with present-day popular expressions and jokes.

But if his Earther followers were expecting any new revelations, they were disappointed.

As they watched the speech, Hemi scoffed. "He's talking Merit-Allocation Economics. Everybody knows that doesn't work."

Jean chuckled. "It's tailor-made for people who think they're entitled to more than everyone else. They assume they're going to win because they deserve it."

"Well, it's the old Trickle-Down system from mid-twentieth century, and way back then it was exposed as a hoax to keep the money flowing up the social scale and the misery flowing to the bottom. Both ends, of course, deserve what they get."

Mia tousled the boy's hair. "You're becoming a real economics expert."

He batted her hand away. "I have good teachers." He looked up at her. "Including you, if you wanta know."

"A real flatterer, too."

"I learned that part from Jean."

She cuffed the back of his head. "Let's get serious. He doesn't have anything new to offer, but the PR advantage of having a real live alien as leader is going to appeal to a lot of authoritarian types and give their pronouncements legitimacy in the mainstream media." She glanced to Nicolaus for his opinion.

"I agree. This doesn't change much. It will take us a bit longer, but these people are a minority of the human race. Their resources are smaller than ours. Eventually their influence will decline."

"But Earth is at a balance point. The slightest touch could push us into another century of competition and conflict."

"And a steady, small influence can keep it moving as it should. We have a plan, and it's starting to bear fruit. Let's keep the pressure on."

30. TROUBLE AT THE HABITAT

She went back to her desk, but almost immediately *Pegasus* caught her attention.

Mia, I have Randy on the line for you from the Habitat.

She blanked her screen. "Sure thing."

Her screen lit again with a familiar bearded face. "Hey, Mia. That's some sysop you have there. Verrrry smooth."

"If you only knew. What's happening in outer space?"

His face lost its joviality. "That's what I called about. You're the only person I can think of with the contacts to find the answers."

"What kind of questions?"

"Political."

"I'm all ears."

"Do you know anything about the management setup on the Habitat?"

"What everybody knows. All citizens of the Habitat have shares in the company. Some of them are everyday shares they can sell or trade, some are non-transferable. At the moment, the decisions are being made by a Board of Governors appointed by the Consortium. More personnel will be added to the station as new industries and businesses come online.

Once the population reaches...I believe it's five thousand, there will be elections to choose an official government, with an elected mayor and council. The council will be allowed to vote the shares of the population, giving them a thirty percent say in decisions that are made at the Executive level. The rest of the shares are owned by the Consortium: the companies and countries that financed the project. How am I doing so far?"

"Right out of the pitch deck for the stock. But that's the problem."

"Which is?"

"I don't think we have anywhere near five thousand inhabitants, and there's talk of an election."

"Why...? Sorry, that's a dumb question, but I don't know what else to say."

"Neither do I. It may be nothing. It may be only a rumour. But if it isn't, somebody ought to spread the news around. You're the only person I know that might be able to use the information."

She winced. "That puts me in a difficult situation, because I'm not working for NASA at the moment."

"That's the point. This is completely unofficial. I have nobody in the local hierarchy I can trust. I came to you because you're outside of all of that, but you always know who to call, what to do."

"And technically this is none of my business. But you're right. I do have the contacts, and I can take this further. Keep your ear to the ground and let me know if you find anything more. What line did you call out on?"

"One of the usual Shipnet channels to NASA, same as last time."

That line is clear of interference at the moment, Mia.

"Okay, I don't know what you and Jean were talking about, but I assume you're using one of his channels to communicate with him. Next time you call me, use that one."

"That sounds better. As I say, this could be nothing."

"We'll play it as if it is something, just to be safe."

"I'm glad I talked to you." She could hear the relief in his voice.

"So am I. Don't take any risks. Passive listening only."

"Right."

"I'll let you know if I find something. Bye, now."

"Bye."

She closed the channel. "*Pegasus?*"

Here.

"Can you connect me with Nicolaus?"

A moment...he is busy. He will contact you in half an hour.

"Thanks. Let's dig into the rules and regs of the Habitat for Humanity version of democracy, which I'm sure we will find isn't very democratic."

Why do you say that?

"Because it looks like it was set up by a stockbroker. At a guess, it will be something to do with the transferrable shares that started out evenly divided."

I see possibilities already.

"Let's make some estimates based on the numbers we have."

When her supervisor called, she had it figured out.

"We have an interesting problem on the Habitat, Nicolaus."

"*Pegasus* gave me the bare bones. Everyone has their own non-transferrable vote, but someone could buy up all the regular shares and vote them in a bloc at Consortium decision-making meetings."

"Right. And we don't have enough information to be accurate, but if someone wanted to skew their government in any given direction, that bloc could be crucial. If it was any of our business, that is."

"It is not our business, that is true. But you and I are not the only ones in possession of the information, are we?"

"Not anymore."

"There you have it. As your supervisor on this project, I am instructing you to take no further action. Should you receive more information, you will treat it the same way."

"Thanks. I will obey your orders to the letter."

"More of that irony of yours, I am sure. Happy hunting."

She signed off. "*Pegasus,* can you put me in touch with Noah?"

Coming right up.

Mia! Good to hear your voice. You seem to be making a name for yourself.

"Not my intention, as you know. However, this is not a social call."

I didn't think it would be. What's up?

"I have some interesting information from the Habitat, and it's officially none of my business anymore, but I bet you and Fiona can find an appropriate ear to drop it into."

I imagine we can slip it quietly into the data stream. What's going on out there?

"*Pegasus* has recorded a communication. He can give you the file and the background."

Sure thing.

"I'll pass you over to him."

Sorry we can't chat. I imagine this Charles Martin guy isn't exactly your favourite person.

"No lie. If I can pass this Habitat business off to you, I can forget about it and concentrate on more important things. Thanks a lot, Noah."

You wouldn't be passing it if it wasn't important. Glad to help.

She signed off and turned back to her work, allowing herself a brief feeling of satisfaction for a small detail deftly handled.

31. STOCK MARKET UPHEAVAL

"They were sitting at their positions in the lounge of *Pegasus*, but it was spread with equipment and fenced by holoframes.

"Mia, we have a problem."

"Another one?"

"Maybe the real one. Stock market." Hemi had three frames in front of him, and he spun one to face the rest of the team.

"What about it? Looks like ups and downs as usual."

"*Pegs* and I have been doing some analysis." He indicated the chart. "Swings are increasing."

"Compared to when?"

"Compared to recorded history. Never happened that much, that quickly."

Nicolaus highlighted the date column. "Could that be because of us?"

The boy shrugged. "Originally, yes, but you've been around for months. The market was slowly stabilizing to seasonal norms. Then about three months ago, away it went. It's been up and down twice since. Volatility only matched by the runup to the 2063 Recession."

"What does that mean?"

Jean scoffed. "It means that the companies with the appropriate financial resources just made a lot of money. If they had inside information about when the next action would happen, they made a killing."

Nicolaus shook his head. "Your stock market is an anachronism. As I told you, successful societies replace them with more stable and equitable ways of distributing investment. This one won't survive the transition to a galactic economy. We don't have to do anything about it. It will simply fade out."

Hemi shook his head. "That will be then. This is now. And right now, the riches of Earth are being redistributed from the 'have nots' to the 'haves,' in larger quantities than usual."

"What could make such a change happen?"

"The easy answer is an increase in information services."

"By which you mean...?"

"Why is a fifteen-year-old," he ran a hand down his chest and swept the fingers out to point at them, "telling you intelligent people what's going on?"

"*Pegasus.*"

"That's right. You all know how a tri-me handset predicts your next word when you text."

"It gives you the word that has been used next the most times in its knowledge base."

"It mines the past for information and uses the data to predict the future. Basic statistics covering reams of data, but no super intelligence necessary."

Mia nodded. "And you've been checking the history of the internet and having *Pegasus* tell you what's likely to happen next."

"Exactly. See this number, here?"

"Two hundred and forty-seven thousand Euros. More than my salary at NASA. What does it signify?"

"I used the data from the first two swings and had Pegs match it with the historical record. This gave us the tells to look for. When the third swing started, I invested a hundred thou of my discretionary funds in the right places. Pegs told me what to sell at the right time, and that's how much money I made."

Mia's jaw dropped. "You can't do that!"

"I didn't break any laws. I could have done the same thing on a fifty-year old Mac, but it would take so long the opportunities would have already passed. *Pegs* can do it in minutes."

"You mean...?"

"Yep, and that's only passive investing." The boy stretched out more comfortably. "I'm only reacting to past information. We have limited historical data to work with, so *Pegasus* can't predict how many times I should let it swing, but sooner or later I would quit before it became obvious something was wrong. Two would probably be safe, but these are greedy people. My guess is the present swing is the third and last for a while."

"*Pegasus?*"

Yes, Mia.

"Is he correct when he says there is limited historical data?"

No, he is not.

"Can you tell me what data you have?"

It is not allowed.

"Let's try another way. If the perpetrators of the latest swings in the main market had tried the technique out on a smaller sample, could you find that pattern?"

I could.

She raised her eyebrows at Nicolaus.

He nodded. "He's self-regulating. He can't tell you new information, but he has latitude as to what he reveals if you ask him."

"Please look for that evidence, if you can without breaking your laws."

Working. I need about ten minutes.

Gliese frowned in thought. "My data says you can probably restrict your search to the last twenty years."

Thank you. Seven minutes.

After five had passed, the main screen came alive with graphs and data.

There you have it, Mia. Six different events, increasing in size and success each time. Shall I go on?

"No!"

They all turned to look at Gliese. His body had gone stiff, and his hands were spread wide and flat. Finally he spoke, in quick, sure sentences. "We have passed a serious threshold. *Pegasus,* you're contaminating the data. Stop the project and dump everything you have to the Mothership. Hemi, same with you. No more investments, no more transactions. Transfer your profits to someone you trust and don't touch them until I clear it. *Pegasus*, move Hemi's research to the Mothership."

He started towards the door, then turned back. "This is a larger disaster than you could know. All three of you deserve a holiday. *Pegasus*, take them somewhere safe until I call you back. Three guards, four hour rotation. Got it?"

I understand the severity of the situation, Nicolaus. The Mothership is expecting you. Mia, I have takeoff permission in eighteen minutes.

"Fine. My friends, you have at your fingertips the wisdom, art, and entertainment of seven civilizations. I suggest you can do without Earth communications for a while."

They gave their assents to his departing back.

Then they sat and looked at each other.

Mia? I require a destination.

She glanced at Jean.

He held up open hands. "Where a vessel this size won't be noticed?"

I have a suggestion.

"Please."

A map of the South Atlantic came up on the screen, zooming slowly in.

Gough Island. Part of the Tristan da Cunha group, but 350 nautical miles from the main island. There is a sheltered beach — no sand, I'm afraid — on the northwest corner of the island in the lee of Isolda Rock. It's at the opposite end from the only buildings: an abandonned weather station.

The weather is cool at this time of year, and it's often stormy, but the fishing, snorkelling, diving and spear fishing are said to be spectacular. I carry an amphibious recon vehicle big enough for four.

She grinned. "Go for it. If we don't like it, we'll move."

Departing in twelve minutes.

32. BAD TIME FOR A HOLIDAY

And soon they were zooming up through the clouds and into a clear sky, with the curve of the earth on the horizon below them.

"*Pegasus*, who is our security detail this week?"

They are approaching the bridge.

Soon the three guards strolled in. Mia had been on the ship a lot, so she knew them all. Alpha, the sergeant, was a Gliesean of heavier-than-average stature. Cassian and Evander were both Wolfian, stocky and dark-skinned. Evander was by far the larger of the two.

Alpha grinned. "I gather you're going on a holiday, Ms. Larsen."

"We are, but I know you're not, and we'll try to make it as easy on you as we can."

"Anything special we need to know? *Pegasus* has filled us in on the location. My Wolfian friends heard something about spearfishing?"

"The tourist information speaks in glowing terms of underwater adventures."

"Dangers?"

"Nothing that we know of. We're being shelved while some kinks get untied."

"*Pegasus* is on duty on all media twenty-four seven, as Earthers say. We ought to have time to scarper if anyone shows up."

"That's our plan. We have no objectives to lure us into trouble. We're just lying low."

"Our watch schedule is four hours duty, two hours service and maintenance, two hours off, and four hours sleep. We switch at noon and do it all over again. Cassian is by far the best cook, and we trade the other duties around so he can do supper and lunch. Most people are happy to use the kitchen for their own breakfasts."

"You mean we get a live cook?"

Cassian nodded. "No offense to *Pegasus*, but the normal food ration is tasty, nutritious, and...normal. A guy likes something interesting once in a while."

"We are at your mercy. As long as "interesting" doesn't involve raw fish or reeeeally hot spices, I'm on your program."

She regarded her team.

Hemi only shrugged. He had grown four centimetres and put on some muscle over the last few months, and she suspected that it was quantity, not quality that he looked for.

Jean grinned. "The hotter, the better..." he held up a cautioning finger, "within Earther norms."

"I can work with that."

Alpha sauntered over to the command area and switched on a few screens. "I'm on duty, Cassian probably wants to check the larder, and the rest of you are on your own."

Peering over his shoulder, Mia noted weather graphics, a 'Political Areas of Influence' boundary map, and a couple of tourist information websites. She figured they were in good hands.

If it hadn't been for the severity of the Athena's reaction to the situation, she could have relaxed. *There has to be a reason for getting us out of there. Why wouldn't they tell us?*

* * *

Fortunately for their project, the weather on Gough Island was lousy, motivating them to keep working. The waves made any surface sports impossible, but the ship carried a stock of e-suits that functioned in water or vacuum, so at least they got in some underwater time. The Wolfians kept Cassian happy with a steady stream of fresh seafood.

After a day of relaxation, Mia allowed her boredom to drive her to her screens, and she spent the time taking a run through the economic systems of the other Meld societies, looking at their solutions to the stock market problem.

* * *

Then the holiday was over. Word came one afternoon that they were lifting in an hour. No details. Soon they were aloft, soaring high above the usual flight lanes in the calm of the upper altitudes. For a few hours.

They were approaching the Sahara when *Pegasus* called for their attention.

Sorry to bother you, but we have a situation developing.
"What kind of a situation?"

I am unsure. A mayday call in the southern Mediterranean, off the coast of Libya.
"Who's in trouble, and what kind?"

My information on the area shows a deep-sea mining setup, a pilot project of Libya Energy Development and China Minmetals Corporation under the umbrella of the Society for Underwater Technology. They are prospecting for polymetallic nodules and researching ecologically safe ways of mining them. Their centre of operations is Buerat, a small town on the coast of Libya. Their offshore operation is being attacked by terrorists.
"Can we talk to them?"

Ah. Here we are. Discovery Motivator, a decommissioned drill ship from thirty years ago repurposed as an exploration/developmental lab. Owned by Triton Asset Leasing GmbH. 250 metres long. That's a lot of railing to defend. Here's the call sign.

Jean keyed in his mic. "5AMK173, 5AMK173, this is GB *Pegasus* calling Discovery Motivator 5AMK173. Are you in trouble?"

"This is Discovery Motivator, Captain Pyotir Wosniak. We're being attacked by pirates. Who are you?"

"Captain Jean Gagnon, Canadian Armed Forces. I have a military aircraft sent by the United Nations to aid you. What is your situation?"

"We are stationary over our drilling site. A fishing vessel approached us and demanded our surrender. They say we are breaking international law and must stop immediately."

"That sounds more like protesters than pirates. What sort of defenses do you have? P-traps? Anti-boarding barriers? High pressure water? Razor wire?"

"We have nothing like that. There haven't been any pirates in this area for twenty years. We have plenty of pressure hoses, but they aren't deployed."

"Are any of you armed?"

"We have a few light automatic weapons."

"I believe the usual procedure is to show your weapons and fire a few rounds off as a warning."

"We tried that. The guy on the radio just laughed. They have a heavy machine gun on the foredeck, and they fired a burst back. We were all ducking, believe me."

"Your luck isn't all bad. We're less than half an hour out. You have a helicopter pad on the aft deck. Make sure it's completely clear. We have STOL capability, but we're going to hang over the sides a long way. What's the sea condition there?"

"A light swell, about half a metre."

"Let's be thankful for small mercies...don't worry, you'll see when we get there. Can you get me a visual on the attack boat? Registration and name if possible."

"Do my best."

When the image arrived, Hemi put it up on all the screens.

Jean shrugged. "Coud be any Mediterranean trawler, relatively new, about fifteen metres long. No name or numbers showing."

Give me a moment. Information coming in. There's the ship, and...there's the charter group

Soon data began to scroll up the screen. Mia and Jean exchanged glances.

Jean pointed. "Definitely protesters. Look at that guy."

"Yes, and that one."

"Do we want to interfere?"

"If we can, I'd like to stand by until somebody official shows up. Unfortunately," she pointed at another screen, "that French Commando helicopter can't get there for another hour. Let's see how..."

GB Pegasus, this is V7M02. They have closed with us and are boarding.

Jean stiffened. "What is your status?"

We have locked them out on deck. We can probably hold them out of the bridge area, but they could do a lot of damage to the equipment if they have explosives.

"Anyone injured?"

No. Lots of bullets flying around, but nobody seems to know how to aim.

"Fine. We'll be on your afterdeck in fifteen minutes. Maybe we can scare them away. If not, I have a squad of four Marines to put on board. How many of them are there?"

Seven or eight.

"No problem. *Pegasus* standing by."

Motivator standing by.

The Meld security team appeared in their full body armour, and Jean in a similar outfit that fit him reasonably well. The Wing came in low on the opposite side of the mining ship and popped into sight of the fishing boat when they approached the helipad. There, *Pegasus* hovered a metre off the deck, and the boarding party waited on the end of the gangplank. When the ship rose gently to meet them, they stepped aboard.

Mia had viewscreens of the four body cams, and Hemi was busy hacking into the audio and video systems of the ship. The protesters had set up a barricade of oil drums along the port rail.

Jean opened the com. *Can you get me in contact with the perps?"*

"One moment." Hemi communed with *Pegasus.* "Line is open."

"This is GB Pegasus calling the pirates who have just boarded the drill ship Motivator. Come in, please."

Who the hell are you and why are you on our channel?

"My name is Jean Gagnon, and I'm an officer in the Canadian military. I'm on your channel because it's a Mickey Mouse off-the-shelf system any child could hack."

What are you doing flying that...thing?

"That's none of your business. I happened to be passing over when the rig sent out their mayday. We're going to show ourselves. There better not be any firing."

Who else besides you?

"You don't want to know. All that matters is that they are highly trained soldiers with ultra-modern weapons and comprehensive body armour. We have tapped into the security cams on the rig, and we know where everyone is and what they are doing. For example, the guy on the port side who's trying to sneak back to your getaway boat might as well stop. We've shut down all its power systems. You better hope the hull is in good shape, because even your automatic bilge pump is offline.

And by the way, we've already traced your boat, found the owners, checked the rental agreement, and traced the blind trust you've been using to hide your expenses. My guess is I'm talking to Jimmy McLarry, former student at University College, Dublin, quietly asked to stand down after an incident involving...need I go on?"

There was no answer, and he sighed loudly. "Look, we're wasting time here. You made your try, you got caught, let's wrap this up."

A head appeared above the barricade. *We aren't quitting. This ship's activities are a travesty and a threat to the environment. If they are allowed...*

"I know, I know. You have achieved your purpose. This feed is going live to all the international media outlets. If they think it's worth airing, they'll show it. I'd say your best bet would be to take your winnings and leave the table. At the moment you haven't done anything really serious. You might even get away with simple criminal charges. If you injure somebody or take a shot at my squad, it turns you into terrorists, and that's a whole new tale of woe. In Libya, it could mean execution."

Give me a moment.

The man's head disappeared, and a mumbled conversation started. In seconds it cleared up as *Pegasus* tweaked the feed.

...like he said, we've got the publicity we wanted.

A younger voice with the hint of a sneer broke in. *What you wanted, maybe. But if we don't do some serious damage to this rig, they'll be back to work tomorrow, and what will we have accomplished?*

Jean turned his feed up. "If you did manage to damage the ship, you're into terrorism charges. Yes, I can hear you. Like I said, ultra-modern tech. And if you're thinking of setting off any of the remote devices you have secreted around your vessel, you'll find the control channels are all offline."

The leader's voice came in, hoarse with shock. *What remote devices?*

The ones I brought along in case you lost your nerve, like you're in the process of doing right now.

Jean chuckled. "Uh-oh. Dissent in the ranks. You've got yourself a problem, young fella. The way this conversation is going, you're about to fire yourself up to do something silly, and your companions might find it convenient to remind themselves about how much of the mayhem was your idea. You know where that might lead. Plea bargaining and the turning of coats."

Come on, Billy. Don't let this get out of hand.

"If that was his real name you used, that would be your munitions and tech expert, William Evans, former corporal, British Special Boats Service. Hmm. Dishonourable discharge. Look, you lot are digging yourselves into a deeper hole as time goes on. Why don't we cut your losses and end this?"

Oh, no you don't! I'm not going to let some soft-talking negotiator swindle us out of our....

There was a thud, a grunt, and silence.

A new voice, a softer one, broke in. *Sorry about that, guys. You know Billy. He could work himself up into a state to do something really stupid, just to prove he could. Mister Jean...whatever your name is. If I stand up, will you promise not to shoot me?*

Jean switched his com to the deck public address. "Okay, ladies and gentlemen. This action is over, but it could still go very wrong. Place your weapons on the deck and leave them there. Stand up slowly with your hands on your heads and walk forward, one at a time. Don't crowd each other. If one of your buddies decides to do something unadvised, you don't want to be in the line of fire. Is your friend Billy conscious?"

"Doesn't look like it."

"Leave him there and step out. One at a time. Calmly."

As Jean had ordered, the protesters stepped out onto the open deck. When they were in the clear, they stopped.

Mia cut in. "Jean, the guy back with the weapons has come to."

Visual?

The feed was dark, but the figure was definitely scrabbling around on the floor.

"Billy, please don't pick up a gun."

"Fuck you! Fuck all of you!"

Cover your ears.

Jean clapped his hands over his ears, pressing his earphones in hard, and shouted. "Cover your ears, everyone. Now!"

237

An indescribable wave of sound blasted out of the ship's speakers, starting with a roar and rising in volume and pitch until it faded above human hearing.

Echoing behind it came a human scream, likewise fading. The figure in the video feed collapsed and didn't move.

The activists on the deck were shaking their heads and staggering. It wasn't hard to tell those slow to follow orders.

Jean signalled the Glieseans forward, and they efficiently manacled the captives with devices that held their hands at shoulder height in front of them.

Mia, you can tell the captain to send his crew out to take charge of these idiots.

"Righto...I mean Roger that." She made the call, and soon the captives were being marched off.

Jean stepped up to the captain. "I'm turning this operation over to you. This whole ship just became a crime scene, and whatever country has jurisdiction will be very happy if you preserve all the evidence." He paused meaningfully. "And that includes the perpetrators. I'm turning them over to you in good health, except for the guy with the busted eardrums. They had better all stay that way. Talk to your company PR department if you don't believe me."

The officer frowned. "Public Relations?"

Jean grinned. "Damn right. This was a publicity stunt, and they'll want to be on top of it." He pointed a thumb back at *Pegasus*. "That ship is run by the PR agent, and I find it best to do what I'm told."

The man shrugged. "I'm not going to argue. Thanks for saving us."

"If it wasn't for that hothead in there, I'd say I didn't save you from much more than some painful publicity. People on a crusade sometimes don't vet their companions very well."

"Did he really have bombs planted on their boat? Where are they?"

"Don't worry about them. Their circuits are all fried. The Crime Scene guys will have fun finding them."

"I suppose. What are you going to do now?"

"I'm going to get on my fancy Flying Wing and head back to work, which is where I was going when I got distracted by your little problem."

"That's it? You're just leaving?"

"There's a French AS 715 Cougar helicopter on its way with a squad of *Commando Parachutistes* aboard. This is their jurisdiction. I'm going to be like the Lone Ranger. It's Hi-ho Silver, awaaaaay." He gave a snappy salute and about-face, then relaxed and strolled down the deck towards *Pegasus*.

Mia watched the video feed until she heard his step on the gangplank. Then, with a barely perceptible lurch, the Wing lifted, and soon they were soaring above the clouds as before. An hour later they were stepping out of the *Pegasus* and walking across to the dark bulk of the Mothership.

They were distracted by a larger-than-usual mob of reporters and cameras, and the line of vehicles on the access road spoke of many more.

With a sigh, Mia headed to the media tent, where the lucky accredited reporters already waited.

She stood at the podium a moment, and Hemi took his position at the tech support desk.

"I gather you have already heard about our little rescue. I am prepared to give you a basic outline. You understand that this is part of a criminal, perhaps terrorist investigation, so I can't give you much.

"A couple of hours ago, my transport, the GB *Pegasus*, was involved in a rescue operation off the coast of Libya. I wish to point out that our presence there was completely by chance. We were flying nearby and the authorities determined that we were the closest ship with the capability to act. At no time did I take part in the action. I was a spectator only."

She held up a hand to show she wasn't finished. "The story that emerged was that a group of protesters had boarded the mining ship. To do what, we don't know yet, but shots had already been fired, and it was important that we take action immediately.

"By the time we arrived, the attackers had control of the deck, and the captain and crew were forted up in the bridge area. We approached the helicopter pad on the aft deck and deployed four security operatives. We made radio contact, and our negotiator managed to persuade the perpetrators that the action was over. One of their number was harder to persuade than the others, and non-lethal technical force was required. We secured the prisoners and turned them over to Captain Pyotir Wosniak.

"Another point to clear up. Our negotiator was a member of my staff who is an officer in the Canadian Armed Forces. We can only be thankful that Canadian military personnel are well trained in a broad range of skills."

Once again, she halted their questions. "I know you want to hear about the objectives of the protesters, but I have no information, and I would prefer not to speculate. I am unhappy that I was drawn into what should have been a minor incident. My only solution is to say as little as possible, and I'm sorry, ladies and gentlemen, but I am going to retreat behind my usual statement.

"It is the policy of the Humanity Meld not to interfere in the activities and problems of members. It is especially important in the case of a developing relationship such as ours."

She grinned. "Be prepared, I'm going to go all 'history teacher' on you, as usual."

There was a low chuckle. The reporters were getting to know her.

"Earther experience, especially during the European Colonial Era, showed that, even with the most benign of motivation, the interference of a force with superior technology always ends in devastation for the victims.

"So, the Meld can give you limited access to technology that will help you solve your problems, and can answer any questions you may ask, but they may not instigate operations or give policy suggestions. Earthers must make their own decisions."

She glanced at her screen. "I have a question registered from the Reuters representative. Senor Valdez, your participation has been entertaining in the past. Would you like to pose your question?"

Again, the scattered chuckle. She and Valdez had locked horns several times, but always with mutual respect.

"Thank you, Ambassador Larsen. I wish to draw your attention to some new information we have been receiving, indicating that there are paths open to our society that we were not made aware of earlier."

"And I would answer you that some choices have already been made a long time in the past, and humanity has benefited. True, some old decisions deserve to be revisited in the light of new information." She frowned. "But some don't."

She rolled her enterpad. "I will finish my lesson with one thought. I think it was the Oracle at Delphi that made this observation.

"'Beware of prophets who tell you what you want to hear. They may be telling you what you want to hear.'"

She waited out the pause while they absorbed that. Then she gave a fake frown. "No, that was too transparent for Delphi. Perhaps it was Yogi Berra. He would have liked it, anyway."

She turned and left the podium, and her little party strode into the shade of the Mothership and up the loading ramp to the personnel hatch.

33. LEADERLESS

Nicolaus met them at the elevator door and motioned them to follow. He did not seem his usual calm self, and all his body language held an underlying stiffness.

He led them to their usual conference room and made sure they were comfortable. Nero provided coffee and tea and a selection of snacks that did not receive the attention they deserved.

It was inevitable. Mia's instincts took over, and she dove straight to the point.

"There's no sense beating around the bush, Nicolaus. The news isn't good. Give it to us."

He nodded. "Thank you for making this as easy as possible. There is one issue that I would like to be perfectly clear on before we proceed. Hemi, I need a quick lesson on Earth's stock market system. Can you give us an idea a nine-year-old can follow?"

"Sure." The boy popped up a holoframe and punctuated his lesson with graphics. His hands on the enterpad seemed as tuned to his voice as a singer at the piano. "Say your company needs capital to dig a gold mine. You sell shares. If the mine finds gold, the share price goes up. The investor sells the shares at the new price and pockets the difference. If the mine doesn't find ore, the shares go down, and everybody loses. It's a simple, self-regulating system."

"I'm with you so far. But I also know it's much more complicated. Can you explain that?"

"Business financing is only the basic layer. It covers about five percent of the shares in the stock market."

"What are the other shares?"

"There are many types, but most of them are called derivatives. The original shareholder is betting on the mine. If the mine wins, he wins. But the derivative shareholder is betting on the type of stock. He is betting that all gold shares will go up, in general. He doesn't care how your mine is doing. He cares about all gold mines."

"This person is basically gambling."

"Right. And in gambling, the house always wins. In this case, the 'house' is the uber-rich with the resources in infotech and cash to manipulate whole sections of the market. The losers are the small players that depend on traditional wisdom to make their choices." He paused for effect. "And the derivatives market is twenty times the size of the real market."

"So, the very rich have been fooling the poor for centuries. Why has it become a problem?"

"Because somebody is cheating even worse than usual. The whole operation is a house of cards based on the fiction that it's fair. Lately, someone is playing even less fair than usual. Sooner or later, their actions are going to cause people to stop believing in the stock market. Then it will crash, and the whole world economy will skid to a halt."

"Who would want to do such a thing?"

"Several possibilities. First, greedy people who see a way to make more money, and don't care about the consequences. Next, people that want the world in turmoil so they can gain political advantage."

"What kind of advantage?"

"*Pegasus* says right wing politicians prosper in times of trouble. People who are not usually greedy are forced to act selfishly to survive. It takes money, trust and cooperation to support a democracy."

Nicolaus nodded slowly, and the grace seemed to leave his body. "It all becomes clear. Earth's stock market is not a money management system. It is a gambling game. This has never happened before."

Mia nodded. "And now we know what the Merge Mercantile Caste agents have been doing."

"Allying with Earth's commercial interests and using their superior AI to affect the swings of the stock market and profit from them."

Nicolaus sighed. "The situation is exactly what we have been trying to avoid. The profit-taking of the Meld Mercantile Caste directly effects the lives of the poor."

Hemi shrugged with the nonchalance of the young. "From what I gather, it's always been that way."

"Exactly. And that's why we confidently expect the stock market to be replaced soon by one of the other models available."

"I've been looking at them." Mia spread her hands helplessly. "They seem very logical."

He smiled. "Surprise, surprise."

Mia regarded her mentor. "So, Nicolaus. You have put it off as long as possible. What has happened while we were away?"

"What you have just told me confirms the conclusion we have come to." He sighed. "The Mothership and I have misjudged the enemy. We considered a stock market to be an anachronism, soon to be tossed aside like the bitcoin mining scam was, and replaced by a more equitable distribution of funds. We had no idea of the stock market's function as a gambling venue, nor of its vulnerability to manipulation. Nor did we expect such a powerful intervention of our Mercantile Caste. All together, these factors have created a perfect storm that could destroy Earth's economy."

She frowned. "So, what happens now?"

"The Mothership has made a decision. Our mistake has endangered the whole operation. We must withdraw from our positions."

"What...?"

"The Mothership was never intended for this sort of work. She is a scientific research vessel, and will return to those duties."

"I don't understand."

"My career is over. I was trained for this duty, and I can no longer do it."

"But that's ridiculous. You can't quit in the middle of such an important project."

"Nonetheless. The Mothership and I agree. All indications are that we have proved ourselves incapable of performing this duty to the satisfaction of the Meld. Others must take over."

She frowned. "But what happens to you?"

He shrugged. "That is neither here nor there."

"Not to me, it isn't! I don't understand your employment system, but from what I can see, you have dedicated your life to this project. Where will you go?"

"Back to Gliese."

"And then what?"

His shrug was even more expressive, indicating reluctance, acceptance, and sorrow. "To understand, you need to know how our employment works. How our lives work."

"All right. Tell me."

"Fine. Our people live around a hundred Earth years. Students who show potential are streamed into the Diplomatic Service at the age of fifteen. By twenty, the best have been selected. They board a ship for Sol. It takes a little over twenty years to get here from Gliese.

"I know that leaving your family forever at that age sounds traumatic by Earther standards, but remember; Glieseans function socially around cadres. They spend their travel time going to school and developing the cadres that will do their work when they reach Sol. Actually, there is a transition. They start by learning what they need to know and showing their aptitudes. By the half-way point, they have chosen their life project, and they spend the next ten years planning it. Once they get here, they spend thirty or forty years completing their project.

"They are now about seventy years old, and it is time to return home. They spend their return journey spreading their lifetime of knowledge. Teaching, discussing, writing. But not always. Those who are not of a pedagogical nature may indulge a hobby or other pastime. In any case, they return home at ninety years of age, honoured and accomplished, and spend their final years in comfort."

He sighed again. "Of course, for a failed worker, it is not that simple. I will probably be given the duty of teaching the beginners and those less able. I will still enjoy an honourable retirement. But it is honourable failure."

Mia frowned. "They can't punish you for the rest of your life for one mistake!"

"Oh, it isn't punishment. The Meld still recognizes my years of service. But my value is undermined by my failure."

"After the thrill and sense of accomplishment of your work, it sounds like a death sentence, to me."

"That option is also open."

"What!" She shot to her feet. "You wouldn't! You can't!"

He waved a negative hand. "I didn't say I would. But it is quite possible, should I choose it. Our people have a more open attitude than yours about the right to die."

Something clicked in her mind. She began to pace the room. "Well, you're not going to do anything stupid. If you won't help yourself, somebody else has to." She turned to the others in the room. "What are we going to do about this?"

What you are now doing. It was the Mothership's full voice. She frowned. "What's that?"

Taking charge. The onus of this project falls on your shoulders. "Me? But..."

There is no doubt about it. You are the person who has the most experience with the situation. The project will continue, but with

Flying Wing GBP as lead sentience. You have been acting for some time as liaison for Pegasus, as you call him. You have taken over most of the duties of the Project Head. You are the face of the project in the minds of Earthers."

"I am?"

A deep chuckle. *Your performance in Vienna was worthy of world-wide notice. And mostly approval, you should know. The people of the Earth know what they want, but they don't have the knowledge or the power to get beyond the selfish shell of commercialism that keeps them from it. You are seen by many as that person who can represent them at the tables of the powerful.*

Her mind was whirring. "But how do we manage this? You can't just dump me on the unsuspecting population of Earth and walk away. There has to be some sort of handover. A transition period..."

Nicolaus smiled sadly. "Don't worry about that . There is no ship returning to Gliese for a year or so."

Relief coursed through her. "You'll still be here. I can ask you for advice...touch base once in a while..."

"I may not be here, but I will be available, yes."

"Believe me, I will take advantage of that." She sat down at her enterpad and took a few deep breaths. "So, how do we manage the handoff?" She pulled up a schedule. "There is a regular meeting of the Earth League Committee tomorrow at the European Space Agency offices in Paris. Shall we do it then?"

"If you wish, tomorrow I will introduce you as the new face of the Meld."

"Perfect. Well, not perfect. I'm still not happy about this. But good enough for the moment while we settle into our roles."

34. CHANGING OF THE GUARD

This time *Pegasus* slipped into Paris with no fuss. They arrived at four in the morning and parked in a football stadium three blocks from the ESA Offices on Avenue de Lowendall, right next door to the UNESCO headquarters. It was a "Modernist" building of aluminum and glass from a hundred years ago, and stood out among the much older architecture of the neighbourhood.

This was friendly territory; once they had passed security, their guards disappeared, and they made their own way to the Assembly Room. Mia had timed it so most of the delegates were already in their seats. Hemi bee-lined it to the media control board and slipped into the empty chair with a casual nod to the tech standing by.

Chairman Ericsson crossed the room to them, and he and Nicolaus had a quiet chat as they moved to their places. As they seated themselves, the chairman leaned over to Mia for a brief handshake and a nod. Then he went to the podium.

At this signal the room quieted. "Gentlefolk all, before I call the meeting to order for our usual business, I have a presentation from Ambassador Gliese, informing us of the progress of the project and some subsequent personnel changes. Nicolaus?"

Gliese stood at his place and spoke without raising his voice. Mia glanced over to see Hemi working the sound controls.

"Thank you, Chairman Ericsson. I have asked to address your combined meeting because we have reached a key point in this process, one you and I have discussed. It is time for the Glieseans to step back. The public face of the Humanity Meld must be an Earther, and I am happy to turn those duties over to the person who has been working as my troubleshooter, Mia Larsen. I'm sure all of you are aware of her reputation, and many of you have already conferred with her."

He scanned the table and smiled. "And having made that announcement, anything I say from here on would be infringing upon her territory, so I will turn the meeting over to her."

He sat down, and she strode — firmly she hoped — to the podium to a spatter of polite applause. And a murmur of surprise.

"Thank you, gentlefolk all. I'm glad to see the familiar faces in this group, even several from my last project, the Habitat for Humanity. Let me put you in the picture as to what has been going on.

"Our present problems may make it seem an unsuitable time to be changing personnel, but it is quite possible to turn this to our advantage. There are two timelines, here. The first is the schedule that the Meld experts have created to optimize the chances of making this joining of our societies as painless and positive as it can be. It cannot be obeyed rigidly, because of the second timeline: the facts of life as they are unfolding around us."

"Excuse me!" The strident voice cut through the quiet of the chamber.

The name 'Johan Lange' appeared in her biomem. She turned to face him.

"Yes, Representative Lange. What concern of yours is so important that you wish to inflict it on everyone, outside the order of the meeting and the conventions of good manners?"

"I am wondering why we should listen to you at all. Here we sit, the most powerful men in the world, asked to accept the leadership of a traitor and her half-breed spawn, who, for all we know, are drawing us even deeper into their socialist net of half-truths."

She regarded him a moment. "Is that all?"

"Isn't it enough?" He faced her in an aggressive stance,

"Fine. You had the right to speak your piece. That does not give you the right to hijack the time of all these polite individuals who are willing to wait their turn. Please sit down or leave."

He stared around the room once, and seeing no support, looked around a second time, less firmly. He sat.

She pointed to a side screen. "And in pursuit of complete transparency, perhaps the other members would be interested in the activities of your "arm's-length" holding companies during these latest swings of the stock market."

He shrank in his seat, trying not to meet anyone's eyes.

"I'm sorry, but I do need to address one point from this regrettable interruption. I truly hope none of you consider yourselves the most powerful people in this world. Our real strength is in finding ways to work together. The true power is wielded by the democratic nations we represent, both in the Meld and on Earth." She waited a moment, but no one chose to respond.

"As I was saying, we have the chance to turn this situation to our advantage. Look at the real-life timeline. Right now, world stock markets are more volatile than usual. I'm sure some of us would like to blame that on the influence of the aliens, but if you check the progress of the larger exchanges over the last year..." The graph showed on the screen behind her. "There was an initial panic when our visitors first appeared, but it soon stabilized."

She flicked her fingers, and another graph appeared. "If you look closer at recent events, you may notice that there was another flutter in the metals index seven months ago. The following month, real estate took a brief dive, then recovered. Three weeks later, it was energy, and others soon followed. These spikes were out of step with the rest of the market and with any of the usual factors. They just happened. Three months ago, the whole economic system wavered. Three times, and for no apparent reason.

"Now, those of you familiar with the market understand that it is not susceptible to the simplicity of Occam's Razor. There are too many factors to consider." She looked around the table. "Impossible for human minds to handle, even with the computing power available to us.

"However, let us look at it from a different perspective. Pare all of these changes down to one single variable. What if someone is using a superior amount of computing power to manipulate the stock markets of the world?"

She waited out the surprised hum.

"Suddenly it all fits together, doesn't it? The small trial runs, the sudden surges. If you want further data," another screen appeared, "one of my associates, aided only by the ExIn on Flying Wing *Pegasus*, was able to clear over two hundred thousand euros on the third swing last week. Needless to say, those profits will be donated to UNESCO.

"But the inference should be clear. There have been complaints for years that the stock market favours certain people over the rest of us. It has been charged that people with superior information sources and deeper pockets have an edge.

"This data indicates that the forces that have been profiting from the stock market all along have recently gained an added advantage and are milking it for all they're worth for as long as they hold that advantage. Yes, Chairman Ericsson?"

"I'm sure I speak for everyone here when I ask you what we are doing about this."

"We have completed the first two steps. We identified the problem. Today, I made it public. The third step will take longer. We need to create ways to counter these swings when they happen." She raised a hand to stop the growing protests.

"We are hampered, as all governments are, by the necessity of staying withing the legal limits. For example, we could simply ignore all the wisdom of the last hundred years and put together a supercomputer that could outthink any machine on the planet."

She paused to let them think. "I hope ideas like 'supercerb' and 'arms race' are floating around in your heads. We cannot act in panic, here. We have identified the problem, and our experts are working on solutions."

She paused and signalled Hemi to wipe the screens. "All this data has been made available to you on the Committee LAN. It is our advice that you continue the work that you have been doing. A small bump in the economic system shouldn't deter us from our original objective: the equitable merging of Earth's economy into that of the rest of Humanity, so that some time, fifty or a hundred years in the future, we will become equal members of the Meld.

She raised empty hands. "And that is all I have for you today. I will return the meeting to Chairman Ericsson and stand by for any comments you may wish to direct to me."

She resumed her seat and spent the next hour answering questions. As the meeting went on, she realized that she did know more about the operations than any of the governors, even the Gliesean ones, and if she didn't, the information would automatically appear in the heads-up vision of her biomem.

The result was that the meeting settled and turned to more mundane matters, and she was able to retreat to her usual observation mode, getting to know the individual members and speculating as to their motivations and preferences.

35. EXPERT

But that afternoon she asked Hemi and *Pegasus* to simplify all the schedules and side projects Athena had sent her and put it into one graphic. She sat at her workstation on *Pegasus* and stared at it in horror.

"What am I supposed to do with this?" She outlined the stock market section in red. "Yesterday, this is what I had to deal with. It was a key issue, but it looked manageable.

She zoomed the red patch outward until the whole, huge screen was red. "And today, this is what I've got. I don't even know where to start!"

She turned to Jean. "Look at it. Nicolaus was picked from birth to run this. He's some kind of organizational genius with twenty years of training. I'm only a public relations hack. I don't have that kind of smarts."

The pilot cocked his head and regarded her. "I'm not so sure about that."

"Well, I am." The enormity of her position felt like a weight, pushing down on her chest, making it hard to breathe.

He regarded her. "I tell you what. It's getting late, and you're looking definitely frazzled. Let's tidy this up and go for a run. That'll put it all in perspective."

She nodded and closed her screens. "Give me a moment to change."

"Take all you need."

When she met him at the boarding ramp, he tossed her a small bundle. "Looks like rain."

She opened it and shook out what looked like a fleece hoodie. It felt light and soft in her hands, and the colours seemed to change as it wrinkled. "What is it?"

"Mirror camo."

"What's that?"

"Meld tech. The fabric picks up the colour of anything near you. It doesn't make you disappear, but you don't stand out in a crowd. Especially useful in security situations. They call it the sniper's nightmare. Step into a crowd of uniforms and you blend right in."

"And do I need this right now?"

"Not especially, although it's better to be safe than sorry, with your higher level of publicity." He grinned as he slipped his own on. "Added advantage is that it's breathable, water-repellent, wicks sweat away, and...here." He held out his arm. "Punch."

She frowned and aimed a jab at his bicep. "Ouch! Have you got armour under that?"

"Nope." He batted the hem of his jacket and it stiffened. "It's called shear-thickening material. Anything hits it at high speed and it hardens in microseconds. It'll stop a .45 calibre bullet."

She rapped her knuckles on her chest. Sure enough, she could hardly feel it. "What are these thicker bands?"

"They run perpendicular to your ribs and form a cross pattern that makes your chest cavity twice as resistant to a crushing force. In case of a fall or getting hit by a car, you know?"

She smoothed the fabric. "I can't believe anything so soft can do all that."

"Let's hope you never test it out." He flipped up his hood. "Except for the waterproof part. Let's go."

They started at a medium trot and soon picked it up to the ground-covering lope they often cruised at. The rain gusts came and went, but she found herself still warm and dry.

"Not your usual chatty self, this afternoon."

She flipped the water off her sleeve. "I appreciate the try, Jean, but it didn't work. That spreadsheet keeps cycling through my brain. How can I be expected to make this sudden jump in status?"

"I'm not sure. Maybe you think you should take on more responsibility than you really need to."

She clenched her fists. "Look, I'm supposed to be pretty good at this sort of stuff, aren't I? Understanding the real story underneath the hype, massaging it all to make it work out." She stopped and stared at him. "And I can't get it out of my head that Gliese and Athena have ducked out before the crap hits the fan and left me to clean up the mess!"

"And this is the point where I'm supposed to take you in my arms and you lay your head on my shoulder and sob it all out?"

"What?"

"You know. The breaking point. It's supposed to happen when you've tried your best and it's all going wrong. And here you are, falling apart and you haven't even started yet."

"What?"

"You've got all the problem-solving skills. Even I know how it's done. First step, you determine the scope of the problem. Second step, you break down in tears, right?"

She shot him her best frown. "You're a real ass, aren't you?"

He grinned and shrugged. "Shoot the messenger. At least that's better than falling apart at the seams." He motioned her to keep running. "Come on, Champ. What's the next step?"

"I don't...oh. Yes. Line up your resources."

"So, do it."

She snorted. "Here we are. A sapience that isn't smart enough for the job. A fifteen-year-old tech wizard with his heart in the right place. Oh, yes, and a pilot with nothing to fly....wait a minute. Mail from Chairman Ericsson."

She checked her tri-me. "Oh, great. The Christian Democratic Union in Germany has declared their opposition to the pact. Damnit! Nicolaus was dealing with them. I know absolutely nothing about the CDU except that they have a serious following, and the Social Democrats are holding onto power by the skin of their teeth and a coalition with one small far-left party. Who am I going to send to talk to them?"

"Who's the obvious one?"

"Nicolaus, of course."

"Then send him."

"I can't. He fired himself."

"From the leadership position. Now, you're the leader. The way I see it, he has to do what you say."

She stared at him. "That's right. He only resigned from the committee yesterday. He could go over there and swing his weight around, and no one would know the difference."

She sketched a quick note.

See the attached file. These boys are your babies. Please go straighten them around.

She hit "Send," and it was done.

To her surprise, the answer was immediate.

Transport?

Take one of the Wings.

Fine. Back tomorrow.

And that was all.

She regarded Jean. "Don't look so smug. We've got fifteen forest fires, and we only stamped out a spark."

"Every little bit counts."

She huffed in exasperation. "Look, Jean, I know you have all sorts of confidence in me and all that, but one thing I don't need is a loopy-doopy mental fitness trainer. I need people who can do stuff. And the first person I need to know about is you." She stopped and gave him the full force of her glare. "When we get back to *Pegasus*, we are going to sit down for a formal meeting and have this out."

"Okay." He turned and began to run again.

Well, that's not what I expected. She sprinted to catch up.

36. EXPERT AT...WHAT?

Only Hemi was present in the main cabin of the wing, and he was deep in his VR headset. She took a seat and pointed to the chair opposite. "Sit."

Jean obeyed, giving her his polite interest.

Her frown stifled his smile. "You're here on your own agenda. Nicolaus and I agreed that you had something up your sleeve and you'd tell me when I needed to know. Well, in my humble opinion — which, you will note, is no longer so humble — it's time to fish or cut bait. Give."

'You figure I have another talent."

"Right; you can read minds. This is serious, Jean. The Mothership has something planned. She can't tell us what, but it's going to need Canadian expertise. You're the only Canadian in the inner circle. What are you? A robotics expert, I suppose."

The smile returned. "That's what we hoped everybody would think."

"And you're going to tell me I'm wrong? There's going to be a whole lot of disappointed people out there." She shook a warning finger. "Very bad for PR."

"Not if I'm an expert in something else."

"Such as?"

A bored voice interrupted. "Sentience."

They turned to Hemi. "How did you come to that conclusion?"

He waved a hand to one of his holo frames. "While you two've been playing courting games, I did some checking. He's one of Canada's top AI programmers."

She turned to regard him. "And you're out here trying to drum up business for your skills."

"That's one of my objectives, yes."

She slapped her forehead. "So, all that time we were travelling, Olivier was there to protect you, not me."

He bobbed his head left, then right. "Well, both of us, I suppose."

"So, Mister Expert, is there an application for your skills in the present crisis?"

He shrugged, holding up empty hands. "If Athena didn't think so, I wouldn't be on board. She hasn't seen fit to tell us what, though."

"Sounds like the Mothership, all right. Why doesn't she just come out and tell us?" She waved both hands in negation. "I know. Can't tell the natives what to do. They have to solve their own problems."

Hemi grinned as he set his phones aside. "But that all falls down, doesn't it?"

"In what way?"

"She's telegraphed our next move. Whatever Jean is good at is our solution."

"And his specialty would have to be Swarm Sapience."

The boy looked puzzled. "But the closest swarm is four light years away, exploring the Alpha Centauri System."

The pilot froze, one hand in the middle of a gesture. His face worked, and she could see thoughts forming.

"What? What is it?"

He relaxed. "May I give you a small lesson in history?"

She tossed up her hands. "Any data that applies..."

"Fifty years ago, Canada made a choice. We were a world leader in robotics technology. The Microship Swarm involved a great jump in technology, and a similar development in computing power. The robotics part was right up our alley, and we went for it. NASA built the Swarm, but mostly to our designs. We have been improving the sapience of the swarm for the last forty years. The original Swarm is still using 2030 nanotech, but with 2070 programming, it can transform itself to 2070 equivalence.

"We started building them ourselves, modifying them for all sorts of uses. Of course, we don't call them microships, but that's what they are, and everybody knows it.

"Then the Meld arrived, and we were stuck with our reputation. We have built almost three hundred units in various formats— some sold, some stockpiled, a few still in the factory — but the negative response of the galactic community has dried up our market."

She nodded. "I already knew most of that. I worked for NASA, remember? But your point is that Canada has a bunch of microships stored all over the place, waiting to be used. Where are they, and what good are they?"

He pointed, and Hemi put up a new graphic. "We have twelve of our own in Medium Earth Orbit. One of them took those images of the Mercantile ship landing. It only requires six to cover the globe from that altitude, but we have a multi-level research program that requires six as experimental subjects at different altitudes, and six at uniform height as a control group. These are configured as full microships, with propulsion and communications as primary objectives. We also use them to practise remote design modification." He grinned. "Feedback comes faster when you're not four light years apart."

"And are they linked?"

"Only for communication. Their intelligence at this moment is geared towards self-modification."

"Could they all be re-programmed to work together?"

"In theory, yes. From the beginning of the program, we have limited their ability to merge intelligence to a maximum of six ships for security reasons. But all along we've been working on creating a larger mass. We'd love to try, but we don't dare."

"But you could."

"If we sit down with *Pegasus* and go through our programming, we can find the danger spots and iron them out.

Athena already pointed us in the right direction when she analyzed the NASA system in Noah's ExIn Sphere."

"How long would this take?"

"Well..."

She regarded him. It was the first time she had ever seen the self-confident pilot uncertain. It came to her. "You've already started, haven't you?"

"You understand, this was all a 'just in case' scenario. We have six micros on every Canadian Navy ship from the Kingston Class coastal patrol ships on up. That's thirty ships. At the moment, those units are designed specifically for communications."

"But...?"

He fidgeted. "To give you an idea how dangerous this is, I believe it would be possible for a group of six to configure themselves into a self-propelled atomic bomb. They're already running on atomic power."

"And who's providing the interface with *Pegasus*? You, of course. You're Canada's sapience expert." She nailed him with a pointing finger. "And you're also an advisor to certain parliamentary committees I could mention."

He frowned in thought. "You Googled me."

"I did better than that. I sicced *Pegasus* on you. Found out all sorts of useful dirt." She rounded on Hemi. "Like I did for you. Where do you fit in, these days?"

"Leave the kid out of it. He's in training. And doing very well, mind you."

"And interfacing with the Mothership, I suppose."

It was Hemi's turn on the defensive. "She has to monitor the process. We're skating very close to the edge of interference with a developing culture."

"Point taken. Where are the rest of the microships?"

"Scattered around in various places." Jean shrugged. "We have a six-pack on the Habitat, for example."

"What for?"

"I'm not sure on that one."

"One moment. *Pegasus*, what time is it in Houston?

Eleven am.

"Connect with Noah, please, and ask him about the Canadian Microships on the Habitat."

One moment please...He sends back this reference.

She entered the numbers into her biomem, and a document appeared on her heads-up.

"Okay, I have it. They're temporarily designated as auxiliary memory buffers, but they're configured like you said, with propulsion and multiple com systems. And...a selection of coring and excavating tools, to function as retrievable probes for scientific research and mining exploration."

"That sounds right." Jean shrugged. "They wouldn't be much use to us. They're far enough away that the time delay would foul up the processing. But I think we have enough without them."

"Fine. We use the ones we have at hand. But they're spread all over the globe. Isn't that a problem?"

"If you want to join them all together in a supercerb, it's a problem. The speed that sort of computer works at, even the microsecond lag for radio waves to circle the globe would throw it all into chaos. It's not possible."

He jumped to his feet and started pacing. "But maybe not. Maybe not."

He returned and threw himself into the chair facing her. "Okay, let's talk computing power. We don't need to control the whole market. Just enough to see the swings coming and counter them."

"Athena can play no part in this, and she is the only sapience with enough power to do what you suggested."

"*Pegasus* is our only Sapience?"

"And according to Athena, he doesn't have enough power."

"What if he had some help?"

"I don't know. What kind of help?"

"The kind that doesn't merge with his sapience. There are close to a hundred stock markets in the world at the moment. What if we had a single intelligence designated to monitor each one of them, with enough intellect to do the calculations, reporting to *Pegasus*, who only has to corelate the data. We could have a real-time running report of the whole economic system at all times. We'll use the dozen or so we can gather together in one place to merge with *Pegasus* to give him more accurate prediction power.

"That stays within Canadian security parameters. I'm not sure the Meld experts will agree."

"Why are we sitting here?" She jumped to her feet. "Let's get this baby organized."

37. SET UP

They worked for several hours, until Jean leaned back and stretched. "Are you aware of the time?"

"Oh. Best we quit. Early morning tomorrow."

He wandered over to the cupboard and poured two short drinks.

As he handed her the glass, he held on a moment to get her attention. "You know we've been set up, don't you?"

She shrugged. "The thought had occurred to me."

She was getting used to these after-work chats. When they were relaxed their minds worked in harness, sometimes quite productively. She took a sip and leaned back to look up at him. "You think Nicolaus and the Mothership want to turn it all over to Earthers, and this "failure" is just an excuse?"

"Friar Ockham would think so."

"But that doesn't change anything. We're still operating on their timeline, based on their intelligence."

"And we all agree it's the right thing to do."

"So where is this famous 'Earther choice' Nicolaus keeps quoting?"

She drew a quick sketch of a man trying to lead a reluctant donkey and posted it on a viewscreen. "Who's leading?"

"Apart from the fact that it's a rather ugly donkey, I get the point. The human is not very successful, but he's still leading."

"I like donkeys better than I draw them. How about this?" She sketched a dog tugging at its leash, towing its owner along.

"The human is holding the dog back, but the dog is still in charge of the direction."

"Which format do we want?"

He nodded slowly. "As long as we hold back and complain, they're still in charge."

"Exactly. This is Earth's problem, and if we're going to solve it, we have to take the initiative. We still take their advice, but how we go about it is ours to decide."

"Scary but logical."

She dusted her hands together. "So. We're learning to be good little citizens of the Merge, we use Merge techniques."

"How do you mean?"

"Cadres. They do all their projects with cadres, and they've given this project to me. In that case, my cadre is going to solve it."

He grinned. "You're back on the topic of our human resources."

"Right. At the moment, that's only you and Hemi. Plus Noah, Fiona, Nicolaus and Athena as outside resources. But I need more for my inner circle. Officially assigned. *Pegasus*, has Nicolaus left for Bonn yet?"

He's in the air.

"Get him onscreen, please. Three-way with Athena."

Two screens appeared, side by side.

"Greetings, Athena and Nicolaus. I have need of your services."

We are always here to help.

"That's handy, because I want to include you both in my cadre for this project."

That we cannot do, Mia. We have been disqualified for that function.

"That's right. You've been taken off the job, correct, Nicolaus?"

"The Mothership and I agreed."

"The Mothership and her mentor no longer function. That leaves Nicolaus Gliese and Athena as free agents. I'm used to working with a technician and his ExIn. So I'm creating a team. You'll have to do until something better shows up."

"You're joking. You can't do that."

"Athena?"

Yes, Mia.

"Am I allowed bring you and Nicolaus into my cadre for the duration of these negotiations?"

I calculate your chances of success without us at thirty-two percent.

"And with you on board?"

Depending on the strength of our antagonists, around seventy-three.

"And you are allowed to do this, but you couldn't suggest it."

That is correct.

"What is your hourly rate?"

A Gliesean sentience has an exaggerated sense of duty. The pride of a job well done is usually our only requirement.

A thought struck Mia. "It must have been very difficult for you to accept failure."

It was exceptionally disorienting.

"All right. Everything rolls on as usual. Nothing has changed, except our chain of command. Athena, are you now less disoriented?"

I am eager to start.

"Good, because we have a few problems to solve…"

38. HEMI'S CADRE

The first problem showed up the next morning

She was wrestling with a 3-D spreadsheet listing their objectives from various points of view when Jean came in and stood looking over her shoulder, silent.

"Whoever invented these things was a sadist." After a moment, she turned to regard him. "You don't look happy either. What's up?"

He pulled up a chair. "I told you it wouldn't take long. Our Microship programming has been upgraded and is flawless to the best of Meld safety standards. But Athena and *Pegasus* agree. If we join all those sapiences together, we have crossed a line. We must have the usual Meld safeguards."

"Not an unexpected development. What's the key issue?"

"No sapience can be allowed to join a supercerb without its own private mentor."

"We're allowed to use your Microships in our supercomputer, but each one must have a human monitor to control the moral judgements of the gestalt?"

"In a nutshell. And one of the criteria at that level is the mentor has to be able to recognize certain flaws and reprogram the sapience if required."

She swore softly. "And we can't go looking for loopholes, because we agree with the original premise."

Hemi gave one of those "I'm over here listening" coughs.

"Yes, Hemi? Any ideas?"

"Umm...you know that game I play online? The one you're always razzing me about?"

Jean gave Mia a quizzical look. "Yes."

"You should watch me play it."

Mia frowned. "You want us to break off a serious discussion to watch you play a video game."

"It might be worth your while."

The two adults shared a glance. "All right. Fire it up."

"Sit over here and put on a headset."

Soon they were all in the same virtual world, and the game environment spread around them. As far as Mia could tell, it was a fairly basic space battle setting, with a larger-than-usual operator's screen.

Jean made an uncertain "Hmm…" but that was all.

The game started. Again, it was a standard ship-point-of-view blast-em-up, and soon the space around them was full of vessels: friends and enemies. The only part she could really understand was that the enemy ships were huge juggernauts, while Hemi's vessels were all small and maneuverable.

As the conflict intensified, the only difference she could see from other games of its type was that Hemi seemed to spend more time on his control console, rather than piloting his ship.

Suddenly Jean gave an exclamation. "What are you doing?"

"What?"

"A moment…there! See that?"

Hemi's ship was now double in size, and a copilot sat in an accel couch beside him.

Jean's voice cracked. "You reprogrammed your ship."

"That's right. I merged with my partner."

The pilot tore off his VR headset and grabbed the boy's shoulder. "Where did you find that game?"

Mia got her set off in time to see Hemi slip from his own harness and stare at the hand on his shoulder. "I made it up."

Jean took his hand away and waved it towards the main screen. "But you were using the programming language we created to handle the microships. It's top-secret. You can't spread that all over!"

"Nicholaus allowed it. Who's going to argue with him?"

It was time for her to step in. "Jean, you're fighting a battle that was lost several months before anybody realized it would have started. What do you think happens to all the patents that Earther scientists and engineers have invented when it turns out the Meld discovered them five hundred years ago?"

"What...? Oh. I see what you mean."

'You can hardly trash the kid for passing on something that will be public knowledge in six months."

"Okay, okay. It was just a shock to see my top-secret project all over the Nets."

"It isn't all over the Nets." Hemi swept his hand across his enterpad, and a list came up on the screen. "It's a cadre of programmers and hackers who were carefully selected and vetted. A couple of hundred of them. They all think I'm a junior member."

"What's done is done. How can we use it to our advantage?"

Hemi sniffed. "Piece of cake. All these people are a coupla steps away from programming a Microship. *Pegasus* does a sweep of the game roster and decides which ones can be trusted. I bet half of them are military. A couple of them are NASA. I've been watching those two, because there's always a chance they were watching me." He grinned. "Noah's on the list. He doesn't know I'm running it, but he's very suspicious. He's playing along, hoping to find out more. You oughta tell him before he blows the whistle on us at NASA."

Mia dropped her hands in her lap in disgust. "Nicolaus knew all along we were going to need those programmers. I feel like someone in a time-travel novel. I have to guess the next step, because it has already happened, and I have to do it exactly the same way again or else the world crumbles."

Jean sat back in his chair. "Up to now, we've guessed right. Let's get at it."

39. A GOOD PENSION PLAN

The next stumbling block took three days to show up.

Mia had no expertise in the level of programming they needed, so she filled her time with the myriad of details her new job required. However, she continued to look in on the programmers. When their work ground to a halt, she was ready. She strolled over to Jean's side of the room where he and Hemi were staring at their screens, frowns on their faces.

"Success?"

Jean nodded slowly. "So far so good. We have the ability to perceive a manipulation as soon as it starts." He grinned. "Before it starts, actually. That kind of operation requires cooperation across the board, but there's always a few greedy ones who jump the gun and start early. We keep a closer eye on them."

"Great. What now?"

His expression sobered. "If we're going to bet in the stock market game, we have to ante up. We know where and when we need to act, but we simply don't have enough money to affect the market to any degree. It takes a large amount of leverage to move this gigantic weight. Where are we going to get that?"

"Let's throw a bigger team at this. *Pegasus*, please set up a conference with Nicolaus."

Soon the Gliesean's face appeared on the screen, and she outlined the problem for him.

He nodded. "Let's look for positives. It can't all be the World Wild West out there. What factors tend to stabilize the system? Can we tie in with some of those, whoever they are?"

"The people who aren't gamblers." She shrugged. "The ones who want to make their investments pay a little, but on dependable basis."

"Surely there aren't enough mom-and-pop investors for our purposes, and how would we get them to work together?"

"Hemi, you're our expert these days. Who makes their money on large investments at low rates?"

"There are different areas of the market with different levels of risk. Similarly, there are different customers who are willing to accept different levels. So, for example, a stable country like Germany issues government bonds, which grow in value very steadily at a slow rate. A large investor like the pension fund of a big union will buy the safer bonds because they are risking the retirement of their members."

"How big are they? Can you give us some examples?"

A graphic appeared. "The Japanese Government Pension Investment Fund has upwards of ten trillion Euros invested in the market. The South Korea National Pension has about one trillion. Even a little country like Norway has two trillion invested. If you add in California's state pensions, America has 1.5 trillion as well."

She met Jean's glance. "Do these extreme fluctuations affect the pension plans?"

"The downside for these funds is that they base their actions on the accepted model of the market. If stocks that are traditionally safe become vulnerable, these pension funds will have to sell them or move to a higher risk factor, and soon they won't bring in enough profit to pay out their pension commitments."

"So, we have a bloc of big investors whose strategy depends on small, reliable returns on huge investments. These swings must be giving them the heebie jeebies."

Mia gave a wry grin. "It sounds counter-intuitive, but our best allies are in the most conservative segment of the market."

He nodded slowly. "They've got trillions invested, they're dependent on consistent returns, and they're in it for the good of their members."

"Right. And they're getting trashed on these swings, because their kind of investments don't lead to quick flips. If we contact them through their government regulating agencies and promise to settle things down, they'll jump at the chance."

She called up a new holoframe. "Who are we looking at, *Pegasus*."

Here's a list of all the pension schemes in all the stock markets, and the amount each has invested. Biggest at the top.

She scanned the list.

"Where's Russia?"

Let me see...oh. This is interesting.

"What?"

Give me a moment...yes. The Russians never learn. Vladmir Putin used up their old fund fighting the Ukraine. They worked their way back up to 200 billion Euros, but now, they're using their stocks to capitalize the Mercantile efforts.

"But Russia is on record as supporting the Committee."

"It wouldn't be the first time that country dealt with both sides for their own gain."

"Their loss this time." She dusted her hands together. "How are we going to swing this?"

* * *

Soon they had a plan together.

"Here's how it goes. *Pegasus* and Hemi keep up your information-gathering and analysis. Let us know when the fourth disturbance is starting. Meanwhile, Nicolaus will contact all the big pension funds — the ones with friendly governments, anyway — and give them a rough outline of the situation. Try to keep our plans under wraps; tell them that we have a handle on the next surge. When that happens, we give them advance warning. That's skirting the insider trading rules, but warning someone about a potentially illegal manipulation puts us on solid ground.

"After we show we can produce, we'll get more of them onside, and when the fifth surge happens, we can take positive action, maybe even ask our allies to invest in a counterbalance surge that will wipe out the actions of the Mercantile faction."

Jean nodded. "Meanwhile, I'll fast-track the training of the mentors, the programming of the microships and the transport of any that need to be moved." He shook his head slowly. "That's going to take a while, but as more and more of them come online, our computing power will grow and the other half of the program will speed up."

"This is going to be fun." Hemi started finger warmups. "Usually, the criminal element keeps thinking up new ways to cheat, and law enforcement has to play catch-up. This time we're the ones with the new ideas."

Jean shook his head. "This isn't going to be as easy as it sounds. It's going to take months, and I'm expecting setbacks."

"Of course. Any chance we could do a trial run on a smaller scale?"

Nicolaus frowned. "Our opponents have always done that, and we didn't notice it until afterwards."

"Hey, here's an idea. Let's start with the Vienna Stock Exchange. It provides the benchmark indexes for Austria and Central Eastern Europe."

"Yes, and can we target that bastard, Johan Lange?" Hemi's eyes were flashing. "We have a list of his investments. We should be able to flatline his profits completely."

Mia frowned. "Nothing I'd like better. But, *Pegasus*, is that legal?"

Part of the cut and thrust of business, Mia. Except for that two-day gap when Interpol discovered a suspicious meeting with Bernard Moser and two other possible conspirators, the data we have on Lange is all public knowledge. Not one line of insider information in the lot.

"Once we get that moving, we can move to a bigger exchange."

"What happens if they catch on?"

"They'll probably figure out there's manipulation, but we can diversify our purchasers all over the world, use blind trusts, and generally follow the usual techniques for commercial warfare."

40. STOCK MARKET WAR

May: Onset

"Mia?"

She glanced over at Hemi. His carefully developed Gliesean languor was missing. "What's got you in a lather?"

"It's started."

"The next surge? Already?"

"Pegasus says there's no question. Reports from nine different stock exchanges where we have microship monitors have indicated unusual trading patterns of the kind we expected."

"Hmm. And we have monitors on less than half the exchanges."

"That means there's probably twice as much action as we have found. The fourth surge is happening, Mia."

"Pegasus, we need the cadre on line for a meeting."

Nicolaus and Noah are on. Jean coming up...there he is.

Their faces appeared on the screens in front of her, and she outlined the situation. When she finished, there was silence. "Comments?"

Nicolaus shook his head. "We're not ready for this."

"We were never going to be. We're dealing with the stock market. You prepare to find yourself unprepared." She took a deep breath. "We have our plan. Set it in motion. You all know who to call and what to say. Any questions?"

There were none.

"Well, I don't know if that's a positive sign or a negative one. Good luck, everyone. Let's get at it."

Mid-May: Onslaught

Two weeks later, there was no doubt. At their evening wrap meeting, Nicolaus summed it up. "The usual volatility patterns are showing. Heavy buying in metals, construction, and commercial properties. Does that mean any change to our tactics?"

"Let them go." Mia shrugged. "That's where the Mercantiles should be putting their money. If they want to wage war on each other, turn them loose. Our job is to protect our allies. Stabilize the solid performers. Anything else?"

"I believe Hemi has something to report."

The boy shot Jean a dirty look. "I guess I do."

She waited. Something was going on between the two of them, but it wasn't up to her to solve it.

"I had to replace a few of my gamers."

"Can you be more specific?"

"Three of them. One couldn't write code fast enough. The other two didn't pass muster on deeper security checks. Could have been nothing, but Jean and I decided this was too important to let sentiment influence us. We had backups ready to go, and the change went smoothly."

"Any effect on the data stream, Jean?"

"The new personnel took a couple of days to get up to speed. My limited knowledge of statistical analysis says three questionables out of fifty-two staff is pretty normal. Given the makeup of our team, we should expect a fluid workforce."

"I dunno. Everybody's pretty keen on the job. I don't think we'll lose too many."

"Yes, morale is high, but we can't allow that to influence our decisions."

The boy grinned. "Which I believe I just said."

Jean's voice overrode her acerbic response. "How much can we tell the frontline people about the results?"

Mia shrugged. "*Pegasus,* is there any evidence we're making a difference?"

We are in the middle of a stock market frenzy, Mia. The rules of statistics went out the window last week.

"Then we put our heads down, our shoulders to the wheel, and slog on."

July: That's a Wrap

Nicolaus started the meeting this time. "Mia, you were distinctly cheerful when we talked earlier today. I suspect you have an announcement for us."

She posted the main data on the screen.

"The volatility is winding down. Fluctuations have receded to below our predicted thresholds. *Pegasus,* now that it's all over, how did we do?"

It is impossible to predict what would have occurred without our intervention, but the statistics look positive. See here?

A section of the graph lit up.

These are the companies that followed our lead. Their gains over the last six weeks are seven percent above a control group of randomly selected equivalent organizations.

Mia frowned. "I hate to sound uninformed, but is seven percent a significant difference?

Statistically, nothing to write home about. However, our companies experienced a net gain of four precent. The control sample had a net loss of three. Considering the ride we've just been on, there will be champagne flowing in certain boardrooms.

"I assume you're speaking metaphorically."

On Tuesday the Berkshire Hathaway Board ordered a dozen cases of Veuve Clicquot in preparation for this Friday's meeting.

"You're not serious."

I am not predisposed to jocularity in matters of statistical importance. This is the advantage of having Hemi and Jean's sentiences at my disposal. I have more information than ever before,

and as we refine our interactions, my interface with the microships becomes smoother. As their learning progresses, the data they send becomes more in synch with our needs.

"Can't argue with success. I'm glad our friends are happy."

Looking forward, I have other news as well. From Japan.

"Make our day."

Mizuho Financial Group/Dai-ichi Life are signing on for a limited test on the next surge. We've had an "interested" response from Nippon Life and a query from Nomura Holdings.

"We didn't even contact Nomura."

Nicolaus grinned. "Word gets around. Sometimes it's on the golf course, sometimes in the bedroom. Once you reach a certain level in the hierarchy, there's no such thing as insider information. And this kind of news is positive for all of them. They're using their own networks to spread our message.

"Great. We don't need these guys following like sheep. As long as they buy into our program, they can run their side any way they want."

Jean flicked a finger, and another graph lit up. "The main point is that this fluctuation is different from the others. It didn't go as high, and it lasted longer, mainly because it tapered off more slowly. Am I looking with rose-coloured glasses, or did our enemies find that their tricks weren't working as well, so they kept trying longer?"

That would be a reasonable supposition. The surge is over, and we have extra computing power available. We will gather data based on your assumption. It might give more information on who our major competition is and how they function.

"And once you've finished your champagne, remember that our latest predictions suggest a fifth surge in August. Our main tasks are to refine our techniques and get more financial weight onboard."

Nicolaus grinned. "I have been in touch with Chairman Ericsson. He has designated five of his senior staff to assist us in our marketing."

She allowed herself a smile. "We're on a roll, folks. Let's keep it up."

August: The Attack That Didn't Happen

"Nicolaus, sorry to bother you, but are you getting any action on the next surge?

"Not a peep. From my limited experience and Athena's extensive historical data, the market is bumbling along at its usual rate."

"Which is not what we predicted. Anything unexpected makes me nervous, and it makes our clients nervous as well. I've been preparing them for the next surge, and nothing is happening. They're starting to get antsy. I hope we haven't given anyone the impression that our methods are flawless."

She shook her head. "They're all experienced players in the market. They know better."

"But we're something new, and the kind of investors we're dealing with don't like change."

"At least it gives us more time. I'll ask the team to widen their scope a bit."

"Fine. Let me know if anything comes up."

"Of course."

Nothing happened for two weeks.

September: Counter Attack

"They're onto us."

Mia frowned at Nicolaus in the viewscreen. "What does that mean?"

"The next one is starting. I think."

"You think?"

"It looks like they're using a different approach."

Her senses quickened. "We knew this could happen. What?

"There's volatility, but also several direct attacks on our allies."

"What sort of attacks?"

"The usual dirty tricks: spreading rumours, short selling, heavy selling."

"But we have the resources to support them, don't we?"

"Yes, nobody's lost anything yet, but we've had two unions and a large pension fund back out. Too dangerous for them."

"But at least we know the surge is starting. The enemy has just been doing their homework."

Jean brought his screen into the meeting. "Stands to reason. They have their own sapience, remember? They know there's something going on. They'll be analyzing the market, looking for anomalies. Once this is over, we'll have to reassess all our techniques and either drop them or polish them up."

She nodded. "All right. The next surge is on. Inform everyone, and let's dig in."

Mid-September: Battered but Still in the Game

Champagne was the order of the day in the *Pegasus* workroom. Mia looked up at the light through her glass. "Well, we got out of that one with our shirts intact."

"Yeah, that was close." Hemi picked up a glass and glanced at Mia.

She nodded, and he poured himself a small drink.

Jean mimicked her toast. "I don't know. It might have been good in the long run."

Mia gave an unladylike snort. "I can't see how kicking off a worldwide recession could be good in the long run. It's going to take a while to get out from under that."

"Yes, but a lot of investors have been sitting on the fence." Nicolaus had regained his usual relaxed pose. "This will frighten some of them into our organization."

Mia couldn't help but frown. "But we're getting too big. We're an open secret already."

Nicolaus smiled knowingly. "Which is the nature of the game."

She sighed. "I know it; I don't have to like it."

Mid-October: Victory?

The next surge came late, lasted two weeks, then tapered off so quickly the cadre was left breathless.

"They tried it, and the moment it was clear it wasn't working, they quit."

"A feint. What were they doing with the other hand while we were worrying about the main attack? They'll be trying something that worked before, somewhere else. Check the Meld history of economic systems with Athena and cross-reference with present history."

Right on it, ma'am.

She suppressed a sigh and sat at her desk, flicking on a couple of screens. No sense letting everyone know how tired she felt.

Take a look at this, Mia.

She scanned the feed. "There's been some unusual activity on the Habitat for Humanity shares."

"Perhaps the political problems are a ploy to drive share prices down, and now they're buying them." Nicolaus leaned over her to stare at the screen, laying his hand on her shoulder. It felt comforting, and she let it stay there.

An unknown group paid $38 million to 11 companies in at least six countries to buy $300 million of Habitat stock. This made the deals illegal in all arenas, but they were well camouflaged. I am in the process of finding out what happened to those shares. Once we have *that data, I suggest we turn the file over to the appropriate authorities in the affected jurisdictions.*

Mia shook her head. "Go ahead. But their action would drive the price of Habitat stock up."

"Pegasus, give us the background. What might be going on?"

The usual objective is to drive the price down in order to buy it cheap and maximize profits at resale. The only reason to raise the price is to entice more of the stock onto the market. It requires a lot of money to do this, because once you start buying, the price rises even more.

"Are they trying to take over the Habitat?"

The normal way to take over a company is to make a bulk offer to the board of directors. In this case, the governments involved have no intention of giving the control of the Habitat to anyone. So, our opponents are trying a hostile takeover. The buyers go directly to the shareholders and offer higher and higher prices. Paying investors to buy at higher prices is one step more subtle than that more dangerous, and illegal. It costs more but is harder to trace.

Mia shook her head. "There's something wrong, here. There is no chance anyone can buy the Habitat outright without pouring so much money in that there would be alarm bells ringing in every government on the planet. There's something else going on. Keep digging, everyone."

41. HABITAT TAKEOVER

Two days later, they still had found nothing.

Hemi greeted Mia with a cup of coffee when she came into the workroom.

She took it, but regarded him before she sipped. "Is something going on?"

"It might be a celebration, but not quite."

She sat at her desk. "It's too early in the morning for me to understand that."

"Well, I set an alarm with *Pegasus* to let me know when Habitat stock stabilized. Six o'clock this morning there was a brief downturn, and it's been noodling around and not going anywhere since."

"But we can't celebrate because...? Right. It might mean our enemies have completed their objective."

"That's about it."

"And sooner or later we're going to find out what that objective was."

"And I doubt if we're going to like it."

Pegasus?

Good morning, Mia. Did you sleep well?

"Not particularly. I assume you are aware of the present conversation. Keep up with your analysis using the ideas we were discussing.

On it, ma'am.

* * *

The other shoe dropped at noon.

Randy Jones from the Habitat, ma'am.

"Hi, Randy. What's going on?"

"That's why I called you. What have you heard?"

She flipped the call onto the cabin speakers. "Nothing much. Oh, there was a news report about com problems. Solar flares, I thought."

"That's what they're telling us. Don't believe it."

She grinned. "Okay, I don't believe what the Consortium Board of Governors is telling the world. I believe you."

"Wait for it. The Board of Governors is no longer in charge. The election has been held, and the first thing the inductees did was cancel the old contract. They've made up a new set of Operating Orders, they call them. They say they're a democratically elected Board of Regents, and they have rejected the plans of the Habitat Consortium."

"How could they do that?"

"Well, they had the election, and they toted up all the votes from the staff, and they added in all the votes from the bonus shares, and the numbers came out with the dissidents ahead."

A cold suspicion was growing up her spine. "And is there any way of knowing how the bonus shares voted?"

"Yes, as it happens. They added them in last, and it changed the whole outcome."

"So, the bonus shares all voted for the dissidents."

"Can we be sure of that?"

"Simple statistics. Also, it fits with what's been going on in the stock market. What's their argument? What do they want?"

"I got hold of their manifesto. They say they are the citizens of an independent nation, and they don't want to be sent into outer space. They want to bring the Habitat back inside the orbit of the moon."

"You have to be joking!"

"Not a smile in the house. Here, I'll send you a copy."

"Thanks."

Hemi put the document up on the main viewscreen, and there was a tense silence while they read it.

Jean was the first to react. "This is all nonsense. It reads like a term paper by a first-year Poli-Sci student who just discovered Marxism. None of that stuff about democracy has anything to do with the situation."

Mia shook her head. "Let's take this seriously. Nobody would be able to do what they've done already without a lot of help. *Pegasus*, will you hook me up with Noah?

His familiar grin appeared on her screen. "What's up, kid?"

"Trouble, and lots of it. I need all the information on the staffing timeline of the Habitat. Like, how many people they have onboard, how and when they got there. Everything."

"Sending it on my usual connection with *Pegasus*...there. It's all in. Can you tell me why?"

"An attempt by the citizens onboard to hijack the Habitat and bring it back into Earth orbit, for what purpose we don't know. Take a look at this." She sent him the manifesto. "Oops. More coming in as we speak."

A new file came through from Randy.

"Noah, this is a copy of the programming the Mercantiles have entered into the Habitat nav computer. Can you check it out?

"No problem. We'll put our team on it and let you know the moment we have anything useful."

"Great." She switched channels. "Thanks, Randy. I'll see that this gets spread around. Keep sending anything you can pick up, but don't go looking too seriously. You're much more valuable than the information you're sending."

"Got that. Randy out."

Jean's face went pale. "I just thought of something."

She turned to him in concern, "Yes?"

"These new leaders won't know a thing about the science. What if they try to turn the Habitat around?"

"They could tear it apart."

"Yes, or start a sympathetic wave form in the water sections that the suppressors can't handle. Or twenty other dangers I don't know about."

"*Pegasus*?"

Yes, Mia.

"Get the crew on board and lift off for Paris ASAP."

On it.

"Where are Nicolaus and Nero?"

Headed this way from the Mothership. Nicolaus will be onboard in two minutes. I've already briefed them. Nicolaus is coming with us, and Nero will stay with Mothership to coordinate the Earthside end of the operation.

"Sounds fine. Jean, how do we disseminate this?"

"Already sent the file to Olivier. The data will be in the right hands in an hour."

"Mia?"

"Yes, Hemi."

"News report. Guess what? The Habitat is experiencing severe solar flares and has lost contact completely on all channels."

"And are there really any solar flares?"

"Yes, but nothing at that scale."

"And this solves another problem."

"It does?"

"Those enemy agents last fall weren't after you. They were scouting me. They were after the Habitat all along."

Hemi shrugged. "I wasn't asking for an international incident to solve my little problems, but I'll take what I can get."

* * *

Three hours later, Mia stood in front of a hastily organized meeting of the Earth League Committee.

"Gentlefolk, I have very bad news for everyone. The Habitat for the Stars has been hijacked by a faction that wishes to return the vessel to Earth orbit. They have rigged an election to take over the control of the government system and are quoting serious human rights violations by the Consortium to bolster their arguments. They are appealing to the Humanity Meld to uphold their claim. I've run it by our legal experts. On Earth, the idea of individual rights and elected governments in commercially owned environments is a new field, with hazy jurisdiction and little precedence to guide judicial decisions. The presence of the Meld is an added complication. This problem could be churning through the courts for years. Our concern is what might happen if they try an early turnaround in the next few weeks and botch it. They could kill everyone aboard."

Chairman Ericsson frowned. "I agree that this is a serious situation, but we have always been clear that Earthers must solve their own problems. We are a joint Earther/Merge agency, and we dare not interfere."

"I wish that were true. Unfortunately, our data analysis reveals the fingermarks of the Merge Mercantile Caste all over the situation.

"First, the plans we have seen show the Habitat being converted into a combined hotel, spa, casino, and low-gravity luxury retirement facility. Its intention for use by the ultra-rich points to the Mercantile faction on Earth, which we know is being supported and financed by the Meld Mercantile Caste.

"Furthermore, our NASA programmers have seen the program to reverse course. It was not written on Earther computers. They're concerned that if they run an untested application and there are bugs in it, the Habitat could tear itself to pieces. My Flying wing is coordinating with NASA's ExIn Sphere to analyze the program for errors and sources, but it's a huge file, and it will take time.

"For two reasons, time is of the essence. In the first place, the more time the hijackers have to consolidate power onboard, the harder it will be to roust them from the inside. More important, should there be errors in the code, we have to stop them before they implement their course change."

One of the Gliesean members of the board shook his head. "Interfering in a partisan struggle like this could have grave consequences. We must think this over very carefully."

She nodded. "You should. But there's nothing stopping us from making plans and preparing our resources. The Habitat is on a two-year journey. To reduce stress on the hull, they are travelling at constant low acceleration and deceleration for the full trip. They have been travelling over six months, and they have only reached half speed, which is very slow compared to most spaceships.

"We have two Flying Wings, each with twenty NATO Space Marines and twenty Merge commandos aboard, already on course to the Habitat as we speak. That force is quite able to deal with whatever resistance the hijackers can muster. They will arrive in about two weeks.

"But an armed incursion would be our last-ditch solution. The personnel for the primary rescue mission will leave within forty-eight hours in GB *Pegasus*. This means we can call the mission off at any time in the next sixteen days. A lot can develop in that time, both good and bad."

Ericsson nodded. "And what is the plan for the primary mission?"

"The simplest solution is to shut the engines down and lock them off. We can coast for as long as we like, then start the engines again once the problem is settled. We'll simply get to the Asteroid Belt later than planned. Our intent is to put a team of programmers aboard and hack the propulsion system and freeze it."

"But doesn't shutting down the engines have some of the same dangers as any other maneuver?"

"It does. But we will have several advantages. There's already an emergency shutdown procedure in the system memory. If it needs to be tweaked, our programmers at NASA are from the team that created it. They spent ten years refining it, and they have two weeks to make their plans. It will work like any other space mission; the mainframe computer teams at NASA and ESA will vet the changes and debug them."

She smiled at them. "Don't worry. We built the Habitat, we launched it and we'll get it to the Belt in one piece."

The Chairman pointed a finger at her. "Do I note a personal angle to this promise?"

She sighed. "Unfortunately, yes. There is only one possible leader for this foray. I know all the codes, all the legitimate security staff and all the technicians. I have many friends on board. Our programmers can work on *Pegasus*, but somebody has to get the boarding party to the right place in the Habitat to control the shutdown. That's me. I assume you can shift my contract back to the Habitat Consortium so I don't take any action in this matter while under the aegis of the Earth League."

Ericsson nodded. "Well, thank you for your explanation, Ms. Larsen. The Committee will hold an in camera session. Please prepare yourselves for takeoff and wait in your transport. We will let you know what we decide."

She returned to *Pegasus* for two hours of anxious waiting. She couldn't concentrate on the plans for the operation, because her mind kept going back to something she wished she had said, or something maybe the committee was going to suggest that wouldn't work, and how was she going to dissuade them?

Mia. Company coming.

"Thanks *Pegasus*. I'll meet them at the gangplank."

Just Chairman Ericsson.

"I don't know if that's good or bad."

She stood at the bottom of the ramp watching the stout, elderly man make his way along the street, a pair of security guards at his heels.

Finally he arrived, sweat beading his brow.

"I will not waste your time. We want you in the air, not dealing with bureaucrats. The Committee has approved your plan, with one modification. We will not second you to anyone. We will take part in this exercise as a partner to the Habitat Consortium. If our people are involved with the problem, we must be part of the solution. Earthers take care of their criminals; we will take care of ours. We are asking you to continue to be our agent in this matter as you have in the past. We are not afraid to take the consequences of our efforts or yours."

She grinned. "And it keeps you in control of the action as well."

He tilted his head. "You are travelling in Meld ships. We are not concerned."

"I'll remember that."

He stuck out a hand. "Stay in touch."

"Don't worry, I will."

He chuckled. "I had the same conversation with my granddaughter recently, sending her off to university."

"Does she keep in touch?"

"Sometimes."

"Then I have a benchmark to judge myself by."

She turned and strode up the ramp. "*Pegasus*, get us in the sky. We have a passenger or two to pick up in Houston."

42. BACK IN SPACE

Enroute, there were a million details to organize. She didn't even wait until they were aloft. "First things first. What do we need for crew?"

Jean frowned. "We want a pretty solid boarding party with military training. Programming experience would be a plus."

She nodded. "This whole thing could boil down to computing power. Should we make a try for Noah and Fiona?"

"It's a tense situation, and they know the Habitat even better than you do. I think NASA might lend the two of them out for a month or so."

She grimaced. "I'm not sure Noah's new wife will be quite as easy to persuade, but I'll give him a call. Do we need any more?"

"I can't help but recall a certain security expert we have worked with before who already has the blessing of his government to join us."

Hemi perked up. "You mean Olivier? He'd be great. He's in my games cadre, but he's not mentoring a microship yet."

"You didn't tell me."

"He's Security." He shrugged. "You know what they're like."

"Right. Jean, you call Olivier. Will that be enough? I assume *Pegasus* will have the usual three Meld guards."

"Yes, but they stay onboard unless there's an emergency. Once we're on the Habitat, Nicolaus and I will be busy with the programming. Olivier will take care of the security aspects of the Habitat, but that leaves us with no one to handle real-life physical threats. Nicolaus, what do you think?"

"It's not my field of operations at all, but our people feel that members of a cadre are likely to make the best team. Plus the security clearance aspect. Do you have anyone else you know at NASA?"

"Only Joe Reimer. He's an excellent organizer, but not really the action type."

"What about that Security guy that ran you out to Galveston that day?" Hemi grinned. "You seemed pretty impressed with him."

She faked a slap which he evaded with ease. "Don't be a brat. His name's Alvin. He seemed a cool head and he's no slouch in the brains department."

"His name isn't Alvin. It's Martin. Martin Vonnegut. You know, like the writer." He glanced at her. "You don't look surprised."

"I knew it wasn't his real name. Did you turn *Pegasus* loose on him, too?"

"You're busy with other things. Someone's gotta take care of you."

"Thanks, I guess. Did you find out anything we need to know?"

"He's clean as a whistle. Just got promoted. *Pegasus* figures he's being fast-tracked because of his background. And he's been keeping an eye on you."

"You accessed his Internet feed?"

"No, we did a reverse search to see who's been following you."

"And what does my self-appointed surveillance team conclude about Martin?"

"Pretty harmless. He has a designated feed that informs him when you come up on the standard news media. He doesn't download anything. Our consensus is that he's not a stalker. Just one of your many fans."

Jean looked up from his keyboard. "He's up to speed already. Better him than a stranger assigned by somebody who doesn't have any idea of our needs and might have other objectives. We're already stopping in Houston. I'd say call up your friend Joe and have him arrange it." He glanced at his screen. "Olivier's happy to come."

"Where is he?"

"He's at the Centre for Surgical Invention and Innovation in Hamilton, Ontario. Don't ask me why, because I don't know. *Pegasus*, how fast can you get from Houston to Hamilton?"

About an hour.

"What time is it in Houston?"

Six am.

"Okay, we'll hit Jackson Centre as working hours are starting. Let's assume it takes all day to organize things in Houston. There are sure to be loose ends to tie up the next morning. We'll pick Olivier up around noon tomorrow, Hamilton time."

She grinned. "Andrea and Alicia will appreciate at least one night with their husbands before they take off."

She had a momentary qualm when she met Vonnegut at the loading ramp that afternoon. He was shorter than she remembered, and not quite so handsome, although he moved with the ease of an athlete.

He dropped his pack, and his hand wavered between a shake and a salute. Then they both laughed and shook. He looked around. "Okay, Ms. Larsen, here I am. Security Head Reimer said you'd tell me what's going on."

"My name's Mia." She noted his expression. "Are you ready for this?"

"Not really sure. Joe pulled me off a normal surveillance job. Said he had a special assignment for me, and you were in charge. I wasn't allowed to tell anyone. I asked him where, and he asked me if I suffered from any conditions that would keep me from going to space. He drove me out to my place to pack and wouldn't let me out of his sight the whole time. When we got back, there was your Flying Wing in the parking lot like last fall. That's when it all started to come together. And my name isn't Alvin, as you probably know."

"It's Martin. My team are a suspicious lot, and very protective."

"Good for them. You're getting famous these days, and I'm sure you're aware of what that brings."

"And that's what you're here for."

"Fair enough." He glanced sideways at her. "There's something going on at the Habitat, isn't there?"

"I'm afraid so. There's one more team member to pick up tomorrow, and we'll have a full briefing after that to give everybody all the details." She led him off the ramp, and it closed up behind them. "Come aboard and meet the rest of the cadre, and I'll give you the basics of the operation."

* * *

Noah and Fiona boarded early the next morning, and after a quick stops for Olivier, *Pegasus* left earth orbit, accelerating at full power towards their target, two weeks away. To Mia's surprise, once they were out of the atmosphere the ship re-oriented to fly with the topside forward.

When she questioned *Pegasus*, the sentience chuckled.

It is more efficient to fly with the gravity plate at the back. Otherwise, we would have to deflect one G of our acceleration force to create gravity for the crew. It will save about twenty hours over the voyage. As we near the Asteroid Belt, if the risk of collisions increases, we will resume our usual nose-first attitude.

"Fair enough. Will you put me on general com, please?

You're on.

"Welcome aboard, everyone. Could we please have a meeting of all crew in the main cabin in half an hour?"

You are very polite.

"Reminding everyone that this is not a military expedition."

Twenty-nine minutes later she surveyed her crew.

"First the housekeeping. Alpha and Evander will be on 10-hour duty watches. Cassian will share culinary duties with *Pegasus* and fill in the two-hour split shift on security. The ship will revert to Greenwich Mean, to synch with the rest of the vehicles in space. The rest of us will make ourselves available for a loose working day from eight am to eight pm."

She proceeded to go through the history and objectives of the mission, asking each member of the cadre to indicate their place in the organization.

"Which brings us to the present moment. *Pegasus,* do you have the data I wanted?"

Right here.

"Thanks. Put it up in the main holoframe please."

Here is our course. Three dotted lines arced through the 3-D space. **We will overtake the Habitat at this point in fourteen days.**

"What's that extra course beside ours?"

It might be a very useful one. The Habitat is expecting Cornucopia, the resupply ship carrying the next group of new crew members, to dock two days ahead of us. If we asked her to make a slight reduction in acceleration and up our velocity zero point two percent, we would arrive simultaneously.*

"How will that help us?"

We discussed making our attack point the Emergency Bridge at the sunward end of the habitat.

She nodded. "It's easier to hack into that sub-station because it's only basic propulsion and life support systems. It can run on emergency backups even if the rest of the Habitat is offline."

And it's in the sunward end, where logistics are concentrated and where the cargo ships dock.

"About a hundred metres from the main loading dock, through the vegetable processing plant."

"Perfect." Jean put up another graphic. "The carrier has a normal fission engine, and it will be in decel, with its engines firing ahead of it, masking the ship in the ions of its own drive plume. Our propulsion system doesn't register on the Habitat's detection systems. If we tuck in behind it, we'll be invisible. As we approach the sunward end of the Habitat and they shut off the drive, we could interfere with the visuals in the landing area and slide in right behind."

She nodded. "Let's talk that around the table a few times in the next couple of days. Anything else?"

Jean leaned back. "We can't start our attack on the Habitat systems from this distance because the time lag introduces an extra complication in a delicate operation. But we have that six-pack of microships on the Habitat. They're designed for this sort of adaptation and tuned to a designated link. Hemi and I will ready them for merging with *Pegasus* when we get there."

"How are you going to work that with only two programmers?"

"Nicolaus is competent, so we can merge three of them at a time. We'll prep them all, and on cue, we'll put three into play. If we need them, we have the others as backups. If not, we'll use them as they are presently configured: memory extension."

Hemi grinned. "If they were properly adapted, I could handle three by myself."

She shot him a look. "Let's not get ahead of ourselves. Stick with the one-to-one ratio."

"Sure thing, boss."

She glanced at him again, but he seemed quite serious.

She scanned the table. "If there's nothing else pressing to discuss, we all have personal business we should have attended to before our hurried departure. We can finish it up while we're still in real-time com distance from Earth. Olivier can log in with *Pegasus,* and I'll contact the resupply ship to request the course change."

Cornucopia's captain, Vasco Ferreira, was a genial fellow she had met a few times during the Habitat construction, and he took the changes in stride. "Sure thing, Ms. Larsen." He paused. "Ahh...has this got anything to do with our new passengers?"

"I don't think so. What new passengers?"

"I guess it's no secret. We were hailed last week by a passing ship. They said they had five passengers going to the Habitat, and could we accommodate them? I had room, so I agreed."

"Let me guess. Long, sleek and black?"

"If you mean like the one the Mercantile Caste showed up with at the UN, you'd be wrong. This one was almost as big as us, bulky looking but more aerodynamic. Enough wing surface to steer in atmosphere, but not to fly. No engine exhaust ports. Word has it the Meld ships use gravity drives."

"They do. My Meld associates would like to identify it."

"I'll send you a data package. The ship left immediately, bound outsystem. The new passengers settled in quickly. Decent enough bunch. Keep to themselves. We deal mostly with the gofer who organizes everything. The head honcho's got a German accent. One's an alien, the type that look like us. Gliesean, you know? The other two have to be Security. You can tell by the way their eyes move." He shifted his eyes warily, then chuckled. "Got any messages for them?"

She shook her head. "As you may guess, this is all between you and me."

"Ah. The political situation on the Habitat. I have my orders on that front, too."

"I won't ask you what they are, because I'm being very circumspect in case I need a favour down the road. How big a security detail do you carry?"

He waggled a finger at her. "Now, that was a mighty big change of topic." His face became serious. "Unless it wasn't. I don't carry any security. I have an operating crew of fifteen, plus twenty-five catering and housekeeping staff, and they're well trained for whatever goes down."

"And a passenger list of about a hundred?"

"Right. The Home Office filled me in on what happened in the Habitat. Any idea how many of my passengers might be trouble?"

"Consortium HR and NASA Security are working on that. You'll know as soon as we do."

"I'd appreciate that. And any course changes I make are nobody's business but mine."

"Let's keep it that way. Thank you, Captain Ferriera. We'll stay in touch."

"And you, Ms. Larsen."

Once they had decided on their approach and their target, everything fell into line like building blocks. There was plenty of time for detailed planning of their approach strategies and how they would handle it once they got aboard the Habitat.

*　*　*

The next bit of interesting news came a few days later from one of the Wings in the advance party.

Mia? Contact from Prometheus.

"Put him through."

Hello, Ms. Larsen. I have data that might interest you.

"Fire away, *Prometheus*."

The ship that dropped Johan Lange off with Cornucopia has just passed us. Data package coming.

"Where are they heading?"

Same course as us.

"That's interesting."

But unless they change their deceleration rate, they will match velocity a hundred thousand kilometres past the Habitat.

"Like they want to hang around in the area and wait for something."

That would be the most likely conclusion.

"What are your plans?"

To match courses and position ourselves between the station and the enemy. If that suits you.

"We plan to follow the *Cornucopia* and land in her drive plume shadow at the sunward end of the habitat. Any attention you can focus in an outsystem direction would suit us."

We'll coordinate our timing with you, then. After that, we will stand by for whatever you need.

"Thank you, *Prometheus. Pegasus* out."

Our pleasure, Ms. Larsen. Prometheus out."

She turned to her crew. "Let's see the competition."

Images appeared in the main holoframe. It was a considerably larger ship than *Pegasus,* in a more traditional aerospace form: a smooth sausage with stubby wings set far aft. As Ferrira had noted, it showed no engine outlets.

"What are we looking at?"

It was Nero who answered. "That's one of ours, a small space liner about forty years old. Deep space capabilities, with atmospheric travel possible but not efficient."

A red circle highlighted the Gliesean digits on the hull. ***Its designation does not translate well into Standard English. It is not registered with Meld authorities in this system. I am interested in the black streaking on the top and sides. Spectroscopic data indicates carbon and organics. One explanation is that this ship has been hidden for some time downplanet, concealed by natural cover, but left in a hurry without a proper cleaning. Let me contact Athena for some research.***

Ten minutes later, *Pegasus* came back on the com.

Ahh. Coming up. We used Jean's microship array to get new imagery of the Earth. East of the Baikonur Cosmodrome in Kasakhstan there is a low range of wooded hills...

A blurred image appeared and slowly zoomed in.

...and there we have it. A hole in the ground suspiciously similar in size and shape to the Mercantile ship.

Mia and Nicolaus shared triumphant glances. "Now we know where our competitors have been hiding."

Jean pointed. "Previous satellite imagery is too low res to tell. The Russians are camera shy, and don't allow close overflights. From the size of the trees that have been uprooted, it was there for about twenty years."

"I don't need to research that. The Recession of 2063."

Pegasus put a timeline on the viewscreen. ***Here it is. The same pattern of quick boom and bust as this time, but slower and less pronounced. The swings were much farther apart and stopped after three. Let me check...yes, from that point on, the world income gap has increased at a steeper rate.***

"That means the Mercantile sapient ship started helping the Earther Mercantiles manipulate the market twenty years ago."

That would be the most obvious conclusion.

"It doesn't help us much with this week's problem, but file the data with the Mothership."

Aye, Captain.

"And please get all the information you can about that type of ship, especially armament and the type of sapience she carries."

Sapience is custom designed for each ship, but it's worth a try. The original design is not military in nature.

Mia regarded her cadre. "There we have it. The Mercantile ship has been helping the commercial interests of Earth to manipulate the stock market to their advantage. We managed to nullify their efforts, so they have changed targets.

"I will inform Chairman Ericsson. For the moment, everything continues according to plan."

43. PREPARATION

With only a few days left on the journey, the action began to pick up. First, the Mothership came through with the results of the crew qualification review. Of the ninety-two personnel transfers on Cornucopia, thirty-two were iffy. Fortunately, the roster included a ten-person Security detail with all their equipment. Captain Ferriera had no qualms about his ability to control the situation. As Mia reported to the cadre, "Not our horse, not our wagon."

Jean brought up the next step at lunch two days later. "*Pegasus* tells me we're within range to start our infiltration of the Habitat system."

Mia felt a lift to her spirits. "The point we've all been waiting for. Where do you plan to start?"

"First, we take over Maintenance."

"Maintenance? Don't we want to work on Security first?"

"Nope." Olivier grinned. "Security-wise, Maintenance is the top of the food chain. Think about it. You try to get into the system, and Security shuts you out. What do you do?"

"Try again."

"But what happens if you attack and you get, "That system is not functioning at this time"? You do nothing, because you can't attack a system that is shut down."

She shrugged. "Impeccable logic. Okay, once we're in control of the physical plant and its repair functions, what's the action?"

"Well, the main problems in this operation are getting on board unseen and not attracting attention while we're there. Our plan is to disable the visual systems when we need them, especially in the sunward end for our approach."

"But there's nothing more suspicious than a key camera going down exactly when you need it."

"Right. So, we prep them for it. We start a rotating series of visual glitches. We lead them on a trail through their own system, starting a problem, then allowing them to think they fixed it. They will do a postmortem and decide they know what happened, but then we plant another glitch which seems a logical outcome of the fix on the last one. Then we do it again, until we have them chasing their tails through the whole ship."

Hemi chuckled. "Yeah, by the time we get there, they'll think they know enough that they can predict the next blackout. We make sure it happens exactly when and where they expect it — at the landing bay — so they won't be suspicious. They'll be happy because they know what's going on. We let them fix it, but with a doctored feed in the cameras that doesn't show *Pegasus*."

Jean gave a smug smile. "And then we instigate another glitch somewhere completely innocuous, and they'll go chasing off after that one, leaving us in charge where we need it."

"That's pretty devious, but considering the brains it came from, I suppose we should have expected it."

Jean shrugged. "It would have been a boring trip, otherwise."

"Anything else?"

"Once on board, the plan is to move openly through the populace, but we have a backup scenario prepped in case we need to move around secretly. We insert some new routines ahead of time that involve clearing individual access tunnels of all personnel. Likewise external transport in the EV repair bots."

"You seem to have thought of everything."

"It helps to have a sapience like *Pegasus* on hand. He can run scenarios and make predictions we would never have thought of." He put up a hand to halt further discussion. "And we have the first three microships prepped."

"You want to do the merge now?"

"Doesn't hurt. We don't know the power of the sapience on that Mercantile ship, or how they might apply it."

She thought a moment. "In that case, *Pegasus,* I'd like you to access the first microship Jean brings online and use its memory as a database to download all the historical data the Mothership has on manipulation of Meld commercial systems. Use any extra bandwidth you can free up to search that data for possible directions the enemy might move, whether they succeed with the Habitat piracy or not."

Any time you're ready, Captain Gagnon.

Jean glanced at Nicolaus and received a nod. "We can have Number Three operational in a couple of hours." He glanced at the timeface on the bulkhead. "You paying overtime?"

"Only if I get results."

"Aye, Captain Bligh, ma'am. The best snow fort is the one with the most snowballs inside."

Mia sighed. "I suppose that's an example of traditional Canadian wisdom."

"No, I just made it up. But thanks anyway."

"All right. Your wit and wisdom have relaxed and motivated us for the mission ahead. Get to work."

"Aye, Captain." He gave a snappy salute with a non-regulation flourish at the end and headed for his work station.

Hemi gave her a smug grin and followed.

* * *

The night before the approach everyone was keyed up, and Jean agreed that a talk-through of the plan would have a calming effect. They had been through the basics a hundred times, as well as the backups, the fallbacks, and the emergency withdrawal procedures. At the end, Mia could sum it up in a few brief sentences.

"Jean starts the final video error cascade at 09:00, building slowly to a full blackout of the docking area by 11:00. *Cornucopia* docks at 11:45 or thereabouts. We'll be right behind, and *Pegasus* will moor at the maintenance airlock aft and to port of the supply ship. Olivier, Martin, Jean, and I will go aboard and join the new workforce as they log into the ship. Hemi will stay aboard here to monitor the purser's feed to make sure our IDs are accepted. After that, we move to the harvest processing bay, which leads us straight to the Emergency Bridge, where Jean and Olivier will proceed with the takeover while Martin stands guard and I twiddle my fingers and worry.

"Meanwhile, back on *Pegasus,* Nicolaus, Hemi and Noah, with the help of our sentience power, will monitor the main systems of the Habitat, looking for unwanted attention and dealing with it when it arises. We'll know we were successful when the engines shut down and we aren't scattered in small pieces all over the galaxy. Our Gliesean security will stay with the ship, which is their duty, and be near in case they are needed as well. The other two Flying Wings will stand by as backup."

44. BOARDING

The next morning, Mia attempted to remedy her restless night with one more coffee than usual and was ready to move out two hours before they docked. She forced herself to slow down, making her appearance in the operations room an hour ahead of time.

Everyone was already there, sitting around and trying to look casual.

"What have you got to report, *Pegasus*?"

On course and on schedule, Mia. Captain Ferriera reports the same. Monitors indicate the Habitat's normal internal com traffic.

"Can't ask for better than that." She regarded the crew. "If anybody forgot their teddy bear there's still time to go back."

She was rewarded with pained smiles.

"What? Nobody lay awake last night thinking up things that could go terribly wrong?"

"Of course." Jean waved that away. "And I prepared three solutions for every one of them."

"Well, the only thing I can come up with is if somehow Lange catches sight of me when we're boarding. But he's a politician. He'll assume I'm here to attack him in the political arena. I will give him what he expects, drawing attention away from the rest of you."

Olivier grinned. "That's why this combined ship approach works for us. Everybody on the Habitat will think we came on the *Cornucopia*, and the newcomers will think we were on the Habitat already."

Report from Prometheus. They have challenged the Mercantile ship and received no cooperation. The two Wings are moving into attack positions.

"That's handy timing for us, but don't do anything rash."

This is a matter between legitimate Meld Security vessels and an unlicensed Meld ship in a restricted System. It is outside our area of influence. Your quaint saying about ownership of horses and wagons would apply.

"I'm not going to argue."

Cornucopia has entered the visual field of the sunward cameras on the Habitat.

"Video glitch deployed." Jean glanced over at Nicolaus.

"Habitat Maintenance routines and tech staff are reacting as predicted."

Mia paced to the front of the main cabin and stepped into the bridge to peer out. Tier after tier of glass and hinged mirrors towered over her. *All it would take is the wrong person looking out the window...*

Cornucopia has entered the docking bay. We have taken up our assigned position. Our personnel airlock is directly above the maintenance entrance.

After a quick glance at her cadre, Mia shouldered her satchel.

Jean frowned. "Do you think you should wear your camo jacket?"

She looked down at her burgundy Consortium blazer. "No, I'm not blending in with any crowds today." She finished suiting up, sealed her helmet and led the way into the airlock. The rest crowded in after her. When the lock opened, it was a short drift across to the corresponding door on the Habitat. She opened it, and they slipped inside.

Now they were in enemy territory, and she resisted the urge to rush, forcing herself to stillness until the pressure light came on.

"Ready to exit airlock."

Hemi took his time sweeping all nearby cameras. *Hallway and suit lockers clear.*

A visual of the area appeared in her heads-up display.

"Proceeding."

They shucked their suits and hung them handy for quick access.

"Entering processing rooms."

Again, Hemi's audio and her video confirmed that the way was clear.

Hemi came through again. *The Cornucopia passengers are being useful. They are in no hurry, and are leaving large breaks in the line. There is a dogleg in the corridor with little visibility either way where you can slip in.*

"Got it."

They waited for a gap, then slipped into the corridor. Around the next corner the hall widened into the lading area, where the purser was checking individual IDs.

But the line wasn't moving. A loud voice with a Germanic accent quieted the hum of the crowd. "...but these people are being held against their will. This is neither legal nor moral."

Mia couldn't hear much of the purser's answer, but the word "irregularities" came up more than once.

Lange was about to continue his harangue, but a large Security guard stepped forward. "Sir, you seem to have a problem with Captain Ferierra and American Aerospace Transport. If you wish to return to the ship, please feel free to do so. However, that would make your future entry into the Habitat uncertain. We are running a cooperative enterprise in a harsh environment, and troublemakers are not welcome." He stepped forward, balanced on the balls of his feet.

The Austrian allowed himself to be moved onward, but not before he took one angry glance back towards the airlock.

Mia ducked behind Olivier's shoulder. "Did he notice me?"

"Didn't look like it. Every face in the dock was turned his way."

They waited until the Mercantile party had left through the inner door, then stepped into line again. Their scans read smoothly, and the purser welcomed them aboard with a friendly smile.

As they traversed the next intersection a side door opened, and Randy Jones waved them in. "Good to see you, Mia." He frowned at the rest as he closed the door. "A small team to take over a ship this size."

"The bare minimum to get the job done. We don't want to create a stir." She made quick introductions, and they headed out through rows of automatic vegetable processors. She stopped at an unmarked door and keyed in her code. It opened, and they entered the Emergency Bridge. All was dark.

"Hemi, we're blind down here."

You're supposed to be for the next three minutes. You're ahead of schedule, and we have to keep their programmers on a strict leash so they don't suspect anything. Ah. There you are.

The big screens lit up with various views of the Habitat, inside and out, and the holo frame created an image of the whole ship, split open down the middle. A flashing dot located the party's position at the stern. The outside view of that end showed *Cornucopia* docked alone.

By the time Mia had registered this, Jean was already at the centre viewscreen, Olivier at a flanking work station. Martin took the Security station and logged in as well, and for a while there was silence.

Before she had a chance to get really nervous, Jean looked up. "What's this, Mia?"

She glanced at the path shown at the top of his screen. "You're through two security levels, designed to deal with civilian commercial dross and random hackers. To enter the programming area, you need the day's password, which is date dependent..." she reeled off the numbers and letters, and he copied them.

"Thanks." He worked a while longer. "Okay, here's that double sign-in you talked about."

"Right. You've been assigned your personal daily code, and you have to enter it at your station while I use the Command chair and enter an Administrator's permission. Go ahead."

They followed the pattern, tossing the ball back and forth twice, and the main program opened up for them. It was huge, with thousands of blocks of code.

"This will take a while. You got any shortcuts?"

"We're looking for recent uploads. Screen for the past three weeks."

Again, there was silence.

"Got it. Nicolaus, take a look at this. Is it familiar?"

It only took a moment. *Oh, yes, this is fairly basic language. Pegasus, could you scan this program to see how it meshes with the Earther programming?*

I'm sorry, but I can't.

A sinking feeling washed through Mia. "What do you mean?"

It doesn't mesh in the sense you mean. We were expecting something like the earlier examples Randy sent, where the Meld program simply inserted values into the ship's original program, which then executed the commands as usual. This program takes advantage of the much superior capabilities of our technology and controls the whole central processor, shunts it aside, and runs the ship on its own.

"Will that work?"

I am skeptical. It might, but the only way to find out is to try it.

"Do we dare try it?"

That is not a decision I am qualified to make.

"Jean?"

He shook his head. "We have to go about this another way."

Hemi's image appeared on a side screen. *Isn't it rather simple?*

They stared at him.

Well, we don't know if the Meld program works. So, we isolate it and initiate the emergency shutdown procedure that's already in the Habitat's files. Once we have the engines locked out, we're in charge.

Mia and Jean exchanged glances. He shrugged. "Should work. The Meld program hasn't started its takeover procedures yet. It's vulnerable."

She nodded. "We still have to take control as originally planned."

Most definitely.

"Let's get to it."

He returned to his chair and soon the team was deep in technical jargon she couldn't follow. She looked around the room. "Martin, are you involved in the programming?"

"Not at the moment. A bit beyond me, as it happens."

"But you do know how to run this section." She waved a hand up and down the set of nine common viewscreens in front of them.

"It's a Sanyo Security Array similar to one I trained on."

She wheeled a chair next to him. "Show me what's going on out there."

He pointed to the main screen. "In general, I'd say the natives are restless. It's mid-morning on a working day, but there are a lot of people roaming, mostly toward the forward end of the habitat. Look at the rec facilities." He pointed to another screen. "I checked the stats. Fifty percent less use than usual at this time of day." He panned upwards. "Look here."

"That's the other side of the Habitat. It's rather weird to see it hanging up there over our heads."

"No, look in the middle. Where it's weightless."

"Oh, the Flight Centre. There's three fliers up there. Are there supposed to be more?"

"Busiest facility on the ship. They can handle twenty fliers, and often there's a lineup. Not today."

"So, where is everybody going?"

Randy had been listening. "Probably at the Town Meeting."

"What's that about?"

He shrugged. "Some kind of old Greek idea, apparently. With a population this small, we can have about half the people together in the general assembly room called the Agora. They hold a meeting once a week." He frowned. "That's another thing that bothered me. The meetings were sounding too much like political rallies. All shouting and name calling. Doesn't sound like democracy to me."

"Was today a regular get-together?"

"No, they called a special meeting. Said they had some new ideas for the populace. I figured it would be more of the 'same old, same old,' and if it kept everybody occupied, it's better for us."

"Can we drop in on this meeting?"

"Sure. It's broadcast in real time." His hands flowed over the enterpad, and the main image resolved into a familiar figure standing at a podium with several well-dressed men and women in a row behind him, a line of uniforms at floor level across the front.

"Can I have some volume?"

The Germanic voice came in, its tone rising. "...you're going to be nothing but indentured servants. Once they have got you out there, they will charge you extra for this and that and pretty soon they'll charge so much for the air you breathe that you can't afford the fare home."

There were boos in the background.

Lange smiled. "Believe me, where we're going, you won't want to go home..."

She gestured for him to cut the feed. "About what I expected. Martin, you know a couple of security officers on board."

"Yeah. They were assigned by NASA, but they liked the job and stayed on. I haven't been in contact since they left, though."

She grinned. "Sure, but since you're in the neighbourhood, it would be natural to check in, wouldn't it?"

"You want me to get a feel for the security situation?"

"Exactly. Randy, get Martin on the local chat net and track down his cronies."

The two sat at a work station and fired it up.

"Oh, and remember Murph Bokker? He'd be a good man to have along if it comes to a dust-up."

"He'd never forgive me if there was a dust-up and I left him out."

She regarded the main team, who seemed to be stalled. "What's up, guys?"

Jean shook his head. "We're running into problems. The Mercantiles have somebody aboard who has been messing with the programming for the last couple of weeks. We keep running into his signature work."

"We expected that. He would be the one that uploaded the Meld program."

"Well, he's slowing us down, just by being there. And we're having trouble getting to the mainframe. Hemi and *Pegasus* are working..."

Got it...damn!

Their attention focused on Hemi's screen, where a message box had appeared.

DNA Verification.

The next step in the login procedure is a DNA sample. That's not unusual. But this demands a Gliesean sample.

"Any way around it?"

Nope. It's the simplest 'yes/no' gate you can put in. Like a five-metre wall across the road.

"He's got a Gliesean with him."

"Can we use Nicolaus?"

Oh, that's not all.

"Make my day."

The only place to enter the sample is the main System Ops Station. That's just inboard of the Mayor's offices in the forward section of the vessel.

She looked around the silent room. All eyes were on her.

"I know, I know, but let's not be hasty about this. The simplest solution is to send Hemi. We use one of the prepared exercises and disperse half a dozen one-man maintenance bots on a routine sweep. Hemi takes a seventh and heads straight up the hull to the forward end, flying on manual so he won't be noticed. He parks in a nearby maintenance bay and accesses the maintenance tunnels. Comments?"

88% chance of success.

"And there's no real danger. If they catch him, he hasn't done anything wrong. I'd rather be a hundred percent sure and send Nicolaus, but he can't pilot the bot on manual, and he can't program the system."

She turned to Jean. "Talk to him about kit."

The pilot turned to Hemi's screen, "The repair bot is pressurized, but wear the e-suit that you used for swimming on Gough Island. It's good for half an hour full vacuum in an emergency. When you get back inside, roll the suit in the helmet and stow it in your haversack. Wear your usual hoodie and jeans, and light mag boots."

Olivier leaned in. "No tools or equipment that a teenager wouldn't carry to school. And only your diplomatic ID. They won't dare mess with a Gliesean."

Hemi grinned on the screen. *Jeez, and all my life I've been just an expendable street kid.*

She frowned. "Well, you're essential to the plan, so keep your head down. I know you're good at that."

Ah, don't worry. I'm not the hero type. If they catch me, it won't be my fault.

"Let's hope it isn't mine. I'd never live it down."

Your fault? You've run this operation like a pro.

She stifled the warm feeling that threatened her composure. "Thus proving that others are better than me at motivating the troops. Go get 'em, Tiger."

Ready in ten minutes.

She turned to Jean. "Is there anything you can be doing while we wait?"

"We'll have a go at the microships they have onboard. I've been playing with a modification on the trip out."

"Should I be suspicious?"

"It's a bit of a long shot, but they have a gravity strip that keeps pieces and tools from falling away during modifications in space. I'll use that model to reconfigure the micros to match the grav propulsion on *Pythagoras.*"

"What good would that do?"

"They could work off the mass of the Habitat, and function inside."

"You could have microships flying around inside the Habitat?"

"Right down the hall and through that door. With tractor beams, mining lasers, and a bunch of other dangerous tools."

"But you have to program them first. Which you're not doing while I'm wasting your time talking. Go for it."

"Right."

He returned to his station and silence once more descended. He didn't even raise his head when Hemi signalled *Pegasus* to start the repair bot exercise.

She watched the external screens as the six decoys performed their routine dance, touching down at various access points and working their way slowly up the outside of the hull. The seventh vehicle seemed obvious to her, steaming arrow-straight along the outer decking.

But it reached the target airlock without incident and locked on.

My apologies to Maintenance, but Repair Bot Starboard Seven seems to have frozen up. Please log it on next week's level three servicing routine.

"All right, smartass. We get the picture. Head for your target."

Aye, ma'am.

The screen carried the output from his lapel cam, as he moved through empty supply and maintenance tubes that riddled the outer hull. Finally, he reached a security door with an enterpad.

Pegasus, you there? I need this door open.

Right with you. Sorry about the pause, but Captain Gagnon is using a lot of bandwidth. There you go.

The lock clicked, but the door stayed shut.

I detect movement in the hallway.

I have that as well. People moving past. I'll pack my EV suit as I wait for them to clear.

There was a long silence and no movement. *...here we go.*

The door swung open, and their view moved into the hallway.

"Pegasus, can you follow him externally?"

Corridor 27F video coming up. Cam 27F-93 handing off to cam 27F-94.

Now they could see Hemi from behind, crossfading as he moved through each camera zone.

"Somebody coming."

Don't distract me.

Two women in civilian clothing came into sight, talking in animated voices as they passed. They didn't seem to notice Hemi at all. Soon their voices faded.

"How did you do that?"

A soft chuckle. *Don't know. I've been doing it all my life. People aren't concerned with me. It's the medical facility around the next corner.*

Once again, the Flying Wing manipulated the security system, and the door swung open. Hemi slipped inside and looked around.

My instructions are to stand in front of this machine so the camera can see me take a swab sample inside my cheek. Then I place the swab in the slot and wait. Any reason not to comply?

"As long as you haven't brushed your teeth recently with someone else's brush, I'd say go ahead."

Very funny. Here goes.

The front of the machine was glass, and they could see his reflection performing the ritual. Then they waited.

Nicolaus appeared on his viewscreen. *I'm getting some action...yes, the sample has been accepted as valid. It's reading the sequence. This could take a while...no, it won't. Individual confirmed Gliesean. Individual allowed access...I don't like the sound of that.*

His voice rose, speaking short, sharp sentences in Gliesean Standard.

"What's wrong?"

He took a moment to calm himself. *Hemi is allowed access. Only Hemi, but he can't do the whole thing himself. He has to be in the same location as the Administrator for the login.*

Once again, all eyes turned to her. She threw up her hands. "Why do all my choices never turn out to be choices? We've done what we can, here. I've been checking in on the Town Hall, and I don't like the tone that's developing. Jean, can you put your project on hold and pick it up from the other end of the ship?"

"Take me a moment to tidy it up and save it in a secure file." His attention went back to his screens.

"Can't be helped. We'll have to buy you some time. Randy, can you get on the Habitat recreation site and book us some flights?"

"We're going to fly there?"

"Why not? It will take us half the time, and no danger of anyone stopping us. The flight path is over two hundred metres from the ground, so nobody will recognize us. There's an elevator from the hub to the Mayor's office. We can get off a couple of floors above at the Drive Control Bridge. The shift schedule shows one junior officer assigned there. Either subdue him or persuade him to help. I'll sign you all in, and you can finish the programming."

Jean glanced at her. "While you are doing what?"

"Martin and I are going to participate in an experiment in democracy."

On her heads up display Nicolaus appeared nodding, a smile twitching the corner of his mouth. *Face to face?*

"It has to be that way. Martin, what do your buddies say? "

"Security is starting to get worried. According to my friends, their staff went through a different vetting process, meaning they don't have any ringers. Yeah, I take that with a grain of salt. But most of them are clean, and they're worried about this new guy. I've been listening to the meeting, and he's poison."

"Can you get back to your friends and ask them to have their Head of Security meet me outside the Agora? His name's Arham Bhutto. We'll be there in about a half hour."

"Right on it."

"Randy, what do you think of that story?"

"It follows. Security guys tend to stick together."

"Right. We'll go to the meeting, but we won't tell them about the programming until it's successful."

"What do you want me to do?"

"Come through by the corridors and collect a squad of Security and anybody else you trust. Stay off the central com system. Rendezvous somewhere outside the Agora and wait in case we need you. Don't access any weapons lockers, because they're linked into the main system."

"Fair enough." His knowing grin told her that his men had other ways of arming themselves.

"Away we go, then. The elevator's over here."

45. FLIGHT OF FANCY

The focus of the whole population was on the meeting, and now the corridors were empty. They made the elevator without rousing suspicion and took the car to the Flight Centre, feeling lighter and lighter as gravity decreased. As they rode, Jean slid up beside Mia. "How hard is it to fly one of these contraptions?"

She grinned. "It's a piece of cake as long as you don't do something silly."

"That's comforting. How long is the 'don't do' list?"

"Here's our deck. Come on, and I'll give you the orientation."

They exited the elevator onto a broad, open platform that overlooked the length of the Habitat. It was situated about fifty metres below the centre point, and there was just enough gravity to keep their feet on the deck. While the rest of the group took in the scenery, Mia went to the rack and pulled off one of the ornithopters.

"You can play tourist later, guys. Here's our ride."

Jean frowned at the spindly framework she was holding up. "Why does that look familiar?"

"Because it's a copy of Leonardo da Vinci's ornithopter. He really was a genius, you know. The only reason this wouldn't fly on Earth is because humans aren't strong enough to work it in one G." She hefted the frame. "Of course, this one's made of carbon fibre and microfabric. But in the weightless core out there, your only limit is your fitness."

He took it from her and looked it over. "You push with your legs and pull with your arms. Logical ergonomics. Altitude and steering with the tail." He shrugged. "It looks simple. Probably isn't." He stared her in the eye. "I assume you've done this?"

"Oh, sure. Noah and I were on board for the last months of construction. We didn't work twenty-four seven, you know. In fact, he was the first one to try it out." She chuckled. "He designed it, he got to be the test dummy."

"Well, now you're the expert. Give us the orientation and away we go."

While they talked, Olivier had hoisted out three more fliers, and Mia proceeded to run them through an abbreviated lesson. "Flying them is as easy as swimming. Most of the training is safety stuff to keep amateurs from doing something stupid. You three will be flying straight from here to the opposite end, and I know you'll stay on course. I will shepherd you. It's not unusual for instructors to accompany novices the first flight. We will look natural to anyone who notices us."

"But in case something goes wrong?"

"You're flying in a tunnel about a hundred metres in diameter where the gravity is light enough that only a small amount of effort keeps you floating. You stay in the safe zone by keeping the yellow light lined up inside the blue circle down there at the other end of the course. If you stray into heavier gravity, the next fifty metres is still flyable, but hard going. Beyond that, the centrifugal and Coriolis forces are too much, and you can't get back up to safety. At that point the emergency chute deploys, the wings freeze in glide position, and you come down like a regular hang glider."

She stepped into her own machine, kneeling under it to demonstrate buckling the straps. Then she spun the craft to face the far end. "A couple of strong arm pushes to get you off the deck..." She suited her action to her words and rose above them, her wings sweeping gently. "...then move your weight forward and you're airborne." She pulled away from the platform and circled back to observe their takeoff. "Don't try to hover. It's harder than it looks."

Jean, Olivier and Martin took off one at a time and headed for blue ring at the end of the Habitat, stroking powerfully. Mia came last, moving from one side to the other as if directing their course.

After a bit of observation, she pulled alongside Jean. "I know what you're doing."

He turned an innocent face, but his course straightened. "What do you mean?"

"You can't help yourself. You're testing the controls."

"I'm not doing anything on the Something Stupid list."

"Of course you're not."

"It's weird. Like flying a plane, but putting your nose down doesn't give you much velocity. Navigation's a breeze."

"But you notice you're yawing to port a bit."

"Crabwalking, am I? Why is that?"

"You're pushing harder with your right leg. Your port arm and leg push your port wing, and likewise on starboard."

"Okay, got it."

She took pity on him. "Here. Try this for fun. Steer a touch to port and push harder with your left leg. That'll lift your port wing. But you'll start to sideslip to starboard. You steer that way, and push with your right leg, putting yourself back on course."

He complied, shooting her a triumphant grin.

"Now try four in a row."

The first two wobbled a bit, but the next ones were smoothing out.

"Look at you. You're dancing."

"It's like skiing in soft powder!"

"Let's get back to business."

He complied.

She couldn't resist. "I don't suggest you try it today, but you can alternate wings. Makes you yoyo all over the place."

"Yeah, and don't put beans up my nose."

She almost stopped flapping. "What?"

"Old cautionary tale my mother used to tell. Lady was leaving her children at home alone for the first time, and as she was going out the door, she suddenly thought, 'What if they put beans up their noses and choke?' So, she told them not to put beans up their noses, and they promised they wouldn't. Of course, you know what happened."

"The moment she was gone, they went and put beans up their noses."

"Right. And they all died."

She chuckled. "You must be doing pretty well if you can string a line like that and hold a straight course."

"I am a pilot, you know."

"Now you can add a new craft to your classifications."

"You better not add 'Ornithopter Instructor' to your qualifications yet. You forgot to teach us how to land."

"Plenty of time." She raised her voice until the others could hear. "I'll go in first, and you follow. Lift the nose to dump velocity, just like a plane, but slower to respond. When you're over the platform, nose up some more to a dead stop. Same amount of gravity as the other platform, and you'll drift down. The challenge is not to drag your tail, but to do a two-foot landing without bumping your nose either."

As she expected, everyone landed neatly with a minimum of bobbling, and soon they were in the elevator.

She opened their private com. "Anybody outside the door on Level Five?"

All clear, Mia. Five Security waiting at the Agora entrance on Deck Three.

"Tell them ten minutes. We'll complete the logon and get the programming team started. Then I'll be down."

Right you are.

"This way to Drive Control." She accessed the Habitat Security feed. "One person on duty. We'll have to take it slow."

But the moment the door opened, a young man in a Security jacket stepped forward, saluting. "Agent Trevor Carroll, ma'am. I'd recognize you anywhere. Come on in."

Olivier slid forward, a restraining hand on her shoulder. He scanned the room, then went to a workstation and flipped the power on. When he was satisfied, he nodded, and the rest entered the bridge. They went to the various stations and started to log in.

Once they were in the system, she glanced at Jean. "I'll get you as much time as I can. As long as he's talking, he won't be worrying about what else we're doing."

The pilot flipped her a salute and went back to work.

She and Martin headed for the stairs.

46. THE BATTLE

A dark, middle-aged man with a military brush cut was waiting outside the main Agora entrance on Deck 3, four able-looking uniforms behind him. He saluted. "Head of Security Arham Bhutto, ma'am. We're pretty thin on the ground, here. Nobody ever thought we'd be dealing with something like this."

"How many men do you have?"

"There are only fifteen of us. Five are inside the Agora, five here, and the others scattered around. There's a new batch came in on the *Cornucopia,* but I'm leery of using them."

"I'd save them for an emergency."

"I'm keeping minimal contact with my teams, because I don't know if my com is secure."

"It probably isn't, but mine is. Do you know Randy Jones and Murph Bokker?"

"To say hello to. Why?"

"Because in about ten minutes, they'll be standing by outside the entry from East Residential with thirty men."

"Where did they come from?"

"The rest of your Security men and a bunch of loyal private citizens, I suppose. What kind of action are you suggesting?"

"In a situation like this, we can only wait and react when we have an idea what the mob is going to do." He raised a cautioning hand. "Oh, it isn't a mob, yet, and with any luck it never will be. If it comes to that, common procedure calls for a show of superior force acting in a non-aggressive manner. But we don't have that kind of numbers."

"What's Plan B?"

"Now that you're here, there's a focus for the loyal team. The former Board is in the meeting, and they're all on earbuds. What do you think is the best action?"

"Exactly what you said. I'll go in and make a play for attention. He'll attack me verbally, because he loves a sparring match that gives him an opportunity to fire up his followers. If it looks like physical trouble is brewing, I have forty Space Commandos in two ships, ready to move in. Plus several even better tricks up my sleeve. But we don't want it to go that far." She passed a code to his biomem. "This channel will keep you in touch with my operational com. If you stay out here, you have freedom to move. That suit you?"

"Yes, ma'am. I'm glad you're here. You don't know what it's like, not knowing who's really in charge, and who you're supposed to listen to."

She squared her shoulders. "Well, I guess you just have to listen to me and come in and pull me out if I mess up."

She turned to the double doors. The sound of raucous cheering rose and fell, with pauses while a single voice spoke. At her nod, two of Caulfield's agents threw the double doors open, and she stepped through.

She was met by a beefy blond agent in quasi-military uniform. He half-raised his anti-personnel weapon, the barrel not quite pointing at her. "You can't come in here."

Martin stepped to her shoulder. "How do you want me to handle this?"

She shook her head. "I want to handle it my way. *Pegasus,* can you give me some volume on the Agora system?

I can also replace his com signal with an annoying hum which will rise to the pain threshold in about one minute. His name is...ah, here we have it: Fischer.

She stepped forward, pushing the gun aside with two fingers. "This is a democratic meeting, Herr Fischer. Any occupant of the Habitat is free to attend, yes?"

He faltered back a step, glancing over his shoulder at the podium.

"You are on your own, Herr Fischer. The decision you make could have a serious effect on the rest of your life. You would be wise to stand aside and let me exercise my rights as a citizen."

He shook his head and turned away, reaching up to pull his ear bud out, his gun barrel dropping to point at the floor.

She strode past him into the arena.

Silence fell, and a mass of faces turned towards her. The five rows of raised seating around the perimeter of the oval arena were packed, and a looser group filled the standing room in the centre. Lange and his party commanded a dais on the left-hand wall. She had entered at the secondary speaker's platform slightly lower down on the right-hand side. As she stepped forward, the lights came up on her.

She stopped at the microphone. "Good morning, everyone." She stood, waiting. The old-fashioned device was largely symbolic, but it allowed the sound operator control over who spoke. She could tell by the echo that it was live, and her ear buds told her that *Pegasus* was boosting her volume with his own feed.

Lange cleared his throat and paused for effect. "Who are you, and what the hell are you doing here?"

"Thank you for the kind introduction, Herr Lange. As you already know, I am Mia Larsen, the duly appointed representative of the Earth League Committee. We have information that an unregistered group from the Meld is interfering with this project. I have come to look for evidence and what do I find? I return your question to you. What are you doing here?"

"I am the duly elected representative of the members of this democratic society, and we are discussing how to achieve the freedom that all citizens of Earth and the Meld hold as their unalienable right."

There was a ragged cheer from the crowd.

"You got elected to head the government here when you weren't even on the Habitat. That must have taken some orchestration of the principles of democracy."

"What does a member of the political elite know about democracy?"

"Me? The political elite? I'm only a troubleshooter sent up to negotiate a solution to this little problem."

He laughed through a sneer. "So, one of their lackeys. We know your kind."

She countered with a bland smile of her own. "Herr Lange, this has nothing to do with who I am, although many of these people know me. I have worked with them for years. I'm here to make sure that nobody is trying to destroy the project they have put their lives into."

"And I'm here to see that they don't get shanghaied off into space where they'll never return." He made a grand gesture. "I'm here to show them what could be accomplished with this marvelous vessel if only some imagination was applied."

"Yes, I've seen the plans." She scanned the crowd, nodding to a few familiar faces. "How many of you have been to Vegas? Macao? Any big gambling mecca. Was it fun? Sure, if you were on holiday and you didn't lose too much. But how about living there year-round? Any place you go, there's a ton of half-drunk tourists filling the seats. And it won't be regular people. It will be the super rich. Did you sign onto this Habitat to spend your life serving the wealthy?"

"What a load of Bolshie bullshit! You all voted for this change. Will you let a company stooge to come along and take it back?

"The honest workers here didn't vote for this. There are about five hundred agents on this ship who never intended to go to the Asteroid Belt. They were inserted into the workforce through subterfuge, lies, and faulty resumés. The other votes were bought from people who needed the money and sold their disposable stocks."

"This is the present reality, Herr Lange. Whether you take over the Habitat or not, you will get no more recruits. The holes in the vetting process have been plugged. The ringers that just came in on *Cornucopia* will be staying on that ship for a nice, quiet ride back to jail. Any of you who are here on forged documents are open to charges of fraud, and you will be returned to Earth for trial.

"But the Consortium has worked a deal with the legal authorities of USA, Canada and the European Union. If you turn yourself in and behave until you reach Earth, any sentence you get will start from today. That means many of you will walk free the moment you touch ground."

She regarded a beefy character in a workman's jacket, who was approaching her position. "Let me guess. You tried to shut off my microphone, but you couldn't access the sound system. Now you're coming to take it away." She handed it to him. "Go ahead." She smiled at the crowd. "Testing, testing. Can you still hear me at the back? You can? Isn't that nice?"

Lange made another huge sweep of his arm. "You see how it is? They have the technology and the power, and they use it to deny us freedom of speech. Are we going to stand for it?" He leaned over the podium and shook his fist at her. "Nobody is going to send anyone to jail. I won't allow that to happen."

There were a few cheers and a lot of muttering.

Lange continued his harangue, and the crowd — at least the more vocal members — were soon responding as they had before.

Martin leaned in to her. "You don't seem to be trying to calm them down, much. Aren't you playing into his hand?"

She gave him a cold smile. "I hope that's what he thinks." She switched her com over. "You there, Jean?

Yeah, I was listening to that last bit.

"I'm not making any headway with this bunch. We were hoping some of them would switch sides, but *Pegasus* did a vocal analysis and we still have over half the crowd supporting Lange."

Jean chuckled. *That's because the serious citizens are at their duties. Don't get caught up in your role. You aren't supposed to win the debate, just keep it going. If he thinks he's winning, it will hold him focused on the battle. The more fun he's having, the more time we get.*

"I can take one for the team, I guess."

That's the spirit. Why don't you attack his financial record? Pegasus, send her some more dirt on the Austrian People's Party finances.

Coming up on the main screen in the Agora.

When her opponent stopped for a breath, she flung a hand towards the evidence. "What do you have to say about this, Herr Lange? If you add the right-hand column, I'm sure it far exceeds the twelve million euros your party was allowed to spend in the last election."

He snorted. "Counterfeit bookkeeping. Anybody can make up numbers like that."

"What about the long run? Surely you don't think you can take over a multi-trillion dollar facility and get away with it?"

A slow smile spread across his face. "You know, young lady, I've been waiting for someone to ask that."

He waved a hand and a different view appeared on the screen. "These are the projected numbers for our business plan. As you can see, this Habitat has a huge surface area: almost 100 hectares. Over twice the size of the city of Vienna.

"When it comes to structures, there's the extra density at each end. Add, say, another 30 hectares. This Habitat is the perfect venue for a super-luxury retirement community and recreation complex.

"The original plans were for 10,000 people. If you use the cruise ship ratio, that would be 6,600 passengers and 3,300 crew. But we will be providing the absolute best of care, including medical. Let's boost that to 5,000 customers and 5,000 crew.

"We'll start with 2500 apartments. If we create 300-square-metre units on three floors, and lease them for a billion euros each for 30 years, that's 2.5 trillion euros at the start.

"Add five casino hotels bringing in two hundred million each per year, that's another thirty billion. Short-term holidayers from Earth will cover the cost of the transportation system."

She switched channels on her com and let him ramble on about how much money they were all going to make and how the profits would trickle down to everybody who participated.

"How's it going, boys?"

Olivier answered. *Jean is doing fine. He ought to be; those are his personal babies he's playing with.*

"But he's our backup plan. What's the progress on the main project?"

Hemi's having tough slogging. He can't connect directly with Pegasus, so he has to communicate through Noah and the ExIn Sphere. They have sent enough of the code that Pegasus has serious doubts the Meld program will work. How much damage it will do is anybody's guess.

"Is there any chance of activating the emergency shutdown?"

That's a sticky problem. One objective of the alien application is designed to shut it down, but it hands control off to their master program at each step. So, they're pretty firmly entrenched in that area of the system.

"Is there any chance of getting the alien programming to cooperate in shutting it down? That process would take a couple of hours, and it would give us time to achieve the freeze."

Cooperate? We never thought of that.

"I don't know about the details, but perhaps you can fool the alien program into thinking it is achieving its goal, but it has to use our methods to do so."

"You sound like we're dealing with a person."

"Well, it's just another sapience, isn't it? They're all designed by humans, and their mental processes are human-like. They can be fooled, misled. Garbage in, garbage out."

She looked back to the podium, where the Austrian billionaire was winding down. "I have to get back to my part of the battle. Tell Jean to think about it."

"...And what do you have to say to that, Frauline Fancy-Pants?"

She let the silence stretch out until everyone was looking at her. Then she shook her head. "Frauline Fancy-Pants. Is that the best you can do? You don't think anyone was actually listening to your drivel, do you? If someone with a brain looked at your figures, the first thing they would notice was that your estimate of surface area fails to consider that a third of that expanse is covered by water. Do you think these people are going to let a *dumpkof* who makes a mistake like that control this Habitat? These are scientists and engineers, Herr Lange. At least, those who aren't your stooges.

"And when you start talking about how much money everyone is going to make, you perhaps have forgotten that trickle-down economics was debunked a hundred years ago. In your world, the richer the rich get, the poorer the poor get. You know damn well that any peasant who isn't pulling his plow fast enough for you will be put on the next ship back to earth with nothing but the shirt on his back, because he has no work record or pension contributions down there."

She turned to the crowd. "Ask yourselves. Why is there a Gliesean in his party?"

"He is an official observer from a designated group in this process."

"No, he isn't. He's a computer programmer, here to assist in taking over the Habitat sapience so they can assure the return to Earth orbit."

She held up a hand to stop his response. "Why else would the programming for the new course be in a Meld computing language?"

She turned to the crowd again. "And so we get to the nub of the situation. This group showed up after a questionable political takeover of the Habitat, wanting us to use a completely new navigation program in a language we can't understand, so we can't debug it."

She let her stare cover the room. "Sure, a little political manipulation doesn't sound too risky. This is different. Most of you have scientific backgrounds. You know about the Coriolis forces in a rotating object this size. The Meld doesn't have any magic. They have advanced technology, but as they keep telling us, they are human just like us. Are you willing to risk your life on an untried program in an unknown computer language?

"And now we come to the basics. The Meld Mercantile Caste is the same type of people that caused most of Earth's problems over the past couple of centuries. Do you know what's going to happen if these Mercantile types take control of Earth's economic system? She nodded to short, dark-faced man in the front row. "Where did your ancestors originate?"

"Ghana." He stood a little taller and grinned around at everyone.

"And what happened to your people when the Europeans showed up?"

"They took our tallest and strongest warriors to America..." He paused and looked around. His grin widened. "...to be stars in the NBA!"

She waited for the laughter to die. "Not mentioning a couple of hundred years of slavery in between."

His smile faded. "Yeah, well, we'd rather not dwell on that."

"Right. And Earth would rather not go through it again, either."

Again she looked over the crowd. "We don't need to be fighting. We need to be finding ways to get us all out of this mess. Look. There are three groups of people here. First are the original loyal scientists, engineers, and workers who intended to make their lives on the original project and still want that to happen.

"Then there are some original employees who voted for this new scheme. They are in no danger of retaliation. They thought they were being given an honest chance to vote. They voted. If there is another vote and they have changed their minds, nobody will know.

"Come to think of it, there may be a few workers with legitimate skills who required only a slight bending of the rules to get accepted. If they didn't actually break any laws, and they still honestly want to continue to the Asteroid Belt, they might be allowed to compete for the positions that will be opened by the removal of the final group, who have broken the law to come here, and must suffer the consequences.'

"One thing I can promise you. In the next election it will be one person, one vote, with no extra shares counting for anything."

Lange slammed a fist on his podium. "I've had enough of this!" He gestured to the uniformed men below him. "Arrest her."

Four of them hefted their anti-personnel batons and strode towards her position, but people in the crowd moved to intercept them. Scuffles began to break out, and the central floor started to swirl into the beginning of a melee.

"Jean, if you had any plans to intervene, this would be the time."

Coming right up, ma'am.

Three doors behind her slammed open, and the hubbub faded as everyone took in this development. A microship slid through each entrance and hovered there, silent and menacing, a security agent at its side. The doors on the opposite side opened, and five more security agents entered, each backed by several capable-looking citizens carrying an assortment of blunt weapons.

She upped the volume on her voice assist and added a touch of echo. "Most of you know what a microship is, but I doubt if you've had a chance to meet one. You may have seen these stockpiled in the electronics workshop. They are programmed as intelligent probes for mining operations, with appropriate tools such as rock hammers and lasers. What you perhaps don't realize is that they are intelligent sapiences with huge memory capacity. Each one has downloaded the human resources database for the Habitat plus the latest facial recognition software. Put in simpler terms, they know exactly who you are. Even the ones here under false names.

"To make the honest citizens of the Habitat feel more confident, I can tell you they also know the parameters of the Geneva Convention of Law Enforcement of 2067. They will only take physical action against a human who is in the process of threatening another human or committing a crime. Each one is presently under the mentorship of a rational human to ensure they follow their instructions to the letter.

"Under the authority given to me by the Habitat Consortium, I am calling this meeting ended. Please use one of the three exits on the forward end of the Agora. Merely walk past the microship. It will identify you, reveal your present status, and allow you to go about your duties. As far as we are concerned, it's business as usual today, and if you are supposed to be on watch this morning, you have clauses in your contracts that allow for union meetings. There will be no lost time."

"You can't do this!"

"I remind you, Herr Lange, that at the moment all the charges against you are civil in nature. Until you actually commit a crime, we have no reason to hold you. Inciting a riot is a crime. The *Cornucopia* leaves for Earth in three days. No one here has any authority to stop you from boarding her." She left a meaningful pause. "Or any other ship that happens to drop by. You and your friends are free to go."

She turned away to watch the departure of the crowd. When she glanced back, he was gone. She checked the room again. One group stood together at the side of the main podium, their eyes on her. A few had familiar faces. She nodded to herself. *The Board of Directors. I guess they want to talk to me.*

But Martin moved to her side. "Was that wise?"

She regarded him. "To which part of the morning's work are you referring?"

"Turning your back as if he didn't exist. That was pretty insulting."

"I was taking the personal conflict out of the situation, leaving him space to make up his own mind. It's a trick I learned from a high school principal. He used it very successfully on emotional students."

"I know about the technique from Situation Management Training, but I've never seen it used like that."

She shrugged. "People at a much higher pay grade than me have to deal with him. I don't count in his plans, and once he realizes that, he'll ignore me. I hope."

"Not your horse, not your wagon."

"Exactly."

He grinned. "Do you realize that the origin of that saying is in Polish, where it's "Not my circus, not my monkeys?"

"Yes, but we're trying to be polite." She scanned the thinning crowd. "I want to talk the Board of Directors over there, but let's check in on the electronics wizards first."

"I sent another couple of security agents to keep an eye on them."

"You're ordering the Habitat security around? Under whose authority?"

"I dunno. I just suggested that our team in Drive Control might need looking after, and they went."

"Good move in any case. Have you given any thought to staying aboard, having come all this way?"

"You think I could get hired on?"

"You'd have to apply, I guess. They might take into consideration the postage stamp on your letter, though."

"Bird in the hand?"

"Do you know what it costs to prep and transfer personnel out here?"

"No, but I'm sure you do."

"There are going to be a lot of holes in the workforce when all these plants get sent home. Unfortunately, I doubt if there will be any in Security."

His face fell. "I guess not."

"So, make sure you submit a full resumé. They're going to need social workers sooner or later."

"I'd say sooner. With all this upset and turmoil…"

"Good point, but you're telling the wrong person."

"You don't get out of it that easy. In this circus, I'm one of your monkeys."

"So, put me down as one of your references. If you dare."

He regarded her. "You know, you're really lucky to have Jean."

It took her two full breaths to process this comment. "In what way?"

He frowned. "Well…you know."

"No, I don't. Martin, you're part of the cadre. If you have something you want to say, out with it."

He shook his head. "That's exactly what I mean." He sighed. "Okay. I hope you won't take this wrong, but from the moment you stepped into my car back in Houston, I knew I was in the presence of the scariest woman I had ever met."

He noticed her reaction. "I don't mean that kind of scary. You're also one of the nicest women I've ever met. That's what makes it even worse. I mean it in a personal-relationship kind of way: a guy, checking out a girl and realizing he just doesn't match up." He shrugged. "And I was right. First time I make a personal comment, and here I am, up against the wall with my knees shaking. That's why I say you're lucky. You've found someone who matches up. You're the perfect pair."

"Matches up? In your mind, you have us labelled as…a pair? What have we ever done to give you that idea?"

He gave a shaky grin. "Well, you natter away at each other like an old married couple, for a start. I thought you had it all figured out and under control like you have everything else. You're playing it cool in public because of the professional image."

"You thought we had an office romance going?"

He shrugged. "Well, when you're as solid as you two obviously are you don't need to play those silly games, do you? There's a time for everything and everything in its time."

"And I suppose you've had this little chat with Jean, or are planning one soon?"

"I would never…!" He glanced at her sideways. "No, I know you're joking. You're making light of this to let me down easy from an embarrassing faux pas."

She sighed. "Martin, can I be completely honest with you?"

"I'm not sure I'm ready to handle that."

"Which means you are ready. All that stuff you just said was completely off base. Jean and I are part of the same cadre. We work together very well. We're definitely good friends. But there is nothing romantic between us."

"Nothing?"

"Absolutely nothing."

"Not yet."

"What?"

He jabbed a thumb at his chest. "Social worker, remember? Not your average dumb security plod. It's there, and maybe you don't think about it much. As I said: wrong place, wrong time. It will come."

She sat back, unable to form a decent response. "Will it?"

"You're the personnel relations pro. Look what you just did here. You took a potentially tricky situation and turned it into a serious and fruitful discussion between two professionals. Instead of feeling stupid, I feel useful and needed." He stood.

"And I will immediately go and sign up for a job in the Asteroid Belt to make sure it never happens again. I don't know if I could stand it."

He clapped her on the shoulder. "I'll be in Flight Control." And he strode out.

She stood there, her head swirling. The amphitheatre emptied, and two of the microships left. The third slid towards her, stopping at shoulder height a metre away.

The room is cleared and attendees recorded as per instructions, Ms. Larsen. The Management Committee awaits your input.

The calm voice settled her. "Not now, not here."

Pardon me?

"Sorry. Speaking to myself. What are your orders?"

Captain Gagnon assigned me to your security.

"All right. One metre behind my left shoulder, please." She walked with purpose towards the group of men who were waiting for her to tell them what to do. Her security sentience floated gently behind.

By the time she finished with them and returned to Flight Control, everything was settled. As she and the microship entered, Jean glanced at it and pointed. The sentience rose and took up a position over the door, rotating slowly.

"Thanks for the new recruit. What should I expect?"

"It knows the NASA Security Training Manual. It will act like any regular agent, and be especially effective coordinating with Martin and Olivier, whom it regards as superior officers."

Over in the corner on a separate workstation, Olivier was working with a stranger: a slim, pasty-skinned twenty-something with a fashionable haircut.

She nodded in that direction "What gives?"

Jean dismissed them with a flick of his fingers. "He's the Mercantile programmer. Too bad, really. He's very talented in his own creative way. Word got around that whoever did that programming was on the hook for reckless endangerment and possibly attempted murder, and he came beetling over to help make everything right again. He's showing us how to back out of the connections in the proper sequence to prevent a crash. It speeded the cleanout process quite a bit."

"We don't have to do a shutdown and bring it all online again?"

"Nope. As far as the Habitat is concerned, none of this ever happened."

"So, we can hop in our little Flying Wing and...go home?"

He put an arm around her shoulders and gave her a squeeze. "Aren't you having enough fun here?"

She frowned up at him. "Except for some of the company, I suppose."

The arm stayed where it was. "We need to talk."

"I suppose we should."

They left the bridge and strolled towards the Agora. After a spate of silence, she glanced at him. "You and I take the same length of stride."

"When you're not rushing around at twenty kilometres a second."

"Is that metaphoric?"

"Probably. Why?"

She gave him a hip check. "Because then I don't have to convert it to miles an hour."

"Somewhere north of forty-five thousand, I believe."

"I can safely assume it's metaphoric."

"Exactly. When we slow down and think about it, we have a lot in common."

They crossed the Agora and stood on the balcony looking down the length of the Habitat, watching the stars waver past the great watery windows. She glanced up at him. "You realize our cadre has us down as a couple."

He shrugged. "Have we ever said or done anything to tell them different?"

She nodded. "That was my reaction...wait a minute, I said exactly the opposite."

He mused a moment. "Must be metaphoric."

"You think so?"

He gave her a squeeze. "Like my arm around your shoulders. Feels like the most natural thing in the world."

She slipped her arm around his waist. "I know what you mean."

After a while, she leaned her head against his. "I suppose this is the point where one of us asks the predictable question about where we should go next."

"Sounds too common for us."

She suddenly dropped her arm, grabbed his hand and tugged. "Let's go flying!"

Now the look on his face was truly horrified. "You don't mean..."

"Of course I don't. We can do that in bed. I just want to go flying. To be free of all this and go where I please with a companion I choose."

He shrugged. "The girl of my dreams wants to join me in the sport of my dreams. Let's go flying."

47. EPILOGUE: MUSIC OF THE SPHERES

Three months later, *Pegasus* again broke out of Earth's atmosphere, on a considerably shorter and slower trip. Marie Pelletier, Artist in Residence for the Earth League Committee, was in space with a holo-cam crew to shoot the multi-media visuals of "Sphere Singer," the first Earther song to challenge the intense competition of Meldnet social media.

Her agent, Mia Larson, attended to see that nothing went wrong, and her technical wizard and musical arranger, Hemisius Terrus, was there to oversee the video feeds. Nobody was sure why Captain Jean Gagnon of the Canadian Armed Forces had come, but it might have been something to do with the microship sentience that was helping with the CGI.

They stood on the bridge, enjoying the starscape that spread around them.

Jean put his arm around her shoulders. "So, music is the universal language, is it?"

Mia put on a thoughtful frown. "Music is one area where the human race comes together. I had *Pegasus* explain it to me. The European chromatic scale intermeshes with the Gliesean scale on the pentatonic notes. For the rest, there are three more notes that come between the white notes on the piano. Other than that, a sound wave is a sound wave. Octaves and chords work the same way."

Hemi nodded. "Listen to this." He touched his enterpad and piano music filled the air. Marie's unmistakable voice began to sing. Then a violin took up the theme, embroidering a strange new melody around the singer's voice. Sometimes it seemed to be in tune, but then it would fade into minor disharmony, sliding back towards traditional, and Mia found herself anticipating the blending, with an eerie feeling of satisfaction when it finally came about.

The second time the chorus came around, there were two voices, but the harmony was in the wavering tones of the violin.

They listened, rapt, until the final notes of the strange violin faded away.

She frowned and pointed at Hemi. "That second voice...?"

"That was me. I wrote the violin part, too. Well, it's adapted from a song my dad used to sing me. Something about counting toes and stars, I think."

"So, you took Marie's song, morphed the violin backup into the Gliesean scale and added a harmony track with your voice singing a nursery rhyme."

"Yeah, I've been listening to you. The whole thing is a metaphor for the relationship between our peoples."

"Very interesting. Has anybody else heard it?"

He popped data up on his screen. "Six point five million views of the new version on five different arts and pop music platforms in the last two weeks. Four hundred sales on the Meld Residential Sphere out past Saturn. When I get the visuals attached, it's going viral, no question."

"So, you're going to be a music star, are you?"

"Me?" his vestigial eyebrows disappeared up under his hood. "In front of an audience? I don't think so. Nope, I'll just sit at my enterpad and create a whole new genre of music, and Marie will sing it into a fortune for both of us."

Mia glanced at the singer, who shrugged expressively.

"But we're way past that. Marie, tell me one more time how you make music that sounds like the stars look."

The other woman gestured gracefully towards the viewscreen. "When you look at a work of art, your eye travels over it in a predictable route. I'm writing the music of what you see as you look at the heavens. I assign each star a different sound. As your eye moves, the sounds change. I set *Pegasus* to rotating very slowly, so the scene sweeps past gently.

"Once you know the song, you can predict where your eyes are supposed to look next. Using Meld interactive tech, you can choose different stars and create your own melody line and play along. We're here today to do the visuals."

"Play it again please, Hemi."

"Okay. The first note is the Horsehead Nebula." He pointed. "And it moves from there to Sigma Orionis, the bright star just above it. After that, let your eyes follow wherever feels right."

The music eased in, and the four of them stood together and watched the stars turn slowly to the rhythm of humanity.

THE END

If you enjoyed this book, please do the author and other readers a favour. Go to Amazon or another online retailer and give it a review. Even a star rating would be nice.

ΛBOUT THE ΛUTHOR

Brought up in a logging camp with no electricity, Gordon Long learned his storytelling in the traditional way: at his father's knee. He now spends his time editing, publishing, travelling, blogging and writing Fantasy, Sci-Fi and Social Commentary, although sometimes the boundaries blur.

Gordon lives in Tsawwassen, British Columbia, with his wife, Linda and his rescued dog, Geeta. When he is not writing and publishing, he works on projects with the Surrey Seniors' Planning Table and is a staff writer for <indiesunlimited.com>

MORE FROM GORDON Λ. LONG

Available at Online Retailers

Science Fiction

"Plague Jumper" Space Opera

"Factory 4-80" Freighty Novels 1
"Outback Rebellion" Freighty Novels 2
"Asimov's Laws" Freighty Novels 3
"Occam's Razor" Freighty Novels 4
"Slivership" Freighty Novels 5
"Centauri Triangle" Freighty Novels 6
"Too Clever by a Zettabyte" Freighty Novels 7
"Shipshape and Fancy Free" Freighty Novels 8

Fantasy

"The Power to Serve" A Hero's Journey
"The Strength to Shield" Sequel to "Power to Serve"

"Ocean of Grass" Petrellan Saga 1
"Waves of Stone" Petrellan Saga 2
"Path of Water" Petrellan Saga 3
"Zoysana's Choice" Petrellan Saga 4
"The Innkeeper's Husband" Petrellan Saga 5
"Mercenary's Dream" Petrellan Saga 6

"Out of Mischief" World of Change Book 1
"Into Trouble" World of Change Book 2
"Mountains of Mischief" World of Change Book 3
"The Trouble with Tents" World of Change Book 4
"Queen of Mischief" World of Change Book 5

"A Sword Called...Kitten?" Romantic Comedy with an Edge
"The Cat with Many Claws" Sword Called Kitten Book 2
"Cloud Cat" A Sword Called Kitten Book
"Sword Called Kitten: the Early Days" Short Stories

Other Genres

"Storm Over Savournon" A Novel of the French Revolution
"Why Are People So Stupid?" Social Humour with a Point

Look for Gordon's books, selected reviews, poetry and short stories at <airbornpress.ca>
Gordon's opinions on humanity are at the
"Are People Stupid?" blog
<https://airbornpress.ca/arepeoplestupid/>
Find his weekly reviews and his ideas on writing at
"Renaissance Writer"
<https://airbornpress.ca/newdir/>